Night Bound

Night Bound

The Soulfire Series

Book Two

Alisar Eido

The Unlikely Spark
Austin MMXVIII

More Information at:

www.alisareido.com

www.alisareido.com/the-unlikely-spark

Cover by Amanda Cavazos-Weems

Logo by Logan Kees

ISBN-978-0-9989741-3-2

First Print Edition, Paperback, August 2018

10 9 8 7 6 5 4 3 2 1

Acknowledgments

My deepest gratitude to everyone who has come so far with me, and for me.
Thank you for being part of the story.

A special thanks to the Beta Readers:

Charlotte Griesel

Amanda Mery

Janet Hancock

Dedicated to those who have survived great escapes,
and found the grass was greener.

Chapter 1

The pincer shape on the map revealed the open mouth of the underworld, poised to engulf them. It had been hours since they'd discovered it. Shocked silence occupied most of that time, studded now and again with brief words that stated the obvious. So far, no solutions.

Verenna sat on the bed where she'd nearly left the world, hugging her knees and watching Mortimer pace. The off key tune his feet played across the creaking floorboards echoed the unsettled mood of the room.

"Do you think we have time to run? If we could just get far enough..." Mortimer muttered into the hand that stroked his beard.

"Maybe," Darius answered without expression, tapping his fingers on the thin arm of his chair. "But we still don't have the last ingredient for the sun serum. We have no cart. No guarantee of shelter for days in any direction. I'd say it's not our best bet."

They went quiet again, letting the click and whine of the floorboards rise to fill the absence of speech.

Verenna picked at a stubborn speck of dirt under her nail. Running was just what they'd been doing for weeks. That's what got them chased to the edge of a city-sized nest of demons. It no longer seemed such a viable option.

Minutes passed.

"We should have stayed at the abbey. At least it's defensible," Fabien's voice startled them out of their thoughts. He sat on the ground with his back to the wall, slowly rotating his blade so the onyx eye of the hawk on its hilt glimmered in the firelight.

"Sounds like a great idea. Ever heard of a siege?" Darius scoffed. "If we didn't bring the fight to them they'd have brought it to us. At least out here we're small, mobile, unpredictable..."

"And without anything between us and them," Fabien retorted, glowering through the hay-blond hair that hung across his eyes. "The only way out now is to fight."

Darius leaned forward to meet his gaze. "Have you noticed that there's only four of us?"

Mortimer joined in with vague hope in his voice. "The village. They might fight with us. This is their home after all. I'm sure at least a few of them would be willing to join us."

"They've got the most to lose. That's for certain," Verenna interrupted. "They can still die." She flicked a last bit of grit out from under her thumbnail and looked up to find shock on the faces of the other three.

"Look who's decided to join the conversation. You wouldn't happen to have any profound insights on our situation, would you?" Darius slumped in his chair and steepled his fingers.

"Well..." Verenna glanced at their expectant faces and shrugged. "You just keep saying the same things. We can't run. They know roughly where we are, so we certainly can't hide for long. Fighting probably won't work because we don't know the numbers. And even if we did, we're not sure what we're up against. We don't know anything about what's inside Bronwell..."

"I said profound insights, not a profound summary," Darius reminded her, rolling his eyes and letting out a slightly overdone sigh. Her jaw tightened, but she ignored him and pressed on.

"What I'm saying is, there's only one of those things we can change. We don't know enough. Let's find out. Let's go scout around Bronwell. Go during the day. It's hard for those kind of creatures to come out in daylight, yes? If we could learn what's hiding in there, or find the source of the creatures that are in the woods, well, at least we'd have something to go on. Instead of sitting around talking over all the things we don't have." The girl adjusted her sitting and looked away from the others in an attempt to play down her kindling excitement at the idea.

"Out of the question," Darius snapped. "That citadel is a festering hive. It's likely the origin of all the creatures we've been trying to avoid. It doesn't matter how many there are in there. Any number is too many. And there may be thousands."

"If we can't die then what's the harm?" Verenna challenged.

The doctor let out an exasperated huff. "We can't. But there are worse things, trust me. Also, you seem to have already forgotten demons aren't the only creatures that rely on darkness. Us too."

Mortimer stopped his walking and placed his palms on the table. "He's right. If I can't find silver nettle then we're not going anywhere in daylight."

Verenna gestured to the old man. "But you can go in the sun. I've seen you. So can I. Why can't we go?" Verenna demanded.

Darius leaned forward to put his face in his hands. "Good God, you are so ready to be stupid now that you think it won't end your life. Yes, you can still stand the sun. That is because you are not truly one of us yet. And until the first dark moon, there's no knowing if you will be. You are The Descendant. Death's little balancing act depends on you being alive. That's the only thing keeping Merlin's eldest daughter in Hell where Death put her. Therefore, immortality may not fully take hold for you. And we should not by any means test for it. If you think you are the one to scout that place you're an idiot."

"I think she's brave," Fabien defended. "Who's got something better to do, anyhow?"

Verenna couldn't help but let a smile creep across her face as she met the warriors approving, green gaze.

"It's too dangerous," Darius insisted.

"So is sitting here," Verenna argued, refusing to let him dismiss the idea so quickly. "What good is it to just stay put? We don't know enough to think up a good plan and the only way to find out is to go see for ourselves. We don't even know what types of demon might be in there."

"You know about their types?" Mortimer cocked his head.

The girl pulled the little blue book from her pocket, rising and tossing it onto the table for the others to examine. "I've been reading it." Despite the punishing journey the volume had been through, enough of the silver lettering was left to glisten an explanation. 'The Practical Handbook for Identifying the Demonic' shone across the cover.

Darius nearly laughed. "And none of what you read worries you? Anything and everything in that book could be behind those walls. Probably is. And you're still willing to walk in and see?"

"I told you. Brave," Fabien boasted.

"I mean, your prophecy says I'm supposed to wash the city clean. How am I supposed to do that if I stay away forever? Might as well see what I'm up against and just...get it over with."

Half of Mortimer's mouth rose into a crooked smile that seemed proud of her. "I'll ask the villagers to help me search for that nettle. I've been trying to keep to myself to avoid questions, but we're beyond that luxury now. We could have sun serum in a day or two with luck."

"Are you joking? It's not just about keeping what we are a secret. Any one of them could be a husk. There could be a messenger among them that would alert Souris. The Sarzen finding out our nature is the least of those problems," Darius protested. But Mortimer met him with reason.

"If there were a messenger, Souris would already know our

location and it would be too late. Yet we're still here. Either Souris doesn't know exactly where we are, or…"

"Or he's waiting for us to walk into a trap," the doctor disagreed.

Fabien joined in to mock Darius' upset. "Well then let's be 'mobile', 'unpredictable', like you said."

"It's just for information. We wouldn't be going there to fight," Verenna added.

"Why do you think that matters? Demons don't care if you're ready for a fight. You'd be walking behind enemy lines! If something finds you…"

"Darius," the solemn, oaken sound of Mortimer's voice halted the arguing. "We're going. The girl's right. We have to know more."

"The world has gone mad," the doctor muttered glancing around the room for signs that the conversation was a dream.

Again Mortimer chimed in with logic. "Regardless, we will still need sun serum. If I get you the last ingredient, will you make it?"

The doctor sat with his elbows on his knees, gently shaking his head. Verenna held her breath. They could go without, but only two of them. And she wasn't eager to be alone with Mortimer after learning he'd been the cause of the initial accident that had put a hole in her side. Safety required them to stay together. That would be impossible without the serum. So would escape, if it came to that.

Darius sat up again defeated. "Do I have a choice?"

ᕦᕤ

The next few days left little time for Verenna to hold grudges. Preparations for their journey into the occupied city made it necessary to break her nearly week long streak of one word answers and dark stares. They had to talk, strategize, think up every outcome they could and try their best to prepare for all of them. She poured over The Handbook for anything that could help, but all of the defenses listed seemed to require at least one item they didn't have. And nothing in the pages came close to addressing a situation the scale of the one they faced. After what felt like the fiftieth time going over the book, she resigned herself to the porch to watch the villagers working to brace themselves for whatever might come of their venture into Bronwell. What small fortifications they had were redoubled, windows secured, food gathered and dried, and the few stacked boats in their possession were cleaned and repaired where needed.

A few of the Sarzen joined Fabien at chopping wood in the shade. Darius sat inside, brewing together the herbs for the sun serum. Mortimer had managed to find the last plants for it with the help of the village children. They surrounded him like a giggling island each time he came back from the woods with more supplies. It was hard to stay angry with the old man, watching him tell stories and comfort the occasional scraped knee. Without the fire of resentment burning in her gut she fell to feeling sulky and useless. She missed reading things that weren't about the Underworld, having a real bed, and clean clothes. The smell of roses drifting through her bedroom window on crisp, clear mornings. They'd be done blooming by the time she got home. If she got home. Summer was drawing to an end. Soon the world would exchange its green silks for the autumn's tarnished gold. She wondered if the note she'd left with the maid at Falseman Inn would reach her parents by then.

"You alright?"

Verenna startled. She'd been too lost in daydreams to notice Fabien's approach. Despite working in the shade his skin was a stinging shade of red. She could see through the gap of his open shirt that bright blue veins had sprung up at the center of his chest next to the healing wound from Enra's knife. She could swear she saw it pulsing. He noticed her wince at the sight and did up the tie that held it closed. "Beginnings of sun sickness," he explained. "Looks like a sunburn from the outside, feels like twice that on the inside. It should calm down if I'm inside for a bit. It's not serious yet."

"If you say so," Verenna shuddered with the idea that she might one day know the feeling. Thankfully he changed the subject.

"They've got the horse, you know."

"What?"

"Yeah. They said they tied it up as an offering the night they captured us. But nothing ate it. All their other animals were taken by demons, but nothing will touch that old sack of bones. They started feeding it. Said it must be blessed or something."

Verenna scoffed. "I'm pretty sure it's just too thin to bother with."

"I think that's more like it, but there's no telling them that. Either way, we'll have it for a quick escape if we run into trouble in the city."

"It can't carry all of us."

"No, just you." He said it with a dismissive confidence, but she could tell that a deep understanding of the risk they would soon take was eating away at his heroic front. She couldn't look at him.

"I wish I knew how to fight. If ever there was a time for it, this would be it," she said with her gaze fixed on the dark patches between the trees.

"You could learn. I could teach you," Fabien suggested with a false nonchalance.

"Somehow I don't think I'd be good enough, quick enough to make a difference now."

"But you're a natural! I should know, with all the times you've clawed me up. Besides, isn't knowing something about fighting better than knowing nothing? Here," he took her by the shoulders and shifted her to face him.

"First thing's first. I want you to punch into my palm. Go on." He took a stance and held up a hand, ready for impact. Verenna made no move, studying him with considerable scepticism.

"It's alright. Throw the strongest one you've got."

Verenna wadded up a cautious fist and flung it into Fabien's open hand with a heavy smack.

"Not bad. From the sting of it that's not the first time you've punched something."

"I used to fight my cousins."

"Well, I feel sorry for 'em. Seems like you'd do a good job at it. Again."

The thwack of her knuckles against flesh satisfied something mean inside her. She liked it.

"Again," he repeated.

With new self-assurance, she pulled back her arm and heaved another punch at him. But her enthusiasm caused her to overbalance. The blow glanced off of his hand and she stumbled into the railing of the porch. She could feel her ears going red. "I'm no good."

"You are, though. And you'll be better if you keep at it. But, make sure you've got a proper fist made before you hit anything. You had your thumb curled up inside your fingers. You'll break it that way."

"And how's it supposed to be?" she asked, struggling to keep the frustration out of her voice.

"Like this." Fabien took her hand and lay it flat in his own. He gently curled her fingers into her palm. His touch was warmer than she'd expected. Though the red of the sun had faded somewhat from his face, its heat still buzzed in his skin.

"My father told me it's like holding a pint. To close your fingers like there's a handle in your hand. Don't think that's as familiar to you, however."

She laughed at the truth of the statement. She'd held a pint once, the night they'd come to the village, and had hated the contents so much that it was hard to imagine picking one up again.

"Close it like..." Verenna watched his face as he searched the ceiling for the right words. The warmth of him seemed contagious. She could feel it rising in her cheeks. She looked down at their hands but the blush kept spreading.

"Close it like there's a secret, written on your palm. Hold it hard," he told her as he tightened his fingers around hers. "Don't let the enemy see. And lastly..."

Verenna swallowed and kept her face downturned. She could feel him looking at her. She silently prayed he wouldn't notice the flush that had seeped all the way to her neck.

"Lock it with the thumb." He nudged her last finger into place and clutched her newly formed fist with both of his hands, as if he'd solidify it with the baking heat of his touch. "Like that."

She made the mistake of looking up. Their gazes met and she lost all memory of how to speak. "Ah...right. Ah..." she fumbled.

His eyes, two splendid emeralds, sparkled at her with a transfixing kindness. It occurred to her she'd forgotten to breathe, absorbed completely in the heat of his hands and his glittering stare, until a throat cleared at the cabin door. Both jumped at the sound. They dropped hands and immediately gazed in opposite directions.

Darius had arrived silent as a shadow in the doorway. He rested a shoulder on the frame, watching them with crossed arms and a calculating scowl. Verenna could feel him look her over head to toe, but refused to acknowledge him. The doctor soon turned his disapproval towards Fabien. He let his glare linger until the young man met it. Darius's lips grew thin, drawn tight to hold back a deluge of scolding. He looked like he might spit.

"The serum will be finished by tonight. We'll head into Bronwell at first light tomorrow. I suggest we not get distracted." On the cusp of harsher words the doctor spun on his heel and vanished back into the dim of the cabin.

Newly alone, Verenna and Fabien glanced at each other once more, all bashfulness lost under the vast foreboding of the next sunrise.

Chapter 2

That night Verenna lay for hours in dark with nothing to mark the creeping pace of time. Finally the sun painted the overcast sky a sallow shade of cream.

She rose with the others to ready what they needed for the journey into sacks. Talk was stifled by the humid apprehension of the hot day to come, heavy with the false promise of rain.

Verenna sat on the edge of the bed and tried to comb her hair with her fingers. She watched the doctor wander the room to meticulously choose hiding spots for three, wax-sealed, clay pots of sun serum no bigger than apples. One in the floorboards, one in the rafters, one inconspicuously placed on a shelf amongst other abandoned jars of the same make. She'd seen him fill a drinking bladder full of the amber liquid just before the daybreak. She would have assumed it was hot honey if she hadn't known better; the way the syrup glided from the ladle down the neck of the container. She didn't want to imagine what it might taste like, sure she'd be forced to find out soon enough.

Fabien took up the map that lay across the table from last night's planning. He checked the fresh marks to be sure they were dry before rolling it with care and sliding it into its canister. She questioned the wisdom of bringing it along but supposed it was too valuable to be left behind unguarded. Especially if things went poorly and they couldn't come back for it.

"Here," a voice grunted. Mortimer knelt beside her. He extended a worn pair of boots with a hole starting at the side. "A gift from the Sarzen. Can't have you barefoot if we need to run."

Verenna took them and nodded her thanks before setting about the laces and hooks. Nervousness had tightened her throat too much for needless talk.

"And this." The old man opened his other hand to reveal a little glass vile on a rough, twine string. "Probably the only bit of glass for miles. No idea where they found it. Wear it. It's filled with the serum. The sun shouldn't hurt you yet but it's better you have some if you need it."

"Um, right," Verenna muttered. She'd felt fairly normal since she'd been bitten, except for her loss of appetite. With the moon growing towards full, it was easy to forget about the impending consequences of the bite.

"Don't scare her," Fabien broke in. "She'll be fine for weeks yet."

"Mind your business, boy." Mortimer's growl caught them all off guard. His peace-keeping manner fell away to show something sharper, meaner than they'd seen before.

"No need to snap," the young man imparted with distaste.

"Mock me if you like, but we're heading off into who knows what. You'll excuse me for trying to make sure we all come back."

For a long moment, motion ceased, resuming when the old man stood abruptly. He looked from one surprised face to the next before storming to the door. "I'll get the horse."

Upon opening it, he halted, surprise stalling his temper.

"What is it?" Darius urged. Hurrying the last of the herbs into a bag as he rushed to see what had so arrested the old man. Verenna shot up from the bed and pushed passed Fabien to have a look for herself.

The whole town had gathered outside. At least half had weapons in hand. Enra stood at the lead. Noticing the door had opened she turned and made a stately approach up the steps of the porch. Verenna held her breath for the woman's first word. Her dark and distant expression gave no clues as to why she'd brought a mob to meet them. Had they found out what they were? The girls mind swam with vague memories of someone mentioning burnings back at Falseman Inn.

Enra halted only a few short paces from the door, stopping sharply like a soldier. It struck Verenna the length and leanness of the woman's frame, the canyon between her furrowed brows carved by the terror of survival, the tarnish of use on the hilt of her knives, and all the sets of eyes that looked to her for an order.

Mortimer moved a protective arm across Verenna. She felt Darius take hold of her elbow, ready to pull her away from the door at any hint of trouble. Behind her came the sly shushing sound of Fabien's sword sliding ever so slightly out of its sheath. Only the breeze moved.

"We're ready," Enra proclaimed.

"For what?" Verenna dared, and felt Darius's grip on her tighten.

"For whatever is behind those walls, Miss. We're coming with you."

Darius pushed to the front of the group. "You don't understand. We're immune to the disease. You and your people are woefully unprotected. Going to the source might be suicide. We don't know what we'll find," he warned.

"I believe I do understand. We discussed it last night and came to a decision. We wish to avenge our dead. We are going."

"You're mad," Fabien whispered. "There may not even be anything alive in there to kill."

"We will see."

"And we can't promise you protection," he cautioned.

Enra smiled ever so slightly. "Good thing no one asked you to."

Mortimer held up his hands, "We're only scouting."

"Perhaps that's what you intend. But whatever is behind those walls may have different plans. If this expedition turns into a fight, we're going to be there for it," Enra insisted. "The old man says there is a pincer move ready to close in around this area. If we don't act soon, it will close in on the village. We have to go prepared to do more than just scout. We must be ready to take any opportunity we get to end this."

"You told her all of that?" Darius hissed at the old man.

Mortimer grumbled in reply, "They have the right to know. It's technically their city. Besides, they gave us shelter and because of it they have an army of demons ready to swallow them up right along with us. The least we could do is let them know what to expect."

"And we thank you for that," Enra bowed her head to him. "Not to be rude, but we should move. The sooner the better. We'll need all the daylight we can get, I hear."

Within minutes they were plodding towards Bronwell. Enra had suggested they approach straight through the floodplain and make a beeline for the front gates. It would be the route with the most sun and therefore the safest. With the sky milky and dull, it might still be dim enough for something to hide in the shadows of the trees and ambush them. They'd agreed to her plan without much argument. If anything was watching they'd be seen, but strong daylight would keep most trouble at bay. They hoped. It didn't keep Verenna's pulse from racing every time the wind ran trails through the grass.

She couldn't help but be thankful for the breeze, however much unrest it caused her. At least the sickening smell of the city was being whisked away from them. She remembered the honey-rot stench that had wafted from the broken gates all the way across the vast fields. She tried not to think of what it might be like to breath once they entered the city.

Desperate for a distraction, she sought conversation, some noise besides the buffet of the wind and rhythmless beat of their shoes. Mortimer walked closest. Though his mood remained questionable, she decided to venture a start.

"What did you mean when you said the city belonged to the Sarzen?"

"I suppose they don't teach that story anymore," Mortimer mumbled. "When this region still had kings, the city was taken from the ancestors of the Sarzen. They were once citizens. Nobles. Brought by a foreign princess when she came to marry the prince. As king and queen, they learned to love each other dearly. Not only that, the marriage brought new trade, prosperity, new knowledge from across the sea. But that wasn't enough to stop certain groups from developing a distaste for the wealthy newcomers. They came to believe that there were irreconcilable differences between them and their new allies. Especially when children came of the marriage. Half dark, half light. It solidified the fear that the queen's people had come not to make alliances, but to take over. To replace them."

"But if the marriage was good for the country why…It doesn't make sense."

"Fear often doesn't. While most welcomed an age of prosperity others plotted for the royal family's removal. From inside the king's court, it turned out, a Lord Camlann Gausterre took it upon himself to see it done."

Verenna trotted a few steps to keep pace with the old man who'd sped up as the story progressed. "Then what happened?"

Mortimer fell quiet and shook his head, his graying locks dropping to shield her from his burning expression. "They got what they wanted."

"Who did?"

"The wrong people. The king was murdered, the queen, and any guards still loyal to them. Then the traitors called court and murdered every dark-skinned one in the room. Except the royal children." Verenna could hear the clench of his jaw in his speech. "They'd need a legitimate claim to the throne. So Gausterre would marry the daughter, Princess Adrinée, and frame the son for the murders. He'd be executed. That would get him out of the way nicely. And it would serve to convince the city that the Sarzen were the savages they'd said. That they were wild and murderous...that they'd kill their own family. Every last one of the Sarzen were forced from the city under threat of execution. Some refused to go. They weren't around long." The muscles of his neck stood out like pillars. She could see the tension of grinding teeth in his hollow cheeks.

"What happened to the son and daughter?"

"The prince narrowly escaped his execution. He was set free the night before by a guard who took pity on him. And the princess, rather than marry, and give the usurper any legitimate claim to the throne...she died by her own hand...before rescue could be arranged..."

Verenna whispered the only words that came to her, "I'm so sorry."

"Sorry..." Mortimer repeated in a smoldering hush. "Why? It was a long time ago."

She swallowed any further conversation, letting the old man stride ahead of her. His posture slumped under the weight of his temper. Something in him had soured this morning. She'd never seen him in a mood like this and frankly, hadn't thought he'd be capable of it. A certain defeated sweetness usually tamped down any sparks of anger that might arise. Not today.

"No regrets, I hope. About the plan?" Fabien appeared at her side almost as soon as Mortimer left it.

"No," she answered, making sure to keep her voice steady and eyes dead ahead. She liked that he thought she was brave and intended to keep it that way. "Why would I have?"

"And why should you?" He affirmed with a hearty clap to her back. She caught his crooked smile in the corner of her vision and tried not to think about how close his hand swung to hers as they walked. She could feel her ears going warm again.

She cleared her throat. "Nothing to be afraid of yet, I suppose." But the words sounded insubstantial even as they left her lips. The breeze took her voice away across the heaving fields of grass to the dark rim of trees. What if something were listening?

"Not yet," Fabien grinned and bumped her shoulder with his own. He seemed to revel in this uneasiness the way children delight in ghost stories. "I have a feeling we're in for a ride."

"You say that like it'll be a great time. Can't say I'm that excited. I'm not scared though. I'm not."

"No one said you were," he winked.

"Fabien!" Darius called from the front of the pack by Enra's side. The doctor motioned the young man forward. The tension between Verenna's shoulder blades went slack as Fabien jogged up to meet them.

The three spoke in hushed tones, exchanging stern looks and nods without slowing. Darius pulled the map from the canister slung over his shoulder and reviewed some element with the other two, now and again pointing to the distance on either side of them.

Verenna scanned the trees again. It would have been hard for even the most practiced eyes to spot motion amongst the breeze tossed limbs. There seemed to be no immediate danger. That in itself was unsettling. Still they plodded on. Their footfalls on the soft soil sounded like the ill timed thumping of a faltering heart.

She studied Enra's troops. They walked on all sides of her, a last ditch barrier between her and anything that might come charging out of the woods. Each maintained a quiet alertness, calm yet ready.

A few tendrils of her hair tickled against her neck in a way that raised goosebumps on her arms. The horse whinnied and stomped with nerves on its lead at the back of the group. Something in the atmosphere had shifted.

She turned her gaze forward again to the trio in the lead. Still nodding, murmuring. Then Fabien raised a hand. Her stomach lurched as it came to rest on the hilt of the sword strapped to his back. He drew it just enough to let the silver of the blade peak above the sheath. Enra raised a fist and the entire troop halted. Verenna turned in a circle and scanned the distance. What did they see that she didn't?

"No, not yet." Darius's low words found her ears and Fabien released the blade.

Verenna couldn't contain her worries any longer. She hurried forward to catch the last of the conversation.

"What's wrong? Did you see something?"

"Nothing yet. And perhaps," Enra's steady response did little to settle her stomach. The girl's nerves were still electric with uncertainty. "I believe we are being watched."

"Watched?!" Verenna rasped. "By who?"

"What." Darius corrected, setting her insides tumbling anew.

Enra mulled the situation over. "It may be wolves, or something like them. I've made this walk enough times to know when I'm not making it alone." The woman looked to the distant city and shaded her eyes. "We're half way through now. Turning back is no better than staying the course."

Verenna almost laughed. "So what exactly do we do?"

"We stay calm, stay close, and we keep walking," Enra shrugged. With a wave the woman ordered them onward.

"Perfect," Verenna said with a manic sort of cheer. "It's perfect. We're fine. We'll just keep walking."

Fabien attempted to comfort her. "If whatever it is hasn't left the trees to attack us, the day may be too bright for it. It's just like we hoped. As long as we're back before sundown it should turn out alright."

"And how long were you going to keep the fact we're being watched a secret from the rest of us?"

"They know. They're used to it," Enra flicked her head towards the group in tow. "It's you we were worried about."

"And just what the blazes does that mean?"

Darius took up the explanation as he rolled the map back into the canister. "Panic makes a mortal flame grow stronger. We can't have you getting flustered and becoming a beacon."

"I am not getting flustered! I'm getting angry that I seem to be the last to know everything. And what do you mean mortal flame? Aren't I supposed to be one of you now?"

"One of you?" Enra repeated with a kind of ponderous curiosity.

Verenna instantly knew she'd made a mistake.

"Undying," Darius jumped on the answer. "She's Undying, like the rest of us. I believe you saw an example when you stabbed this one here." He pointed a thumb over his shoulder to Fabien.

"Again, my apologies," Enra bowed her head to him.

"I'll live," he answered. Verenna smirked at the joke but no one laughed.

Enra's eyes narrowed as she considered what had been said. After a few moments consideration, just when Verenna thought she'd let the subject go, the woman spoke again. "I'm not one to question prophecy. Our stories tell us that the Undying would come to aid us in reclaiming our home. Seeing as I haven't had anyone else take a knife to the chest and walk away, the stories are doubtless about you four. If it isn't too intrusive to ask, how did you get that way? You look normal enough. What exactly are 'The

Undying'?"

Darius did not let the question hang, spitting out an answer before any further blunders could be made. "We are on your side. I should think that's all that counts for now."

Enra gave a stoic nod and the group plunged into silence.

Verenna looked back they way they'd come across the peaceful ocean of undulating grasses. Though it was all too easy to imagine something erupting from it.

Before the quiet grew awkward Fabien started on a different subject. "We should fill out our plan. How much do you know about the conditions in Bronwell?"

"Not much," Enra answered, a grim hum to her voice. "All we know for sure is we've been under attack for months. About two months ago the last of the people leaving Bronwell were gone. Few stayed, except those without the money or connections to make another choice. We haven't seen anyone coming or going since. It's like the whole city died. Pretty sure we heard it the night it happened too."

"What exactly does that mean?" Verenna edged into the conversation, unsure if she wanted the story she asked for. Everyone walking in earshot adjusted their gait. Some stood straighter, others looked away, some looked to each other with weary eyes, short of sleep.

"One night, when most of us were gathered in the main house looking after our sick, we heard a noise. A great groaning. And then a snap, like the crack of a whip a hundred miles long. It came from the direction of the city. We didn't dare go outside to see what had happened. We'd learned the hard way that the night is dangerous. Then we heard the screaming. So far off that at first it seemed like the whine of insects. It took a while to realize what it was. When we did, we stoked the fire so the crackling drowned it out. Then, the earth shook. Hard. It lasted only seconds but we were sure the roof would come down. No one's yet been able to make sense of it. All anyone could tell was that something was happening to Bronwell and there was nothing we could do."

"Then what?" Verenna quavered, rubbing her arms to try and soothe the goosebumps there.

"Didn't you ever go see what became of the place?" Darius pried.

"We weren't near strong enough at the time. The night you arrived you saw all of our healthy number in the main house; about forty, many of them children. We're hardly above a hundred total. That means over a half of our number were either ill or charged with the care of the sick. We were too weak to risk approaching the city. Besides, in a few days the wind picked up. You could smell death on it. There may be some still living. But we had no resources to save them while struggling to save ourselves."

"And the difference now?" Verenna inquired.

"First, thanks to your doctor, those of us who are left are well. We are a hundred strong. Secondly, we have you." Enra smiled towards Verenna who allowed the corners of her mouth to rise into what she knew was an unconvincing mask for her apprehension.

"Still not sure what good that'll do," she murmured to herself, letting the conversation move on.

"Of course, we should still take precautions," Enra continued. "We should split up at the gates. Two groups with two of you, fifteen of mine. We'll go in opposite directions down the two main thoroughfares. That way if one group is attacked or runs into trouble, there's a rescue party." Enra's voice carried a hardened confidence.

"Absolutely not," Darius sputtered. "That was the whole point of us bringing the girl. So if we have to make an escape the four of us are all together. What did you think, we brought her in case of a fight? Extra muscle?"

Verenna cleared her throat to remind him she was there, but he didn't seem interested.

Enra's response came across as steady as her decision. "No offense, but I have a bit more practice at keeping people safe against this type of threat."

"As you should, seeing as you seem to want to put them in harm's way," Darius barked, only to have several of Enra's rank step in. One glowering man with a beard and boulder-like shoulders looked like he might take Darius by the collar and throw him.

"You watch what you say. We've done fine for ourselves so far."

"I'm sure you have. I suggest you keep up the streak by not splitting the group."

"What experience do you pretend to have?" Another with a wide scar across his neck chimed in.

"Experience curing half your population of one ill or another. You'd think I'd have earned the right to be listened to."

Enra held up a hand to cool the hostilities. "We are listening. You're just wrong. We appreciate you immensely, doctor. But you can't always be in the lead."

In wordless astonishment, Darius made the mistake of turning to Fabien for support.

"It makes sense to split the group. I was a scout for a time. I've lead war parties too. It's the best way in case we end up needing reinforcements. It makes your forces look smaller if you're seen. Makes the enemy underestimate you."

"Good God," Darius muttered, a palm to his forehead. "And you've got nothing to say, I take it?" He motioned to Mortimer who walked a little ways separate from the group with a pensive gaze that never left the distant city. "Nothing Enra hasn't said."

"We should meet back at the gates around noon. That will leave us plenty of light to get back," Enra recommended. "If there's a threat, start making as much din as possible. The other group will try to find you."

"Excellent. Fine," Darius pouted. Verenna almost giggled at his squirming, but kept quiet under the weight of imagining what 'trouble' might mean.

The lack of words allowed something else to rise on the wind. A far off moaning, thunderous and impossibly deep, trembled through the air. Verenna perked her ears, unsure she'd heard anything at all. "What is that?" she whispered so low she could hardly hear herself. She looked at the men and women surrounding her. Their faces held no curiosity. Either they knew the sound or hadn't heard it.

Finding Mortimer near by in the crowd she moved over to him and murmured, "Mortimer, do you hear that?" He gave no reply. He continued to march with his hunched, brooding gate as if he hadn't noticed her. "Mortimer?" She said a touch louder. He looked empty. Even in profile his face seemed inanimate. The perpetual wrinkle of worry between his brows had smoothed. In fact, his face as a whole appeared smoother and more pointed somehow. Perhaps it was due to the patchwork of ragged facial hair that had sprouted over their stay with the Sarzen that hid the lines of his face.

"Mortim-," Verenna tugged at his sleeve but before she could fully utter his name he'd ripped it out of her grip and took a quick step towards her. She gasped and stumbled back. He fixed her with a furious stare that looked straight through her, his eyes narrowed, chin down, teeth clenched. It lasted only a moment. He glanced around confused, but himself again.

At her gasp the group had turned urgently inwards to investigate. "What's going on?" One of the men pressed. "Are you alright?"

"Y-yes. Yes." Her heart beat out of her chest as if she'd been running. Searching Mortimer's face for any sign of the fury she'd witnessed the instant previous, she found only a pleading helplessness that told her to lie. "I stepped on something. That's all."

The company exchanged skeptical looks.

"Why have we stopped?" Enra demanded.

"It's nothing. I'm sorry, I-I stepped on something and gasped and- I'm fine. We should keep moving."

Without fodder for argument, the group resumed their march. But Verenna caught the concerned look that passed between Darius and Fabien. There must be some other secret they hadn't seen fit to tell her.

"You were saying something?" Mortimer breathed, his voice tinged with guilt.

"Um, yeah. I thought I heard something. Something like a low moan. But I don't think anyone else heard it."

He looked to the still distant fortress with heartbreak. "It's the gates."

Verenna didn't understand until they'd come right up to the entrance of Bronwell. The rumbling she'd heard had swelled as they approached. And now at the source, it chilled her more than ever. The titanic gates hung open like dead arms offering a final embrace. Her father told her once that it had taken a hundred oaks to build each door. Yet they'd been torn open like flimsy shutters in a storm, one of them lolling at a an angle that threatened collapse. The stronger gusts of wind awoke the sound. The moan of strained hinges grieved the failure of the gates to safeguard the city. She dared not think of what tore the massive barricades from the stone.

Beyond them a vast city square expanded in desolate grandeur.

The beautifully paved patterns of blue and white ran up to an imposing facade with spires that peaked higher than the city walls. Carved above its grand, arched doorway were depictions of peasants, nobles, monks, all bent in various states of respect and pleading towards a figure in the center; an angel with a demanding expression. She held aloft two scales with the other hand pointing skyward. Two streets split off from the square, cobbled with common, brown stones, and lined with buildings, boarded and abandoned by those who kept them. They hadn't been gone long. Despite the utter emptiness, the city was still tidy. The ravages of nature had not yet taken hold.

"Two even groups," Enra called and her party broke into halves. "And two of you stay with the horse at the gate. Hooves will make to much noise with the place this quiet." She turned to Darius with a raised eyebrow, as if challenging him to split forces as seamlessly. She leaned into her hip, resting her wrist on one of the twin knives she kept on her belt.

"Right, Mortimer with me. And as much as I feel I'll regret this decision, Verenna, with Fabien."

The two must have looked surprised. "Please don't think it's about anything beyond the fact that he's got a sword he loves swinging. It's for protection. And she'd better be protected," the doctor finished through gritted teeth.

"She will," Enra added, stepping over to the party that contained Verenna. The knot in the girl's gut loosened a bit. She hadn't realized until that moment what a comfort the woman's competence was. "Camon," she called and the bearded man with the wide shoulders turned to her. "You lead to the east. We'll take west. If something goes wrong, send us a signal. We'll come running."

He nodded once and set off.

Fabien shrugged, "Off we go then?"

"You seem eager. Don't," Enra instructed and as she lead their party west. "We've got to stay alert."

"I'll do my best. It's exciting, is all. Might finally find a fair fight."

Verenna shared none of his enthusiasm. As the two groups parted ways, she couldn't ignore the feeling she was balancing on a wire. Like the lightest motion in either direction might send everything toppling.

Chapter 3

Without any sign of life to soften them, the buildings seemed to jut from the street like the uneven teeth of a vacant skull. The wind changed and moved like rancid breath through the empty streets. The shops, the vendor's stands, public squares were relatively free of it, but the homes...The stench of dead flesh reached out to them as they passed. Even boarded windows and locked doors could not spare them the smell. Verenna gagged.

One of Enra's number nudged her gently and passed her a cloth.

"Here. Tie it around your nose. We soak them in lavender water. It'll help."

She looked up into the face of a young man with a wide, warm smile, and ears that stuck out just slightly too far. "That's not your only one is it?"

"Nah. I've got a few. We had a feeling we'd be needing them."

She took the gray rag from his well-callused hand and tied the cloth around her face, uttering a muffled thanks from beneath it.

"What's your name?"

"Oaam".

"Verenna," she returned.

"Oh I know. You're all anyone's been talking about since you got here. I eh, wanted to offer a personal apology about snatching you from the road though. I was one of the party what done it."

"Well, I guess it turned out as best it could." She reached to push back a loose lock of hair, but dropped her hand when her fingers grazed the gnarled place where a Sarzen arrow had taken a piece of her ear.

"It's alright. It's not all that bad," Oaam comforted. "We've all got scars. They make for good stories. Think of it. If anyone ever asks you about it you'll get to tell them you were kidnapped by masked men in the woods and survived."

"People where I'm from don't tend to like scars or adventure stories," she grinned, thinking of Willoughby's reaction. Hopefully, the new shape of her ear would be just ugly enough to end his attempts at courting her. "Even if I tell them I doubt they'll believe me. That is, if I make it back to tell them." Her face drained of all amusement as her mind gathered the image of her father shaking his head in disbelief as he polished his reading glasses. How could he ever fathom what she'd seen? How could anyone do more than shake their head at another one of her outlandish stories?

Seeing the gravity of the situation return to her, Oaam placed a hand on her shoulder.

"I don't think anyone will notice. Not with all that pretty red hair to look at."

She huffed, one cheek rising into a half smile. "Thanks." No compliment would be enough to fully distract from the ominous surroundings.

Verenna felt a presence at her opposite side. Fabien had appeared beside her, smirking at Oaam.

"What? Can't your fighters take the smell of death? That few fights under your belt?"

Oaam's eyes narrowed above the rough edge of cloth over his nose. "It's pointless to smell it if you don't have to. And I wouldn't worry about our count of battles."

"It just seems like you'd be used to it is all. Toughened up." Fabien shook his hair out of his eyes and gazed off into the distance with a stoicism Verenna new he did not truly possess.

"The 'toughened up' don't need to prove they're toughened up," Oaam retorted, matching Fabien's far away look.

"Focused," Enra called back to them. "We need everyone focused. Verenna come walk with me."

Happy for the invitation she hurried to join the woman. Something about the way she walked and the keen, observant dark of her stare made Verenna feel that she'd be her best bet for survival if things went awry. "Ignore them. We need all eyes sharp."

"For what?"

"For anything. Mostly for movement."

A shudder danced down Verenna's spine. From then on every stirring leaf made her heart pound like it might burst.

The buffet of the wind across her ears made her strain to hear beyond it for any coming danger. They reached a bend in the wide street where the main thoroughfare curved to follow the ramparts. She could hear the sound of rushing water and knew the river must be on the other side of the stones. Her gaze wandered upward along a thin stairway to the top of the wall. Distracted by the sheer scale of it she failed to notice the roots that extended into the street. A dead stump protruded from the base of the monolithic stones of the facade. It caught her foot and she lost balance. Enra caught her by the arm as she headed towards the ground with a muttered 'careful'.

The girl mumbled her thanks and tidied her dress to keep down the flush of embarrassment that threatened to dye her red.

When Verenna looked up she found they were at the edge of another square. This had surely been the last bastion of hope for the people of Bronwell. Feeble wooden barricades attempted to stand at attention around the shambles of a meager market. The defenses were hasty constructions, built by people who in the frenzy of mortal fear, had flipped carts of goods to block the street from some advancing threat. What little they had had been spilled in the street and left to rot. Just beyond the boards and tables and pieces of broken wagons, the breeze swirled something dark into the air. Verenna took a few steps back as the Sarzen around her braced themselves for a fight.

"What is that?" one of them whispered.

"Could be nothing," Enra growled. "Let's not assume."

The group crept forward until they could get a full view of the scene beyond the barricade. "Bodies," someone breathed.

Strewn about the ground were the corpses of the fallen. Some lay in black and red, opened by carrion. Others dissolved into the wind as ash, hollow, as if burned from the inside out.

"Husks," Verenna hardly heard herself say it from under her own hand. The stench had infiltrated the lavender soaked cloth and it was all she could do to keep the rancid air from making her wretch. "We saw one on the way to your town."

Enra spoke over her shoulder from the lead. "Are they dangerous?"

"Not anymore. But whatever made them might still be around."

"Doubtless," the woman sighed.

"Do you really think there's anyone still alive here?" a wiry young man hushed from the back of the troop.

"It's possible. Some of these aren't long dead," Fabien informed them, his complexion green with the full effluvium of the corpses.

Oaam nudged him with a rag he could no longer refuse, noticing aloud, "Look how they fell. They were all running towards the barricades they set up. Like they were trying to get past their own defenses. Why?"

"There's a broken side of a building across the way. The cobbles are all turned up..." another chimed in.

Verenna couldn't think how she'd missed it. On the other side of the market there lay a vast hole in the ground, large enough to swallow a house. The stones of the street were thrown about like pebbles on a beach. Something had scraped them aside to bore into the earth...or dig its way out of it. Another voice quivered, "What happened there?"

"It seems we are the ones fated to go and see." With that Enra set one daring boot forward.

Something rumbled. The sound bounced around the empty space confusing them as to its direction. It happened again. Louder. The shifting of earth and rocks. A tremor toppled a board from the barricade. It clapped to the ground bringing every knife out of its sheath, knocking every arrow. Again, rocks tumbled somewhere unseen.

The troop pulled in tight around Verenna who clung to a fistful of Fabien's shirt. Then, out of the wind-whipped quiet rose a sing-song voice. "Hellooooo little mouse."

The walls themselves seemed to sing it. Her ribs locked up, a cage for her lungs that would only allow her frantic sips of air as she remembered the nightmare that had named her 'little mouse'. The two glowing orbs above a wire thin sneer that had appeared to her in the dark. The vines that had wound themselves through her hair and around her neck. The mocking voice that had called to her to come fight and lose.

Another rumble sounded, this time closer, hidden behind the corner they'd rounded minutes ago. Something slithered out along the ground, like fast growing roots. The lifeless things Verenna had stumbled over had become animate. The tendrils spread towards them, following the grooves in the stones, until Verenna realized they were not roots at all. They were the long, cracked, twisting, fingers of a an ever growing hand.

More appeared high up on the side of a three story building. They chipped off bricks and crushed the windows of the second floor like fine china. The troop stood transfixed by the sight, unable to fathom what unfolded before them as the ever-stretching hands pulled the rest of the monster into view.

Two milky lidless orbs sat above a jagged line of a mouth. A wide head on a crooked, vulture neck, topped a spine that curved like a crescent moon. Sagging skin so thinly draped its bones that the blades of its shoulders stood out like tombstones. How it had hidden its whole form as the stump she'd never know. Even hunched over the creature's head rose to the level of the second floor. It uprooted one of its hands and took an oozing step forward. Its dry, sore-riddled lips peeled back over icepick teeth the gray color of steel.

"I see you've accepted my invitation. How kind of you to come." It chuckled. "This will be more fun if you run."

"What is that?" Enra gasped.

Verenna answered from instinct. "Souris."

⁂

The silence didn't sit well with the eastern group. Mortimer's fickle mood and Darius' obvious pout at not being placed in charge of the troop made for a tense lack of conversation.

Camon walked in the lead, the rest fanned out behind him, eyes up and vigilant. One of the younger members walking with them spooked at the rattle of a tumbling leaf and fired an arrow. Her sudden jerk of motion had all weapons drawn and bristling in a flash.

But the shot thumped pointlessly into the dirt between the paving stones, pinning the leaf with a weak crunch. A grumble went up from the ranks as they stowed their knives and clubs on their belts once more.

"Calm down," one of the men groaned.

"It's a leaf, Adrinée. A leaf," another grunted as they walked on.

The girl slung the bow across her body. "I know that now. It could have not been a leaf."

Mortimer broke his sullen silence to congratulate her. "It was a good shot."

"Thanks," she answered, surprised to hear the old man speak.

"You're talented like the princess you were named for."

"Really? I've been told she was a great lady. Not a fighter."

"One can be both." Mortimer gazed down at his feet with a subtle melancholy. "Who taught you to shoot?"

"My brother."

His eyes darted up to the girl's freckled face, his expression a mix of heartache and hope. "What's his name?"

"Oaam." The girl seemed perplexed at his crestfallen reaction.

"It's a good name…" his words trailed off.

"Well, it's his middle one."

"Is it?" Mortimer tried to hide his urgency.

"He doesn't like his first. Says his first one makes him sound old. Don't tell him I told you but it's Mortim…" she clapped a hand over her mouth as she realized her brother shared the old man's name.

He laughed. "No offense taken. I am old. Very, very, old."

"Ahead!" Camon called. The troop drew weapons and focused in on a figure stumbling towards them. No answer came. Adrinée notched another arrow alongside two other archers. They held their bows down at the ready for a nod from Camon.

"Who comes?! Identify yourself!" Darius shouted to the approaching form. As the newcomer drew near it became clear it was an old man. He walked as if he sorely missed a cane. He did not speak but raised his hands to show he meant no harm.

"He's hurt," a thin, young man with wiry limbs uttered, stepping forward like he meant to go to the old man. Darius stopped him with an arm across his insubstantial chest. "Not yet. Let him get closer. We have to be sure it's safe."

"We came looking for survivors, didn't we? Shouldn't we help?"

"Kaybin, listen to him," Camon instructed. "Hang back."

The young man hesitated but did as he was told and rejoined the ranks. The man hobbled nearer, his shaking limp turning into a staggering sort of jog. The archers raised their bows.

"Not yet," Camon whispered and held up a hand. The scowl he wore under his dense beard deepened as the stranger's rasping breaths reached them.

"I said identify yourself!" Darius demanded again with significantly less confidence in his voice. No reply came. The man hauled himself along even faster until the scraped knees that peeked through his torn pants finally gave out and he toppled into wheezing exhaustion in the dust twenty feet away.

"Oh come on," Kaybin muttered and jogged to help.

"No...no!" Darius found himself sprinting behind the young man, just in time to catch his hand before it alighted on the old man's heaving back. "He could have the fever that ended half your people. Stay. Back. And try not to do anything else stupid."

Darius had hardly finished when Camon reached them and pulled the boy up by his shirt. "I told you, boy," he scolded. Even the leader's scar speckled face could not hide the traces of genuine fear for the youngster.

As the group looked on the doctor turned the old man onto his back.

He was filthy. If the city itself didn't have such a stench about it, surely the man would have reeked. His wisps of gray hair moved like weak smoke in the breeze. He was gasping something meant to be words. A gnarled hand with chapped white knuckles took a trembling hold on the breast of the doctor's coat.

"Mortimer, water," Darius waved for him to approach. Mortimer uncorked a bladder of water as he ran to them, dropping to one knee in a slight plume of dust to feed it to the man on the ground. He spluttered but managed to swallow enough create a meager whine.

"It grows," he coughed. A baffled glance between them said that neither Darius nor Mortimer knew what the stranger meant.

"It grows...in the rocks. In...the walls."

"What does?" the doctor asked as Mortimer gave the man another sip of water.

"It brought them. It...it cracked the ground. Pouring out...pouring..." the stranger fell into dry, hissing coughs.

"What on earth?" the old man whispered.

"Souris. What else could it be?" Darius offered.

Mortimer settled a hand on the man's brow but flinched and withdrew it almost immediately. "Fever. He's burning. I've never felt anyone that hot before."

Even to the doctors practiced touch the man was impressively fiery.

Just then the withering stranger whispered something so low both of them craned their necks to hear.

"Kill," he exhaled like steam.

"Kill? Kill who?" Mortimer urged.

"Me."

With that the man let out a rattling scream. His jaws split wide and out roared sparks and tatters of ash.

"Back!" Darius screamed at the troop. "Get back he's a husk! Get back!"

Both men threw themselves away from the creature shrieking its anguish. Mortimer was not fast enough to avoid the embers in the man's burning breath. He gasped and swatted the side of his face to put out the cinders that settled in his beard.

The husk rolled to its stomach and began to crawl towards the Sarzen, its fingers crumbling as it gripped the ground to pull itself along.

Adrinée let fly an arrow. It thudded into the creatures calf, which split it with a crack. It fell into halves like a burnt out log revealing the spark laden interior of its body. Still the creature dragged itself onwards, disintegrating with each inch.

"Hide! Get around the corner!" Darius shouted. "It's at the end of this body. It will be looking for a new host. Go!"

Most of the group fled for cover, leaving Camon to shove into motion those too shocked to run.

In the moment Darius looked away the burning shell of a man made its way to him and gripped his leg. He spun and ripped it away, but with too much force. The doctor overbalanced and hit the ground, the maps leather canister softening his fall enough to keep the wind in him. He kicked the smoldering remains of a hand off of his ankle as it seared through his clothes.

"Gah!" he scrambled back but the creatures other hand caught ahold of his shoe. With the last of its dying strength it heaved itself on top of Darius. Just as the heat pierced his clothes a resounding whomp sent ash in all directions. Mortimer, face bloody from the sparks, landed a kick that rolled the creature off of the doctor. He pounced on it and with a blacksmith's swing, thrust his knife into the beasts back. The husk writhed and spewed more sparks, catching the corner of the old man's coat. He rolled aside to put it out, leaving the creature all but dust.

The wind caught the ashen remains, stripping them away to reveal a churning, molasses blot, that squirmed in the daylight, squealing like hot oil cooked out of meat. It shrank as it convulsed until finally the spasms stopped. The remaining puddle seeped into the dirt, leaving no more than the faint suggestion of a puddle.

Mortimer rose and signaled the all clear to the Sarzen.

Camon was first to return. "Is that...is that what's in the woods? Is that what's out there at night?"

"Sometimes," Darius panted from the ground. "But this one was weak. Desperate enough to risk daylight. The ones that have been bothering you are much stronger I'm afraid. Much."

Camon shook his head. "Are you two alright? You don't look like it."

Mortimer dismissed the comment. "Just scratches really. They bleed a lot but they'll heal soon. Darius?"

The doctor went to stand but collapsed back to the ground. He'd doubled over on his knees one hand on his temple, the other clutching his stomach.

"Is he gonna be sick?" Adrinée puzzled.

"No, of course not," Darius managed to splutter against the threat of vomiting. "It's Verenna. There's something wrong with the other group."

"How do you..." Camon began, but Mortimer stopped him.

"That answer another time. We have to go find the others..."

As the old man gathered Darius to his feet, a rumble coursed through the ground. Then another. Then a third, accompanied by the distant sound of rocks shifting. Shivers of the commotion ran through the soles of their feet to raise chills on their skin. Somewhere else in the city, faint and far away, a horn sounded a long, unwavering blast.

Mortimer looked to Camon with unmistakable terror. "Now."

Chapter 4

"Run! I'll hold him off!" Fabien bellowed as he dashed towards the titan, his sword singing out of its sheath. Oaam followed in his tracks, sprinting so fast he might have been flying.

"What are you doing?!" Verenna shrieked and went to follow and stop them. But a hard hand closed around her forearm. It was Enra.

"Scatter and signal!" the woman commanded her tribe and they blew away into the cracks of the city like leaves. "Come on," she grunted and hauled Verenna across the threshold of the dead market square.

Verenna tried not to see the sprawling corpses as they bolted past. She pushed her legs harder in desperate strides to reach the cover of the next street. Battle cries rang out behind them. She heard Fabien's voice over the din just before it vanished under the deafening scream from the monster. Her head swam.

She turned to look back but Enra gave her arm a yank. "Don't. Keep running."

At an unrelenting pace they rounded a corner and streaked down the next thoroughfare, keeping out of the shadows of the buildings and away from darkened shop windows. Souris' distant laugh resounded behind them. Verenna's legs spasmed with effort as she struggled to keep up with Enra. Gasping for air, she panted, "Where are- we going? We can't - keep - this pace."

"There's a way out. A back way," Enra puffed. "Just keep - going."

The laughter sounded closer in their wake, more frenzied than before, punctuated by the sound of falling rocks. "Mouuuuuuse," it called. "Mouse, where are you?"

"It's closer," Verenna wheezed. The crack and rumble of breaking bricks thundered out of a thin alley as they blazed by.

"We can make it," Enra insisted. "Don't stop."

The bones of Verenna's legs ached with shock as she forced her feet to pound against the unending cobbles of the street. The two of them tugged the lavender rags away from their mouths to suck in air as they demanded the impossible from their lungs. What had happened to Fabien? Oaam? The rest of the Sarzen? The other group? Someone had to warn the group that went east.

"What about- what- about," Verenna couldn't finish but Enra understood.

"They'll know. They'll hear it."

"What?"

A single blast of a horn sounded behind them. The echo of it bounced off every wall, surrounding them with the solitary note as it flooded passed them.

Enra smiled with an open panting mouth. "That."

The thunder from another tumult of collapsing brick sent a tangible tremor along the thoroughfare followed by another outpouring of deranged laughter.

Unable to resist any longer Verenna glanced back down the long, arrow-straight street. Something curled around the corner. Fingers. Weaving themselves into the stones of the wall. Her gasp turned Enra's head in time for her to catch the last rootlike digits gripping the building.

"There!" The woman pointed ahead to a sliver of a sidestreet hardly visible from the main avenue. "In there. Faster." With a miraculous last burst of speed they threw themselves into the gap in the wall and hurried to hide around an upcoming bend.

As soon as they'd turned the corner they fell in a heap at the edge of a small, stone courtyard surrounded by the boarded windows of the little homes that used to share it. They tried to silence their heaving breaths with hands over their mouths, knowing the space would amplify the slightest noise. Pressing their backs against the wall there was nothing to do but listen to the creatures approach. Another tumble of rocks. Silence. A ripping, uprooting sound. A single, heavy footfall. Repeating. Closer and closer.

"My mouse, my mouse, she's here. I know it."

Verenna couldn't even blink her eyes. Fear held them too wide.

"Myyyyy mouse. Where are you?"

A light touch on Verenna's shoulder sent a lightning shock of terror through her. One of Enra's hands had alighted on her, the other pointed to a gated door at the other end of a tunnel through the wall. She motioned the girl to follow.

They crept towards the opening, heads bobbing in an attempt to peer past the darkness for danger.

"Is there anything in there?" Verenna mouthed the words so they were barely audible.

"If there is, it's probably better than what's behind us." Enra dipped into the shadows, her steps soft and cautious. Verenna took a deep breath to steady herself and ducked in after.

The passage smelled mossy and damp. The breeze eased through it, cooled by the shade. Verenna clutched her skirts to insure the material wouldn't flap. As they passed the darkest part of the tunnel she could see something hanging near the iron latch of the gate. A lock. She swore silently and prayed Enra would have a solution other than doubling back.

As they came to the gate, the woman knelt and took out a thin strip of metal from her belt. She took the lock in hand to pick at the keyhole. Verenna winced at every subtle click. Not even the thud of her own pulse in her ears could drown it out.

Verenna stared down the empty hall behind them and listened for their pursuer. The crush of breaking rock and the weighty, rip and boom of the monster's steps had vanished. Wisps of hair brushed against Verenna's cheek. The touch made her shiver. With her back against the cold stone of the tunnel she watched the gray of the day beyond.

The light wavered as if a thick cloud might be passing overhead. The shadow deepened. Verenna squinted, half expecting to see rain until the entirety of the light was blotted out. Two milk orb eyes spread a dull glow down the tunnel. It had been on top of them.

"I've found you mouse!" Souris hissed.

Verenna screamed for Enra to work faster as the monster's muscles undulated, rearranging the bones of its shoulders to fit down the passage after them.

"Go! Hurry," Verenna wailed.

Enra took up a rock and hammered at the unyielding lock. "I'm. Trying," she grunted between clanging strikes. Souris filled more and more of the shaft, his grinning toothy face looming ever closer.

"Mine now," he taunted as he slithered to end them. "Mine forever. Mine, mine, mine."

The beast's mouth had drawn near enough that she could feel the rancid chuffs of its breath riffle through her hair. Verenna took in the vomitous aroma with the air for another scream just as the lock broke open. Enra kicked the gate wide and grabbed the girl, throwing her out into the street ahead of her.

Verenna went tumbling into the day. Souris howled in the darkness as Enra charged out of the passage to escape. But before she made it more than five paces from the door, a bone thin appendage with four bulging joints like the knots of trees shot forth and wrapped her arms to her body. It snatched her off her feet and smashed the woman into the wall at the edge of the opening. Enra gulped for breath but the vine-like finger constricted her chest.

"Got one!" Souris' delight shone in the bulbous eyes that floated disembodied in the dark. He cackled. She could see the shine of daylight off of each of his long, gray teeth.

Verenna heard a crack and saw Enra's face go pale with pain. She scrambled to her feet. Without knowing what drove her, Verenna dove for one of the daggers hanging on the woman's belt. Yanking it from its holster without a thought she plunged it into what little, wrinkled flesh hung around the creature's bone.

Souris bawled, his mouth opening wide to release an effluvium of flies. They pelted Verenna like tiny rocks, a few clinging to bite her arms and neck. Another crack and the girl knew Enra's ribs were breaking.

She tugged the knife from the creature's appendage and struck again, this time at one of its knuckles. More flies pelted her face and hands as she continued to hack at the grotesque phalange. Verenna didn't bother to swat at the flecks of pain that dotted her entire body. Nothing mattered but getting through the tentacle crushing Enra. Dark blood spattered the front of her dress like tar until finally the piece of Souris' hand fell to the ground.

The hand recoiled into the tunnel. Enra collapsed in a half conscious heap. Verenna abandoned the knife and scrambled to haul the woman out of the monsters reach. She wrapped her arms around her chest and began to drag her away, inch by inch. The deluge of insects and wailing faded out, replaced by the rattle of crumbling mortar. Verenna pulled faster until they were around a corner. Only then could she hear Enra's weak commands to stop.

Verenna set her against the wall and pressed an ear close. The woman could hardly breathe. "It's not after me. Don't carry me."

A loud rumble announced the fall of larger stones. Verenna

dared a glance from whence they'd escaped. Roots, a dozen of them, had sprouted between the rocks to pry at the structure. She gasped, "We have to go," and grabbed Enra to start dragging her again. But Enra grabbed back with a shocking strength for someone so injured. The way she took hold of Verenna's arm forced the girl to halt and listen.

"It will leave me, if you leave me. Take the other knife. Run." Enra gave a nod to the hip that still carried a blade.

"No. You'll need it," the girl heard herself say.

The world slowed around them as the tremendous anxiety of striking out on her own set in. If even Enra, who's every action dripped with the natural prowess of a survivor, lay before her unable to carry on, what chance did she have, knife or no?

Dreamlike, Verenna rose. Her measured steps took her to the edge of the wall protecting them. She peeked around. Another tremor darted through the earth. Yet more carriage sized stones gave way to the struggling beast lodged in the wall. She could see its perfect glowing globes just beyond the tunnel entrance. Enra's first knife lay halfway between her and Souris.

She started for it. One slow step into the open. Some instinct in her said fewer motions might keep the creature from detecting her. She could feel the grit of the street grinding under her boots and took extra care to stay silent. A few more quiet steps. She could hear the beast's heaving breaths as it rested in preparation for its next great push against the stone that trapped it. Its gaze seemed fixed on her, but without a pupil it was hard to tell if it saw her at all. Another layer of stone boomed to the ground. Verenna ducked and covered her head, fearing she might be in range. Once the rubble stopped rolling her eyes darted about for the glint of the knife. If a stone that size covered it there would be no getting it back.

She caught sight of the blade, ahead no more than ten feet. Still hoping that her creeping would keep her from the monster's notice she started to crawl for it.

"I see you mouse."

She froze. The wire thin smile had reappeared in the shadows below the floating eyes.

"I see you. I have seen you for weeks. There is nowhere to hide that I cannot see if I choose. Nowhere."

Against every fiber of better judgement, Verenna inched further towards the blade, towards the monster's reach.

"Take the knife. It will do you no good. You are all alone. All of your friends have already succumbed to me and my horde. There is no one to defend you and no one for you to defend."

Verenna stopped her crawling. The other group. What was happening to them? Or what already had?

"Thaaaat's right," the monster's voice soothed. "They're gone now. Aaaall gone. Same as the citizens here. You saw them. Dead in the street. Easy work for my shadows. I didn't tear a hole in the earth to leave survivors wandering around."

She felt sick rise in her throat at the idea of being alone. Truly alone.

"No one will ever know what happened to you," Souris glowered under the tremendous grating sound of brick about to give way. "No one will ever know what happened at all."

Her eyes stung with tears, blurring the shine of the knife just a reach away, a dream hazy glimmer, like memories of polished silver, the flicker of the sun off the bird bath she would watch from her bedroom window, the buttons of her father's waistcoat and her mother's knitting needles. She squinted and shook her head.

"Liar…" she whispered.

"What did you call me?" hissed the beast from the chasm.

"Liar," Verenna said it louder, her vision clearing of water enough for the shine of the blade to grow keen again. She lifted a hand. It hovered ever so slightly in the direction of the weapon. Perhaps they were gone. Perhaps everyone was gone. But why should she believe it from the mouth of a Horseman?

"Insult me all you like, it won't bring them back. When I give the order, the horde I raised will descend on this city. They've been waiting for you to arrive. They'll be hungry. Very hungry. No one in these walls or miles outside of them will be left to tell your story. Not a soul left alive."

"You're lying," Verenna cried, hoarse with effort.

"You challenge me, mouse? Me? The fever that came for Bronwell came from me, my army. I have swallowed whole kingdoms in sickness. You have seen my work first hand. And still you doubt me? I, Souris, Devourer of Cities, who has brought the whole countryside to its knees? I do not lie. Call for them! Call for your friends and see who answers!"

Three of the creatures roots burst from between the stones and took hold of the cobbles before her, cutting the distance between them in half. Verenna startled but didn't move back. The root slithered forward, seeking her. Seeking the knife. There was no more time.

"I don't believe you," Verenna breathed. She launched herself at the blade, her hand scrabbling to clasp it until, her fingers closed around the smooth hilt.

"Then I will show you the truth myself!" Souris roared, sucking in air for a paint peeling cry. A torrent of flies belched from the dark space in the wall. Verenna scrambled backwards, trying to shield her eyes while floundering to her feet. The sound made her head swim, her forehead hot, made her clumsy, dizzy, sent an ache through her joints, as if she'd come down with fever only for the duration of the noise.

Just as she managed to gain her balance and stand, an avalanche rang out behind her. The wall that held the monster had collapsed. Souris reared above the rubble and bellowed once more.

The whole world seemed to spin. Verenna took off running despite her wobbling legs that threatened to bring her to the ground at every step. She had no time for a plan. No time to think of where she was headed. Even if she had, her knowledge of Bronwell's layout was next to none.

"Run mouse. I'm right behind you," Souris called to her, giddy with power. The fever feeling vanished. She sprinted harder until he shrieked again. It sent her stumbling against a building.

Something crashed above her head. A shower of rubble rained down, landing blows on her shoulders and collarbone. The edge of one of the stones struck a gash across her forehead. Darkness closed in. The impact of hitting the ground shook her awake again. Blood streaked her forehead, blurring the vision of her left eye.

From where she fell she could see the monster. Souris beamed as it readied itself to lob another chunk of masonry. She squirmed from under the pile of fallen debris to the menace of his cackling.

"What's wrong? Take a tumble?"

She heard the whoosh as a new projectile left his gnarled hand. Verenna hurried forward as best she could, half blinded by the blood tumbling from the gash on her head. The cool of a shadow fell across her body. She covered her head, expecting to be crushed. The crash of impact sounded a mere arm's length away. The boulder had missed her by nothing more than luck.

She rolled for the closest cover of what appeared to be a short wall. Only when she'd tossed her weakening body behind it did she realize that it hid a flight of worn stairs. A path to the battlements. Keeping low, she started the crawl skywards, sinking Enra's knife into the cracks to help pull herself onward.

"Hide and seek! I'll count." Souris shouted in ecstatic delight as he began to croak a tuneless melody. "One, is Disease who will eat the whole town. Two, Famine lays waste to the ground." His song cracked into wheezing laughter, closer than ever. The rip of pulled roots signaled his steady march towards her hiding place.

Battling the pulsing pain ricocheting around her skull Verenna managed to haul herself to the top of the steps. She couldn't think straight. An unshakable wooziness was settling in. Creeping along the ramparts and keeping out of sight were all she could think to do.

"Three, is War to break what's left," Souris taunted. By the sound of it he'd reached the bottom of the steps. He was closing in. "And four, the goodnight, when you go to meet Death."

Chapter 5

Darius hadn't run so hard in living memory. He lead the eastern group by a length, Camon and the others charging close behind him as they rushed towards the distress signal of the western party. Every impact of heel to earth provoked a vomitous jolt in his stomach. Something had gone terribly wrong for the others. A whole range of sounds had lead them along their way. Rumbling, distant cries, deranged laughter and loudest of all, something shrieking.

"We can split up - when we reach - the Western Market - find the way they went," Camon panted. Darius tried and failed to draw enough air to respond. Camon shouted something else but the doctor couldn't hear it over an unearthly scream. The noise grew in intensity until it had infiltrated every crevice of consciousness. It slowed their pace and had them clapping hands over their ears. Each scream disoriented them, sent chills through their flesh, and wracked their limbs with aches like fever. The group pressed on against the sickening sound and crested a hill in the road. The doctor could hardly have run another step but forced himself onward, eyes down, until a thick hand seized his arm and drew him back hard.

One of the Sarzen had caught hold of him just in time. Before them lay a gaping hole in the earth. Vacuous. Darker than daylight should have allowed it to be, and wide enough to swallow a house.

"What in the world..." someone murmured.

"Must be the reason for that tremor we felt at the village. This thing opening up," another Sarzen shuddered.

"Or being opened," Mortimer suggested stepping forward to gaze into the abyss. "It could be a Hellmouth. Souris probably cracked it open to come up onto earth. From the look of it, he brought up reinforcements." The group followed the old man's pointing, noting for the first time the bodies strewn about the square. They'd died while fleeing from whatever it was that rose from the ground.

Darius could hear the breath catch in the throat of one of the troop. "How long ago did they...how long have they…" Someone whispered.

The wind lifted the smell of decay to them. Between the stench of death and the deep, twisting feeling that Verenna was in danger, the doctor did all he could to keep from retching as he answered. "Weeks. The bigger worry is what killed them. Can anyone tell where that sound came from? That shrieking?"

"I couldn't place it because of the echo," Mortimer answered. "It came from this direction but it's hard to say more than that."

"Well, which road from here?" someone urged from the back of the pack.

"That way?" Adrinée suggested, indicating a pile of broken stones across the square. "It looks like the trouble started there. Look at the fallen bricks. It would explain all the rumbling we've been hearing."

As she said it, something stirred near the rubble. What all had assumed was a corpse raised a hand into the air, an off white sleeve billowing around it like a flag of surrender."

"Nock!" Camon screamed. The archers whipped their arrows into place and took aim.

"Wait, no!" Darius held up a hand. He skirted the cavernous hole in the street and rushed towards the figure on the ground. It was Fabien.

The rest of the group trailed behind him as the realization spread. Darius skidded to a stop and knelt. Fabien's face was splattered black and red. Something like tar clung to his cheek and he spat out the blood oozing from his regenerating teeth. His leg crooked at a strange angle under the fabric of his pants. "What happened here?" Darius demanded.

"Attacked," Fabien wheezed, clenching his jaw and groaning as one of his ribs popped back into place. "Souris. He hid as a dead tree growing out of the wall. Bastard uprooted himself and surprised us. We stayed back to fight while the others ran. Enra took Verenna. That way," he made a feeble jerking motion with his head to indicate where the women had escaped. "We tried to hold him off. Me and Oaam. Oaam…"

Fabien attempted to twist onto his side, but hissed and fell back as his leg shifted in the dirt. Adrinée followed his gaze. A ways off lay another bloodied shape. Her brother; crumpled like discarded paper. Wordless, she sprinted for him. The Sarzen rushed in and crouched around the young man. They showered him with all manner of attempts to wake him.

"Is he breathing?" Darius called. For a searing moment no answer came. Finally one of the group shouted, "Yes. Barely."

Before another word could be uttered Camon took charge. "Half of you, search for others. Get anyone who's injured back to the gates. The rest, particularly those with arrows. We're finding Enra," he commanded.

"Sword?" Fabien gasped, managing to get himself sitting.

Darius shook his head, "What?"

"SWORD!" He screamed as he shifted his leg into place. He let a few gasping breaths pass before explaining. "Where is it? I'm coming too."

"On a broken leg?" Mortimer blurted.

"On any leg I've got. Our girl's got a helluva fight on her

hands. It'd be a shame to miss it."

The old man found the blade dulled with more of the slick black spatter that dappled one side of Fabien's face. He passed it to the man on the ground who used it to pull himself to standing.

"Go with the injured. You'll slow us down," Darius insisted.

"Then run on ahead. I'm right behind you."

"We don't have time for this!" Mortimer snapped. "Let's move."

Camon was already waving half of the troop towards the street Fabien had indicated. "Stay close. And hurry." His grunted orders spurred them onwards into the corridors of the city. They picked up speed only to be stopped mid stride and be bent double by an ear-splitting cry. The sound clanged inside their skulls.

Darius's stomach lurched as if he might throw up his own heart. As soon as the ringing cleared, he spoke. "We may be closer than we thought."

એ

Verenna held her breath in a slim shadow that she hoped would be enough to shield her from the monster's notice. The cool of the stone against her head helped clear the haze. Still not enough for any escape ideas to take hold. The thud of falling bricks meant he grew closer, peeling apart the wall to get to her. Two orb eyes appeared directly above her, milky, centerless, unblinking. "Got you now," Souris smiled, his strange misshapen head filling her whole field of vision as he leaned close to laugh. She tried to scramble backwards but the creatures vine-like fingers grew through the edges of her skirt.

Trying to keep her vision straight Verenna struck at the smirking face with Enra's knife. To her surprise the blow landed. A thin slit raced across the beasts eye. It sent shimmering white liquid spilling over the front of her.

Souris reared and screamed. He clutched at the destroyed eye with his free hand, trying to find a way to mend the skin that now hung like an empty blister.

The roots that held the edge of her dress contracted and Verenna slid across the stones on her back right up to the edge of the stairs. She tried to slash at his fingers but there were too many. Each hand sprouted tiny tendrils that had begun snaking their way into the fabric of her clothes. They'd bind her legs soon. But only if she stayed in the dress.

In wild desperation Verenna sliced through the front of her bodice and into the waistband of her skirts. With a rip she was free. She forced herself up, to her knees, then higher until she was leaning over the stones that guarded against the long fall to the river below. She watched a few drops of blood from the gash on her head plummet and vanish on the bank. She pressed up until she stood.

The wind made her underskirts weave around her legs as she turned a stumble into a run. Every wailing cry the creature let out threatened to buckle her knees, to overcome her with the symptoms of fever. But something in the wind, something faint and familiar, reached through the cacophony, urging her on. Voices. Shouts she recognized.

She threw a glance towards the city as she ran and saw shapes on the ground running with her. Darius sprinted in the lead, screaming at the top of his lungs for her to speed up. He gestured ahead to another set of steps. If she could get down to the rest of the group perhaps there would be a chance for survival. Or at least a good fight.

The few Sarzen with bows were firing everything they had at the raging beast. The arrows sank deep but did little to immobilize the monster.

"Go! Go! Go! He's-" Verenna lost the doctor's warning as something enormous crashed into the wall behind her. The force of it turned the section of the battlements behind her to rubble. A look over her shoulder showed her the source. Souris had torn off a piece of a nearby roof and smashed it in her wake, destroying any hope of doubling back.

She focused her wavering vision ahead as another crash shook the stones beneath her. This one came closer on her heels.

"Run, run, run, Mouse. I smell you. Run, run, run," Souris chuckled to himself. She pushed harder for the steps. Just as she seemed to be gaining on them the battlements ruptured before her with an explosion of fragmented stone. Souris' gnarled fist came up through the walkway in a flurry of mortar making the path impassable.

She skidded to a stop, letting herself fall to avoid sliding right onto the collapsing section of the ramparts. A peal of manic laughter sent panic ricocheting around her brain. She scrambled away from the latest blow, back the way she'd come, pointless though it was. Another eruption of brick cut short her path as Souris brought his other fist down once more. Again she scurried backwards, only to be confronted with another burst of stone. The creature was chipping away at each end of the section of battlements that held her above the river. Each strike landed closer and closer. Every shriek of laughter rang louder than the last as his blows closed in on either side of her, eating up her space to dodge and run.

She leaned over the side of the wall. The river seemed impossibly far down. Could she jump? Could she leap far enough to clear the shallow water? How deep was it anyway?

Her head wound spilled a few more ruby drops. They vanished into the rippling blue below. It might be her only chance. And it had to be better than whatever was about to happen...right?

"No, no. Don't you jump," Souris teased. He cackled, a merciless, grating sound, that turned into rumbling coughs. "Not unless you want to meet what's in the river."

There was her answer. Before, a simple cut on her forearm had raised the water into boiling rapids that had nearly drowned them all. Something in it had a taste for her. Perhaps it had a taste for other things too.

"Wash the city clean," she whispered. She wiped a hand across the hot, red stream streaking her brow and flung the drops towards the lapping current below. That couldn't be enough, she thought. She grabbed a piece of broken stone, wiped her bloodied hand on it, and launched it into the river.

"Silly little thing. What's this? Do you think I'll follow that stone? Do you think I'll mistake the splash for you jumping in the river? You only took one of my eyes, child. I still see you. I've always seen you."

His fists busted loose more fragments of battlement on either side of her. She took them up, one by one to paint them red with blood and send them hurtling into the water. Verenna leaned out over the rampart again to check the distant trees for the same sway that had announced the tumult of water the first time. The river seemed lifeless in comparison. The shouts of the Sarzen reached her as if from a distant memory. Some single word. Again and again. Finally she understood it. 'Fire'.

An arrow clattered to the ground beside her. A whizzing noise and a pinch in the arm later and her shoulder went hot with pain. She let out a yell and dropped to her knees, clutching at the wooden shaft jutting from her flesh. A few drops of black tar spattered around her. Souris had been hit as well. At least nine arrows stuck out of his arm, shoulder, and neck, protruding from his skin like the last ragged feathers on a nearly plucked bird. A last well placed shot sunk into his cheek right below his good eye.

He roared another wave of flies and turned away from her to swat at the others. It left her alone long enough to summon the courage and pull the barb free from her shoulder. She screamed so hard it tore at her throat. But surely this would give her all the blood she needed to make the river rise. It had to be enough.

She hung her arm over the side of the wall and rolled up her sleeve, let the rivulets of blood stripe down her skin and trickle into the placid currents. Still nothing. Not a single wave out of place.

"Come on come on come on," Verenna muttered through gritted teeth. She watched the distant trees where the river vanished. Her eyes combed the gray sky for the plume of frightened birds that had marked the coming of the last flood. She shut her eyes and tried to listen between the noises of the fight below her for the far off thunder of swelling rapids. She opened them on shattered hope. If anything the water seemed to be drawing away from her, shrinking in its banks, abandoning her.

The white hot pulse of the hole in her shoulder made her head spin. Perhaps if she threw herself in whole, that would be enough to call the rapids. She gazed down into the rippling gray for a moment. The shouts and battle cries of her companions quickly made up her mind. If it might save them, she'd have to try.

Verenna clambered up between the merlons of the battlement. She swayed with the push of the wind, teetering. Standing on the edge made the wall seem infinitely higher than it had looked moments before.

Another blow crashed beside her making her crouch and cover her head. Having dealt with the Sarzen's attack, Souris' returned his attention to her, ready to put an end to their twisted game of chase.

"Oh mouse, you've made a mistake." He ripped his hand from the rubble he'd created and pulled himself higher up the wall, bringing the empty white socket of his vanquished eye to her level.

She made a slash at the other but Souris loomed just out of range. "Nowhere to run now."

Another chunk of wall fell away, met with shouts of warning below. Dizziness made two blurry faces out of the one that sneered before her. Again she struck out. The blow missed but nicked the monster's sagging jowl, tipping the knife with black. He hissed. His tattered lips bent into a sickle of a smile to frame his rows of needle teeth.

"You'll pay for that," he let a fist fall and collapse another section of rampart. "And for my eye." He swung again and even more fell away. He'd shaped the battlement into a stone island no more than twice her length in either direction. The last rocks clattered into the river. The next strike would destroy her. It had nowhere else to land.

"Any last words, mouse?" Souris raised his knotted fist to finish her.

Verenna felt her ears going red with ire at the certainty in his voice. "Go to Hell."

"Oh, that is exactly where I'm taking you. There's someone who would love to meet you."

Her body shook with the tremor of rage that this was how she'd end. Crushed and powerless. The tremor grew until it felt as if the whole ground, the whole world, were shaking with her. Perhaps it was.

The broken stone below her began to clatter into the river. Shouts rose from the group on the below. They scattered, racing for higher ground. Something thundered against the column of ramparts that supported her with a boom so deafening it wiped all sound from the air. The river was rising.

Souris' face fell into panic. His mouth opened to shriek but the whoosh of the building river overtook his cries. Verenna turned for a look over the battlements and saw water rushing to meet her. She pulled herself back from the edge moments before the seething spray burst over the top of the wall. The water climbed skyward, impossibly high, and in it, the face she'd seen before. The one that had stared and gaped as a hundred hands had tried to ferry her down its throat. But this time its bubbling eyes were not focused on her. They were locked with Souris. The wave seemed to pause at its zenith to gather strength before rending wide the watery abyss of its mouth and leaping towards the horseman. Verenna lay flat and pressed herself into the stone to keep from being swept up in the pummeling cascade of water.

As soon as the wave fell away Verenna sat up sputtering. Below her the river surged into the streets, swelling and wrapping itself around Souris. The monster squalled his dismay, clinging to the pillar he'd carved from the city's wall. His frantic grip ripped yet more boulder sized pieces from the structure holding her above the frothing torrent. His body was submerged up to his middle and around him the water seemed to be boiling. A closer look revealed the commotion to be the thrashing of thousands upon thousands of rats. Souris' legs, back, bones, skin, all of it were dissolving in the rivers grip to become them. The waves around him teemed with them as the fought to swim to safety.

Verenna recoiled at the sight but a single vine like finger whipped out and caught her uninjured arm, almost knocking the knife from her grip. It dragged her to the brink, to look down upon the withering face of Souris as he disintegrated.

"You think you've killed me? You cannot kill me! I am sickness. Disease. Malady. I am forever! As long as man goes on, so do I. You cannot win. You will...not..."

"Get off!" She pried at the binding around her forearm as the root tried to grow into her skin, struggling to get at the blade in her pinned hand. A cracking sound and her perch shifted. The pillar of wall was giving in to the force of the water as the flood receded. It gathered with it the wreckage of the city; broken wood and stone, and bodies, along with the tumult of fleeing rats.

"I will rise again,"Souris wheezed. "My armies will await me!"

The ground beneath Verenna tilted. The remaining structure would not hold out long. Souris' grip loosened on her wrist and the stone alike, the water melting him to his shoulders. But the damage was done. This pillar would fall.

"You belong to me. To the Underworld! The Beyond!"

"I belong to no one!" she screamed as she pushed his coils farther off of her arm. With a last heave, the root fell away and Souris' hand plunged into the retreating river. A meager laugh whined out of him as he sank to his neck, his mouth filling with water.

He gurgled a last taunt. "How little you know, mouse. How little...how little..."

In seconds the splashes of the rats overtook him. His final grip on the stone wall wilted into the river. But without his support, the pillar swayed and took an alarming angle. With the river back in its bounds there were only two clear landings; a soft one in the water, and a deadly one on land. The stones sank away from her feet, leaving her weightless as she launched herself towards the water.

The impact slapped the wind out of her lungs and stung her back, sending what felt like a ripple of lightning though her injured shoulder. Her body collided with the riverbed hard enough to jar her, but the slowing layer of water had spared her most damage. As soon as her face broke the surface she set about gulping down air. Her feet found the muddy bottom. A mixture of disgust and fear of what she knew the murky swells contained had her lunging for shore. Anything to be out of the water.

"She dove! She went under," a call rang out. A closer voice

called her name. Someone splashed towards her. Sturdy hands took her by the shoulders. Human hands, brown like the leather of a book. Mortimer. She winced and clutched at her injury, still gasping to inflate her lungs. He let go amongst profuse apologies. Wrapping his coat around her, he lifted her from the water, and carried her onto the bank. The old man helped her over the last of the fallen stones into the waiting arms of the others.

She stared down at her own two feet, hardly able to believe she had life enough to stand. Around her a drenched group of Sarzen celebrated, whooping with joy. None of it felt real.

A bursting laugh and Fabien rushed up to her. He limped heavily and his face was a patchwork of dirt and blood. But he beamed to see her all the same. He looped his arms around her and squeezed. "You did it! Vivie you did it! I told you. Didn't I tell you you're good at this? Haha!"

She half smiled, half grimaced. His embrace awakened every bruise on her. "Enra," she panted. "Enra was…"

"We found her on our way to you. They took her back to the gates. She's got plenty of broken ribs. But she'll live."

Verenna breathed a sigh. "Good," she managed, a lump forming in her throat. She couldn't tell if it would yield tears or why it might. Nothing made sense yet. She wasn't sure if it ever would.

"Where's Darius then?" she asked as another throb wracked her shoulder.

She'd answered her own question before anyone else could. He stood behind the celebrations, bent double, his hands on his knees, looking at her and shaking his bedraggled head in disbelief. The flood had soaked him, making his clothes cling to his thin frame. His ordinarily sleek hair had been scrambled into something that resembled seaweed. There was no sign of the map he'd carried, but the loss had been eclipsed by something like gratitude. None of his usual sourness existed in the exhausted flush of his cheeks. He straightened up, came to her and took her face between his hands, searching every detail of it as if he intended to memorize her freckles then and there.

"Don't you ever, you understand? Don't you ever."

The corners of Verenna's mouth crept into a smile she didn't understand. Seeing him concerned felt like a joke. "Well, if you're just going to stare at me why don't you see about the gash on my head?"

His fingers moved her sopping hair aside. "It's already healing up. Nasty though. What happened?"

"Hit over the head. Souris was throwing rocks. Well, whole sides of buildings, really. It's already closing?"

"You'll heal faster now you've been bitten. Being one of us has a few advantages. Very few. Are you dizzy?"

"I was. Not so much now."

"Good. Your pupils are the same size. You may have had a concussion but it's likely fixed itself by now."

Verenna huffed, perplexed by her own body's sudden ability to weave itself back together without her notice or attention. "I suppose I'm cured?"

"I suppose so," he answered, though his hands did not relax their gentle hold on her face. His eyes had stopped roaming her for injuries and locked with hers. She'd never noticed they weren't black, but the most subtle shade of velveteen brown.

Uncertain what to say next she pulled Mortimer's coat away from her shoulder and pointed out her other injury. "A stray arrow got me."

He instantly released her and took the slightest step back. "Yes, I see. Well, um. It's stopped bleeding. But I will need supplies to fix it up. No sense risking infection. You may be healing quickly but I'd rather not find out the hard way that you're still mortal."

The march back to the gates seemed like nothing compared to the march into them. A weight had lifted from the city, freeing the wind to sweep relief through the streets. The newly wetted ground cooled it, breaking the fever that had plagued the citadel for months.

Arriving at the gates held comfort but no victory. All who'd come had returned, but not all of them breathing. Five Sarzen lay motionless. Oaam among them. Adrinée ran and skidded to her knees beside him, her face streaked with weeping. She clutched his hand as a few men shifted him onto a stretcher they'd fashioned from broken pieces of the market stands destroyed in the flood.

Verenna clapped a hand over her mouth as if to hide the fact that she was empty of words. These people had followed her here. They'd followed with the hopes they'd be saved.

"It's not your fault, you know," Enra murmured from her position propped up against the gate. "We came knowing the risk. All of us."

The girl took a seat beside her as her companions set about assisting. Mortimer placing a consoling hand on Adrinée's shoulder. Fabien limped over to help put another stretcher together. Darius inspected the many wounds earned in the fighting and the flood. "I'm so sorry," Verenna whispered. "I didn't mean for this. I had no idea. I should have...I should have never asked..."

"You didn't ask. You lot tried to stop us coming. We insisted."

"But they're dead because of me. And you nearly died saving me. It's all my fault."

Enra stopped her by taking her hand. "We've been living a life with no guarantee of a tomorrow for a long time. For us, even the night can eat you alive. What happened here will make more tomorrows possible for our people. The prophecy promised you'd come and cleanse the city of this plague and that you did. And tragic as it is, we had the honor of being part of it. Of taking back what should have always been ours. They aren't sorry. And I certainly am not."

The girl couldn't restrain the silent downpour as she watched a troop preparing to set off towards the village with their dead. Even Enra could not remain dry eyed and stern. She took a hesitant breath, trying not to disturb her cracked ribs. "As for me saving you, I believe the opposite is true. As I recall, you came to my rescue with the knife when that thing had me. I wouldn't be sitting here if it weren't for you. I know I wouldn't."

Verenna hadn't realized but she'd kept her white knuckled grip on the dagger the whole walk back. "I didn't know what I was doing," she sniffed as she unrolled her stiff fingers. She passed it back to Enra.

"Few of us ever do. But it worked and I thank you. My people will thank you. You, my girl, have the loyalty of the Sarzen, if ever you should need it."

"Th-thank you," she stuttered, wishing she could come up with more to say. Before inspiration arrived, Fabien limped over, his face significantly less swollen and purple than it had been an hour ago. Mortimer followed shyly in his tracks.

"We've got a stretcher for you Enra. Don't want those bones any more jostled than they already are." Fabien managed a pained grin.

Two of the Sarzen moved the woman onto the bed of tightly lashed boards. She swore a storm but eventually lay back and let herself be hoisted onto their shoulders. "Move out!" she murmured. Camon heard and called it to the rest of the troop. Even from her sickbed her orders were instantly obeyed. The group started the long walk home; Enra carried in the lead, the living in her wake, Verenna beside a hobbling Fabien, and behind them, the dead.

The girl shivered and pulled Mortimer's coat close about her. She found him walking close and attempted to thank him, though he refused to look at her. His face seemed more drawn and stubbled than ever. He stared blankly at his own marching feet. The old man gave a vague grunt of acknowledgement and removed himself to the outskirts of the group.

She couldn't place it but something about him, something small but vital to him, had gone missing. And new darkness had replaced it.

Chapter 6

"Without a leader, I suspect they'll fall back and start to disappear," Darius hoped aloud as he dressed Verenna's shoulder by the fire in the Sarzen's biggest lodge.

"No sense in being an optimist just yet," Enra warned. "Until we can be sure we should all keep staying together in the main house. We're safer in these numbers."

A murmur of agreement went around the room.

After the woman's announcement the dull hum of subdued conversation swelled again. Verenna tried to keep her eyes down. She didn't want to find out how many of the Sarzen blamed her for what had happened that afternoon. Enra's words had been kind but she could not stop the tide of guilt that rose within her. Especially given the continued kindness of the village.

They'd given her new clothes to wear. A simple olive green skirt and a brown vest that let the sleeves of her chemise show. It laced up the front and made the task of dressing easier than she'd ever experienced. She'd also found herself instantly in love with how easy it was to breathe. Still, it didn't feel right to take more from people who'd lost so much in one day.

The Sarzen had already managed to bury the dead. It had to be done before sundown to avoid the creatures that came out after dark. The tribe had seen to it with an efficiency that Verenna knew came from practice. The weeping had calmed, aided by a cask or two of mead cracked open to settle nerves, and the heavily spiced stew that a few of the elder women put together in a massive cauldron. The girl marveled at how these people had withstood so much loss. They'd spent hundreds of years banished to the trees beyond the walls where they were once royalty, carving a living among the many entities that stalked them in the woods, then losing over a third of their population to a relentless disease, all the while maintaining the hope that an ancient story would come true to save them. It had come true. And yet more lay dead.

"A toast," someone said. Verenna woke from her reverie to the smooth wood of a carved cup being placed in her hand.

Camon stood with a pint raised high over his head. "To those we've lost today. And to everything they helped us gain. We honor them as they honored us. May darkness bring day."

The whole room repeated his last words in unison and fell silent in the shallows of their cups. Even though the taste curled her nose Verenna did her best to swallow down a few gulps of the bitter liquid. She hoped to find some of the comfort everyone else seemed to gain from it.

"Thought you didn't like the stuff," Fabien whispered just behind her.

"I don't. Seems right to drink it now though. If ever."

He smiled. Less than usual. His teeth hadn't fully replaced themselves yet and vanity wouldn't let his lips part too far. The bruising around his eye and cheek had almost vanished, leaving yellow traces around the socket that matched his messy hair. He downed the remains of his cup. "Seems right to me. Right enough for another." The young man moved away through the milling crowd about their nightly tasks.

Darius tugged the final knot to secure the bandage around the arrow wound. "That should hold if you don't fuss with it. Or do anything else suicidal. It may even be closed in the morning. You're healing even faster than I thought." Verenna watched his attention shift to the place where Enra sat propped up against bags of grain. "Now if you'll excuse me."

He'd gone so suddenly distant that Verenna couldn't rein in her curiosity. The doctor went and knelt at the woman's side. With what stealth she could muster Verenna slunk into a closer chair to listen.

"I'm very sorry for your losses today. It's not fair or right."

"Nothing is. And thank you," she murmured. "If you four hadn't come along we'd have lost a lot more than the five. Turns out you're quite a healer after all."

"That's what I wanted to talk with you about. Your people have been able to do something I could not. This population has a higher survival rate for Cold Fever than anywhere else on the map. There are no recorded survivors anywhere but here. How are you doing it? It's nearly a miracle."

"We have powerful gods. Powerful rituals."

"Yes, quite," the doctor fell silent to rework his question. "If I may, what exactly do these rituals entail?"

"It's long. Complicated. And not something we usually discuss with outsiders," Enra discouraged.

"An overview then? I don't mean to tread on sacred ground, but sharing the knowledge might save countless lives."

Sighing the woman began. "It's basically this. When someone is dying, when there is nothing else to be done, all of our doctors gather. They sing old songs, and pray, and give the sick one an extract made from Zahralla. It means Godflower. It's how the gods decide who will go with them and who will stay. They give the patient the draught, and hold vigil while the sick one falls into a deep sleep. A sleep like death. If the gods are not ready for them, they will wake within a day. If they do not, we can rest assured they have gone peacefully into the afterworld."

"A sleep like death…" Darius pondered. "I have a last favor to ask. May I, with your permission, have one of these flowers? One of us, well, one of us may need it in the coming days. You see…"

His voice dropped so Verenna could hardly hear and she lost the rest of what the doctor said.

The girl leaned back in her chair and strained for another clue. Why was he so certain he'd need 'a sleep like death' on hand? Before she had any success gathering more information she noticed Mortimer by the door. He stooped against the wall as if his back were in agony, his brow glistening with sweat. As if feeling her gaze he snapped to attention and surveyed the room. She could have sworn she saw him sniff the air. His features seemed sharper than ever before and his brows heavier. Then as if nothing had happened, the familiar creases of his face returned. Worry, bordering on panic washed over him and he moved for the door. The old man's steps were measured but his whole body was stiff with tension. No one else took notice. As he cracked the door and slid into the night, Verenna saw a green flash in his eyes that vanished like a spark as he turned his head.

She'd seen it once before, in the hall at Falseman Inn when he'd brought her dinner. Though she hadn't thought to explore what it meant. He'd been acting strangely all day. Curious and concerned for him, she crept to the door, knowing full well how outraged Darius would be if he caught her trying to sneak outside. But the doctor was still wrapped in urgent conversation with Enra, allowing her to slink out and investigate.

"Mortimer?" she called in a whisper. No sound reached her but the simmering of leaves in the wind and the rhythmic pulse of crickets. "Mortimer!?" She hissed his name a little louder.

She found him sitting on the steps with his head in his hands, the bulk of his shoulders silhouetted in the light of the newly full moon. He made no reply. She took a few steps closer, the tap of her shoes on the wood of the porch amplified in comparison to his quiet.

"Are you alright? What's wrong?" She reached a hand for his

shoulder but withdrew it as she remembered his temper from earlier that afternoon. She could feel a strange heat rolling off of him, like he'd just come in from the sun. It radiated through the leather of his jacket. Only then did she notice how fast his ribs were moving; in and out in quick bursts of breath, as if he were panting.

"Please say something. Please?" Her stomach rolled with gnawing tension. Something wasn't right with him. With as little noise as possible she seated herself beside the man. Despite her care the steps creaked under her weight. The night smelled like water and the green of cooling trees...and blood. The iron tinge on the air startled her nose. She checked her bandage. She hadn't bled through it.

The odor came from Mortimer's hands. Each finger had split at the cuticle, allowing his nails to broaden and stretch until they hooked over his fingertips. All of the joints of his hands were kinked backward as if his tendons had shrunk. Verenna's eyes went wider than the moon. "What on earth? Mortimer, your..."

He turned his head to look at her. The old man's face had transformed once more into the animal visage she'd caught a glimpse of earlier that day. But this time it did not fade. It held no apology. There was no room for it. Not next to the seething, hungry, rage that sunk his eyes into the shadows of his skull, that pulled the bones of his face into a mean point. His wide nose narrowed, his jaw grew long like that of a jackal, cradling a perfect 'v' of meat shearing teeth. Mortimer was gone and whatever stole him wanted her too.

The girl couldn't scream for shock. She tried to rise but toppled and landed in the feeble grass at the bottom of the steps. His focus never left her. With a predator's grace he reached out one soundless arm, then the other, and crawled towards her, perfectly balanced on the palms of his hands and the balls of his feet. His shoulder blades jutted up like hackles under his coat, two competing mountains, one rising as the other vanished. His head drooped, neck thickened with new muscle, his lolling tongue dripping saliva that shone silver in the moonlight. It glistened off of his stretching canines as he stalked ever closer.

She inched backwards, keeping her motions slow as her mind raced for what to do, for any thoughts at all besides the all consuming realization that the man she knew, the man who had saved her, cared for her, befriended her, was also the beast before her. A werewolf.

"Mortimer? Please, hear me." She whispered in the vague hopes that he'd recognize the sound of his own name. "It's Verenna. Vivie. It's me."

Her words meant nothing. All of the gentleness in his features had dissolved. He hovered before her as a new being, completely unidentifiable, half way between a man and a massive gray wolf. The creature took a few deep huffs of air, sensing her, and let a low, thunderous growl rumble forth from its chest. Verenna's mouth went dry. She glanced to either side for a place to hide or some object she could defend herself with. Her hands searched the ground on either side of her as she began to scramble backwards. The wolf matched her speed, honed in on her every move and closing the distance between them.

How long until Darius noticed she was gone? How long until someone came to look for her? And what would they do to this creature before they recognized it as Mortimer?

The beast tightened its body to lunge. But he stopped just short of springing. His ears perked. He raised his head and froze. Then, sensing something beyond her perception, he bounded into the darkness of the woods.

Once certain her life was not at stake, her heart broke for him. Somewhere inside her friend lay trapped and helpless against the persuasion of the moon. She staggered to her feet and started after him. "Mortimer!" she yelled at the border of the forest. But something else answered. A cold laugh glided out from some hidden place in the trees. "Oh you won't be seeing him for a while."

She gasped and whirled to see where the voice had come from. But as soon as she turned her back to the trees the tip of a blade pricked her spine, rooting her to the spot. "Don't you move now. Not before we have a little talk."

The pressure changed and the night around her went cold, as if she'd been plunged into icewater. "Who are you?" Verenna demanded.

"My name is Lord Gawshire. I'm sure you've heard the name."

The girl didn't need to see the man to tell he wore a smirk. "I'll scream."

"Good. My hounds are hungry."

Before Verenna could ask what he meant she noticed three shapes at the edge of the trees, darker than any shadow had a right to be. As her sight adjusted she caught the glint of animal eyes above double rows of bared onyx teeth.

"What do you want?" she glowered, trying to put as much courage in her voice as possible.

"That's easy. I want you."

"Why?"

He stepped in so close behind her that she could feel the cold of his breath ease up her neck as he laughed. "The same reason they all do. My dear, do you have any idea what you are worth? You're the ultimate hunting trophy. You defeated a Horseman. Souris himself. To catch what a Horseman can't... Now that, is a true prize."

"So you want to kill me?"

"Oh, no. That's not what I want at all. And if you cooperate I don't think it will be necessary."

Verenna swallowed hard and tried to steady the uncontrollable shaking of her knees. "Well? What will keep that unnecessary?"

"That's the spirit. Let's make a deal. My proposal is this; come with me to my manor. I promise you safe passage and fair treatment. You will be a guest in my home."

"Otherwise I am your prisoner, I take it."

"No, dear," he whispered as he dug the sharp edge of a weapon into the small of her back. "I do not take prisoners." He twisted the point making her gasp. "I do hope I make myself clear. Come with me, and all is well. Or, you and all of those lovelies in there will die tonight. And you'll be last."

Verenna made an attempt at nonchalance. "Oh? You're going to kill all of them with just you and your three dogs?"

"It's possible. But I don't like the odds. That's why I brought reinforcements. Would you like to see them? Or are you satisfied that I am in fact poised to destroy all of you?"

The girl said nothing.

"Wise," Gawshire smirked. Verenna's eyes watered as the frigid tip of the knife sunk a little deeper into her flesh.

"Decision time," the cold breath warned. "You'll find I can be generous, though from time to time, I'll admit my patience does wear very, very thin."

She shuddered, contemplating if a scream might travel faster than he could end her life. Even if it did, warning them wasn't the same as saving them.

Verenna nodded until she could manage to force words from her fear parched throat. "I'll go." As she issued the words a feeling like drowsiness overcame her.. Her legs wavered. Her knees felt numb. A great weariness had taken hold, growing from the spot the knife had pricked in her back. She remembered falling, but not being caught. Floating. Being lifted by what felt like smoke.

The loping motion of a horse at a gentle, unworried gallop.

Howls rippled through the maze of her half conscious mind. Bestial cries over a great distance. They'd close in and fall back, ebbing like the tide of sleep that broke now and again to show her the moon and reveal to her the darkness that cradled her.

Coal could not describe it. An utter lack of light, blacker than pitch. When her head lolled back she could see the outline of her captor's face in the deep shadow of his wide brimmed hat. Two red glimmers winked like far off stars just under its edge..

In what fragments of thought remained with her, she wondered what the man's manor held for her. Death, almost certainly. But what would come before?

☙

A panic took hold of the cabin as those gathered realized the girl was gone. Not only that, Mortimer couldn't be found either. And the full moon suggested the worst.

"How did you let her out of your sight? Weren't you supposed to be doctoring her?" Fabien shouted.

Darius snarled his defense. "Yes. Doctoring. Not babysitting. What was I supposed to do? Sit and stare at her all night?"

"We will get nowhere like this." Enra's interruption quieted the entire room. "Most likely she's with Mortimer, yes? I'm sure that affords her some safety."

Fabien and Darius exchanged looks. "You'd be right ordinarily. Just not right now..." the doctor trailed off.

"What do you mean?" The woman commanded. "I've seen the way he treats her. He'd never harm her."

"He's not himself, so to speak," Fabien added.

Enra inclined her head and fixed them both with a stare that demanded elaboration.

Darius took the lead. "You asked me once what we were. Why we were Undying. Well, Mortimer...even if you knew I doubt you'd believe it."

"We saw the first Horseman of the Apocalypse today. I'll hear anything out at this point."

Fabien took a deep breath and launched into the inescapable. "He's a, well, a lycan. You know, a..."

"Werewolf," Enra finished. Everyone in earshot shifted with unspoken distrust. "We've heard of them. They used to live in these parts the elders say. They were much more common in those times. Before the last round of burnings."

"They're mostly peaceful. Mostly." Fabien insisted.

"And you?" Enra inquired. "Is that what you are?"

Neither man could bring himself to speak or meet her eyes. A startling awareness of all of the sharp objects in the room settled over them. The fire glinted off of farm tools hung on the walls, knives dangling form belts, even the woman's gaze seemed sharp enough to cut.

"No," Darius whispered with hardly any air left in his lungs. "We are, um," he cleared his throat.

"Honesty would be appreciated, boys," Camon added with a protective step towards Enra.

The doctor fumbled for a term that wouldn't upset the room full of armed onlookers. "I don't think you'd know any other term but Vampires."

The whole gathering withdrew to the walls, hands on weapons, hugging children close.

"You? You are Night Bound?" Enra breathed.

"It's true," Fabien forced himself to stand taller. "But it's also true that we have been fighting on your side, and healing you, and doing you no harm at all."

None of the villagers reacted. In the silence the two men prayed their good deeds would be enough to protect them from centuries of gruesome reputation. Murmured discussion stirred all around them. Both Darius and Fabien turned in place, trying to find some ally.

Enra held up a hand. Her jaw set, stern and judicial, for the decision she would have to make. "I hope you know that your kind have not always been decent to us. I am actually quite shocked that you're among their number. Each time we've encountered one of you before, it's been a slaughter. Once a decade some deranged creature comes tearing out of the trees to murder whoever's in sight and drink their blood. That doesn't seem to be your way, but I'm sure you understand our concern."

"Of course, but please," Darius began as Adrinée cut him off with a snarl, face still streaked with tears for her brother.

"Please, what? Your kind kill our kind. How can we trust you?"

"Those are rogues. On the first dark moon after being bitten, our kind goes through something called blood lust. Because the person's never fed before and isn't familiar with the urge, things tend to get out of hand. If the one who bit you doesn't stay, and if you haven't been lucky enough to find a clan to help you through your transformation, you're loose in the world and reduced to little more than a rabid animal. That's what you've witnessed. I'd bet anything. But those rampages vanish with time. Fabien and I, we've been this way for centuries. We belong to a clan. We can control ourselves. There is nothing to fear from us."

"Maybe so, but you've kept this from us for weeks. If there was nothing to hide, if you're not dangerous, why would you hide what you are? Do you really expect us to feel safe?" Camon added with an aggressive step towards the two. Enra signaled and he halted.

"I suppose not," Darius wanted to look away from the multitude of judging eyes encircling them, but challenged himself to meet every stare. Fabien took the opposite stance, looking down at his feet and gently shaking his head under the weight of shame.

"What would you have us do?" Enra's question blanketed the room in a profound quiet punctuated only by the crackle of the fire.

"Whatever it is you see as just, I suppose. We can't ask more of you than your conscience would allow," Fabien gave a respectful nod to the woman, knowing that anything more might condemn them both. "Honor is honor, wherever it grows. You've got my respect, for or against us."

"As well as mine," Darius hushed. He doubted that these people would have the knowledge to correctly dispose of them, but that didn't meant the tribe couldn't make them wish for death. An appeal to honor might be one of the only ways out. But as the silence dragged on the doctor found it harder and harder to hold his tongue. The girl had vanished and he could feel the time they'd have to find her shortening by the second like a fuse. Camon leaned in to whisper something to Enra. He strained his ears but did not catch it. Bursting with frustration, he blurted, "Whatever your decision, make it quick. Verenna is gone. The girl who came to save your city is out in the dark somewhere and we have to get to her before who knows what else does. I seldom beg ma'am, but I will if it means you'll let us go so we can find her."

Fabien chimed in with his own plea. "Please, you've got to realize, we aren't asking for us. We've only faced one Horsemen of four and Verenna's the key to that. There are so many more people like you who will need her very, very soon. Let us go so we can find her and bring her to them."

Enra calculated the story with a hawkish intensity. They could hardly tell what thoughts swirled within her but her people held their breath to hear them. The night would either end with a desperate search for the girl or a bonfire made of their bones. Each second meant an instant less to seek and save Verenna from whatever had befallen her.

Fabien's sensed the tensions peak. His hand itched for his sword. It rested near the hearth, the flickering of the cooking fire giving it a pulse of its own, as if it were alive with the urge for use.

Darius didn't dare move. The slightest motion could be interpreted as aggression. He watched Enra's mind working behind her mask of composure until his own morbid guessing became to much. He shut his eyes and tried to find hope. But when he did, his mind conjured images Verenna, and all the permutations of possibilities that could have befallen her by then.

An eternity later, Enra came forth with her decree. "In light of what we've seen today, I do not think we have a choice."

Chapter 7

The stale air of a shuttered house called to Verenna from somewhere beyond sleep. Next, the sour taste of unclean teeth greeted her accompanied by the watery warning that she was about to vomit. Rolling off whatever couch she'd been placed on she reached for a bucket someone had thought to place beside her and proceeded to empty the meager contents of her stomach into it.

"Good morning," a calm voice spoke from somewhere she could not see over the rim of the pot.

Verenna spat and sat back against the creaky chaise with a brand new appreciation for how hard her head was throbbing. She tried to speak but fell into coughing.

"There's water. Drink. It's not poisoned," the disembodied voice instructed.

She glanced up and found an ornate goblet perched on an elegantly legged table. She knew she shouldn't take the word of a stranger, but she'd become so thirsty in her sleep that she gulped it down regardless.

She closed her eyes and leaned her head back on the chair as the water soothed the sting of acid in her throat. "Where is this?"

"My home."

"Where's that?"

"Don't you remember our talk? You are an honored guest of the Gawshire Manor."

Frantic to find the source of the voice, she searched in all directions for the wraith she'd seen the night before; the man with coal eyes and the wide hat. Instead she found a rather ordinary gentlemen, at least in that he didn't appear to be made of concentrated midnight. A dignified man sat in an ancient yet ornate chair, legs crossed, fingers steepled. He had on clean clothes, well pressed, made of rich yet understated material. Pepper gray streaked the faded brown of his hair. He looked about fifty, but the lines that should have creased his face were strikingly absent in all but a few cases. A strange newness hung about his features that made the girl feel tricked. He could have been handsome if it hadn't been for a certain ruthlessness simmering just below the surface of his pleasant, thin smile. All together, his looks were an ingenious disguise for malevolence.

Verenna's heart sped up and she felt her hands go clammy. This was the man that had slain one of his own at the gates of Falseman Inn just to gain entrance. The one who sent a posse with hell hounds out to catch them. And, above all, the one who controlled the beast called Fumus.

"What did you do? What did you do to the Sarzen?"

"Alive and well. All of them. As I promised."

Memory strained and stretched in her aching head. She could see the night he'd stolen her as if seeing it through the ripples of stained glass. She had no concept of how long ago she'd seen these things but the last thing she truly remembered was the pinch of the knife in her back. Then everything melted into darkness and howls, trees whipping past the face of the moon.

"And what did you do to me?"

"Nothing. You are safe and well. Again, I have kept my word."

"I don't feel well," Verenna turned to heave fruitlessly into the bucket.

"Of course you don't. I drugged you. The tip of the knife had a powerful sleeping draught painted on it. For your safety and mine. Couldn't have you fighting me the whole way here. I also couldn't have you remembering the way out." He smiled with a false innocence that made Verenna's skin crawl. She rubbed the tingling spot on her back where the blade nicked her skin.

"Well, what do you intend to do with me, then? You've got me. Now what?"

His smile broadened and he let out a dignified chuckle. "You are quite the fighter aren't you? Most don't recover fast enough to be asking this type of question so soon. For now, relax. I will see to it that my servants cater to your needs. Remember, you are a guest, not a prisoner."

"A guest who can't leave is a prisoner," she growled, the pain thudding behind her brows translating into a fury she hoped he heard.

All of the pleasantries fell from his visage. He glared, lines appearing from nowhere to mar his placid expression with thinly veiled rage. "Or is it that prisoners who play along are guests? Don't play word games with me, girl. You'll be treated only as well as your own attitude affords." Verenna shrank from him but his anger passed faster than a summer storm. He rose with grace and resumed his mild manner. "Well then. I will leave you to adjust to the situation. Make yourself comfortable."

Verenna took in the space for the first time. She got the impression that the room may have once been arranged for entertaining, but hadn't seen guests for decades. There were no homey or comforting elements about the place that were not covered in dust or dilapidated. Couches and chairs lay about in no particular arrangement, worn and bulging with lumps. The only piece that wasn't listing to one side was the couch she'd been placed on. A fireplace with copious amounts of ash in it did very little to help light the room. Dim daylight did most of the work. Tall windows once lined three of the four walls. But they'd been covered over with masonry, leaving only their pointed tops to let in hints of the day outside. In between, dense, sullen curtains hung over angular shapes that she assumed must be paintings. It felt like a trap.

Gawshire chuckled. "If you wanted to know how long you'll be a guest here all you have to do is ask."

"Well, consider me asking."

"Perhaps a week, maybe two. There is plenty to be done."

"Like what?" Verenna inquired, though she knew any answer would likely be a lie.

The man paused and thought, folding his hands neatly behind his back. "I'm preparing for a, well, a party of sorts. There are a few business associates of mine who would love to meet you. I need time to arrange the proper meeting place, that's all. But more on that later. For now, drink that water, lay down, and wait till that headache wears off. Fair warning, you won't be any good at walking for a while, but that too will wear off. Anywhere from a few hours to a day or two. Be careful until then. I can't have you falling and knocking yourself into worse condition."

Verenna followed him with a smoldering glare as he swaggered towards a sturdy, oaken door implanted in the opposite wall. He added over his shoulder, "When you feel well, I must insist that there be no exploring unaccompanied. I feel that in exchange for my kindness you might at least afford me my privacy. I hope you understand."

He swung the door aside without a sound, turning back to wink at her before vanishing into a torch lit passage beyond. The door shut with a delicate click and left her in silence. Verenna listened for the sound of footsteps to assure herself the man had left, but none came. She didn't hear the clang of a lock either.

She stood, wary of her shaking legs, and used the furniture to help herself across the room. She put an ear to the door and listened. "Hello!" she called, well aware this could be a test.

Gawshire could be waiting on the other side to see if she'd disobey him. She knocked. "Hello, I need something. I need, um, more water!" No one answered.

The girl stood in silence and let the minutes roll passed as she contemplated the rusted handle. She lay a hand on it, keeping her touch feather light, and gingerly pressed the lever with her thumb. A slow scrape and click and she could feel it shift. It was open.

Heart in her throat she gave it a tug. It swung towards her. Some strange child of panic and joy flooded her as she leaned around it to peek into the hall. But in doing so, she nearly smacked her forehead against yet more wall.

Verenna heaved the door wide. Her jaw dropped. The doorway had sealed up with brick. She rushed her hands all over it, sure it would be fake. She'd just seen Gawshire step through a very real doorway into a very real hall. Utterly baffled, she plopped down on the floor to contemplate the magic trick she'd just witnessed. There must be a way to open it.

The girl only realized how long she'd been staring when the light from the windows shifted to a deep, rainy gray. She shook her head and struggled to her feet, no wiser than when she'd sat down to think over the problem. With what small strength she had she slammed the door closed over the infuriating section of stone. She almost sent herself toppling. To take her mind off of the mystery she decided to explore the rest of the room.

With a gait like a lame horse she hobbled to the curtained walls and pulled the first one aside. Behind it she found an ancient painting of a woman in royal attire, the corners of its frame decorated with thick cobwebs that swayed in the breeze created by the pulled curtain. Verenna blew gently to clear some of the dust from the woman's face. Beneath it, a familiar pair of eyes. Cracked as the paint was, the features held such a striking similarity to someone she knew that she stood transfixed.

Kind, dark features, hair streaked with gray, pulled into an elegant bun, brows that bore the weight of caring. Verenna studied the woman for a long while, searching herself for how she might know her.

Hoping for a clue, she moved to the next. An imposing man with a sharply trimmed beard and angular nose gazed upon her with stern wisdom. But his eyes captured her the most. Unlike the rest of his face, there was a softness to their hazel gray that made him seem friendly. He too felt familiar in a way she could not describe.

The rest of the paintings seemed to depict various generations of the same family, spanning centuries and differing wildly in richness. Some looked to be gilded, others hung in simple wooden frames. But none stood out to her like the first two. Until she made it to the opposite side of the room.

Only one curtain hung on that wall, hiding a single painting. A wash of realization came when she pulled back the drape. A girl perched like a delicate bird in front of a young man who stood behind her with the posture of a sentinel. They were obviously siblings and the perfect mix of the man and woman in the first two paintings. Even the pounding of her head dimmed with incredulity. The young man was Mortimer.

She placed a hand over her mouth. The story he'd told on their on the walk towards Bronwell had been his own. He was royalty. A prince. And the sweetly smiling girl painted beside him, his sister, Princess Adrinée.

Verenna turned to the room, aghast at the idea that everyone in the paintings had been killed in the same massacre Mortimer described in his tale. But if this manor had once belonged to the royal family, did it now belong to their usurper?

She sank into the nearest lopsided chair, feeling woozy. The one who'd judged the family unfit for the throne, the one who'd ordered them slaughtered and framed the prince, might still be alive. She fought to remember the name Mortimer had told her. It hung just behind the veil of memory, but she knew it had born a strange resemblance to the name Gawshire.

The tiny hairs on her arms and the back of her neck prickled with the chill of horror. She thought she might be sick again. To know the truth, to be caught up in a feud so ancient, had a certain thrill to it. But not without the overwhelming sense that the brutality inflicted had not ended with the family. That it had continued to simmer in the manor house, reincarnating through the ages in the form of burnings, inquisitions, and now, whatever fate Gawshire concocted for her.

There would be no surviving whatever evil he'd plan for her. She'd have to find a way out or destroy him, if he didn't get to her first. With a new sense of urgency she redoubled her clumsy efforts to find a way out. She checked every inch of wall, opened and closed the door, scoured every piece of furniture for some secret until her legs would no longer hold her and she was forced to slump onto a musty chair to recover. The futility of it all was even more exhausting than the searching itself.

Refusing to give in to hopelessness, she made herself as comfortable as she could on the run down furnishings and began to count all of the ways she could think of to leave a room. Eventually weariness won over discomfort and Verenna drifted into an uneasy sleep.

When she awoke she found herself immersed in almost perfect pitch darkness. She stretched her eyes to make sure they were open and sat bolt upright, worried she'd been relocated into some new trap.

The musty smell and the feel of the uneven stuffing in the upholstery assured her she was in the same place she'd lay herself down. As her eyes adjusted she noticed a single glimmering candle left a ways off on a table, next to something that resembled food. The smell of meat reached her. Her stomach turned in a new fashion entirely. Though the scent of the food enticed her to a distracting degree, a feeling more akin to anger than hunger turned her gut. Regardless, distrust wouldn't allow her to move towards the plate.

For a moment she held her breath and listened for anyone else, anything else, that might be concealed in nights wrappings. She watched the little flame, waiting for it to bend the way the candles in the church had, into the mouth of some waiting creature she couldn't yet see. It hardly wavered. It wasn't much comfort but it helped settle her.

She pulled her knees up to her chest to avoid the sneaking feeling that something would grab her from beneath the chair. With nothing else to distract her from the appeal of the meat, she turned to watching the stars drift by the meager windows. Her fingers ran around the loop of twine Mortimer had given her with the vial of sun serum suspended on it and she soon lost herself in wondering where he was. Where they all were. As much as she'd like to be rescued, half of her heart hoped they'd stay clear. The only thing keeping her safe was Gawshire's mysterious need for her. He'd have no mercy for anyone else.

As the night wore on the moon rose and threw a timid beam through the glass as if offering her a rope too silken to climb. It cast enough of a glow throughout the room that she could be sure nothing waited for her. She watched the dust move through the moonlight like smoke. The light was nearly bright enough to show the russet colors of the decaying rug sprawled in the center of the clutter.

Inspiration electrified her. She hadn't thought to search the floor.

Verenna flung herself onto the rug and began rolling it up. Her hands traced the lines between stones, checking for cracks, a trap door, something to push on that might open one of the walls.

She took on the whole room the same way, realizing half way through that there were five rather massive rugs carpeting the chamber. By the time she'd rolled them all up and out again her brow dripped with sweat. With the last of them flattened she lay out panting. Nothing.

There had to be a way out. She'd try with daylight on her side.

Dawn's gold glowed against the amethyst underbellies of storm clouds. She'd waited the whole night awake for the instant the room grew bright enough to continue her search.

She rolled over on the couch to find the plate gone and candle burned to the base, still smoldering with recent fire. She sprang up and took stock of the space. Someone had managed to come in and out without her notice. They'd come so close to her and yet she hadn't heard so much as a whisper. She shuddered. It both horrified and enraged her to know that they must have opened the door she'd been looking for without her notice as well.

"How," she breathed. "How, how, how, how, HOW!" The last one rang out so loud it almost echoed in spite of the fabric lining the walls.

"Do you need something?"

Verenna whirled to find a blank faced servant, dressed in burlap rags and utterly emotionless.

"Wha- I, how...how are you getting in here?"

The servant did not answer. Upon closer inspection, Verenna recognized long chipped fingernails and the nest of tangled locks though someone had clearly tried to chop it back with careless hacks. This was the woman from Gawshire's possy. The ones that met them on the road after Canterford. Though the woman held none of the menace the girl remembered, it was unmistakably her.

Verenna circled her once to take her in. The woman hardly

blinked, keeping her vacant focus on the distance. Her nostrils and mouth barely twitched with breath. The girl might have guessed her dead if she hadn't just heard a voice.

"Is there something you need?" she repeated.

Of course there was, plenty. But somehow, faced with the direct question Verenna couldn't find the right request. "Well, yes but.... I don't think you'll actually…"

With next to no inflection the woman replied. "I'm here to take care of you. What is it you want?"

Verenna hesitated to answer for fear that anything she asked might reach Gawshire's ears. She couldn't very well ask to be shown the front door, but there might be a way around that. "I want to go for a walk."

The woman lingered in silence so long Verenna thought she might not have heard. The sound of the answer startled her. "Where to?"

She honestly hadn't expected to get that far. "Well, erm, I don't really know where I am, so, I'm afraid you'd have to tell me."

"You're in the home of Lord Gawshire. You are an honored guest."

"Yes, so he's told me. But, where can I walk? Where am I allowed?"

"You're allowed any comforts I am able to provide." The woman said it like some line from an over rehearsed play.

"No," Verenna growled. "I don't want any comforts, I want to walk. Where can you take me?"

Again the woman paused. When her silence became too frustrating Verenna prompted her again.

"Here, I'll pick. Outside. I want to walk outside. For fresh air. Can we do that?"

Still the woman maintained her quiet. "What is unclear about that?! Can you or can you not take me for a walk? It smells like mold in here and I'd like to step out. Please!"

"I think I understand," the servant said with a distance that made Verenna doubt it.

She turned on a heel and stepped past her towards the door. "Do...do I follow you or...", Verenna shrugged and moved in the woman's wake. A frantic anticipation told her she was about to learn the secret to leaving the room. But as they approached the only apparent exit, Gawshire's voice sounded close behind her and she whirled around, ready to defend herself.

"Good question." He managed to enter unnoticed too.

"Do you always sneak up on your 'honored guests?" Verenna snarled.

The syrup of his laughter coated the chamber with a deceitful sweetness that made her ears go cherry red with ire. The click of a door latch brought her focus back to the servant. She turned to catch the woman opening the door but she'd already gone and shut it again without Verenna's witness. The girl wanted to scream.

"I do apologize. I only stepped in because it seemed you'd confused the help. I've only commanded them to perform certain tasks. Bringing food and clothing, cleaning, answering basic questions, and avoiding certain others." His pointed look told her he knew what she'd had in mind. "That was some clever phrasing. Most ask directly for the way out. Of course, my servants will easily refuse to answer that question. You, my girl, are a touch smarter than those who have preceded you."

Verenna could feel her face flushing. Her fists clenched at her sides, fighting against the urge to throw one of the punches Fabien had showed her. "So you were having me watched all night?"

"Heavens no. There's no need. Is there?"

Fearful he'd post a guard, the girl changed the subject. "I remember that woman. She was one of the ones traveling with you. Now she's, just, blank. What happened to her?"

Gawshire's eyes took on a vicious sparkle. "The same thing that happens to everyone who fails me."

"And what's that?" Verenna straightened herself and tried to appear unshaken.

"They become husks, naturally. If they cannot conduct their bodies in a manner useful to me, I can certainly find some other creature that will. You know what 'husks' are by now, I'm sure."

Verenna nodded, trying to ignore how terror had dried her mouth. She swallowed.

"Of course you have," Gawshire continued and began to stroll the room at a leisurely pace. "I'd be shocked if you didn't run into at least a few in your travels thus far. This region is absolutely festering with them. But to your question, yes, they become husks. The demon inside them owes me its servitude in exchange for my raising it out of the pit. And voilà! Servants. That is, until the body crumbles. But that's not too large an issue. If I wish to keep them I give them another. It's beautiful if you think about it. A naturalist might call it symbiosis. Two creatures, better able to live thanks to one another. They escape damnation for whatever time I allow, and I gain much needed help around the house."

Verenna didn't know what to do with her disgust. "Keep those creatures away from me. I don't want them around. Isn't there anyone alive who can do the job?"

"Oh, but living help is so much trouble. They run away, get defiant, plot against you. And they have so many needs."

"Fine," Verenna huffed and resigned herself to the idea of being waited on by demons. "Can I make a request?"

"Of course."

"A book or two? Something? I'm bored in here."

"I doubt that."

"Why?" Verenna said too quickly as a dizzying rush of blood

pressure made her blush.

"Well, dear it would seem you've been fairly busy trying to get out." He nudged the edge of a rug with his foot. She hadn't realigned it. The clean stone the rug had been covering for a century or more gleamed compared to the dust faded floor around it. Horror drained her limbs of warmth as she braced for his reaction.

"Don't worry. It's only natural to resist. But! I have a feeling you will very much warm up to the idea of staying over dinner tonight. A proper dinner. Until then, I'll send for a few books. And perhaps a change of clothes. What kind of host would I be if I didn't allow you to dress for dinner?"

Seeing a potential opportunity for escape Verenna inquired, "Will that be held, um, in this room?"

"Heavens no! In my personal chambers. It's much nicer there, I think you'll agree. We'll discuss the terms of your stay at that time."

"So I'll be allowed out," Verenna pushed for confirmation.

Gawshire shrugged. "Naturally."

She didn't know whether to feel relieved or further concern. She wanted out, but there would be no way to know if it would better her situation until it happened.

The books and clothing took quite some time to arrive. Another blank faced servant entered, set them down and didn't so much as acknowledge her thanks. She watched the man who'd brought the items to her carefully, hoping he'd show her how they operated the door. She tried speaking to him, asking for a name, but Gawshire had clearly instructed this one to be silent. Every time she made an inquiry all the figure would do was motion to the books.

Resigned after what might have been an hour of trying, she picked up the first volume; a history of wheat farming in the area.

The second was a story about a girl angry with the man she'd naturally, in the end, marry. By the time she'd skimmed the first few pages the man who'd brought them had slipped out.

She threw the book across the room in frustration and took up pacing. Each turn around the room brought her no closer to an idea of how on earth the door kept opening for everyone but her. She might find out when they came to bring her to dinner, but with Gawshire there was no guarantee. He'd likely find a way to hide it from her even then.

As the sun set through the skylight she examined the dress that had been left for her. Rich red, and draping off the shoulders, something she would have coveted at home. Her parents would never allow such a garment. But with a man like Gawshire requesting she wear it, the gown lost its appeal. Besides, she had nowhere to change. People had been walking in and out unannounced the entire time she'd been there. Deciding not to risk it, she laced the gown on over her dress. She slid her arms out of her sleeves and tucked them under the finer fabric so they wouldn't show. Just as she finished a throat cleared behind her and made her instantly glad she hadn't fully undressed. Three servants had appeared, two men and a woman, all in matching burlap tatters. They didn't seem to be watching her. Or anything. Their unfocused gazes stayed on the back wall until the woman among them addressed her.

"Miss, if you'd turn around." Verenna eyed the her with considerable suspicion.

"Please Miss, if you will turn around."

Verenna took a few slow steps to face the opposite wall.

"I don't see why this is necessar-"

Everything went dark. A hood thrown over her head tightened and pulled back, throwing her off balance. She toppled, sure she would hit the floor. But two sets of hands caught and lifted her, one seizing under her arms and the other taking her ankles. She struggled and clawed and kicked. Her nails dug into flesh multiple times until she felt the wet of blood on her fingertips, but neither of her captors flinched or made a sound.

Moments later she felt stirring air. A draft. They must be leaving the room. She made to yank the bag off of her head to see what mechanism they used to keep her prisoner, but found it had been tied at the nape of her neck. As fiercely as she tried she could not reach the knot. The heat of her own panicked breath filled the bag as she was carted off into the unknown.

Chapter 8

Verenna fought and swore until she exhausted herself. The stoic creatures never once loosened their grip or altered their pace. She could tell by the incline that she'd been moved up a series of stairs. Finally, the path flattened and she could hear the harsh echo of their footsteps in what she guessed must be a long corridor.

The grating tune of rusted hinges announced their entrance into a chamber. The two that carried her released their grip and she plopped unceremoniously onto stone. Someone tugged at the string that tied the sack over her head. She snatched it off before the servants had the chance. The light from a roaring fireplace assaulted her eyes.

They'd brought her to a grand study, not unlike the one Darius kept at Falseman Inn if he abandoned it for a few hundred years. The shelves looked like they'd been looted of most of books. Those that remained were discolored with age and strung with cobwebs. Decaying paintings of royalty past decorated every wall, an audience for whatever ritual would play out that night.

On a small table near the fire sat a plate of fruit, a carafe of wine, and a roast chicken with steam still rolling off of it. None of it called to her.

She checked the room for Gawshire but found herself alone with the servants. The three had retreated to the door to block any escape attempts. With their duty complete, they seemed unconcerned with her. She stood and used the edge of the red dress to clean the blood from under her nails as she took better stock of the space.

There was only one place in the chamber that looked recently used. A wide table with papers spread across it. She stepped towards it, checking over her shoulder to see if Gawshire's servants would try to stop her. When they did not move she knew she would be free to investigate.

She peered at one of the pages left lying about, but found that it was written in Latin. All of them were, except one. Spread across the table, with a dusty tome weighing down each corner, was a water stained map. She rushed to read it and found the delicate, scrolling penmanship of Darius. The scores of tiny x's had been blurred somewhat, but it was for the most part, intact. Her mind spun at how it might have gotten there. They'd lost it in the flood at Bronwell. Gawshire must have been watching the whole time. That or one of his creatures found and brought it to him.

Alongside the doctor's marks, a strange handwriting etched the page like runes. Harsh marks made with quick sharp strokes interrupted Darius's tidy notes. These too were in Latin, but by their placement she could guess their meaning. There were notes by Bronwell that included the name Souris, and Canterford bore a small paragraph. A large x had been scraped into the page over a city to the north by the name of Turim. She'd learned all about it in her schooling, though she'd never been. It was the seat of government and the largest city in the region. Another cross lay over a region called Ferox. That land lay in the northernmost part of the country, with little population and a large degree of autonomy. In between the two the largely uninhabited miles of green were marked with a single word Verenna did not understand. Many more markings dappled the map but with no idea when Gawshire would arrive her thoughts turned to stealing it.

Her guards didn't seem to notice her excitement over the

discovery. But she'd need to distract them if she were going to take it. She shoved a pile of papers to the ground and kicked them around. "Oh dear! Look. How silly of me."

As planned the guards came awake. Two of them glided across the room, unperturbed and began collecting the papers. The third and largest stayed at the door. Verenna grimaced.

Looking around her mind found something missing from the dinner table. Keeping her hand on the edge of the map she turned to the third husk. "I would like water. Go get that, please." The creature blinked slowly to acknowledge her and turned to follow her order. The moment he'd turned his back she hastily folded the map and crammed it into her bodice, pressing it as flat as she could to minimize the lump it was sure to create. As soon as she'd stowed it she knelt and lifted a handful of papers onto the table and spread them around to hide the empty space her thieving created.

Just when she thought she'd managed to get away with it Gawshire's smooth voice rose close behind her. "I see the dress fits well."

She spun to face him but said nothing. Certain she'd been caught she braced herself for the worst. But no anger came. Perhaps he hadn't seen her take the map after all. "Thank you," she said following the prolonged guilty silence.

"Please, sit." He pulled a chair for her at the dinner table and indicated with a wave that she should join him. Afraid to refuse, she took the place he offered and allowed the attendants to serve her. Their motions drifting and measured.

Gawshire watched the ghostly shells he'd made like an artist, glowing with pride at his own masterpiece. When they'd finished pouring wine and making plates, the servants gathered by the fire to roost like crows on a fence. The three of them sat on their knees in an evenly spaced arch, staring into the blaze. The flames bulged towards them as they breathed in steady unison.

Gawshire took a bite from the plate set before him. "See? It's not poisoned. Aren't you going to eat anything?"

"I'm not hungry," she answered without taking her eyes off the four husks by the fire.

"I insist. You must keep up your strength," he pressed.

"I really don't want anything." She startled as Gawshire slammed his dinner knife deep into the table.

His easy expression hardened and his eyes grew wide as he snarled, "I suggest you accept what I offer you now because my next will not be so pleasant."

Verenna didn't move though her heart knocked at her ribs. She took up her knife and fork. With deliberate mannerly motions she took a bite of the roast chicken. It had looked delicious but by the time she'd chewed enough to taste it she found it had hardly any flavor. She managed another bite, keenly aware of Gawshire's unyielding gaze. That seemed to appease him. As quick as he'd snapped he came back to himself again. He toyed with the hilt of the knife in the table and lazily wiggled it free. "You know, I do find it encouraging that you're willing to listen."

"You've made it pretty clear I haven't got a choice."

"Don't be silly. You have a choice. And so far you have wisely chosen to be cooperative." The man chuckled and took another bite, leaning back to stare at her as he chewed. She kept her focus on the plate and cut a few more pieces of meat that she didn't intend to eat. After a painstaking pause Verenna could no longer stand his intense scrutiny and prompted the discussion she'd been promised. "You said you wanted to talk to me about my stay and why you needed me."

"Indeed. To the point. I wanted to explain the fascinating situation we find ourselves in from my perspective. There is much you do not know that I think would give you a fuller view of your future. One with significantly more prospects than you have right now," he trailed off with the slightest scowl denting his brow. "Eat," he reminded her.

She took another bland bite. "What prospects?" she said around the mouthful.

"Glad you're interested. As I am sure you know by now, you are the Bright One, the prophesied descendant of Merlin, born to stop the ride of the Horsemen. You may not know that there is one other direct descendant that doesn't like that plan very much at all. One of Merlin's daughters is awakening in Hell."

"The one that killed the others," Verenna finished for him.

"You know of her. Very good. Apparently I've underestimated the knowledge of history among the creatures you've been traveling with. They're hardly more sophisticated than animals, most of them."

Verenna filled her mouth with more food just to keep from snapping at him over the insult.

He sighed and swirled wine up the sides of his cup. "Regardless, you see the problem. Only one descendant can live at a time. If she ever wants to get herself out of the afterlife you have to die. If you were to say, fall ill, or if some terrible accident should happen, she would rise immediately to take your place. And that puts a high price on that pretty head of yours." He tapped a patient rhythm on the table with long, well kept nails. "If I were to kill you, better yet turn you over to her, it would buy me not only safety when Hell rises, but an army of my own. A kingdom, perhaps. I could ride with the Horsemen across this world and do as I pleased for the rest of time."

"So? Where exactly is my choice in it? It sounds like you'll get everything you want when I give up the ghost." The girls mouth went dry. The way the firelight glinted off his knife brought the memory of being stabbed to the forefront of her mind. She took a greedy drink of the water the husk had provided in an attempt to stay calm.

"Ah, but I could have even more with you alive."

Verenna's eyes narrowed as she considered for the first time that he might not know she'd been bitten. He didn't seem to sense that she was anything but mortal. Her gut told her that this would afford her some advantage later if she could keep him from finding out. She let him continue without interjecting.

"You see, if I kill you or give you over, and she rises, I will serve her for eternity just like every other being on this earth. But, if I keep you alive and well, she will never be able to claw her way up to the surface." He took hold of her wrist in a way that demanded she look at him. His unblinking fixation unnerved her to the point of trembling. "I will hold the key that keeps her locked in Hell. And no one, nothing, will ever rise above me. She will continue to send all of her armies to this plane. And I will capture and control them. Her army will become my army until she has poured out the entirety of Hell and sits in the depths alone. Still unable to rise to this plane. All because I have you."

He beamed, intoxicated with the idea of such unfathomable power. Verenna cleared her throat and took up her wine cup as an excuse to remove her wrist from his grip. At least he seemed more excited about the prospect of her living than dying.

"And what happens when I die? I'm going to one day. Then where will you be? You'll have betrayed the queen of Hell and she doesn't sound like the type to forgive you."

Gawshire rose to inspect his servants at the mouth of the fire. He cocked his head and considered them as if he might kick one of the poor creatures into the flames. They did not stir or bat an eye as he approached. "Do you know how old some of them are?"

"I didn't think to ask."

Gawshire ruffled the ill-cropped hair of the tallest man. "The oldest here is two hundred years."

Verenna struggled for the response that wouldn't get anyone thrown into the fire. "How did he manage that?"

"He didn't. I did. Because I chose that he should live this long. I cared for him. Gave him what he needed to walk this plane for two whole centuries now."

"Generous," Verenna ventured with a tone that laid bare her suspicions.

"It is really. If only they offered sainthood for this sort of thing. The world would be a much different place indeed." He let out a sigh, tucked his hands behind his back, and walked a pin straight line towards her seat at the table in the wake of his long reaching shadow. "And would you like to guess how old I am?"

Verenna tried to excuse herself from answering. "It would be a bit rude, wouldn't it?"

Gawshire let out a single cough of laughter. "No child. When you get to be my age you tend to be proud of it. I am one thousand and seventy four years old." He spread his arms wide and gave a turn that made the gold threads of his vest catch the light. "Could you tell?"

"Never would have guessed."

"I could do the same for you, you know. Death does not come equally to all." His shadow fell over her as he said it. With the fire at his back he seemed to be made of nothing at all, coal dust and smoke, like night itself hung with lavish clothes. "You do not have to die, if you choose to rise above it."

"And how does one do that?"

"Join with me. I will show you."

"I don't-"

He held up a hand. "I offer you a seat at the top of this crumbling world. A seat that will save you from an eternity of servitude and pain. You will be a queen, and treated as such. You will sit beside me as I preside over our world."

"If this is a marriage proposal-"

"No need. I do not wish to marry. And there is certainly no need for an heir if you're to go on living forever. You will already be giving me everything I could want just by agreeing to an eternal life as royalty. That doesn't sound so hard, does it?"

"It doesn't sound…" Verenna trailed off as she caught a flicker of gray out of the corner of her eye. A gray clad gentlemen appeared in the farthest corner of the room, watching them, with tight, thin lips. Corvudeus had returned.

She took in a little gasp that set Gawshire on edge. "What is it?" He turned but in an instant the image of the gray gentleman evaporated.

The girl scrambled for a lie. "I thought I saw something. A rat. I don't like them."

"Many shadows crawl in this house. But do not worry, dear. You are perfectly safe. Especially from rats. My servants eat them when larger souls are in short supply. Regardless, I shall have one of them check. Norik!" The shorter of the two men shot up as if fired from a spring. He made a tidy about face and awaited an order. Gawshire instructed him in Latin, and he hurried to search the place where Death had been moments before. Verenna wondered what would happen if the servant found him.

"Back to business," Gawshire said, laying back in his chair and taking a long pull of wine. "How are you feeling about my offer?"

Desperate to keep him believing she'd consider it she spat out a question. "So, I'd be like you? You'd make me what you are and I'd live a thousand years?"

"Far more than that. I'm only getting started."

"What's it like becoming what you are?"

The man's lips parted into a feral grin. "The most overwhelming sense of freedom you could ever imagine. You fly where the world can never reach, you run and the world will never catch you. More power beats through you than your mortal heart could ever provide. You are endless, timeless, eternal. Does that sound appealing?"

She shivered and looked down to her where her fingers wove and unwove themselves in her lap. Gawshire stood so that his shadow eclipsed the firelight once more. "Nothing else to eat?" he indicated with a gracious sweep of his hand. She shook her head.

"Very well." As if the words were a cue the servants rose to clear the table.

"What are you?" Verenna uttered under her breath.

Gawshire seemed genuinely surprised. "Pardon?"

Verenna dug to find the courage to say it louder. Something told her he wouldn't like the question. "What are you? If you want me to agree to be what you are, I'm going to have to know what that is."

The man smiled politely in a way that did not include his eyes. "I am many things." Her inquiry put an edge in his voice.

"And what are those things?" Verenna insisted.

Gawshire licked his lips as if deciding whether or not to humor her. "I am a Houndsman, as I'm sure you heard. I had my humble beginnings in raising and keeping hellhounds. I am considered a master of that craft. I am a bit of a bounty hunter, of men and beasts alike. Though I do find hunting beasts far more enjoyable and rewarding."

"That's not what I mean. When you took me the other day you didn't look like you do now. You were made of this, well, like smoke, but darker, like ink. And your eyes were glinting red."

"Hm," the man considered her before moving towards the fire to think.

She watched him process her demand and dried her sweating palms off on her thighs. Her plan appeared to be working. It seemed he had bought the idea that she was interested in his offer. The more she convinced him she might play along, and the more she knew about the type of creature he was, the safer she'd be. "I won't agree to help you until you tell me what it is you'll turn me into." He didn't show any signs that he'd heard her, so she phrased her guess as a question. "Are you, like the servants? A demon?"

He spun to face her the moment the words left her. His speech came faster and increasingly heated as he poured out a tirade. "I am not like them. I am so much more than some common filth from the pit. I am greater than that rabble could ever dream of being. I am of the Old Guard. The highest order. Only gods can match me for power. They lived, they died, and now they are bound to the underworld. They are nothing more than helpless nobodies made to serve. I, however, have lived, and through my own genius, have never died. I am bound to no one and nothing. I pay my debts to the Queen of Hell in full for the use of her creatures, my creatures, and I am no one's slave."

"Debts?" Verenna ventured timidly.

Gawshire straightened up, tight lipped, and nodded to his servants. Verenna had been so fixated on the man's rant that she hadn't noticed the three of them gathering behind her. They took hold of her arms and raised her struggling to her feet.

"That's enough for tonight," Gawshire commanded. "Take her back to the room. She's got a lot of thinking to do, and a very limited amount of time."

"What does that mean?" Verenna panted. "You said I had time to decide!"

"You do. But unlike me, you don't have forever."

"So what, you'll have them kill me if I don't decide fast enough for you?"

"No, child. If you were going to die, I'd kill you myself."

Her mouth moved noiselessly but could not shape a reply in time. The bag was thrown over her head and knotted again. They hurried her from the room, chased by the sound of his laughter.

Before she had the chance to orient herself of make any sense of what direction they'd gone, she was dumped like a flour sack in the dim twilight of her holding room. She tore off the bag but could not get it off in time to see how the servants left the room.

"Wait! No. No, I need something come back!" She'd hoped to see whatever trap door they'd come through slide open again, but even as she called out she knew it was useless. She stood and ranged the room for something to break that wasn't already broken. She kicked over an uneven table. It felt right somehow. She scattered a few molding books, knocked over several armchairs, attempted a couch and eventually fell to yanking herself free of the ornate red dress she'd strapped into for the evening. Empty, she flopped down onto the chaise she'd been sleeping on and let out a sigh that matched the couch's defeated creek.

She stayed there a long while, feeling the stillness of night nest around her, creeping in like a cautious child. In the absence of any daylight she noticed a little fire in the hearth that painted the room dusty amber.

"You should be careful," a voice echoed, jarring Verenna into a state of alert. Someone leaned against the mantle. She sat up ready for the next fight until the smell of Canterfords bakery wafted off the fire. The safe, familiar scent of the flower shop, the fields and trails into the woods calmed her instantly and made known that Corvudeus had arrived.

"Why are you here? I thought you renounced me or something," she scoffed.

He shrugged. "What can I say, I like spectator sports."

She tilted her head, lips pursed and sour.

"Be as angry as you like. I came to warn you."

"The danger's pretty obvious now, thanks. I would have appreciated the help before the kidnapping. It's happened three times now. Three! And where were you?"

"Watching."

"Oh? Sunday off?"

The corner of Death's mouth perked at her ire. "You know I can't interfere."

"But you can warn me?" she doubted, glaring at him.

"I can advise to some degree. The decision must belong to you, however."

The girl rolled her eyes and crossed her arms. "I await your wise counsel."

"Do not take Gawshire's offer."

"And you think I would? I am not a complete idiot. All he wants to do is turn me into one of whatever he is and use me for hundreds of years."

"I'm very glad you understand. Even if you cannot die, there are things worse. And that man is capable of them. My books are rife with his endeavors." Corvus righted one of the chairs she'd thrown over.

"I'm sure they are. That's why I've been trying so hard to find a way out of here."

"That's why I came. To tell you not to run just yet. Rest and wait, and escape will come to you. This manor holds horrors and traps that you are not yet ready to face alone."

"Or you can just tell me about the traps. Obviously you know what it would take to get out."

"That, my girl, would be planning. That is not advice. Just bide your time here. Escape is coming."

"So what, am I supposed to sit around and hope I'm rescued?" Verenna marched to him and made a point of shoving the chair he'd fixed back onto the ground.

"All I can say is that it would be prudent to not attempt anything alone." Corvus strolled to another piece of fallen furniture and set it straight, then to the next, with the grace of a waltz.

"That makes no sense. If the others try to rescue me and we're found, Gawshire has no reason not to kill them. If he hasn't already. He said he'd let them live if I came with him. Did he? The Sarzen, and Fabien, Mortimer, Darius...did he kill them?"

"Well those last three certainly aren't dead, so there's that news," Death chuckled.

She toppled the next chair he'd set right with a swift kick. "That's not funny."

"My apologies. Their immortality is my mistake. I've learned to laugh at it. But yes, Gawshire let them alone once he had what he came for. In fact, the Sarzen are better off than they've been in some time thanks to you vanquishing Souris. Without him his armies are directionless and confused. They won't last long without leadership. You rearranged quite a few of my ledgers with that bit in Bronwell the other day. I should congratulate you."

A lump formed in her throat. She hadn't really counted it as a victory. Not with that cost. "Not sure congratulations are deserved..." Her voice came out softer than she expected.

"You saved more people than you lost. Thousands of names fell out of my records. They're all alive because of you."

"Still doesn't feel right to celebrate."

"Of course not. It is only at a great distance that one can see the true results of individual deaths. Too close, and the greater design is clouded by it."

Verenna rubbed the place where the arrow had landed in her shoulder. It hardly hurt. But checking on it gave her something to do besides acknowledging Corvus. He had his head cocked like a bird, sharp with inquisitive attention, as if she were some new bit of shine he'd come upon.

"Do we have an agreement? Will you learn this place before you try and escape?"

The girl glowered. "I'll think about it."

"Why do I suspect that that is the best I'll get tonight?"

"Because it is." She could see him shaking his head from the corner of her eye. "I suppose it will have to do." Corvus gathered himself and traced his path back to the fireplace.

In the silence the girl felt something shift in her bodice. She'd almost forgotten she'd stowed the map inside.

"Wait, can you help me read this?" She reached into her shirt to produce the roughly folded square.

"That I cannot. That would be help."

"Fine," Verenna tossed it down with a satisfying slap. "Can you at least show me how they've been getting in and out of this damned room? I've been tearing the place apart."

"And you're right on top of it," Death responded.

She immediately dropped to her knees to search the floor at her feet. Finding nothing but blushing rage she looked up and shouted, "That's not helpful!" But he'd already gone.

Shoulders sinking, she took up the map, unfolded it and settled by the fire to try and make sense of the marks Gawshire added. Hours later with the fire dwindling, she retired the map into her shirt once more and trudged to the couch, flopping down dejected, exhausted, and no wiser for her efforts.

But as she tried to get comfortable on the chaise she noticed something about its creaking. It wasn't the chair. The sound came from somewhere in the floor. She shifted again to test what she'd heard and the noise came again. The subtle creak, not of old wood, but of strained rope.

As if in a dream she stood and moved to the door. She opened it to find stone barring her way. Leaving it open she rushed back to her seat and tossed herself onto it to see what happened.

The section of brick that blocked the doorway lifted, revealing a hall with a sputtering sconce just beyond. The girl launched herself for the newly open door only to have it slide neatly back into place as soon as she left couch. She sat and stood a few times over and watched the portal open and close until an idea struck her.

Rushing around the room she began dragging every piece of furniture she could lift and stacking them one on top of the other to add weight to the chaise. A precarious pile of chairs and ottomans later, she'd raised the trap door just enough to squeeze beneath it.

Death's warning echoed in her mind but the idea of freedom was too sweet to stop her wriggling through the opening she'd made to the hall beyond.

The sconce was close to going out, but bright enough to illuminate two narrow sets of steps with low-ceilings. One leading up, the other leading down. She'd been hauled upwards to get to Gawshire's study. That meant the best bet for an exit was the stairs leading down.

Verenna gazed into the darkness below. It undulated with the flickering light of the torch on the wall. As if it were possessed with a life of its own. As uneasy as it made her, she knew the way down was her best shot at freedom. She jostled the torch free of its brackets and started down the steps.

Verenna moved only as fast as she could while keeping her footsteps silent. Each time the passage curved she found a new impenetrable darkness waiting there. The light of the torch did not splash against the walls. It seemed to be using all its might to keep the darkness just above her head. The damp, mossy smell of a cave strengthened as she moved ever downwards.

A sound sang out of the black, making her jump and cling to
the wall. The thought of being discovered paralyzed her until the
noise rang out again. The pretty, musical drip of water somewhere
ahead chimed down the hall, calling her further. One hand traced
the smooth stones as she pressed on, the cool of deep earth seeping
through them into her fingers. It startled her when they can across
something jagged.

On closer examination she found a massive chunk of stone
missing from the corner where the passage twisted again.

She ran her hand along it. Moss had not yet softened its edges.
The damage must be recent. She shuddered to think what could
have broken through the rock that way. Nearby white lines
streaked the grime and lichen. Claw marks. Most small, no higher
than her waist. Some large, like the ones Fumus had carved into
the church pews as the beast had thrown them about searching for
her. It hadn't occurred to her that the creature might live
somewhere other than nightmares. But she could not turn back
now. Not so close to escape.

The torch did a flailing dance. The slightest stir of air shifted
the edge of her skirt. She must be near an opening. Hope hurried
her forward only to find a new place for her stomach to drop.
Another set of stairs twice as steep as the first descended into the
unknown depths.

A breeze moved against her brow, a soothing cool against the
fever heat of the torch. The light itself seemed to shy away from
spilling down the steps in front of her. But the way the air moved
told her there must be an exit below. Where else would a breeze be
coming from? Checking over her shoulder to make sure nothing
followed, she took the first step into the midnight before her.

She followed the sound of slow dripping water deeper and
deeper. The tunnel squeezed in as the path sunk, the ceiling
dropped, forcing her to carry the torch in front of her. It blinded

her to the passage ahead, but with unflagging determination, she continued driven on by the promising breeze.

She could smell it. The green aroma, not of a cave, but of water and trees at night, of open space. She could not resist the cool, clean taste of the air. She wanted it more than anything. Verenna followed the scent farther.

Without warning the stairway opened up. Nightblind from the torch she held it away to try and get a better idea of what she'd come upon. A truly cavernous space yawned before her. The ceiling glittered with wet, black, rock. Iron bars lined the walls; portcullis' the size of cathedral doors. Before her the thin staircase continued without the assurance of railings. And up ahead, directly opposite her in the cavern, an unblocked archway glowed with the faintest trace of moonlight.

Verenna rushed for it, nearly toppling off the steps several times in her hurry to know what she'd found. Finally her foot met hard ground instead of another step. Slick, wet stone made it hard for her feet to gain purchase. She kept her head swiveling, checking all sides, even above her for any potential attacker. Nothing stirred accept the occasional drip-splash of water from somewhere unseen. Verenna raced onwards towards the dim, white light. She'd dashed much farther now than she thought she'd have to. From up high on the steps the distance hadn't seemed so long. She chanced a look back the way she'd come.

A patch of lichen underfoot made quick work of her balance and she hit the ground. Her knees knocked hard against the cavern floor and sent a shock to her jaw that knocked her teeth together. The torch rolled away from her towards the iron bars lining the cave. Thankfully, it did not go out. Lifting herself from the ground with the thudding pain of impact in her wrists, she moved for it, then froze as the puff of breath sounded from somewhere in the dark. An animals waking huff and yawn.

Unable to pin down the direction it came from she turned in a panicked circle. When nothing came for her she stooped for the torch and met two shining circles like cats eyes in the dark just beyond the bars.

She snatched the light and backed away, swinging the fire at the faintly glistening orbs. They blinked lazily. As hard as she commanded her eyes to search she could not see the creature they belonged to, only its opalescent eyeshine. The whining yawn of a dog came from her left. The air that passed her reeked of decay.

Another pair of eyes flickered open beyond the lengths of iron. And another, and another, until there were so many they might have been fireflies. Whines, huruphs, the shifting of bodies stirred and spread to every corner of the room. She could make out the subtle gloss of the light across the bulk of muscular shoulders and jaws. The bars were cages, holding score upon score of Hell Hounds.

Unsure if they could see her she took a deliberate step in the direction of the opening and stopped. The eyes followed, winking with curiosity, though none of them barked. She took another step. They followed her, some rising to pace, others emitting distrustful growls.

An idea struck her. Instead of taking a next step, she swayed the torch. Half of the eyes followed it. Still a good many fixated on her. They could see her, but were not certain of what they saw. None sounded any alarm. They simply watched, tilting curious heads that were hardly distinguishable from the night around them.

Careful to feel the grip of her shoes before each move, Verenna ventured farther towards the moonlight. One of the animals grunted. She stayed motionless until the discontent settled. If any one of them set to barking the whole castle would hear it echoing out of the ground.

She edged up to the dim glow, the breeze as strong as it had ever been, tugging the sleeves of her shirt as if begging her attention. But instead of a door she found a shaft straight down into black waters peaked with the white light of the moon. The reflection had created the hazy brightness she'd pursued.

Jumping seemed like the only option but what body of water would she be jumping towards? The river? A moat? Could it be they had reached the coast in that night of riding and this was the sea? Regardless, the splash she'd make might set the dogs baying.

"Verenna," a voice hissed. She swung the torch to investigate the source and met a face painted with drastic, angular shadow in the light of the fire. Her balance wobbled and she felt a heel drop off the edge of the shaft. Luckily a hand shot out of the dark and seized her arm before she could topple into the water. Another hand appeared and took hold of the torch. A wise move, as she had cocked it back to take a swing at whoever the night disguised.

"Don't," an urgent whisper begged. "Verenna! Vivie! It's us!"

All of the fight drained out of her when she recognized the lilting way Fabien said her name. She suddenly understood why Corvus had told her to stay put. Help had in fact come to find her. With the torch held steady she could see Fabien and Camon beside him, holding her arm. The face that had frightened her in the moment faded into view as Darius stepped into the small pool of torchlight. Verenna threw her arms around Fabien with a relief so great she could have fallen asleep then and there.

"Glad to see you too," he murmured.

"Why the Devil did you come down here? This is the kennel. You know, where he keeps the Hellhounds?" Darius scolded to end the embrace.

"I'd noticed," Verenna retorted. "I was just trying to find a way out."

"Unless you want to jump, there isn't one." Camon added with a dry humor. "And I'd avoid that. You don't want to know what he keeps in the moat."

"How did you get in then?"

Darius explained, "We snuck across in a boat and came in through a window. After that, as you can tell, we got a bit lost."

"Time to start back tracking," Camon muttered as he gazed over the hundreds of curious watchers in the cages.

"Please tell me you remember something about the way you came." Verenna couldn't keep the bite of frustration out of her voice.

"Vaguely," Darius said as he joined Camon in examining the cells full of hounds. "We had to run when we heard someone coming down the passage. That turned out to be you."

"But that isn't," Camon hushed and pointed to the stairs. "Someone's coming."

The words had Verenna's heart in her throat and her stomach in her shoes. Sure enough, she heard the sound of confident footsteps trekking down the stairs.

"Hide," Camon urged.

"Where?" She rasped.

"Anywhere." Darius took her hand to pulled her into the crag of a wall.

Fabien dumped the torch down the shaft and ducked into a similar shadow. A distant splash, followed by thrashing and dry-throated croaking ensued. "What is that?" she mouthed to Darius. He put a finger to his lips and shook his head. The footfalls drew ever closer. Verenna could feel the fear in Darius' hands as they pressed against her back, drawing her closer to him. She hadn't thought about it but she'd taken a fistful of his vest and had it in the white knuckled knot of her grip.

The steps stopped for a long while. Verenna's ears perked in the new silence. The dogs had hushed. It was as if they'd imagined the newcomer. The cavern had been taken by a quiet so deep that the eventual drip and splash of water might as well have been thunder.

"I thought this might be where we'd end up." Gawshire's voice bounced off of every wall until it filled the whole space with his presence. "It appears you were pretending to consider my proposal only to appease me. Actions are much, much more reliable than words."

Verenna looked up into Darius' face, her expression asking if they'd been discovered, if he could see them hiding. He shook his head ever so slightly, unsure.

"I must commend you on your hiding place. I can't see you. And I can always see you."

Verenna squeezed in tighter against Darius, knowing that the only reason Gawshire hadn't immediately spotted a mortal flame in the room was because it was tucked behind an immortal one invisible to him.

"You did not jump. I know you are here. You were clever to throw something, but believe me, I recognize the way a body hits the water from here." Gawshire considered the silence. "You did not jump," he repeated, with considerably less conviction. "You did not…"

The pressure changed. Everything went cold. Her face, toes, fingers chilled instantly as a painful rash of goosebumps ran rampant across her arms and body.

A substance like ink drifted to the opening to examine the waves below. Two coals neatly lit the spaces that should be eyes. She watched Gawshire over Darius' shoulder, the smoke of him forming and unforming, suspended and undulating.

Verenna shut her eyes. If they were discovered she had no doubt the man would release his dogs. She remembered being told that if they worked en masse they might even drag immortal souls to Hell for a time, not to mention certain dismemberment.

Unable to stomach her own imagination she forced herself to look into the swirling night of Gawshire's form.

He hadn't taken his focus off the water for some minutes. He watched the tiny lapping waves, perhaps hoping to wait her out if she were holding her breath under the surface.

The shadow raised itself from its stooping posture and drew to its full proud height. The figure turned to the room. If he'd glanced even the slightest degree to his left, he would have seen them.

A dog whined. Gawshire drifted forward, soundless as fog. He said something in Latin to soothe the animals complaint. Then, silence. For longer than she could count. Just the whisper of the breeze and the far off lap of the water. Even after the dogs settled, even when she knew Gawshire must have gone, she still clung to Darius, fear having frozen her muscles in that position.

Moving at a creeping pace he let go of her and checked over his shoulder. Verenna snuck forward, eager to see that the man had actually left them, desperate to know if they'd avoided capture.

Verenna squinted into the dark of the cavern. It appeared empty until two red spots winked open in the middle of the cave. They gave off just enough glow to highlight the slender curve of a hungry smile.

Gawshire's whispered "I see you."

Chapter 9

"Come out. Your friend too."

Verenna edged out of the hiding space. "Forward," Gawshire commanded when she hesitated. She could feel Darius close behind her. He gripped the back of her dress, prepared to pull her out of harm's way.

The smoke form ordered them onward until they stood directly before him. The dogs stirred, exuberant with their discovery. Several paced quick routes just inside the bars while others packed up against them to watch.

"So, who is it who's come to save you? Hm? Speak," Gawshire commanded, as if to one of his animals.

"My name is Collins. Dr. Collins. I'm from Canterford."

"You're a liar is what you are. You are Doctor Darius Defoe. From across the sea, via Alma, living outside of Canterford."

She heard Darius swallow hard. Gawshire chuckled without merriment. "Lie to me again and see what becomes of you." He began circling the two of them. "Doctor, I have noticed two things just now. One, is that I cannot see your soulfire. Two, one of my favorite hounds seems very excited to meet you." He pointed to the dog pacing fastest. "That is Phoebe. She is a prized possession of mine because she is unmatched at spotting Vampires. Something about them brings out the most beautiful fury in her. Tell me, Doctor, is that what you are?"

Verenna could feel his hand shaking on her back. Darius did not answer. Either fear or defiance had muted him.

"So quiet. And here I'd heard you have such an ego. Well? Are you or are you not a Vampire?"

"You should know the answer. Are you stupid or just toying with me?"

Gawshire laughed; a hearty, a real one, as if he were genuinely enjoying himself. The space that should be his mouth split open wide to accommodate it, revealing embers studding the shaft of his throat. "You see, that is what I like about your kind. You develop such a wonderful humor over the centuries. It ages like fine wine. Almost a pity to open the bottle."

Something silver glinted in the moonlight behind Gawshire. The shine had been too strong to be the eye of an animal. Fabien's outline appeared, looming large like a coming storm. She tried not to look, not to show Gawshire that a threat approached, but he'd seen the flick of her eyes.

"What's that? Do you have more friends I've yet to meet?"

Fabien's sword plunged into the gathered clouds of the wraith's body. Gawshire shrieked, more with rage than hurt, as he turned and took hold of the young man. He threw him so that his body bashed into the bars of the nearest cage. He hardly had time to roll away before a host of snapping jaws reached through. The dogs barked and howled a strange, off tune chorus, half the cry of wolves, half like the wind moaning through a crack in a house.

Another glint of silver struck low. Camon had joined the fight. Gawshire roared and the fog of his body lunged for the man. Camon dodged but slipped on the slick floor. The smoke form condensed and fell upon him. Verenna raced towards the brawl. "No!" she screamed and struggled against Darius's attempts to hold her back from the fray. If another one of the Sarzen died for her...she couldn't stomach it. The tussle on the floor ended. Camon lay prone, his weak panting the only sign of life.

Gawshire rose just as Verenna broke free of the doctor's hold. She ran at the wraith while he still had his back to her. Throwing herself at him full force she tried to sink her fingers into the congealed ink that made up his flesh. A thicker version of air ran through her fingers, the tears healing instantly as she clawed at him. Without a sound he spun and grabbed her by the throat. "Thought you could ambush me? Thought you could escape? You aren't half as smart as I thought you were. Now you need to listen very, very carefully." The print of his hand around her neck had gone ice cold and tightened, making the muscles of her neck and tongue sluggish and incapable of speech.

Verenna heard Fabien take up his sword somewhere in the dark. Gawshire held up his free hand, "Do it and I release the dogs!" The words echoed and all motion ground to a halt. Even the dogs stopped their pacing and came to attention.

"If any one of you moves without my permission, I will set the hounds free and they will decide what to do with you. You can deal with them or you can deal with me. Your choice."

Instinct froze them all as they balanced on the razor edge between hunted and caught. Satisfied, Gawshire continued. "Now. You will all follow me. You will do so without any fuss or upset or attempts to fight. Remember this. The only thing keeping the hounds where they are is my command and the water dripping down the bars. They can't cross it. But they don't have to if I let them out. Understood?" When no more threats arose Gawshire's coal eyes narrowed. "Good. Upstairs. All of you. Bring that one too." He nodded to Camon's barely conscious body.

"What did you do to him?" Verenna smoldered.

"Gave him Cold Fever, child. Doctor, this should excite you. You'll get to watch the progression first hand. It's utterly fascinating. Now move."

Fabien knelt and helped Camon to his feet while Darius snuck forward with a hand outstretched for Verenna's. Seeing this Gawshire protested.

"Oh no, no, no. That won't do. I don't trust you near the girl. You'll walk separately. I want all of you to remember, good behavior is the only thing keeping those gates closed." He gestured towards Phoebe. The animal salivated, its body so lightless that even its wet teeth struggled to glisten. "It's up to you however. Bad behavior will at least make the dogs happy."

Gawshire kept his hand around Verenna's neck for the entire march, driving the others ahead of them on the winding route to the upper part of the manor. The chill of his presence became painful the longer they walked. Darius lead the group, with Fabien helping Camon along behind him.

Climbing ever upwards, they passed more and more windows. A faint royal blue had already begun to spill across the edge of the world. Dawn would break within an hour. She could only hope daylight would be as much of a complication for Gawshire as it was for Darius or Fabien.

At the top of an extremely steep spiral staircase, the group halted at a beautifully carved door. "Open it," Gawshire demanded. She could feel the reverberations of his voice in the gauzy dark encircling her neck.

Darius obeyed and pulled the door out of the way. The deer that adorned it seemed to flee as it swung aside.

"Inside," he ordered, and ushered them into a tower room with vast windows on three sides. The sapphire morning lit just enough of the world for Verenna to see that moors stretched out on all sides. To the West they ended in a distant line of ink dark trees that must be the woods they'd come from. To the East, the land reached for the horizon with no obstacles, just flat miles straight to the coming sun. A large cage waited at the eastern window, gate open like the mouth of a waiting predator. Others of varying sizes lined the western side of the room. A few lavish chairs dotted the space, most facing the cage. On the mantle above the fireplace sat a glittering row of objects Verenna had never seen before. Sparkling stones, some like crystals with veins of copper running though, others like twinkling ice with rivers of gold and silver, dazzling in their brilliance even in the weak blue of early morning. More hung above them, strung on lines into the most ornate chandelier Verenna could have imagined. Their radiance, even in the lowest light, astounded her.

Verenna felt the collar of Gawshires hand loosen. Reaching up she felt flesh in place of the night stuff he was made of. He'd resumed his human shape. "Like those, do you?" he asked, noting her awe at his sparkling decorations. "Do you know what they are?"

Cautious of her answer, Verenna shook her head. A quick glance to the others told her she wouldn't like what he'd tell her. Darius's whole body shook, his fists clenched at his sides, the muscles of his jaw twitching under his skin. Fabien, still holding up a wilting Camon, struggled to keep his welling tears from spilling down his face.

"These, my child, are souls."

"Souls?" Verenna repeated, to incredulous to form her own words.

"Yes. Not just any souls. Crystallized ones. Immortal ones. Just like those inside your friends here. Well, two of them anyway. They are quite valuable. Largely because they are hard to come by. But as you can see, I have become quite adept at gathering them over the years. They are trophies, testaments to my skill. However, as beautiful and costly as they are, the real prize is in the harvesting."

Verenna felt like spitting at him, but with the memory of the hounds still fresh in her mind she couldn't bring herself to take the risk.

He released her and moved to the mantle. The clack of his

boots resounded through the space with no rugs to stop the ringing. In the center of the dazzling souls she'd hardly noticed a large urn. Gawshire took it by its handles and lowered it onto a little table by the fire. "Come. Let me show you something."

Verenna took a few hesitant steps as commanded. A footfall behind her made everyone startle. Darius had made a move to stop her but froze when Gawshire looked up. "Now Doctor, the girl has a right to learn. I want to provide her the best education."

Gawshire sneered at the helplessness of the girls protectors. He lifted the porcelain lid. It brimmed with gray dust. "And do you know what this is?"

"Ashes," Verenna ventured, her eyes flicking between the vase, the other three, and the gleeful smile of the man before her.

"Yes. The ashes of the creatures who so kindly caught fire to grant me them." He swept a hand towards the mantle.

Heat surged in her ears and she knew they must be going red."That's sick. Why...why would you...?"

Gawshire gingerly lifted a palmful of ash and let it stream through his fist, back into its jar. "Because ash made from the living, can raise the ashes of the dead. Throw a bit of this into a fire, and you can summon what you like, right from the Beyond. And the one who summons is the one who controls. I believe you have all met my favorite, Fumus."

Everyone in the room winced. Gawshire chuckled at their concern. "Don't worry. He takes quite a bit of work to maintain. Many, many souls. I only wake him for special occasions. Do not make this a special occasion."

Verenna couldn't hold back her rage any longer. "Those are people! How many? How many people are in there?" she shrieked.

The man shrugged, unshaken by her outburst. "Quite a few. Perhaps half. The rest are from things like them. That," he spat the word through clenched teeth as he pointed to Fabien, then

Darius. "And that. Are not men. They are monsters who cheat creation. They do not die so they have no right to live."

"And what are you? You've lived a thousand years you said, how are you any different?"

"Because I worked for what I have. I paid for it. In blood and toil. I earned this, and I must keep earning it. And yet these abominations walk the earth eternally for free? What did they do to deserve it? They belong to Hell and I intend to send them there."

"You'll have to kill me first," Verenna snarled.

"Don't tempt me."

"Vivie," Fabien started some warning, but Gawshire turned on him.

"Silence beast!"

"I won't let you hurt them," the girl challenged again.

Gawshire's anger swung back like a pendulum, refocusing on Verenna . He slammed his hands on the table at either side of the vase and fixed her with a hypnotic stare. He could hardly contain himself in his human form. The ends of his hair smoldered and midnight fog seeped from the corners of his eyes.

"I think it's time you made your decision. You will either become like me and rule, or I will deliver you to the Queen of Hell myself and watch you destroyed. Your time has run out."

The heat of rage simmered low for a moment as she looked to the other faces in the room. A bitter thought settled in her heart. "And what will you do with them?"

"Does it matter?"

"It does. If you want me to stay, they get to go."

"Oh child, you have no power here."

"Don't I?" Quicker than he had a chance to stop her she snatched the urn from the table. It nearly slipped from her fingers but she managed to heft it over her head.

"You will all die for this!" Gawshire roared.

Verenna could hear the others whispering for her to surrender but it was far too late for that. "Unless you let them leave. If you let them leave I'll put it down and stay with you."

The unexpected nature of the challenge forced him to consider it. "They leave, you put that down safely, and you stay?"

"Yes," she breathed, feeling the strain of holding the vessel beginning to build. To her eternal shock he agreed.

"You three have to the count of ten to get out of my sight."

"We aren't leaving with-" Darius began, but Fabien stopped him, using the arm not supporting Camon to wrench the doctor towards the door.

"She lives if we go," he murmured. "If we don't he kills her too. Don't be a fool."

Gawshire crossed his arms with the glutted look of victory. "You've made a good choice."

But as Verenna went to lower the urn one of the delicate handles cracked under the weight of the ash inside. The vase tumbled from her hands and shattered on the ground in a billow of gray. Gawshire gasped as if he were drowning. The rest of them covered their faces to avoid breathing dust. "What did you do? What?"

As soon as his mind caught up to his distress, he rounded on her. In an instant his body had dissolved into the nebulous black shape he'd been before. The coals of his eyes flickered with new heat as his voice burst from the darkness in a spray of sparks. "You will all pay!"

"Come on!" Darius called, taking Verenna's wrist and starting for the door. But before they'd taken a second step Gawshire barred their path.

He lunged at Verenna and seized her by the hair. Shoving Darius away from her, he tossed the girl, slamming her into the stone hearth. The world spun. In the rattlings of sound she could organize into speech she heard the doctor cry out.

Gawshire threw her about like little more than a doll, landing her in the shatters of the broken urn, the porcelain shards stabbing into her back. As quick as it had begun the attack ceased. She rolled over to find Fabien gathering Camon out of harm's way behind a few chairs, and Darius on his knees.

"What is this?" Gawshire rasped. He stormed across half the distance between them for a closer look at the fallen doctor. "What is this?!" He shouted, sending pain reverberating through her pounding skull.

Verenna shook her head, her vision clearing in time to see Gawshire realize their connection. Then his voice grew soft and inquisitive. "You. You bit her didn't you? Recently. She hasn't changed yet. That's why I can still see her fire. You're still linked in to her pain too, aren't you?"

Darius made no move to answer, only glowered up at the wraith. Gawshire drifted to Verenna's side and pressed what must be his foot down onto her fingers. She groaned. Across the floor, she could see Darius's hand twitch with the feeling, though he did his best to hide it.

"I had always wondered if the bond of the bite were true. If creatures like you could feel for each other." He kicked Verenna just under her ribs and it sent all the air out of her. Darius too curled to one side as if he felt the hit. "Interesting," he added, grabbing her wrist and dragging her closer to the doctor.

Verenna tried to struggle free but it was useless against a form she could not even fully take hold of.

"I want you to know what you've done doctor. You have made her next to worthless. If she cannot truly die, how can she be reborn to serve me? If I cannot control her and rule, and I cannot give her to the Queen to buy my power, exactly what use is she to me? You have thrown out your last bargaining piece. It seems the only fun left to me is to watch you all burn. You first, doctor." He dropped Verenna and heaved Darius into the cage by the eastern window, slamming the lock closed behind him. "I want you to see this. All of you. This is what happens when you take from me."

Only then did Verenna realize the purpose of the cages, the seating, the windows without curtains. All of it was meant as a theater to watch creatures suffer as the sun came up.

Gawshire opened the window with a flourish. "For the smoke."

Darius seemed too shocked to struggle. His breath came fast as he ran his hands over the bars, mesmerized by his own helplessness.

Verenna stumbled to the cage door and began tugging at the lock, turning it, shaking it as if her own will might be the key. Fabien skidded to his knees to fumble with the metal alongside Verenna. The drag of wood on stone interrupted them as Gawshire pulled up a chair. He sank into the cushions and resumed his human form, crossing his legs and steepling his fingers. He considered them with relaxed delight. "I'd suggest the two of you step away from the window. Dawn will not be kind."

Fabien rounded on him with his sword drawn, but Gawshire crumbled into swirling smoke before he struck. The sword slid uselessly through him and into the upholstery. Ripping it from the dark coils of his body, the man wrenched the blade from Fabien's hands and sent the point for the young man's ribs. Fabien threw himself backwards, missing the blow by an inch or less. Gawshire let the blade clang to the floor. "Stupid boy."

The sky had been painted pale enough to swallow the stars and dim the moon to little more than an ashen circle. Fabien had taken to checking the bars of the cage for a rusting weak point.

"The serum. Didn't you take any?" Verenna asked as she struggled to turn the keyhole with her nail.

"I forgot. In the rush to leave I…you were missing…there was no time to think. No time to go back."

She grunted as the burn of a torn nail set into the tip of her finger. "You?" She looked to Fabien, praying that she wouldn't be the only one left intact when the sun rose.

"I did. How the blazes did you forget!?" He growled as he put his whole body into yanking at the most feeble of the bars.

"I had a lot to think about!" Darius spat, searching the bars of the floor for any faults.

The clanging and chatter of their attempts had muffled the sound of Gawshire's slowly building laughter. Verenna checked the window. An orange line split the earth from the sky, swelling by the second.

She took stock of the room. There was no way the lock would come open or the bars would give by sunup. There had to be another solution. Then she felt the rub of twine at her neck. The vial. She rattled the lock again to keep her words hidden under its clanging. "Darius, here. Quick. Take my necklace off. It's a vial of sun serum."

Darius leaned in as if assisting her with the lock, slipping one of his hands underneath the fall of her hair to undo the knot holding the vial. "Hurry!" she uttered to him under her breath.

"I've almost got it. Hold still!" he whispered.

"He'll see what you're doing if I hold-" her words turned into a gurgle as Gawshire took a handful of her hair and wrenched her off her knees onto her back.

"You're blocking the view," he pouted. Pulling her along behind him he took hold of another cage. A whoosh and the iron box flew through the air and crashed against the opposite wall, pinning Fabien beneath it. Every muscle stood out as he tried to shift the weight of the trap. It moved only a fraction at a time. All the young man could do was watch as Gawshire dragged Verenna to his seat. Her head thunked against the wooden leg of the chair.

"Look at that sunrise," he sighed, content with the oncoming gold.

"Let go of me! Let go! I said I'd stay with you, I said! Let him go." Verenna pulled at his fingers but still they did not budge.

"Oh I know you will. I'll still take you to the queen. I want to see what I can get for you."

Inside the bars Darius had begun to sweat and curled over onto his side. He made no sound, but as the light touched him he convulsed and let out a cough of steam. Verenna's one hand clawed at the fingers holding her hair, while the other worked furiously at the knot in the twine. The doctor groaned and turned over, pulling himself in tight to become as small a target as possible for the piercing rays.

Daylight intensified as the great orange ball of the sun broke free of the horizon and burst upon the world. Darius's moaning grew louder, swelling into screams. Verenna's vision blurred with smoke and light and tears. She took up gnawing at the string around her neck, anything to free it and throw the vial to him.

"My Lord," a voice as glassy as a still lake interrupted the wailing. The woman with the rats nest hair arrived to deliver expressionless news. "There are intruders approaching."

"I know, twit. I have them. You know not to interrupt me here."

"There are more, My Lord. Marching up to the castle. They may be preparing to enter."

"Well, go kill them," the man fumed.

"We tried, sir. They have flaming arrows. They sank the boats and burned the dock."

Gawshire hesitated, allowing a deep rip of frustration to build in his throat. He shoved Verenna's head towards the ground as he stood. "Guard the door. They do not leave."

Before exiting, Gawshire paused and pointed to the fire. With the other arm he made a swift sweeping motion over the broken pot of ashes. The ashes jumped from the ground and whirled into the blaze. The instant the dust met the flames they went searing white. The orange light returned in moments but twice its previous size, and with a strange white core suspended in it, the size of a large pendant.

"Enjoy the company," he smirked. "This will all be over shortly."

As soon as the clack of his boots vanished beyond the oaken door Verenna scrambled to the side of the cage. A raw, red line zipped into the flesh of her neck as she tore the twine away, uncorked the vial and strained through the bars to reach Darius's open, gasping mouth. He gulped the golden drops and within moments he lay still.

"Darius…" Verenna called, trying to reach far enough inside to shake him awake. "Darius!" she rattled the bars.

Beside them, Fabien had finally managed to free himself from the crush of the cage. "Back up!" he shouted to Verenna as he took up his sword. She recoiled to stay clear of a huge, arching swing. It landed squarely on the lock. Another and another, blow after blow, wracked the air with the sound of crashing metal. Finally the lock gave way. Verenna fumbled it off the door and flung the cage open.

"Darius," she begged, crawling inside and seizing his shoulders. The heat of him forced her to let go. His body was hot as a kettle. She had no idea how his clothing had not caught fire.

He winced and wheezed, alive, but barely. Fabien lifted him and set him out of the sun near Camon, who'd come awake with the racket.

"Gods," Camon whispered upon seeing Darius' blistering skin and peeling face. The doctor opened his mouth to speak but his tongue was black with char and too dry to form words.

"What do we do?" Fabien muttered. "The door is guarded. I can't carry them both fast enough to make a run for it."

"I can walk myself," Camon insisted, trying his legs with the support of the wall. They shook violently beneath him. "Not fast mind you."

"We won't be able to run then. We can sneak out if we can distract the guard," Verenna spoke without taking her eyes off of Darius. The red of his skin, the scorched marks at the corners of his eyes and his blackened nails transfixed her with hurt for him. "How did you get in again?"

"A boat. We docked ours near the drawbridge and burned all of theirs. The plan was to meet them back at the front gate."

"Them?" Verenna held her breath.

"The Sarzen. We didn't come alone, miss. They told us to be out by sunup or they'd be coming in."

Frantic Verenna rushed to one window, then the others, checking the ground for the Sarzen. "They can't! They'll die! The hounds!"

"Then we'd better get out quick because there's no stopping 'em when they want a fight. Gotta respect that about the crazy gits. I just don't know how we can get down unnoticed with half of us injured."

Something popped in the fire. The white core had grown to the size of a fist and began to pulse like a heart. Whatever Gawshire had summoned would be arriving soon to finish what he started.

An idea glowed into the girl's consciousness. "When you got here, how deep would you say the water was?"

"We didn't check. Wait, why?"

"Deep enough to jump and not break anything?"

"No. No, we can't swim out of here. There's monsters in the moat, Verenna. Dead things with mud flesh that scream and drag you under. Even if we could get past them, you know I can't swim."

"We won't. We just need to land in enough water to soften the blow. We'll climb back out as fast as we can onto the bank."

"She's right. It's the best way," Camon agreed. "I don't much like it but it's better than finding out what's guarding the door or what's coming out of the fire."

Fabien took hold of his chin as he considered the height. "Everything Gawshire has is likely focused on the Sarzen's attack. I hate it, but we'll have the best chance if we go now." He stooped to gather Darius. Verenna helped Camon to his feet. She struggled to keep him from the ground as they staggered to the window together.

The water below looked considerably murkier than she remembered. Verenna undid the latch and shoved the glass aside. They situated themselves on the precarious sill. Whatever was in the moat, they'd just have to be faster.

She looked to Fabien. He'd gone green with sick. He scoffed with embarrassment at her notice. "Let's get it done with."

"It's not so high," she lied. "It'll be...fine." She hesitated as the arm Camon rested across her shoulders went limp. She looked at him just in time to see his eyes roll back and consciousness leave his body. The man swayed. Verenna tried to keep him steady, but his knees gave out. He rocked forward and sent them both plunging towards the water.

Chapter 10

Verenna hit the surface on her side, shooting water into her ear, and jarring them both as they slammed into the silty bottom. Despite the shock of cold and the impact she managed to kept her hold on Camon's shirt. Before she could get her bearings a warped, whooping chorus of screams struck up underwater. Finding purchase on the bottom she lunged for air. She gasped it in as soon as her mouth and nose broke the surface. Dipping below the surface to kick off the shifting mud, she pulled hard to haul her charge onto the thin bank that lined the base of the castle.

A splash broke the quieting ripples. A bright blonde head erupted out of the water to gulp in frantic breaths. Fabien floundered along in her wake.

Verenna turned Camon on his side and thumped his back hard. He spat water and groaned. Breathing. She dashed back to the water's edge to aid Fabien.

"Take him!" he gurgled, shoving Darius towards her. Verenna got a hold on the doctor's vest and yanked with her entire weight until the unconscious man slid onto the bank. Furious thrashing exploded around Fabien as he struggled for land. An eyeless face surged above the water, mouth open and screaming with teeth that looked like the edge of broken wood. He unsheathed his sword and bashed the creature with the hilt. It dropped below the surface, but three more rose to replace it.

Fabien fought against an ever growing ring of grasping hands made of muck. One of the creatures sunk its teeth into his forearm as he finally managed to stand. He let out a roar and decapitated the beast. Its head spun off and sunk. He began hacking wildly at the water to keep the creatures from dragging him under.

With a last heave to bring Darius fully out of the water, she searched frantically for anything she might use to help Fabien. Two daggers in Camon's belt caught her eye. Enra's daggers.

Verenna snatched one of them and started slicing at the frothing water near the shore. Fabien had managed to gain ground even while four of the creatures gnawed at him. He ripped one off of his shoulder and flung it. He pushed for the bank and caught Verenna's free hand. Just as hope sprang up, so did another beast, directly between them. It latched on to Fabien's throat. Without a free hand he could not tear it away.

She pulled with all she had but only slid farther into the water. Feeling herself losing the tug of war with the myriad of lake-slime hands she did the first thing that came to mind. She stabbed the creature that hung around Fabien's neck. The knife sank into its muddy flesh and it went limp. Able to breath again Fabien made an arch with his sword, curving the blade from one side of his body to the other, snapping the groping hands from his body like twigs. Before another round of hands could take hold of him he made a break for the shore, pulling Verenna up onto land with him.

To their horror the creatures began to follow. A mound of mud broke the water, all faces and limbs, a body made of other congealed bodies.

One of the beasts took hold of Darius foot and tried to steal him into the moat. Verenna slashed it off and threw it at the mass of angry gnashing heads. She and Fabien gathered the two injured men. Fabien helped Verenna get Darius off the ground and draped him against her back with his arms over her shoulders. The doctor had far less muscle to him than Camon making him much lighter. Fabien would have to carry him. They pressed themselves against the castle wall to avoid the slowly encroaching beasts. There were only some five feet left between them and the creatures.

"You didn't say they could come on land," Verenna said and kicked a frontrunner back into the water.

"How should I know what they can do? I don't even know what they are!" Fabien bellowed. His eyes had stretched so wide with fear they looked like green islands in a sea of white. He thrust his blade through an advancing head with a sound like a spade sinking into earth. "We can't keep this up forever. We've got to stop them coming up here." He stacked two more skulls onto his blade and swung it hard to cast them off.

They'd crawled most of the way up the bank, leaving at most an arm's length between their feet and the farthest reaching hands.

"Distract them?" Verenna offered.

Fabien struggled to keep his footing with Camon leaning heavily on his shoulder. "With what? We've got nothing!"

In the moment it took her to look around for a solution, one of the mud beasts caught her ankle in its mouth. The feeling of a thousand splinters being driven to the bone sent a white hot flash of pain up her leg. She howled. Letting Darius slide down with her, pinned between her and the wall, she landed Camon's dagger straight through the monster's head. The strike pinned it to the muck with the shining hilt jutting from the top.

To her surprise, the monsters refocused entirely. They turned to the blade and began to caress it with a strange reverence. With another blinding shock of pain she wiggled her leg free of the creatures dead jaws.

"They like it. They like the shine," Fabien noted with disgusted awe as the mud hands worked to free the knife from the slain beast.

"Your sword, Fabien. That's why they went after you, not me. They saw the light on your blade."

"Well, they aren't having it. Best slip out while they're distracted with this one. That bites not too bad for you to walk is it?"

Verenna looked down and grimaced at the damage. She pulled one of the splinter-like teeth from her flesh and shivered. "It'll have to do. You can't carry all three of us."

The creatures had managed to get the knife free, raising it on many hands and turning it over in the sun. Their screams and croaks turned into quiet, contented hisses as they carried their prize into deeper waters.

Fabien nodded to a patch of bank the creatures had abandoned. "There. We can slip past them."

They moved as fast as they could across the slick banks, stumbling and nearly ending up back in the water countless times before they rounded the North side of the castle.

The bank tapered and vanished, ending in a rotting dock with three smoldering boats tied to it. The work of the Sarzen. More importantly, the dock attached to a doorway in the outer wall. The two took a moment to rest before slipping through it. The inlet let out onto a paved courtyard. From the look of it, it wrapped the building on three sides. The front gate must be straight ahead, just beyond their sightline around the corner. The sounds of shouting confirmed that they must be close. A window shattered overhead and a burst of tinkling glass showered the ground.

"Let's go. Hurry." Verenna took a step into the open but Fabien barked an order.

"Hug the wall. If you move across open ground you'll be too easy to spot. I have a feeling not all of those windows are empty."

He indicated the perfect rows of windows, still heavy with morning shadow, glittering like the onyx eyes of a hungry spider.

"Lead the way," she told him, adjusting Darius across her back. They set off but froze at the sound of a far off screech. Not like the ones that came from the creatures in the water. A cry she remembered. A sound that still rolled around in her nightmares. A single roar woven from a chorus of pain, like ten men in the throes of agony. Fumus was free.

"Go, go, go, go!" Verenna urged. Fabien seemed to sprint effortlessly even with Camon in his arms while she struggled along behind, half falling, half running. She strained to keep Darius draped across her back and stay on her feet at the same time. The intense heat of his burned skin tingled through her clothes.

They followed the wall until it turned to reveal an even larger space; the centerpiece, the drawbridge. At its base two figures huddled together in the morning shadows, laboring over something between them. Adrinée stood beside them keeping watch.

"That's them. Come on." Fabien whispered. They made a break across the open square to join the trio. The three snapped to attention, ready to fight at the sound of their approach. Recognizing Verenna and Fabien they resheathed their weapons.

"What happened?" The woman who'd been kneeling darted over to help Camon the moment they reached gate.

"Camon has Cold Fever. Gawshire's work," Fabien said, setting the man against the wall.

"What about the other one? Is that the doctor?" Adrinée couldn't keep a pale wash of horror from her face. She clearly hadn't recognized him underneath his injuries.

"That's him. Gawshire did that too," Verenna recited, her voice smoldering with hate.

"We're going to get you home," the woman hushed to a barely

conscious Camon, though Verenna wasn't sure either man could understand.

"How far along are we?" Fabien asked the man, crouched and tinkering with something on the ground.

"Almost ready," said a man with burn scars down one arm. He called out to the woman hovering over Camon. "How's the winch?"

"It'll be useless soon. I made sure of it," the woman answered, joining him in their work. "The chains should slide right into the moat when they try to let the gate down. It should keep them busy trying to fish them out. What with all those mud people in the water."

"What are those things anyway?" Fabien asked from his place ducked against the wall.

"Golem. Or River Banshees. Depends on where you're from," the woman answered without looking away from her work. The woman had a missing ring finger and an impressive mass of curls tied back with a leather string. "How's yours coming?" she asked her compatriot.

"Just about ready." He turned to her to answer giving Verenna a view of how strikingly similar they were. Save for the scars, they were almost duplicates of each other down to the last freckle. The girl allowed herself to get lost in curiosity until a deep, worried voice sounded behind her.

"The damned banshees got the second boat. We'll have to make do with one." The hair on her arms stood on end. She turned to find Mortimer emerging from a discreet doorway in the wall.

She hurried too fast for her feet and stumbled into hugging him, breathing deep the book-leather scent of his coat.

"Thought you wouldn't forgive me," Mortimer whispered.

"I just can't believe you came back."

"Always do. Bit happier to be back than usual however."

She looked up at him in time to catch the smile that creased the corners of his eyes, reminding her so much of her own father's grin the last time she'd seen it. It felt like years.

"No sign of discovery yet?" Mortimer inquired.

Adrinée answered him. "No, Sir. The distractions kept them occupied so far." The way she looked up to the windows told Verenna that their safety was a guess at best. "We're almost finished with-" she stopped mid sentence and plugged her ears against a curdling scream that resonated around the plaza.

All attention shifted to the front steps. Fumus, fully formed, hovered in the darkened doorway, a silver nightmare incarnate.

"Oh gods," the man with the burned arm muttered and started praying over his frantic work.

"What in the Hell is that?!" Adrinée had backed all the way up against the gate.

"Time to go is what it is!" The other woman barked.

"Let's go then!" Fabien said, taking up Darius.

"We can't," the man interrupted. "We're not done. If the pivot doesn't fail, the drawbridge may still be able to function. It has to go or they'll be able to follow us."

"And they will," Mortimer added. "Fabien, I hope you're feeling up to fighting."

The young man lay the doctor down and took out his blade, using his free hand to shake Mortimer's.

"Glad to see you back, old man. And I always fancy a fight. Though the sun should do some of the work for us." No sooner had he said it than the beast set a foot beyond the shadows, oblivious to the morning light. "Oh...no..."

"How?" Mortimer groaned.

"Doesn't matter. We're killing it." Fabien took up a fighting stance in front of the group.

The old man took out his dagger and joined him. "Work quickly, please," he added to the Sarzen.

An arrow whizzed over their heads from Adrinée's bow. It landed between the creatures metal gray ribs as it stocked towards them. The sinew of its sides twitched once and the arrow fell to the ground with the clatter of a useless stick. Her jaw fell open.

"Adrinée, get Camon and Darius in the boat," Mortimer suggested. The words were hardly out of his mouth and the girl had already looped her arms under the doctor's shoulders, lifted him with surprising ease, and dragged him through the thin opening in the battlement.

Verenna checked either side of her as if she'd find a weapon. Her hands were desperate for something to do, to help the two men fend off Fumus.

Fabien caught her in the corner of his eye. "Go. Get in boat."

Verenna might have listened if she hadn't seen the remaining dagger in Camon's belt. "Oh no, I'm helping."

"I told you. Get to the boat. What are you doing?" Fabien scolded her.

"I'm not leaving till you do."

"Don't be an idiot. Run," Mortimer insisted without taking his focus off Fumus.

The beast seemed to delight in teasing them, pacing like a lion just out of striking range, sizing up its challengers. Now and again it made a false start only to pull back with huffs of exhilaration that almost felt like laughter.

"No. I'm not letting anyone die saving me again."

"We'll have died for nothing if you don't get yourself safe," Fabien argued. He called over his shoulder to the two Sarzen hard at work. "How are we coming on the explosion?"

"It's not lighting. The fuse is wet."

"How the-?" Fabien stopped himself, shaking his head and

refocusing on the adversary at hand.

The man called out the answer. "It must have been splashed when the golem tried to turn the boat over."

Just as he finished, Fumus seemed to note Verenna's presence. It reared and shrieked with redoubled excitement. Unable to restrain itself any longer it lunged. Mortimer stepped in front of the girl, dagger brandished. Fabien jumped forward, sliding under the leaping creature to draw a deep gash in the creatures belly. Its cries took on a different tone and it tumbled instead of landing.

"Here! Here you great lug!" Fabien called to it, knowing it could not see him. Fumus gained his feet and followed the sound of Fabien's voice. "Come on over and we'll dance a while!" His jeers kept the monster distracted enough for Verenna to start thinking. If they couldn't hold the hungry abomination off long enough to light the fuse they would lose not only their lives but leave the drawbridge functional for the rest of the Sarzen war party to lose theirs.

Fumus pounced again, this time taking Fabien to the ground. The young man howled with pain as he barred the animals gnashing jaws with the length of his blade, the edge digging deep into his palm. Mortimer left Verenna's side long enough to stab at the monster's head. His knife raked across the creatures ghostly skull. Fumus lashed out to grab the old man but he dodged and fell, leaving Verenna open.

She angled herself so its next leap would land well clear of the Sarzen still crouched by the gate. There were no candles to hide amongst this time, and the only thing to set on fire as a distraction wasn't lighting. Her decision to stay suddenly felt like a mistake. The beast came for her. She moved fast, but not quite swift enough to avoid a claw catching her cheek. She heard the rip of her skin and clutched the side of her face. For a creature made of what seemed to be liquid smoke, it had enough solid qualities to do considerable damage.

"Work faster!" Verenna bellowed.

Her distraction had allowed Fabien to gain his feet. He took the creatures attention again, dancing around it and dodging pounce after pounce.

"There's got to be a better way to stop it. Blades aren't working. You stabbed it in the head and it hardly noticed." She looked to Mortimer, hoping he'd have some clue she didn't.

"If knives and the sun won't stop it I'm not sure there's a way. Not like we can talk to it."

Something clicked inside and she had an answer. "Maybe you can," she puzzled. If Mortimer had been part of the royal family he would have been educated as such, which explained his eloquence. And a prince surely would have learned other languages. "Mortimer, do you speak Latin?"

"Well, I, I mean, yes. It's been hundreds of years, but....why?"

"Try it. Gawshire orders his servants around in Latin. Say something."

Fumus gained an upper hand on Fabien. The creature swatted the blade out of the young man's blood slick grip. It clattered against the gate, narrowly missing the two Sarzen. The beast keened a victory cry and prepared to finish the fight.

"I don't- I can't-", Mortimer struggled.

"Do it, old man. You'd better." Fabien warned, his fingers moving gently with readiness, poised to roll away from the next attack.

"We've got it," the Sarzen woman called. "Let's go!"

"Say something this thing understands," Fabien demanded through a clenched jaw. Fumus crouched, moving his haunches like a cat ready to spring.

"Fumus, Audite me."

The beast came out of its crouch and looked for the source of the words.

"Audite me," Mortimer repeated. "Prohibere."

The animal stood slowly and faced him. Its head tilted and it took a single step forward.

"Get to the boat," the old man whispered.

The two Sarzen slipped through the doorway as the three of them backed towards the only escape. Fabien scooped up his sword and took her hand, ushering her towards the exit.

"Keep talking, Mortimer. Tell it to sit or stay or something."

"Shut up, I can't focus," Mortimer hissed. "It's not a dog."

As soon as they were through the opening Fabien all but lifted her into the boat, clambering in after. Their added weight sat the boat uncomfortably low in the water.

Mortimer hung back in the archway, one hand out towards Fumus as if warning the monster to keep away. He glanced over his shoulder to check that all had made it into the vessel.

"Vos nos non movere," he instructed as he backed through the door himself. At first she thought Fumus would not fit through such a small space, but the creatures body melted through the opening seamlessly.

"Get in," Fabien rushed him.

Adrinée balanced on the prow, ready to push away from the shore with a paddle lodged in the bank.

"Mortimer, we're in. Come on," Verenna begged.

The old man continued his steady pace, one foot feeling behind the other for good purchase on the shifting bank. His leg bumped the side of the boat and he nearly toppled in. Catching himself just in time he swung one boot in, then the other, unable to sit for lack of room.

"Manere," he instructed the creature. Fumus cocked his head in the opposite direction. Verenna couldn't imagine such an entity would feel anything but hunger, pain, and the thrill of murder, but the beast looked outright baffled that anyone besides its master could speak to it.

Before Fumus could move past confusion, Adrinée gave a gentle push and set the vessel drifting towards the opposite bank.

Verenna would have felt relief, if the boat hadn't sunk a hand and a half with Mortimer's bulk added on. They were dangerously close to taking on water. A sway in either direction would sink them and awaken the golem that lurked in the murk below.

Adrinée steered the vessel with rippleless swings of her single paddle; the deft skill of a child born by the river. The whole troop of them drifted speechless towards the other shore, as if a single word might weigh enough to sink them. Half way across Verenna felt her fear shift. They had put a good distance between themselves and Fumus, but below them, she could sense the living lake bottom. Her toes curled inside her shoes at the thought of the mud and weeds squishing between them. She shuddered at the memory of the slimy grip that had seized her ankle.

In the distance she could hear the Sarzen coming around the side of the manor to join them. Drumming, the clatter of weapons, and the occasional volley of arrows and rocks, had made a suitable distraction.

Something plucked the surface of the water to the right of the boat. They didn't dare turn their heads to look for fear of tipping. The small peck could have been a fish catching an insect. But another light splash to the opposite side made her reconsider coincidence. Then with a whizz and tock, an arrow punched into the little boat, right between Adrinée's feet where she perched to steer. Somehow she kept her footing.

"Who's shooting?" she demanded.

"There," Mortimer guided her gaze up to the top of the wall over the drawbridge where stood six of Gawshire's servants. "We'd better hope those barrels go off soon. If they're able to lay that bridge across..." He didn't bother to finish. Eight people in a canoe with no defenses except stillness and quiet did not need to hear listed the things they might be helpless against.

Fabien reached across the small distance between himself and Verenna and took her hand. She sensed in the squeeze of his fingers that he'd needed the comfort as much as she did, though in words he'd never say it.

Another arrow zipped by Verenna's head and sank into the shallows. She ducked lower. One of her ears had already been clipped by such a shot and she wasn't about to let the other match. They were almost to the reeds. To safety. Then she noticed Darius hand. It drooped over the side of the craft, balanced on the edge of the boat, ready to topple into the moat. He was too far out of her reach. It splashed into the water with the smacking sound of a struggling fish.

The woman with the missing finger saw the problem and pulled the doctor's arm from the water. It was too late. A sudden commotion underwater sent up ripples that lapped at the boat. One made the leap over the side and sloshed around in the bottom. Another tiny wave broke against the vessel. An even bigger slop of water surged in. A third and a fourth splash of water pooled at their feet.

Mortimer took charge to calm them. "Don't panic. We're almost there. We will be in the reeds by the time the golem come up. We will be alright, just stay still."

Something thumped against the bottom of the boat. Adrinée let out a tiny shrill as her balance threatened to give in to the newly rocking water. She shoved her paddle deep as she sensed herself toppling. Verenna reached up and grabbed a handful of her billowing shirt, pulling hard to keep the girl from falling. Instead of careening into the water, the girl flopped directly onto Verenna's lap and across several others packed into the dingy. The last shove the girl had managed sent the boat skittering for the bank, but in its wake, an eerie howling chorus rose to chase it. The river banshees had awakened.

The boat crushed into the reeds just as a muddy hand gripped onto the side of it. A multitude arose after it, taking hold of the boat and pulling it down. Water gushed over the sides and the craft began to sink. Mortimer slashed at the tide of jaws and hands that swelled from the deep, shouting for the others to get out of the boat. The two identical Sarzen took up Camon and leaped for shore, flouncing messily through the plants. Fabien tugged Verenna's hand and got her standing. "Go," he said, giving her a starting push towards land. She plunged knee deep in the reeds and reached back to help the wide eyed Adrinée off behind her.

The tugging hands had the canoe half way under. Only three were left aboard; Mortimer still slicing at the enemy, and Fabien with Darius draped between his arms.

Fabien made a jump and fell, barely managing to keep Darius's head above water as he floundered forward. Terror had him up again in a flash and running through the rushes for dry land. Last of all, Mortimer made his escape, just as the last of the boat was consumed by the greedy horde. Verenna knelt with her palms to the earth, again finding herself infinitely grateful to have escaped a watery grave. A look to the rest of the group dashed all feelings of relief, however.

The two who had worked to rig the drawbridge stood with Camon draped between them, their rapt attention on the gate, waiting on the fruits of their labor to detonate. "It's got to. It must," the man whispered to himself.

"It will. Just watch," the woman said without a shred of confidence in her tone.

A clang announced that the drawbridge winch had loosened. The gate was coming down.

"No," Mortimer murmured, his face drawn and weary with disbelief. The explosions hadn't come. The chain functioned seamlessly.

"What did we do wrong?" Adrinée looked to the old man, pleading.

"We did what we could." His answer seemed to soothe the girl enough for her to obey his next order. "Ready whatever weapons you've got. They'll be coming for us."

Verenna's skin went cold. She weighed Enra's remaining dagger in her grasp. She couldn't say for sure if it would be any use against the kind of creature that would pour forth from the gates, but it would have to do.

The clanging of the chain through the stone outlets increased in speed. They grew faster until the chains lowering the drawbridge fell away in one, long, resounding string of clanks. The moat swallowed them. The hungry masses below the surface stirred and reached for the flash of metal. There would be no lifting the bridge, but it had come down relatively intact, splintering slightly at its middle with the impact.

"It's got to, got to, got to," the woman repeated. Still no explosion came.

The Sarzen who'd been putting up the distraction were rapidly closing the distance between them to help defend against whatever horde would pour forth from the open gate. So far, only a single figure blighted the doorway. Gawshire in his wide brimmed hat, with Fumus circling him like an affectionate housecat.

The man held up a hand and ranks of servants formed at either side of him. Forty maybe, though more filed in, armed with axes and clubs.

Mortimer shook his head in disbelief. "Here they come."

Chapter 11

Fabien passed Darius into the care of the Sarzen as they arrived. Camon too was taken up and hurried away from the site of the impending battle. The young man's sword sang out of its sheath. "Ready as ever. Looks like this is as close to a fair fight as I'll ever get."

Verenna stepped up so that she stood even with her two companions, Enra's knife ready in her palm.

"You won't quit will you?" Fabien cocked an eyebrow at her.

"Not till you do I imagine. That man tried to kill us. If you think I'm not going to try and kill him back you're crazier than he is."

Both men grinned at her false bravado.

The Sarzen filed in around them like an incoming tide. They set themselves in ranks and braced for action. Somewhere in the crowd Verenna could still hear the woman praying for the explosives to catch fire as Gawshire's forces continued to gather. There were now at least sixty. More than twice their number.

Enra emerged from the crowd and stepped to the front lines. Verenna startled to see her, broken, bruises, scrapes and all. "Why did you come? You're hurt!"

"What kind of leader would I be if I stood behind my troops for protection? Besides, I won't miss this. I was informed that this Gawshire controls demons and lets them hunt in our woods. We will never be truly safe until he's gone. It's as much our fight as yours." She turned and shouted to her gathered ranks. "What do you say!"

A few whoops rose from the crowd, so Enra called again. Verenna couldn't keep her heart from her throat as the woman called out to the Sarzen, despite what had to be rending pain in her sides. The metallic power of her voice laced the air with a contagious courage. "I ask my people, will they fight?"

The gathering roared a response in unison, "We have the will!"

"I ask my people, who will stop us?"

"None but the Gods!" they answered her.

Enra took a proud breath against the pain of her broken ribs. "I ask my people, of whom will history sing?"

Their cries soared as if the clouds were the rafters of a church. "Sarzen!"

"And who are we?"

"Sarzen! Sarzen! Sarzen!" they cried, the sky the only boundary of their spirit. Just as their shouts faded, the thunder of a charging horde broke out on the drawbridge. The husks, near a hundred of them, came pouring down the planks towards their meager forces.

With their pride at its peak, Enra gave the command. "Charge!" They rushed to meet the husks at the end of the drawbridge. Verenna sprinted with the frontrunners, carried by some terminal bravery towards the thick of a clash. They ate up the distance in seconds, but as the first of the horde reached the middle of the bridge, a resounding crack sent them skidding to a halt and falling back towards the safety of the shore. Fire erupted in the hinge that held the bridge to the castle's side. The far end plunged into the water, sending the horde of husks sliding back towards the castle. Their faces blank, even as the hands of the river banshees pulled them under.

The drawbridge folded into two, useless pieces, and vanished into the moat.

The Sarzen, Fabien, Mortimer, all of them looked from one to another temporarily stunned. Slack jawed, with their weapons hanging loose in their hands, they watched the army of husks crumble.

Gawshire watched the catastrophe, unmoving, save for the trembling of his clenched fists. Under the brim of his hat Verenna could see that his face had turned into the suspended ink he'd been made of the night he stole her, his rage so great he could no longer contain it in his human body.

Recognizing that the change might herald a new and different danger, Fabien shouted for the group to pull back. They made a quick retreat with the momentum for a battle they'd narrowly escaped. Mortimer did not follow. He watched Gawshire, transfixed by the smoke man, wavering in the archway of his castle turned island.

Verenna stopped when she realized he hadn't run with them. "Come on!" He did not hear. She jogged back a few steps and took his sleeve. "Come on before they figure out a way out of there."

"He's still alive," Mortimer whispered. His expression looked as though he might faint though his whole body was knotted with tension. He spoke as if in a trance. "He's still here. Gawshire was Gausterre. Camlann Gausterre. He killed them. All of them. He framed me."

Verenna found herself frozen next to him, staring across the divide at the murderous entity. The wraith stared back. His evil had been festering on the earth for over a thousand years, and it had all started with the end of Mortimer.

"We have to go," she whispered without moving so much as an eyelid herself. "He'll get out soon enough. We've got to be far away when he does." She tugged his arm.

Until Gawshire turned away Mortimer would not flinch. Even after the man disappeared with Fumus into the secrecy of the manor, the old man refused to go. Fabien joined them and placed a hand on Mortimer's shoulder. "We've got to get to safety. Enra's not leaving without you. None of them are... My Lord."

The title made Mortimer's head turn. "They told you then?" he asked the two of them.

"I had my suspicion before," Verenna acknowledged. "But the paintings in there have you in them. Gave it away."

Fabien scoffed. "Well bloody hell, they just told me. Did everyone know you were a king but me?"

"A prince," Mortimer corrected. "I never got to be king."

The young man clapped him on the back. "Well you are now, let me tell you. Those people there think so. And you're keeping 'em waiting." He gestured to the Sarzen. Mortimer nodded, a slightest smile a poor disguise for his brooding mood. He looked to the distant crowd with a melancholy fondness that faded to stony determination.

"I can't leave without revenge. I can't. Now that I know he's alive..."

"He's not," Verenna interrupted. "He's a demon. The Old Guard, he said. He won't be easy to kill, I imagine, and he certainly can't die of natural causes. You'll have another chance. Camon might not."

Mortimer shivered and shook his head. He took a last, longing look at the manor, then the keen edge of the knife in his hand, then back to the Sarzen. "Let's go."

&

On the long march back to the distant woods, Verenna was plagued by the urge to check over her shoulder. She expected to see creatures pouring out of the castle after them. She knew Gawshire must be watching them go. Little by little the manor shrank into the distance until it was only a blot on the horizon.

But the girl didn't let her guard down until they'd reached the shelter of the trees.

A smaller group of Sarzen waited for them in the woods next to a supply cart and the shabby horse. They made room for the injured on the wagon and set off towards the village. Someone had managed to rouse Camon with some water, but his grip was failing him and he had to be helped. Darius looked no better at all. The miraculous healing of his kind had come up absent.

Verenna caught up with the cart. A closer look deepened her worry. She'd been warned that the sun was one of the only things that could destroy their physical bodies; their crystal souls refracting the light and burning them from the inside out. He might be as close as one of them could come to dead. Someone had taken pity on his blistered skin and lay a coat across him. She hoped he was still alive enough to feel the relief of it.

The girl's cheeks throbbed with sun. The walk across the miles of green had turned them bright pink. The afternoon bore down on them. Even the flicker of light through the leaves felt like nettles, making the mercy of evening seem like a fantastical wonder.

A breeze struck up as the sun sank into the nest of a golden evening. Someone called a halt from the front.

"What's going on?" Verenna whispered to Adrinée, assuming there would be some new threat up ahead.

The other girl seemed amused by her skittishness. "We're checking an old camp site. We've got supplies buried. If they're still there, we'll set up here for the night."

"Is it safe? This close to what we just came from?"

"Safe enough," Adrinée shrugged. "Or at least as safe as anywhere else."

Mortimer overheard and agreed. "It will take them a while to get off that island. The manor is built on top of a freshwater spring. They can't cross the moat without a bridge of some kind. We destroyed the boats and the drawbridge so we've bought a little time. That water is great protection for them, but it can also be a trap. I assume that's how Gawshire keeps his charges from running off."

"And we'll need a place to treat those two," Enra added with a nod to the cart.

Verenna looked around. "You can do that here? Don't you need medicine?"

"This is where our medicine comes from anyhow," the woman said as she surveyed the woods. "We've got a few with us with the skill to help Camon. I'm sure they can find something to try for Darius as well."

Someone whistled from in the brush and the group set off in the direction of the sound. The cart hassled through the ever tightening trees with greater and greater adversity. The woods grew together so snugly that it became impossible to see more than the few people directly beside her. Then with a flourish, the trees opened into a meadow. The Sarzen were already clearing brush with a mix of blades. Near the center of the clearing Verenna could make out a stone circle that had once been the border for a campfire. All around her people set to work without so much as a word of command. Seamless, they fell into roles gathering wood, clearing the space, unpacking small kits of medicine and other useful items that had been strapped across their backs, and at the edge of the activity, digging. Adrinée showed her how to gather tinder. It seemed insignificant when surrounded by the abilities of the Sarzen, but it helped her nerves to have something to do.

Once the supplies had been unearthed and a decent fire constructed, a Sarzen healer took to mixing the Godflower remedy to save Camon. By her estimation, he'd make it. A strong man without too many years on him had a better chance than most.

Verenna watched the medic from a discrete distance, waiting for her to do something for Darius. One of the Sarzen returned with a few fistfuls of gray-green lichen. The woman made a poultice and coated as much of the doctor as she could with the mixture.

Fabien placed a hand on her shoulder and joined her vigil. After a wordless while he spoke, "I thought maybe you'd want something to eat? I don't know if your appetite's left you yet." He held out a few strips of dried meat from the unearthed supplies.

She took the slices and looked it over without interest. It hadn't occurred to her but she hadn't so much as thought of food since Gawshire had demanded she dine with him. Even then she hadn't wanted to eat.

"I take it that's a part of becoming like you?" She asked without looking at him.

"Unfortunately. Still, you've got to eat until the transformation happens. If you go into it hungry it makes it worse."

"How long till that happens?"

"Dark moon's in about two weeks. We'll be ready though. You won't go it alone." His hand tightened ever so slightly on her shoulder.

"I haven't thus far." She gazed up at him with a weary fondness. "Thank you for coming to get me. I don't know what I would have, how I would...You're heroes. All three of you."

Fabien's mouth curved with a gentle tinge of pride. "You'd do the same. The way you charged towards that drawbridge today, I'm sure you would."

She looked down and massaged a non-existent twinge in her arm to avoid the growing sparkle of his eyes that threatened to turn her face red. Not wanting her ears to go hot she watched the doctor finish treating Darius. Guilt crept in at the edges of her. In the room with Gawshire, he had been able to feel her pain. It seemed unfair he carried his alone.

"Why was he able to feel what I felt?"

Fabien's tone grew solemn. "There's a connection between the one who bit and the one who was bitten. At least for the first few years."

"Years?" she couldn't disguise her shock.

"Remember you've got a whole lot more time than you did before. Years are nothing."

Verenna searched herself for the right way to ask. "So, you think he'll come out of this then? I mean, if they're treating him they must think he can be saved."

"Of course he can." But Fabien's confidence lacked conviction. Verenna took a big, ripping bite of dried meat to fill the silence between them and let him change the subject. "Come on. Enra and Mortimer are starting to sort out our next move. Figured you wouldn't want to miss having a say."

They seated themselves in the grass beside the two leaders already deep in discussion of Gawshire.

"He won't be stuck there forever," Enra sighed as she watched the first flames of the evening's fire lick at the underside of the larger logs. "He'll come for revenge."

"Perhaps," Mortimer considered. "But his first objective will be to find and recapture Verenna. If he has our girl, he can settle all other matters later. She could be the key to his whole future. He could buy his way into kingship with her life."

"But he didn't," Verenna interrupted. Enra and Mortimer seemed to notice her for the first time. "He said he'd rather keep me than kill me. Told me that giving me up would make him a king, but keeping me for himself and not letting the underworld have me would make him some kind of god. He said that if I turned into a creature like him forever, the Queen of Hell could not rise. He even mentioned the story Fabien told me about Merlin's daughters."

Mortimer took up explaining the story to Enra. "The queen we speak of is the daughter of Merlin, in your lore. For the Queen of Hell to rise, she must first empty the underworld onto this plane, and then kill the only living descendant of Merlin. As long as Verenna is alive, she cannot complete her ascension. There can only ever be one living descendant. Corvudeus makes sure of it."

"Corvudeus?" Enra questioned.

"It means Raven God. Death," Verenna's frank reply made the woman go pale. "Not to worry. He's on our side. Most of the time."

The smell of the slow curling woodsmoke filled the empty thoughtful quiet between them. "I suppose it's encouraging," Enra speculated.

Mortimer brought the conversation back to its point. "Regardless, the more head start we get on Gawshire the better. We have more pressing issues that will be better dealt with without his distraction. We need to find the next Horseman. The sooner the better. The earlier they are in their ride, the easier they'll be to defeat."

Verenna's heart suddenly sank. She hadn't thought of it but, now that the old man had reunited with his people, or at least their ancestors, he might not be coming. And after learning the man who destroyed his life lived only a day or so away, how could she ask him to go with her? He had too much unfinished here.

"Well," Fabien joined, scratching his head. "It would be helpful to have that bloody map. Darius had notes about where he thought it would be, didn't he."

Mortimer sighed. "We'll have to do without. We lost it in the flood at Bronwell. There's no finding it.

"Wait," Verenna said and pressed a hand to her chest, feeling the damp lump beneath it. "I've got it."

"What? How?" Fabien exclaimed.

The girl reached into her bodice and produced the worn page to the incredulous mumblings of the onlookers. She herself was shocked she hadn't lost it plunging into the moat. "I can't say what condition it'll be in but, here," she said, flopping the map open for inspection.

Water had taken its toll on the edges, making some of the marks illegible, but in large part the ink had kept enough shape to understand.

"Where on earth did you find this?" Mortimer asked, running a finger along the map to assure himself it had actually appeared.

"Gawshire's study. He had it laid out on a table. He made marks of his own but they were all in Latin. It looks like most of them washed away.

Mortimer's shoulders sank and he rubbed his temples. "This means he knows everything we know."

"True, but you also know at least a few things he wouldn't like you to," added Enra. "I'd bet he wrote his notes thinking you'd never see the map again. These marks, if you can manage to read them, will be true, because he assumed he'd have no one to hide them from."

Her optimistic spin spurred the discussion.

"Well, what can you make of these, old man? With Darius knocked out, I'm pretty sure you're the only one who can read Latin."

"I can try, but the water had its way with most of them. They're too washed out to read." Mortimer leaned close to the page and scanned the thick, black lettering Gawshire had printed. "Good news first. That pincer move Souris had around us? He's scribbled out the ends of it. Hopefully that means retreat. If not, at least it doesn't seem they're ready to descend on us anymore.

He's got forces on most of the main roads. See these tally marks? I'd bet that's how many he's stationed there. He knew about Souris, and, let's see, paid particular attention to this city here. Turim. Hm...Something starting with an M, that might be Malagrir. Turim could be housing our next Horseman. And here..." the old man paused his puzzling. "He's got an X over Canterford."

"What?" Verenna pulled the map closer to see for herself. "What's that mean?"

"I can't say. The words are too far gone. But he's got the same mark over Bronwell, Turim, and here in the far north. Whatever it is, it's something all of them have in common."

Verenna's mind raced. Her parents, relatives, everyone she knew had been circled by Gawshire's hand and marked. She could feel her heart thudding in her throat at the thought that they might have been taken up in his plan to capture her.

"Let's not assume," Mortimer urged. "We have no evidence that that means something bad has happened there. These could be plans for the future."

"Speaking of future, we need to get our doctor to a doctor if he's going to have one." Fabien thumbed the direction of the cart that held the injured. "Even if Malagrir is in Turim, we need to get Darius back to Falseman Inn."

"He is seeing a doctor," Enra corrected, her expression sharpening with indignation. "Our healer is seeing to him."

Fabien held out his hands to halt the misunderstanding. "I didn't mean to offend, it's just that you're doctor deals with humans. We're not quite, well, you know."

Enra seemed to settle, but kept a slight air of resentment.

The old man closed the conversation. "Then we'll have to plot a way back to the Inn. I'll study more of this overnight. By morning I should have more out of it."

"I can draw you a few different routes back. The kind that aren't on maps. They might be faster." Enra offered.

"We'd thank you for it," Mortimer remarked. "We really should thank you for everything."

Fabien chimed in, "Aye. We would have been done for without you and yours."

Verenna felt a swell of gratitude and sorrow. The Sarzen had given so much, paid such a high price to help them, and all the words she could find for their sacrifice was a bashful, "Thank you."

"Nothing else to do but what need be done. Besides, how could we refuse to help our king? We've only been waiting a thousand years."

Mortimer lit up, filled with a pride she'd never seen in him. Enra stood with the old man's help, careful of her injured ribs. "I'd suggest getting some rest. Who knows what tomorrow has for us? May the night be good…"

Mortimer finished the saying under his breath. "Or merciful in its evil."

With that Enra departed to bed down for the night. One by one the Sarzen made pillows of their coats, arranging beds of leaves, and settling in. Their doctor and an attendant kept watch over Camon and Darius, who lay prone in the bed of the cart. Verenna could hear the soft snuffling and occasional shifting of the horse tied to a nearby tree for the night. For the first time in a long while the woods felt calm. She couldn't feel the tingling uneasiness of being watched that she'd had every mile of their travels. Surrounded by the soft breaths of sleep, a few stoic lookouts, and the occasional snap of the fire she felt at home in a way that made her sick for her own. She lay awake with the thought that her family might be blissfully ignorant of the danger coming to them. If it hadn't destroyed them already. They'd have to pass Canterford to get to Falseman Inn. If Gawshire had had his way with the town, she'd find out first hand.

The trees sighed the scent of green into the breeze. The air softened the humidity of late summer, gentling the night with a warmth like tea and cream. The lullaby of crickets made quick work of most of the troupe, sending each to their own worlds of slumber. But despite the sweet songs of evening, sleep would not claim her. She kept looking to the cart where the healer tended Camon and Darius. She knew there was nothing she could do for either of the men, yet she could not shake the impulse to go and see.

Her body hummed with exhaustion but her mind raced. Thoughts of her home, images of the day, and worry about the condition of her friends assaulted her until finally, unable to make herself even the slightest bit comfortable, she decided she'd pay the two a visit.

Verenna traced her way through camp with soft steps, picking her way around twigs and dry brush so as not to wake anyone. She paused for a moment near Adrinée. The girl might have been related to Enra in some way, a cousin or a niece. The line of her jaw and the hawk like fierceness of her dark eyes matched the older woman, though the girls features were still soft with youth. Verenna felt a pang of guilt at the sight of the girl's glaring brow. A battle-worn child. Even in sleep she fought. She'd lost her brother only days ago and still she'd marched to the next fight. Adrinée couldn't be much younger than she herself. Maybe a year or two. How different their lives had been. Verenna shook herself from the reverie and continued her slinking path towards the injured. As gruesome a sight as it might be, she wanted to see them.

She stalked around the fire, quiet as a cat until she reached the side of the cart. Her shadow hid most of Darius' face. But from the light that fell across his forehead and eyes she could tell that he too wore a grimace in his sleep. She glanced over to Camon. At least he seemed at peace. His chest moved with the light rise and fall of sleep. At first she thought Darius might be breathing too, but it was just the wavering firelight tricking her eyes.

Still she wanted to be sure. Her hand ventured towards him. She retracted it, feeling eyes upon her. The Sarzen doctor had noticed. The woman took her in, and with one slow, owl-like blink communicated her permission to touch her patient.

A slight heat rose in Verenna's face. She felt exposed, caught in the act, though she could find no crime in visiting the sick. The woman turned and sank into a deep crouch to continue mixing her potions. Verenna let the heat of embarrassment fade from her cheeks and shifted so she could see Darius' face. He seemed entirely new, hardly recognizable as the pale, dapper, smirking man he'd been not even a day before.

Her stomach twinged as she reached for him, wanting so badly to discover him breathing. She found herself hoping he'd sit up, scold her for taking too many risks, or for being a brat or poke fun at her for not knowing the answer that he'd then make sound so simple. She held her fingers above his mouth, drifting them lower when she felt nothing. Studying the features she began to notice things she'd never seen before. A faded scar at his hairline. The ever so slight crookedness of his jaw. How had she missed them? It felt like reading secrets, investigating the details of a life lived two hundred years ago that he'd surely never tell her. She wondered if this same uneasy feeling had been what made him recoil from her when she'd woken too quickly from her fake fainting spell. Perhaps he had been studying her the same way.

The breeze brushed between his mouth and her hand, so she lowered it even farther to make sure the warm wind would not trick her. Her fingers hovered a hope's space above his lips. When

she found no sign of life a weight settled in her chest. What if he
didn't get up? If they lost him? If they lost any of them. All three
of the men she'd traveled with had almost been taken from her;
Fabien in the river and Souris, Mortimer to his own condition,
and now Darius. Not to mention her own deaths by knife and by
Cold Fever, both of which she'd survived thanks to the three of
them. She couldn't fathom how she'd get on without any of them.
But in particular, without the doctor.

He knew the prophecy the best, and medicine, and seemed to
have some grasp of the creatures that had plagued them thus far.
They'd might manage and march on. Fabien was excellent
protection, and Mortimer learned and diplomatic. She'd managed
to fight herself out of a few situations on her own with her own
wits, too. But without Darius' cocky self-assurance, each step
forward would hold the weight of hesitance. They'd be slower. An
easier target. If Darius wasn't awake by morning, they might be
lost.

Chapter 12

Morning lumbered across the horizon, sluggish and gray. By the time Verenna awoke, a few Sarzen had already reburied the remaining supplies and were busy decorating the disturbed earth with fallen leaves and branches to hide their cache. Two crouched by the meager remains of last nights fire with something boiling in a pot. It made a distinct slopping sound when stirred. Though food held no more appeal than it had the night before, she knew Mortimer, Fabien, or some other good intentioned soul would insist she have some.

Shaking the sleep from her head she wondered how she'd ever drifted off with so much on her mind. And against the wheel of the cart no less. Remembering what had brought her there she scrambled up to check on Camon and Darius. Camon's place was empty. She spotted him a few yards off with the healer, awake and being fed. That relief quickly melted into dread when she saw Darius' state hadn't changed at all. He hadn't so much as shifted in his sleep.

"Morning, miss," Fabien stepped up to greet her. Noting her crestfallen quiet, he attempted to lighten her mood. "He still sleeping, the lazy git?"

She shook her head without pretending she felt any better.

"I brought you this." He extended a cup loosely constructed from a broad, waxy leaf. It was full of a steaming gray mush. "I know, I know, you don't want it. Just do me the favor will you?"

She took it. The warmth in her palms was nice, though the sour smell of the mash made her slightly queasy. "What is it?"

"Some root they smashed up and boiled. I wouldn't ask beyond that."

"Thanks," Verenna sighed and choked down some of the flavorless, lumpy mixture. She forced herself to swallow.

"How is he?" They turned to find Enra making her way through the breaking camp with the map rolled in her hand and Mortimer close in her wake. "Any luck?"

Verenna shook her head and cast an eye over the doctors unconscious form. "Not yet."

Seeing the worry in the girls face Enra changed the subject.

Noticing Verenna's distress, Mortimer placed a hand on her shoulder to bring her out of her thoughts. "Someone at Falseman Inn's got to know what to do about this. The quicker he gets there the better. It's near time for our groups to part ways."

Verenna looked up at him, searching the kindly creases of his face, remembering every time they'd brought her comfort. A pang of something akin to hunger rang up from her stomach. She didn't want to go without him. Her mind fumbled for an excuse to keep the old man with them, at least for another day while she worked on a plan to keep them all together.

"What about the sun serum? We'll need more," she blurted.

"We brought most of it from the village. There will be plenty for the way back," Mortimer assured her.

Verenna heard a dull thud and rounded to find a few, rough, burlap bags being slung into the cart beside Darius.

"No, I mean, but..." Verenna struggled again for a way to hold off their parting. "Shouldn't we wait a while for everyone to regain their strength? We don't have the numbers for a fight. The least we could do is make sure everyone going is rested."

"Hopefully we've found you a way back that won't require any fighting. You should avoid all roads you've traveled before. In this case, the long way is the safe way."

Mortimer took the map and lay it out on the ground before them. They settled around him to listen. "See here. Enra's drawn us a back route. Hardly anyone knows about it and if they do they don't use it because it adds at least a day to the trip. Probably more due to the rough road. But we're least likely to be followed or found this way."

"Will we still pass through Canterford?" Verenna inquired, bending to examine the hair thin line Enra had scratched onto the map with ash from the fire.

Mortimer tilted his head side to side, hesitating to get her hopes up. "Yes, but we shouldn't stay long. Gawshire may know you have family in Canterford. They'll be safest if we make the trip through town brief and don't give him a reason to turn up there."

Enra joined in, tracing her line on the map. "You'll dip through this bit of woods here and wind along the coast. Then take a turn and come inland until you reach the Inn."

"I don't like the coast." Fabien burst into the conversation. "That bit there," he motioned to a patch of coastline where the cliffs dipped down into flat lands. "It's no good. It's haunted."

"It's better to face enemies that are already dead than ones that need killing," Enra argued.

Mortimer took up her logic and continued. "There aren't any better ways. Main roads will be too dangerous, especially once Gawshire gets off the island we made for him. He'll be sending everything he's got after us. Everything."

Verenna studied Fabien's face. His lips had grown thin under his glowering brow. His eyes looked anywhere else to avoid meeting those around him. He snapped, "I just don't like it. It's more trouble than it's worth."

She'd hardly ever seen him truly cross much less so suddenly. "Why?" she inquired, head tilted in confusion.

"Why what?" he barked.

"I mean, we've been facing demons this whole way. Why would a haunted spot on the coast be any more worry than that?"

"Ghosts and demons are different. Demons you can get rid of, destroy em if you've got to. Ghosts ain't really here so there's nothing you can do to 'em...or for 'em."

Verenna considered it for a moment, but when she opened her mouth to question him farther, Fabien quit the group altogether. "Gah, leave it will ya?"

He stormed off to make himself useful in erasing the traces of their camp.

"There's no better way back," Enra shrugged.

"I know you're right, and so does he," Mortimer sighed before he turned to Verenna. "And what say you? It's you we're trying to protect, after all."

A twitching feeling took over the girl at the thought of being responsible for choosing the route that could either save them or endanger them further. She let her gaze follow Fabien for a moment before pushing her hair behind her ear and forcing herself to focus on an answer. "It makes me nervous. What if he's got a good reason we shouldn't go there?"

"If he had one he would have told us. It's personal I'm sure." Mortimer shrugged.

"And there's really no other way?" she pressed.

"Well, yes, but," Mortimer cleared his throat. The response was so endearingly like her father that he might have been the man in disguise. Her heart broke a little more at the thought of leaving him behind. "No one's seen the condition of those for years."

Enra chimed in to agree. "They exist, and I could draw them for you. But we have no way of knowing if they're even passable. It's been so long since any of us have been those ways and they were hard to travel under the best conditions. If you chose the wrong one, you'll lose too much time turning around and starting over. You can't afford to turn back with your friend in that condition. Cutting along the coast is the quickest backroad with the fewest risks."

Verenna's lips thinned with thought. She scoffed, "Just when I finally get to make some choices, there aren't any. The coast it is."

The Sarzen loaded the cart with as much as they could spare and fixed it to the horse in a time so short Verenna wondered if she'd fallen asleep in between. Before much else could be said they'd started their trek to the crossroad where they'd part, perhaps forever. Fabien walked at the back, sulking and kicking any tuft of grass that ventured too far into the road. Enra walked in the middle of the pack, speaking to Camon who limped along supported by two of his people. But Verenna couldn't stop watching Mortimer's shoulders roll under the old leather of his jacket. The coat seemed fuller now, his shoulders grown thicker with the pride of having regained some small piece of the life he should have lead hundreds of years ago. He belonged with them and she knew it.

As if sensing her troubles, he slowed to walk beside her. "I suppose now is as good a time as any to apologize to you."

Verenna paused and puzzled over the statement. "For what?"

Mortimer tried and failed to look her in the eye. He folded his hands behind him and focused on his feet. "For the way you saw me the night you were kidnapped. I'm usually better about leaving before I transform. With everything that happened, I suppose I was distracted. And that put you in danger."

"Not like you could help it," Verenna shrugged.

"No, but it shouldn't have happened so close to everyone. I should have been paying more attention to the moon. I'm sorry."

"You didn't hurt me. There's really nothing to forgive."

That seemed to soothe the old man, allowing him to look at

her again. Verenna debated a moment over a question that bubbled just below the surface. But just as she decided to ask it, someone whistled up ahead.

They came upon the barren patch where the road split in two. Enra held up a hand and the group gathered around at the fork in the path. "Please know how grateful we are to be able to walk in our woods again. Thank you. All of you. That being said, I would prefer to know you are not traveling in such small numbers. I ask you, Sarzen, if any among us would like to join our friends on their way home."

Verenna jumped in before any of the band could volunteer. "You've lost so much already. It doesn't seem right to put more of you in danger. You don't have to."

"We know," Adrinée silenced her. "But some of us want to. I want to finish what my brother started."

"I'll go." A young man stepped forward. His long, wiry arms and crooked nose, and the slightest auburn tinge to his dark hair lent him an awkward charm. "Oaam always looked out for me. He died protecting you. We owe it to him to make sure it wasn't for nothing."

Three more took a step out of the crowd. The twins who'd set the explosion at the gate also came forward. "We feel the same," said the man with the flame shaped scars up his arm. His sister confirmed his words with a salute.

Tears made of equal parts gratitude and foreboding brewed at the edge of Verenna's lashes. Her stomach turned with joy at such a show of support after all that had happened, but sank with the fear that history might repeat. *Thank you*, she mouthed.

Enra let her daring features soften at the bravery of her tribe. "Then I bid you the best of all fortunes, and a safe return when you've done all you must. Lastly, Verenna," Enra stepped forward and with one deft flick of her hand unbuckled the belt that held her remaining knife. "For you."

The girl instantly recognized the glinting hilt of blade she'd used to hack Enra free of Souris' grip. Her eyes strained wide.

"Take it. Consider it a token of gratitude for saving my life," Enra instructed. "You do good work with it. I like to think you'll save a few more lives with it on your way."

She ventured a cautious hand and slid the dagger from its sheath. "I, I can't," Verenna spluttered, studying the way the horseman's black blood had caramelized the silver of the knife in splotched and swirling patterns. "I'd hardly know what to do with it."

"I wouldn't worry too much. You've got a natural sense for it. I have a feeling you'll know exactly what to do when the time comes to use it." Enra winked and flashed a half smile.

The girl took the blade and replaced it in its sheath as if she were trying not to wake it. Seeing Verenna's hesitation the woman added to her reasoning. "Besides, it's a small gift for the one who returned our rightful leader to us."

Mortimer smiled at the ground to hide the gray twinkle of his eyes. She would miss the comfort of his steady presence. She tried to keep her lower lip from quivering.

"I am glad to have come back," he said with an air of relief. "But I am not needed."

The slight lines around Enra's eyes contracted with confusion.

He looked around at the crowd. Every one of them hung on his words. "These people do not need a king when they already have a leader. It's been you. It is you. And that's how it should stay."

Verenna watched as Enra's stoic persona melted into flustered faltering. "Wha- you are a prophesied king returning to us hundreds of years after the banishment of our people. You… you're meant to rule the Sarzen."

"I was. A thousand years ago. But not now."

Excitement welled up to the breaking point in Verenna's throat and she glanced to Fabien. His brooding had been erased by shock. Judging by the gaping mouths the Sarzen were equally surprised. Mortimer seemed to grow taller at the mere utterance of his announcement.

"This is a unique circumstance, of course. But seeing as I am the sole survivor of the royal lineage and I am without an heir, it is my duty to pass my title to the one I see most worthy of it. And I name you, Enra. Kneel."

Verenna reached out and took hold of Fabien's forearm without thinking. Her heart raced as an awestruck Enra took a knee before the old man.

He produced his ornate dagger from his coat and watched it glisten in the morning light. "My sister's knife. It seems fitting. She was a fighter too." He cleared his throat to keep a lump from forming there. "Now, then," he paused and closed his eyes as if to remember. With oaken depth in his voice, he spoke the lines of an ancient coronation from memory, tapping both her shoulders in turn.

"I, Mortimer of families Avonceau and Sarzen, name you, Enra Larine Khal, the Queen of our people, rightful and true. To serve and command with courage, wisdom, and compassion for those who follow your lead. Let your will be theirs, and their will be yours, united in common pursuit for the good of all, as long as you may rein. Arise, Queen Enra Larine Khal of the Sarzen. Long may she rule."

Enra managed to gain her feet in silence before the entire gathering erupted in cheers. The woman's stoicism had returned but not without wet streaks running down her cheeks. Mortimer clasped her hand in a strong shake. "I am more glad than you will ever know to have met you. But they need me now." He lifted his chin towards the road to the sea. Verenna only became aware she was smiling when her cheeks began to ache. She bounced over to Mortimer and threw her arms around his neck and squealed with delight.

"Didn't think I'd let you go wandering without me, did you?"

All she could do was beam up at him as he turned to the Sarzen for the last time. "May the night be good," he began. Enra raised a hand in salute and finished the farewell. "Or merciful in its evil."

With final goodbyes exchanged, they started the horse and cart down their chosen path home. Verenna couldn't help checking over her shoulder as they meandered away. The Sarzen stood at attention until the trees swallowed them out of sight.

≈

By the time the sun started to droop in the sky, Verenna could feel the thud of each step reverberate up her legs. Her boots seemed to tighten around her toes and she yearned for some end to their walking. They'd hardly stopped all day, taking turns riding on the cart to rest. Fabien had managed to rig a kind of tent over Darius to keep the dappled sun away using a branch and another blanket the Sarzen had given them from the supply cache. Though they had given the unresponsive doctor more sun serum, there was no way to know if it would do him any good now. He showed no outward signs of improvement. He still radiated an unearthly amount of heat.

Finally an evening breeze picked up, chilling the sweat of their necks with the prickling whisper of coming night. Mortimer called a halt at a break in the trees. Verenna could feel the group embrace exhaustion as they settled round to make a fire. The twins darted off into the woods to hunt, leaving the rest of them to rub their tired feet and nurse their raw heels.

Verenna plopped down and yanked off her boots, not even

bothering to unlace them. Her feet throbbed at their new freedom. She lay back in the grass. With the heat of the day still fresh in the ground it might have been a featherbed. One hand rested on her knife while the other shielded her eyes from the blazing orange of the setting sun. She had just dozed off when she felt someone settle beside her.

Mortimer had unrolled the map and lay it out in front of him with considerable care. "Good news. We've made good time. If we keep up at this rate we'll be home in less than a week."

Verenna sat up to see for herself exactly how far they'd come. Mortimer's finger hovered over a spot disappointingly close to where they started. Verenna groaned.

Adrinée stepped back from her work at the fire to join them. "We'll have to move even faster tomorrow. We'll need to cross this valley before next nightfall. There's a lot of wolves said to live there." She indicated a point on the map that sat dishearteningly far ahead of them.

"Fantastic," Verenna muttered into her hands as she tried to massage away a newly forming headache.

"Seems a bit ambitious," Mortimer commented.

"It is. But we'll have to do it." Adrinée's curt tone told of her confidence in this judgement. "We would go hunt there sometimes. But we'd never stay the night. Too close to the dens."

"And you're sure there are no dens here? We aren't really that far from the valley," Verenna interrupted.

Adrinée shrugged. "I mean, you can't know exactly where the wolves are, but there's a little lake down there and so much to hunt that they hardly ever feel the need to leave."

"Hardly?" Verenna pressed.

A rustle sounded from the trees. A chill jumped up her back and her hand shot out to clutch Mortimer's sleeve as two figures emerged.

Adrinée giggled at her reaction. "It's Thessa and Renaud. Don't worry unless you have to. You'll tire yourself out."

Verenna dropped her grip on the old man and let out an embarrassed huff as the twins settled near the fire with a few woodpigeons.

The Sarzen gathered to pluck and cook them, perhaps understanding that those they guided would not need a share in this meal. Mortimer looked on and smiled at the little group. But Verenna caught herself staring off to where Fabien sat on a rock, sharpening his sword. He had the same grimace he'd been wearing all day. He'd had no jovial remarks along the way, no off key traveling songs, or showing off his swordsmanship on unsuspecting branches. Whatever made him hate the road to the coast must run deep. Then there was Darius to consider.

Noticing the girl lost in thought, Mortimer lifted himself from the grass. "I'll see to the horse," he said with a departing pat on her shoulder. As if reading her mind, he added, "Why don't you check on Fabien? He still seems upset."

Verenna watched the young man for a while longer, listening to the scrape of a sharpening stone on a blade and studying his scowling face. She pushed herself up onto her sore feet and made her way closer. Unsure if he noticed her, or if she should break the steely focus he put into his work, she took a seat a little distance away. The grind of rock on metal made a repetitive, tuneless music. She'd almost lost herself in the rhythm when he spoke.

"Come to pry?"

She paused and tried to think of the ways he had attempted to soothe her when she'd been angry. She tried on his roguish grin. "Yes," she said, she scooted closer.

The deep crease in his forehead shallowed a bit, but he did not continue.

Eventually Verenna grew restless in the silence and blurted,

"Look, you can't just tell me something is haunted and expect me not to be interested. Do you have any idea how long I'd sit and stare out my window at Falseman Inn? Not even the abbey itself. Just the smoke. Curious isn't a big enough word."

Verenna glowed as the corner of his mouth tucked into a slight dimple. "I'm surprised, given what you know now, that you want to know any more."

She leaned back on her hands. "I like to be prepared. I also like stories."

He stopped sharpening and stared straight ahead. The night held back the breeze in anticipation of his words. Just as she thought he'd decided against explaining, he launched into a story.

"It starts like they all do. Far away, across the sea, a long time ago...a very, very long time, there was a clan called Gortheyrn. Winter had fallen hard on them and sickness followed. On top of their hardships, children had begun to go missing. They thought it might be the neighboring clan, a bitter enemy, but the winter was harsh for everyone. The scouts sent to spy said their enemies were spending everything they had in survival and were in no shape to be stealing children. Besides there was no signs of anything larger than a snow hare passing the settlement."

"Who did it then?"

"*What* did it," Fabien corrected. "One morning when the snow had fallen without much wind, two sets of tracks appeared. Very large tracks, that lead to the body of one of the missing children, drained of all his blood. Those well enough to fight set out in pursuit. They marched for days. Then weeks. Then months. Following the trail, losing it, finding and losing again. Until finally, far away turned into very close by. Just a few miles ahead of us now, on the cliffs. That's where they found it."

"What?" Verenna whispered.

Fabien stared at the ground, a great distance growing in his gaze. "A beast. It walked like a man, perhaps it had once been. But its skin had gone gray. Its fingers longer than they should have been and tipped with ragged broken nails. Its lips and gums had pulled away from its teeth, giving it a heinous, never closing grin. Two fangs had sprouted in its mouth and a strange red lining encircled its eyes, as if it had been blinking away blood. This creature had taken the children. That was what we'd been tracking."

"So, you were there?" Verenna tried to hide the excitement in her voice. As eager as she was to hear how the tale ended she noticed the ache in him as he told it.

The line of his mouth went flat with frustration at having revealed himself. "Yes," he confirmed with some hesitance.

"And then?" Verenna encouraged, hoping to move him past the moment.

"Then we fought it. The brute was stronger than any of us expected. It hurled two of our men right off the edge of the cliff. My father took a blow to the chest that near shattered him. A man considerably larger than me."

Verenna tried to imagine what a man would have to eat to top Fabien's impressive height, but shook the thought away as the story spiraled towards its end.

"Seeing him down, the beast hovering over him, I lunged. I wasn't thinking. I was too far away. The creature had time to turn and grab me. It lifted me off the ground and bit into the side of my neck."

The girl clapped a hand over her mouth.

"I survived, of course," he joked with a trace of his usual humor. "We won. The beast fell. We tried to find our fallen friends at the base of the cliff. But the fall was too far. Unsurvivable. I know they're not at rest. I know it in my bones. But what can I do? Go after them? I can't. They're with the ancestors now. Somewhere I'll never reach."

"What happened after that? To you?"

Fabien's brows knitted together again. He went back to working the cutting edge of his blade, his strike emphasizing the parts of the story that still left him sore.

"You already know."

"I don't. And I want to."

He ignored her request.

"If I'm going to change into one of you soon, I want to know what to expect. Come on. I've got good reason to hear the whole thing."

"Everyone's different. It might not go like it did for me."

"Fabien," she pressed him, moving closer to beg.

He let out a defeated sigh.

"We headed home. We chopped the beast to bits, burned the body, and took its head as proof of our revenge. It didn't take long for things to go wrong. We were still traveling the coast. My neck was healing nicely, even my father looked as if he'd survive his injuries. But as the nights got darker with the fading moon, I started to feel, different. I didn't want to eat, I got restless, couldn't sleep. Then the moon went out..." he stopped. His lips curled in between his teeth and he shut his eyes. "Blood lust took over. I attacked my own clan. My family. I didn't know what I was doing. It was only blurred flashes of memory, my father's horrified face, and two fresh corpses of my former friends to tell me what I'd done. It took me days of wandering the woods alone to remember even that. I could never go home after what I'd done. If the punishment had only been death I would have taken it. I deserved it. But that wasn't all. If you kill one of your own, they strip you of your name. Your honor. Your title, if you've got one. You're renounced by your family and buried in an unmarked grave instead of with your ancestors and your clan. It's worse than death to die in dishonor. I couldn't go back until I found a way to make amends. I swore I'd fight enough of our enemies myself to be forgiven. Risk my life a thousand times to prove my worth to my family."

The sharpening stone raked along the blade, sparking under the pressure of his hand. "Then, come to find out," he ran the length of the sword so embers splashed into the grass below his work. "I couldn't die. And there's no honor," he struck the blade again. "In a fight you know you'll win." The metal sang below his stone, a hungry sound. "'*No honor without chance*'. Those are our words. A warrior's worth is in the risk of losing. I still haven't found a way around that." The blade keened and glinted as if it might come alive. The stone ran its length again, Fabien's teeth gritting as he spoke "I still haven't found a fair fight. And it's been damn near eight hundred years."

His last strike slipped and his hand slid against the edge. He swore and shook blood from his fingers.

Verenna gasped and reached for him, but by the time he unrolled his hand the gash had started to close. "I had no idea. I'm sorry," she murmured, venturing a comforting hand on his knee.

"Don't worry about it," he grumbled.

The girl moved the conversation away from Fabien's hurt to the only piece that had confused her. "Why was the beast like that? Why was it so different from what you turned out to be? It sounds nothing like you. Like any of you."

"That's what happens over time if a Night Bound creature doesn't find or isn't accepted by a clan. With no one to teach you and help you through blood lust, you go, sort of, feral. You get that way again and again, each dark moon. Without help, each time gets worse. Hunting becomes about slaughter more than survival. You end up killing your victims instead of just taking what you need. And the cycle just keeps going until eventually, you're always that way. Little more than a rabid animal...." His story trailed off and his shoulders sank.

"That's horrible," Verenna whispered. For a moment they both watched in silence as the gashes in his hand smoothed over with new, pink skin.

"I was starting to go feral when I found the abbey. Falseman Inn saved me." Fabien glanced at her from below the rough line of his hair. "That's why I think it will be so different for you. You found a clan before you were even bitten. The first dark moon is hardest, but you'll be at the abbey, surrounded by people who have seen it all before. Who know how to help. You couldn't ask for better circumstances."

Verenna tried to enjoy what optimism she could about the impending transformation. "I think I've already started to change." She tapped a finger next to the wound on his hand. "That cut would have made me vomit or pass out or both before. Now it's nothing."

"Ha!" Fabien let out an unexpected bark of laughter. "What a surprise you'll have for 'em when you get back. That's usually how it goes when you leave home though. You're stronger than when you left."

Their gazes locked for a moment. The evening was settling into the emerald woods around them, making the green of his eyes seem like pieces torn from the edge of dusk. One corner of his mouth drew up like a slow curtain, laying bare a certain mischief, the dimple of his cheek a secret she wanted to know. She didn't want to look away, but as red heat rose in her ears she averted her eyes and hunted for something to stare at besides the young man before her. She toyed with a blade of grass, then turned to watch the Sarzen laughing near the fire, then to the wagon where Darius lay. The blush she feared died in her cheeks.

Fabien followed her gaze to the cart. "Truth is, if he goes, I'll miss him. But if he doesn't, don't you ever tell him I said that. He'll be a twat about it for the next fifty years." He wiped his blood from the sword and stowed it in its sheath. "But if I'm really honest" he added. "I'm just mad at him because somehow, even when he's sleeping, he still stops me from kissing you."

Verenna's eyes nearly popped from her skull. A wash of bright red embarrassment ran a course from her face to her neck, all the way down to the lower half of her arms. "Wha- I…" she stammered, unsure what to do with him grinning at her. His smile grew into a crescent moon carved into the slight golden stubble on his chin. Nerves choked her until she gracelessly blurted, "I have to go", and hurried over to the fire, kicking herself all the way for such a stupid exit. There was nowhere to go but twenty paces away in any direction.

It was dark enough now that the woods started to edge in and constrict the clearing, gathering them closer together with the threat of what might happen outside the reach of the light.

She settled awkwardly next to Adrinée and tried to act like she belonged there. The thoughtless words bounced around her head. After all her years wanting to kiss the boy in the Canterford flower shop, here he was in the woods, on an adventure with her where they could be separated or killed in a thousand different ways, and she'd run away from her chance. She tried to settle her mind by focusing all of her attention on the conversation she had walked into.

"I'll take the first watch," the young man with the red tinged hair proclaimed, in a way that told her he was eager to impress.

"I'll take second watch after Kaybin," Mortimer raised a hand to claim the next shift as lookout.

"Third," Verenna almost shouted it. Amongst the ponderous stares, she cleared her throat. "I, erm, I'll take the third watch."

"Fourth," Fabien called as he joined them by the fire, seating himself directly across the flames from Verenna as if nothing had happened. She looked down and played with a loose thread that hung off her sleeve.

"So, how fast do we think we can move through the next leg? We can't stay on the cliffs," the young man insisted.

Adrinée piped up to inform him. "With some luck we'll pass them tomorrow around noon."

Fabien cast his eyes down the path ahead of them. The overgrowth jutted down like teeth in an open mouth. "And without luck?"

℘

The moon slunk above the treetops and lay like an opal against the satin of the evening sky. Each of them bedded down with one of the rough blankets the Sarzen had provided. The earthen smell of being hidden underground still clung to them. Verenna wrapped hers about her shoulders and propped herself up against the cart's wheel. She couldn't bring herself to lay down. The goosebumps that covered her arms and legs told her the woods were watching.

To keep her mind from getting lost in the gaps between the trees she watched the world darken and counted the stars as they arrived. She shut her eyes and listened. Soft snoring drifted to her from somewhere close. Very close. Something inside her perked as her ears tuned to the sound. She glanced around for the nearest sleeping form. They seemed too far away for her to hear such a subtle noise. A sudden hope wriggled inside her. It could be Darius.

With what stealth she could muster despite her rush she hopped up and hurried to the open back of the cart to crawl inside. She leaned down close and put an ear by the doctor's mouth, biting her lip to quiet the scurrying excitement that he might be breathing.

Disappointment swallowed her joy as she sat back on her haunches. Nothing. Not so much as a whisper of breath from him. Listening with more care she heard the noise again, somewhere beyond the makeshift tent atop the cart. Verenna settled into defeat against a few bags of provisions.

She couldn't truly tell in the shifting, low light that broke through the tarp above them, but it seemed his face might be changing. She didn't dare guess if it were for better or worse, healing or decay. But she tried to take heart in the absence of the honey rot smell that had greeted them in Bronwell.

The girl pried her eyes wide as if it might help her see past the dark that embraced them. Maybe, if she watched long enough, she'd see the burns on his face wane with the moon.

The next thing she was aware of was waking to the sound of short, sniffing breaths from close at hand. Neck stiff and groggy, she turned to the opening of the cart. Something watched them.

Another stocky shape lumbered to join the first. More huffing, and low grumbles. The sound of curious dogs. Her sleep weary eyes focused on the open end of the cart. Three sets of eyes glinted back at her. Wolves.

Chapter 13

Verenna started. So did the beasts. Like instinct her hand went to Enra's knife. "Here! Over here!" she screamed. The creatures retreated, snarling at the sudden disruption.

Immediately voices rang out around her. "Who's there?!" She heard Fabien roar.

"Weapons!" Adrinée cried, beneath the terrified whinny of the horse.

Clatters and clangs broke the quiet. "Stir up the fire! It's wolves!" Thessa called to her brother.

"Get out of here, you!" Mortimer hollered at the creatures as he charged, waving his arms to frighten two that had ventured close. A third animal sprang from out of sight to nip at the old man. Mortimer backed away fast to keep himself from being surrounded. Against the churning fear in her stomach, Verenna scrambled from the cart, knife out and ready.

"Verenna!" Fabien grasped her arm and pulled her towards the fire. "Get in the center," he commanded before shouting to the others. "Circle round! Don't let them get behind you! Backs to the cart!"

"Someone grab the horse!" Mortimer shouted. Adrinée made a break for where the animal had been tied away but had to fall back as more of the snapping animals surged from the treeline. A snarling mouth lurked near the knot in the rope. The horse reared and kicked, nearly catching the wolf's back and sending it scurrying to regroup.

Refusing the middle of the protective ring Verenna stepped in to become part of the perimeter between Kaybin and Renaud.

"Where was your head boy? You were supposed to be keeping watch!" the man scolded.

"I'm sorry. I, I just, I'm sorry."

"Bigger problems, boys, bigger problems," Thessa reminded them. "The hell is wrong with these things anyway? They're all ribs. It's summer."

"No young ones. They may have eaten them," Mortimer added.

"Good god, why?" Verenna asked between frightened pants.

Fabien answered. "They're desperate."

Adrinée protested in confusion, "But it's summer. There's game. What is this?"

"I don't know, but there are a whole lot of them," Mortimer grunted as more eyes lit the edges of the trees. Excited yips and whirring whines stirred in the brush, an alien chorus. One by one dark shapes seeped from the shadows of the wood to join the pack in surrounding them. As far as Verenna could keep count there were fifteen. Ice surged through her blood. They were outnumbered. Nearly two to one.

"Noise! More noise!" Thessa shouted. The group flung curses, kicked rocks at the creatures, screamed, but still the beasts edged in.

Verenna's hand tingled with nervous energy and she feared she'd drop her knife. "I don't...I...How do you fight a wolf?"

"Patience," Adrinée told her, as she took careful aim with her bow at a wolf that paced too close. "If you hold strong for long enough, they'll see it's not worth the effort and they'll leave you alone. Mostly."

"Beautiful. *Mostly*. Right." Verenna let out a manic laugh.

"Kaybin, what the blazes were you doing on lookout? Didn't you see some of these coming?" Fabien resurrected Renaud's complaint.

"I was watching!" he insisted. "I can't very well see through wood and nails. They snuck up behind the cart."

Adrinée paused to punch him in the shoulder. "You fell asleep, I know it."

"Did not!" the boy argued. The distraction gave one of the pack opportunity to strike for his legs.

Seeing the creature lunge Verenna brought her knife down, gashing the snapping head and making it retreat before it could take hold of Kaybin's ankle.

"Thanks," he gasped with eyes like milk saucers.

The injured wolf's yelp set off a series of yaps and howls. The pack were working themselves towards a frenzy, edging ever closer. Now and again one would lunge and make someone jump back, tightening their circle even further.

Verenna's insides rolled with chaos. No matter how hard she panted she couldn't seem to draw enough breath. She didn't know where to focus with so many animals milling around them. As soon as she looked one direction a set of teeth nipped at her from the other. She turned just in time to catch a wolf springing for her, its mouth wide to catch her thigh. Frantic, she kicked, and felt her foot land in the fur and sinew of its starved mandible. The beasts jaws came together with a crippling clack. Her toes ached with the contact and she wished she'd put her boots on to sleep.

Nearly shoulder to shoulder with the cart at their back, there could be no more retreat. "What now?" she asked Adrinée.

"Well," the girls voice had a surprising calm to it. She flicked a loose curl away from her dark eyes. "They'll charge soon. Then it's a fight."

"What?!" Verenna squawked.

"You asked," she shrugged.

As she said it Renaud let out a battle cry and took a swing at one of the frontmost wolves. He missed. His axe plunged deep into the ground and lodged there. Seizing the opportunity for revenge the animal went for him. He pulled back in time for the bite to miss his neck and land right above his elbow. He shrieked and swung with his free hand to try and beat himself free of the creatures grip. Before the wolf could drag him to the pack Fabien's sword ended the struggle, slicing the animals head clean from its hackles.

Thessa pulled her brother behind her. "Stay against the cart!" she screamed. "They smell the blood. Brace yourselves."

The jostling pack readied themselves to swarm them. Every one of the brutes shoving the others to get the first taste of the feast to come. The one she'd gashed across the face appeared again, lip curled and licking its teeth, blood staining the white of its eye crimson. It honed in on her. She could look nowhere else. The knife felt clumsy in her hand, her limbs loose and disorganized. If the creature pounced she'd be done for.

Without warning the snarls turned into curious yips, sounds that died out into confused grunts and low growls. The animals abandoned their fighting crouches. Ears perked. Noses lifted to the wind. They heard something.

Verenna found herself following their lead and listening hard to the night. What was it that called them? Somewhere far, she heard a sound so faint she wondered if she were hearing anything at all. Something high pitched and blaring, like the squalling of an infant. It could be the packs pups, but some quality told the girl it must be human. The noise called to her, pulled at her insides in a forlorn way that made her want to chase after it, to soothe whatever cried.

Just as she began to search the treeline for a source the wolves turned and fled into the abyss of the underbrush, rushing to find the distressed creature and devour it.

"Did you hear…" Mortimer began.

"A baby?" Verenna finished for him. "What on earth?"

No one in the group moved for a moment. The breeze whipped the silence between them into a frothing tension no one wanted to address. What creature wept in the woods?

౭∽

A pained hiss broke their contemplation. Renaud's arm was bleeding badly. Thessa tested the bend of his elbow. "Not broken. Just ugly. Kaybin, get the bandages from the cart. It's the smallest bag. There's herbs to pack the wound. Make yourself useful."

He blushed with frustration but did as she told him.

The knot left Verenna's stomach as it set in that the threat had passed. She looked to Fabien who towered over the wolf he'd decapitated. If the body hadn't been so thin the creature might have outweighed him. He'd peered onto the patches of impenetrable night between the trees.

Verenna joined him, putting a hand on his arm. Her touch startled him out of his thoughts. "Don't…don't do that."

The girl immediately retracted her hand. "Sorry…You heard it too, then? The baby?"

"It weren't no baby. It's something, but it ain't that," he mumbled with a distance in his tone that matched his far away look.

Thankfully Mortimer spoke and distracted them from speculation with a plan of action. "We need to go. We can take turns resting on the cart like we did getting here. I would hate to be here if the pack circles back."

"The horse," Adrinée reminded them. She and Verenna both rushed to examine the animal for injuries. The creature had taken multiple bites to its legs, one on its chest, and another on its haunch.

Mortimer joined them, swearing under his breath, a thing Verenna never thought she'd hear.

"How bad do you think it is?" Adrinée asked. "Is she lame?"

The whole troop instantly stilled, all action suspended in anticipation of the dreaded answer.

The old man let out a long breath. "Yes."

A collective groan struck up from the group. But Adrinée called their attention back to the animal's injuries. "Wait...look at that."

"What's happening?" Verenna joined her, crouching with the other girl to examine the tear in the horse's pectoral.

"It's healing," Verenna breathed. "It's...sewing itself shut. How is...What?"

Even Mortimer looked surprised. Fabien stomped over to see for himself. His grimace melted into shock. "She's healing like we do. It makes no sense. Look at her legs!"

They gathered round, and with a mixture of rapture and bewilderment, watched as the mare's injuries closed by themselves.

"He's right," Renaud murmured. "It fixes itself just like when Enra put that hole in you."

Fabien rolled his eyes, his sour expression reinvigorated by the memory.

"How though?" Adrinée, demanded. "I thought it was only you who were like that. I didn't know animals could be Undying too."

"Honestly, neither did we," Mortimer admitted, stroking his whiskers in wonder at their luck. "I'm not sure now is the time to question it though."

Thessa was the first out of awe. "Well...let's hitch her up."

Mortimer rose, his mouth a pensive line. "Suppose we should."

Verenna stood next to him to watch the last of the wounds close up and vanish under the animals dark hair. "Corvus mentioned something about the horse. He said I should ask

Darius."

The old man looked as confused as she was by the statement. "Well, if you get the chance, let me know his answer. Whatever he knows he kept it a secret."

They packed up camp even faster than they'd set it up. The potential of returning wolves sped every action to double time. Once Thessa had Renaud's arm bandaged, they worked together to chop an armload of branches from a broad leafed tree at the edge of their camp. Adrinée showed Verenna how to score the branches in a braided pattern to release the greatest amount of flammable sap. Once ignited, they burned with a vigor even the wind could not shake. When a torch faltered its carrier simply scratched more grooves in its bark to keep it burning. They clung to the flaming sticks as they walked, like children holding a mother's hand, each of them afraid of awakening the dark.

Verenna walked close to Fabien, careful to keep from startling him again. He didn't seem to notice her. His senses were busy translating the subtleties of the night woods. She tried to pinpoint the sounds that kept him on edge but beyond the rustle of the leaves she could hear nothing.

After what seemed like hours of trudging through the night Mortimer whispered her name. "Why don't you take the next rest on the cart?"

She nodded and sped up to get into the cart, settling against the side near Darius's feet. Verenna couldn't help but check again for breath. Still nothing.

Discouraged, she slid off her squeezing boots to try and tempt sleep to her. But as she got comfortable, she felt a dull stab from in her pocket.

The book. She fought it out of the folds of her dress. Its silver title glinted in the faint light of the torches that made it through the tarp hung over the cart. She smiled at the feel of its water warped cover. The curling edges of the sun dried pages rustled like crinoline at the stroke of her thumb.

She tried to make out the table of contents, tilting the little book in all directions to see if she could catch enough light. She wanted to check for anything she'd missed that might explain what they'd heard that night. At a gap in the hanging blankets she managed to catch a beam from Kaybin's torch. Verenna poured over the different descriptions until her eyelids refused to keep open.

ℝ

The next day they made it to the valley Adrinée had sworn would be teaming with game. They didn't see so much as a bird their whole walk through, which made for a miserable dinner of boiled root from the supplies the Sarzen had sent with them. Even the day after that was suspiciously devoid of life. They dared not stop for longer than an hour to cook and eat for fear of becoming a sitting target for whatever had caused the animals to flee the region. Mortimer persuaded the group that they'd stop for a true night's rest when they reached the cliffs.

The third morning of their march smelled like the sea. The air tasted ever so slightly of salt. A humid breeze tugged at their clothes and coated everything in an invisible type of dew. Verenna could feel it in the frizz of her hair when she woke from a nap in the cart.

As soon as she became fully conscious she turned to check on Darius. Lifting the cover from his face she squinted to search for signs of healing. The weak light of early morning kept any improvements a secret. Her mood sank. Only then did she notice Thessa and Renaud perched on the back of the cart.

The twins muttered to each other, pieces of sentences, filled in with shared silence that seemed to carry just as much meaning as the words they exchanged.

"Morning," she grumbled, her voice still raspy with sleep.

The twins nodded.

"No wolves?" Verenna asked.

"No, not since camp," Renaud replied, rubbing the bite on his arm.

Thessa leaned against the railing of the cart. "It's gonna be nice to have an actual camp. It'll be even nicer to get back to my own bed."

Renaud grunted his agreement. "That will be a relief. It'll be easier to sleep when we get back too, knowing the children are safe and all."

"You have children?" Verenna inquired. It seemed strange to her that mothers and fathers would be out on adventures such as this.

Renaud spoke first. "Two. Two girls. Their mother was taken with the fever. One of the first to go."

"I'm so sorry."

He shook his head. "This world is a hard one. At least they've got a sweet ol' auntie to help raise 'em."

Thessa gave her brother a playful shove. "Someone's gotta teach those pretty little things to fight. They'll get good practice with my son." She turned to Verenna with pride. "You might not have known but Camon is my husband. That crazy lug almost got himself killed being too brave. Now he's home safe and it's my turn, I suppose."

Verenna felt the urge to apologize again. Camon wasn't dead, but the half-botched rescue mission had been a close call. "I didn't get a chance to thank him, really. Will you tell him for me when you go back?"

Thessa nodded slow, then shook her head at a memory. "I'll tell him. I know what he'd say though. That he doesn't need thanks when all he's doing is the only thing that's right."

By mid afternoon the trees had fallen away from the road and the sun lay into them. They slept in turns in the shade of the cart to spare their skin from burning.

Fabien's mood had deteriorated even further to the point where no one dared speak to him. Even his shadow seemed angular with ill humor. Finally, the cart came to an ambling halt just off the road.

Mortimer called to the group from the lead. "Congratulations ladies and gentlemen. We have made the cliffs." A palpable relief washed over the troop. "Let's take a rest."

"I'll check on the doctor," Kaybin offered.

"I think he's better off if you didn't," Thessa warned.

Kaybin glared and challenged her. "You know I'm good with herbs. I've been taking lessons from the healer and I'm actually getting good."

"Maybe so, but now's not the time to test yourself," Renaud said, rubbing at his elbow.

"That's swelling isn't it?" the boy retorted.

"No," Renaud clutched his arm to his chest. "It's just, irritated is all."

"Alright. It's irritated," Kaybin repeated, and turned to instruct Thessa. "Next time you wrap it for him, crush garlic into the poultice. I put some in with the bandages. It's good for keeping wounds from festering. Do it. See if he doesn't feel better."

"How about you cook, garlic boy," Thessa suggested with a sceptical brow. She tossed him one of the larger sacks off the cart.

Kaybin's jaw tightened. "Fine. Just trying to help."

As the boy wandered off to make a fire, Adrinée came to his defense. "Stop picking on him, will you? He's good at some things."

"What?" Renaud asked under his breath. "Seasoning me like a roast?"

"Oh, shut up. He's got plenty of talents."

"Lookout's not one of them," Thessa whispered making her brother stifle a laugh.

Adrinée rolled her eyes and quit the conversation to help her friend construct the fire.

"See to the sick?" Renaud invited his sister, and they departed to tend to Darius.

Verenna watched them vanish into the cover of the cart as Fabien freed the horse from its harness. A hand alighted on her shoulder. "Come," Mortimer urged her towards the rising green distance. "Don't rush up to it now."

The girl wasn't sure what he had in mind but she followed his lead. She yearned to take her shoes off again and feel the grass between her toes. The blades look so soft. Maybe it was just the way the wind washed over them. The incline grew steeper and her tired legs made her wonder about the point of this march.

Some crashing noise like distant thunder reached them and she paused to listen. Mortimer ushered her on. "Just a bit more and we'll be at the top."

"The top of what?" Verenna whined, but saw the answer before the old man had the chance to speak. A brilliant light blinded her for a moment and she glanced down, finding herself on a ledge.

The land ended as if it had been cut with a knife. It was not some hill they had climbed, but the rising edge of a cliff. And at the bottom, a frothing, frigid, sea gnawed at the base of the soaring rock. The waves broke so far below them that she had to tune her ears against the wind to hear their roar and sigh. And beyond that, the splendor of the evening sun; a copper plate spilling vengeful red across the horizon scattered tumbling gold across the restless water like thousands of glinting coins. If he hadn't shown her to this peak, she'd have never known the ocean lay so close. Anyone could assume the rise was just another bump in the land.

"Oh," she let a gust of wind fill her lungs. The breeze came strong at the top of the rise, lifting her hair and wrapping her skirts around her legs.

"It's nice, isn't it?"

"More than nice."

He smiled. They stood in silence and watched the glaring sun soften into little more than an orange smudge between sea and sky.

Finally Verenna spoke. "I won't get to watch many sunsets when I turn will I?"

Mortimer tried to keep his answer nonchalant but a quiet sadness dampened it. "Maybe not all of them. But from what they've told me sun serum takes away the danger and a good amount of the discomfort. If you want to see the sunset bad enough I'm sure Darius will be able to mix some up for you the way he does for the rest of Falseman Inn. He'd probably charge you less too."

They got lost in the glimmer of the water for a few peaceful minutes, before an unanswered question bubbled up in Verenna's mind. "Mortimer, if you don't mind me asking, how are you immortal? Are werewolves like that too?"

The old man scuffed a foot in the grass. "Well, no. Werewolves aren't usually immortal. At least none of the others I've ever met. In all honesty, I'm not so sure I am truly among the Undying myself. I do age. But very, very slowly. It's took me near a thousand years to look older than forty. Yet of all the injuries that should have killed me over the centuries, I haven't yet succumbed. It's hard to say whether or not I'm truly eternal." He looked down to the rocks below as if he wished to join them.

Her mind whirled for a way to keep her next question polite. "Can I ask how it happened?"

Mortimer sighed. "A very poor decision." He pondered a moment before continuing. "When my sister died, when I was forced from the city, I wanted revenge more than anything. But if I returned to get it, I'd be killed or captured on sight. The whole of Bronwell was against me. If I were to ever avenge my family, Gawshire would have to come to me. One thing I knew of him, was that he loved to go on night hunts when the moon gave him enough light. And his favorite targets were wolves.

"So I, being desperate and young, and if I'm honest, stupid, set out to find a healer I thought could help me. She lived as a hermit in the woods. When I found her, I gave her everything. My clothes, pendants, my sword, anything I had left of my royal life, in exchange for rags and a curse. I asked to take on the form of a wolf under the full moon. Every full moon. Until I had the revenge I sought. I wanted Gawshire to come looking for me, and when he did, I'd be ready.

"The healer obliged. Of course, as with most curses, there were many unintended consequences."

"So you were cursed instead of bitten," Verenna mused, comparing the tale to the stories she'd heard as a child.

Mortimer's shoulders sank. "I couldn't have been bitten. I was the first."

"Really?" Verenna tried to keep her fascination out of her voice, knowing that the old man took no pride in it. His answer wavered as regret clenched his throat.

"Unfortunately, yes." His story fell to all but a whisper. She moved in closer to hear the end. "Under a full moon, I'm so blinded by rage that I tend to mistake anyone I come across for the one man I seek. I attack them, bite them, then at some point realize they weren't Gawshire. But by then it's too late. They're already cursed, infected with my anger, my bloodthirstiness. They do not become immortal as I am, but they have to live the rest of their days with a burden that should have never been theirs. I don't think there's a way to be forgiven for that." He attempted a smile but it faded with the last winking piece of the sun. Unable to think up any words that might comfort him Verenna simply laced her arm with his. They watched in silence as the day drained below the edge of the world.

It wasn't long before Fabien beckoned them, waving with considerable urgency towards a spot a little ways off the road.

As they gathered with the others they were greeted by a strange sour smell. At their feet lay a mound of bones and fur, roughly in the shape of a large dog, and covered in a thick, wet grease.

Verenna held her nose. "What is that?"

"It's one of the wolves," Fabien answered as he squatted to examine the fallen beast. "But it's been drained."

"Drained?" Renaud grunted.

"Look," Fabien took the tip of his sword and lifted the creatures fur. Beneath it, the bones had been stripped clean. Verenna winced at the gruesome sight. All of the animals insides were gone. Flesh, organs, everything. All that remained was a matted pelt, and a jumble of cracked bones.

Thessa gagged. "How?"

"Looks like it was torn open here on its side, then the rest, maybe, dissolved? Maybe it's something to do with the slime covering it." Fabien shrugged, clearly unfazed by the gore.

"If I didn't know better, I'd say something tried to eat it. Whole," Mortimer mumbled under his hand as he tried to keep the pungent, metallic odor from his nostrils.

"What the blazes is big enough to do that?!" Verenna squawked, dreading whatever new species they might be introduced to next.

The group exchanged looks, shrugs, and mutterings. "Don't rightly know," Fabien responded, bewildered. "But I'm rethinking staying on the cliffs for the night. Or any longer than we have to…"

"I won't argue with that," Thessa agreed.

"Another night marching?" Adrinée protested.

Kaybin countered. "Do you really think you could sleep easy wondering what kind of monster did this?"

"We'll post lookouts," she insisted.

"Even with someone standing guard, I'm not sure there will be enough of us to fight whatever it is. Not without casualties. It has to be enormous," Renaud pondered, shaking his head in wonder at the idea of such a beast.

Verenna piped up in support. "If it ate a wolf, it must have taken on an entire pack and come out on top. We should go. Soon. Now would be best."

"Are you kidding me?" Adrinée groaned at her.

"You aren't scared of what did this?"

"Of course it's scary. I just don't know how we're going to stand a chance if we try to go the whole way without a real night's sleep," the younger girl pressed.

"We've made it this far," Verenna reminded her.

Adrinée threw one hand onto her hip. "And you think that guarantees us something?"

"No, I…"

"It doesn't. Luck isn't in endless supply. You only get so much before something happens. We shouldn't rely on being lucky."

Verenna snapped back at the girl. "I think we know. We're not idiots."

"You're not wrong, Adrinée," Mortimer chimed in. "But our luck is more likely to run out staying put than it is if we keep on the move."

The girl glanced around the circle of her silent companions for support. Finding none she flung her arms wide. "Fine. How should I know anything?" With a last glare at Verenna, she stormed off to sulk by the growing campfire.

"We'll take a rest and then move on," Mortimer suggested. "Can we all agree to that?"

The group muttered their weary approval and meandered to the fire to nurse sore feet.

Verenna hung back with Fabien a moment longer, staring down at the disemboweled wolf. "Does Adrinée remind you of anyone?" he asked without looking up from the carcass of the animal.

The girl shrugged. "Should she?"

"I should think so," he turned to her, eyes wide. "You."

"You're joking."

He shook his head and insisted, "Am not. That was you a few months ago."

"She's being a child."

"A child not all that much younger than you."

Verenna rolled her eyes and crossed her arms.

Fabien turned to her, then glanced to the pouting girl by the fire. "I'm just saying, I'm surprised you're not friends. You even sulk the same way."

"Shut up," Verenna mumbled.

He let out a low chuckle. "I'm telling you, together, you'd be a force to be reckoned with." He made his exit to join the rest of the group. Verenna would have continued to pout on her own but an eerie prickle at the back of her neck sent her scurrying to follow him. If the night had eyes, she didn't want to be caught alone.

⁊

That night's march was harder. Much harder. Clouds rolled in off the sea and stole the moonlight that had aided them the night before. The humid air wrapped smothering hands around their sap branch torches. Now and again when the wind swelled to gusting they'd blow out entirely, leaving them in the pitch with the distant rumble of the ocean and the click of flint until the resin sparked again. Verenna kept her ears tuned to the night, especially in those agonizing minutes of darkness. The flash of a frustrated face in the light of a failed flint strike was all there was to prove they hadn't fallen out of existence. Mired in that nothingness, Verenna could swear that somewhere in the far reaches of the night, she could hear a baby's cry.

Some time past midnight the sky grew vengeful. Thunder growled the heavens ill mood, dwarfing the sounds of the sea with booming complaints so close over their heads they could feel the grumbling in their chests. By the time the first signs of dawn graced the horizon the clouds had made good on the threat of rain.

A deluge soaked them to the skin. Thick fog sprang up as the cold rain battered the warm earth and turned the road to mud. They could hardly see the vague path before them as they trudged doggedly away from the coast.

It was Verenna's turn to rest in the cart. The blanket managed to repel most of the rain, though it sagged ever lower with the unending downpour and let the occasional heavy droplet through. She sat with her knees to her chest and watched Darius' still form with a blank, tired face, letting the jostling of the cart sway her as the wheels dipped into the ruts of the road. Squeezing her eyes shut, she tried to shake the memory of the faint cries she'd heard half the night. Fatigue replayed them in her head, so well she thought she might still be hearing them.

As she was about to doze off, one of the group called out from up ahead of the cart. Verenna cocked her head and listened. It sounded like Thessa, though she could not make out the woman's words. Before she could hone in on what was being said the cart dipped hard on one side into a deep puddle and came to an abrupt halt. The motion knocked her into the sideboards. But as that startle ended, another commanded all of her senses. A gasp sounded from below the blanket.

Her heart pounded wild as she lifted the sheet that covered Darius' burned face. Below it, she found the doctor breathing. Not just breathing, panting. His eyes cracked open and found her. They were horribly bloodshot. His eyelashes flaked into ash as he blinked up at her.

"Darius!" she managed to wrangle her slack jaw into the shape of his name. He'd been what anyone would have considered a corpse just moments before.

He croaked out some attempt at words, but the calls from outside the cart and the continuous whoosh of the rain drowned whatever it was he'd said. Desperate to know, Verenna leaned in. Even then his sounds were hardly language. She scrambled for the two large bladders of water sloshing near his head. Fetching one of them she struggled with the top before tearing it off with her teeth and dripping some of the liquid across his lips. He swallowed it down and spoke again. His message had cleared ever so slightly. Almost comprehensible. She fed him more water, nearly dropping the whole container when the cart rocked drastically forward. The group had tried to heave it out of the rut, but it slid back with no success.

The saturated blanket above sent a trickle of collected rain down her spine. She spat out a piece of her wet hair that had clung to the edge of her mouth, tensed and waiting for the doctor's next attempt to communicate.

"Chry-yuh," he fought to form the sounds.

"Cry?" Verenna repeated. She listened. Someone outside was weeping something terrible. It sounded as if an argument had broken out, making it even more difficult to hear the man. "Yes someone is. Why do…" she stopped as she saw him ever so slightly shake his head.

"Cr-ie-rr," he croaked.

Verenna repeated his sounds out of confusion, hoping her own mouth would form the message her mind could not. "Cry-er…Crier?"

Darius shut his eyes and breathed a touch easier. That must be the answer.

Only when she'd pronounced the word a second and third time did she realize that all the sound outside the tented blanket had ceased. No one shouted anymore. The cart did not rock. All that remained were the shushing sheets of rain, and the blaring cry of a baby.

Chapter 14

Every hair on the girl's arms stood up like its own watchtower as she realized what the doctor had awoken to tell her. The creature that stalked them must be a Crier.

Verenna nearly tore her dress as she ripped the book from her pocket and flipped through once more, frantic for a passage she'd missed that might tell her how to react. As the wailing wore on she felt herself pulled to answer it. Something about the weak, helpless, bawling of the creature made her want to comfort it. She glared at the pages. She must have missed something. There had to be something she could know to keep them safe from whatever came next, but she could hardly keep her eyes on the page. She wanted to run to the injured creature that howled so mournfully. The sound seemed to come from all directions, filling her skull until she thought she'd go mad with it.

Using every ounce of focus she had left she managed to find a small note at the bottom of a page that she had missed. As soon as she'd found it she tore the soaked blanket from its hangings and shouted to the others who had all gathered with their backs to the cart, weapons drawn.

"Criers!" She shouted over the noise, beads of rain flying from her lips as she read aloud. "Beasts that use the sounds of children to lure human prey. Fast, and cunning, but feeble once their physical form is defeated!"

"And how do you defeat one?" Fabien called.

"It doesn't say."

"Perfect."

"Maybe we should go see…" Renaud's voice could hardly be heard over the brush of the wind.

Thessa grabbed his arm. "You can't be serious."

"We should…" he whispered. Renaud's eyes had grown glassy and distant. "If it's a child. We need to help it. We have to…" He took a step towards the woods at the side of the road only to be flattened against the wagon by his sister.

"You're out of your mind! It's a trap!"

"No! We have to save it!" He screamed, froth gathering at the corners of his mouth as he fought to free himself of Thessa's grip. Mortimer came to her aid and the three of them toppled into the mud.

"Stop it!" Adrinée commanded as she and Kaybin dove in to help break up the fray.

"We've got a bigger problem! Pay attention!" Verenna added to the mayhem. "I said, we've got other problems! Quit! If you… quiet!"

Her final shout got the group's attention enough to call them all to the fact that the babies' cries had stopped. Renaud's fighting went slack as if he'd just come out of a trance. Everyone else paused mid action, every muscle tense and listening to the absence of the cries.

"What's it mean when they stop crying?" Mortimer whispered.

As if in answer, a shadow fell across Verenna. She turned and looked up just in time to see an open red mouth large enough to engulf her whole. Its sides were lined with row upon row of teeth, glistening with slime. She shrieked and threw herself to the floorboards of the wagon.

The same sour smell that had clung to the dead wolf surrounded them in a hot cloud of breath. She could hear the others shouting beyond the cage of the creature's mouth, and the whinny of the panic stricken horse still bound to the cart.

The creature's jaws were held apart only by the splintering sideboards. Verenna turned her face and found the thousands of serrated teeth only a hand's space above her. And at its center a gulping throat. She tried to grab her knife but it was pinned beneath her, and the hovering mouth gave her no room to maneuver. It undulated above her as she tried to turn over, eager for her flesh. Its teeth pricked the back of her arm. There was no way to fight without turning over.

Bracing herself for the sharp sting of its fangs, Verenna twisted hard and flipped herself onto her back. The teeth raked her arm and shoulder, leaving scores of tiny cuts in organized rows. She gasped and swore as an acidic sensation overtook the limb and seeped up into her neck. A sensation like lemon and salt thrown on an open blister filled a quarter of her body. But she could reach her knife. Pulling it free she jabbed it into the folds of the creatures throat. It heaved and released the cart. She saw sky again as rain spattered her face.

With her right arm rendered useless she struggled to her knees to check on Darius. Though his eyes would hardly open he seemed unharmed.

Head spinning she looked around for the attacker. She heard the flicking sound of a fired arrow behind her and turned to find Adrinée aiming another shot at the strangest being Verenna had ever seen. Its face was long like that of a deer, but the places where its eyes, ears and mouth should be were completely wrapped with skin and unable to open. It had horns like a buck, with muscular arms and legs that were horrifically human, save for the fact that they ended in three grasping toes with gnarled nails. Its most striking feature by far was its massive barrel of a chest. For such odd proportions, the creature possessed shocking agility.

Fabien rushed the creature with his sword high. The Crier reared. On its back legs it was twice his height. As the young man drew close, it opened the orifice that had clamped down on the cart. A long, jagged seam ran the length of its underside, allowing its ribs to hinge open into the ghastly array of teeth. Fabien dug his heel into the mud to keep himself from hurtling headlong into the creatures jaws. He fell and rolled aside as the beast balled up its three pronged hand into something like a fist and brought it down in the muck where he'd just lain. It shut its chest and hugged the ground, circling them in a swift, crouching crawl.

"Get on either side of it!" Fabien hollered to Thessa and Renaud as he heaved himself from the mud. "I'll come in for the kill."

Verenna was nearly knocked from her feet by the tilt of the cart as the horse panicked against Mortimer's best attempts to calm it, the lodged wheel the only thing keeping it from bolting. Fighting for control of her stinging arm and side the girl managed to stagger off the wagon and join the others. She wasn't sure how to help. With a dagger and next to no practice, there wasn't a thing she could do that the trained fighters who challenged the beast couldn't do five times better. Even Kaybin had pulled out a slingshot and opened fire on the creature with whatever rocks hadn't been swallowed by the soft soil of the road. She felt useless.

She glanced around for something to throw. The only rocks she saw were far too large for her to heft. But at the sight of them, something struck her. She rushed over and began to roll one of them along the ground, stooping low to push it. It might not be a good weapon, but if she placed it right, it could get the cart free.

Her face burned red with exertion as she placed the first stone in the rut. Again she returned to the patch of rocks. This time she gathered one under each arm and waddled back to pack them into the sludge in front of the wheel. She set them into the wet dirt and scurried for more. In her hurry she did not see what watched her.

As she pried another rock from its sunken place in the ground she thought she heard the snap of a branch but the sound was swallowed by a roll of thunder. She scanned the treeline and saw nothing. Then came the sound of something large shifting its weight.

Verenna pushed her soaked hair from her face and blew away the water running across her lips, checking again for another aggressor. Still nothing.

She heaved a flat piece of stone from the ground and hugged it to her body so it would not slide from her tired grip. This might be the piece to get the cart moving again. If the fight didn't end soon, they might be able to run for it.

Only when she'd turned and made for the cart did she see what she'd missed. Out of the corner of her eye she noticed a shape that did not quite fit with the forest. Her head whipped around. Another Crier. Its perfect stillness had disguised it. A few broken branches tangled through its antlers. Rain slid down its head, pooling in the soft skin-lined sockets where its eyes should be and overflowing like tears. If she didn't move, would it see her?

She held her breath, unsure if a scream to alert the others would be worth it. With one battle already underway, they wouldn't reach her before it did.

Rows of slits where nostrils would have been opened and closed with long, slow breaths. The creature let out a huff that sent a horizontal splattering of water across Verenna's face. It took a step forward, walking on its knuckles on all fours, parting the undergrowth with the bulk of powerful shoulders. It came within arms reach of her. The girl stayed motionless, though she could feel her heart knocking against the rock she clung to. Its gill-like nose flared again. Its body tensed. It had found her.

Before she could take so much as a step the beast sent out its front arm to wallop her in the chest. The blow might have cracked ribs if it hadn't been for the rock she carried. She fell back in the mud, winded. The beast's fist came down hard, pinning her between the slick ground and the stone. It leaned into her, pressing until she could not breathe, until she thought her bones might give. The jaws in its chest opened to accept her into its throat or stomach, or whatever fleshy prison was beyond the thousands of peaking fangs. She kicked and scraped in all directions, trying to find something to grab onto to pull herself free. But the ground all around was turning to soup with the rain.

As she felt herself about to pass out, a hissing followed by a meaty thud sounded above her head. A rock struck the beast's forehead, gashing it. The creature withdrew in surprise and the pressure relented.

Gasping Verenna rolled aside, out of the beasts reach. Another rock bashed into the creatures nose, setting free a trickle of what Verenna guessed was blood from its breathing slits. Shaking off its injuries it sank low to the ground, its limbs coiling to spring.

Fabien came charging around the cart with his sword already above his head. At a full run, he prepared to land a brutal blow to whatever part of the creature he could reach. To Verenna's surprise the Crier did not dodge when he swung. Instead it caught the sword in the trap of its antlers. The blade snapped off a piece of horn before it sank into the bone and was stuck. Fabien did not let go though the creature bucked its head to throw him. He kicked it in its long snout, inciting another hiss that sent a spray of blood across him.

Coughing, Verenna stumbled up to help. She drew her knife, but the beast heard her coming and pivoted. Fabien skidded off towards the trees, tossed like a child by the Crier's unearthly strength. It had closed the distance between them in the second she'd blinked. She struck out with her dagger, vision blurred by the downpour, aiming for the creatures fleshy eye socket. She missed. An antler caught her in the side. Her feet left the ground as she was thrown into the side of the cart. She felt the sideboards crack against her back, and slumped onto the ground.

Fabien came back for another round wielding the rock she'd dropped as if he'd be fast enough to bring it down on the beast. The Crier turned its attention back to the crazed young man long enough for Verenna to get her bearings.

The sound of coughing stopped the world spinning and brought her back to reality. Darius. She clambered onto the cart to see that he hadn't been hurt. He gasped and choked but his weak stabbing gestures might hold the answer. Verenna crawled to him and came close to hear his strained instructions.

"The horn," he croaked. "Stab it. The antler. Knives...metal...stone...don't work."

It was as if the words had brought the sun out. Verenna bounded from the cart with all she had left and began frantically searching the mud for the piece of antler Fabien had broken off with his first swing. Clawing through the mire, her fingers found every stick and stone, each one raising and dashing her hopes.

She checked that Fabien was still standing. He'd managed to dance around the creatures far-reaching strikes, still with the rock above his head, trying to lure the beast close enough to crack its skull and retrieve his sword from its place lodged in the Crier's horns. But as he circled, he fell. The Crier leaped upon him. Verenna screamed his name into the dirt as she trolled the mud for the one thing that could save him.

Her fingers found something smooth and curved, warmer than the rocks she'd come across. Pulling hard against the vacuum of the dirt, the muck yielded the missing branch of antler. She scrambled to the spot where the creature had Fabien pinned. Its ribs open. It sunk low, ready to envelope him. Somewhere beneath the creatures bulk she could hear his shouted curses.

Without a second thought she leaped on the Crier and brought the point of the horn down on the back of its neck as hard as she could. The blow landed and stuck between the beast's vertebrae.

Its body shuddered and it tried to buck. Verenna let herself fall and rolled out of the way. Fabien slid from under the beast just in time for it to collapse in a twitching heap.

For a moment both of them sat there panting. Verenna feeling the sting of a hundred tiny cuts and scrapes she hadn't noticed in the chaos of the fight.Eyes wide, he looked at her and let out a blaring victory call. "You did it! She did it!" He took her face in his hands and planted a kiss on her forehead before rushing to rip his sword from the horns of the dying beast.

He braced his foot against its skull and yanked it free. Hacking off another piece of antler he tossed it to her. She barely managed to catch it. After breaking off his own bit of horn, he cut two more and tucked them in his pocket. "They're still fighting the other one," he panted. "Let's go."

Verenna staggered up, wondering how anyone ever fought a war if a single fight was this exhausting. With ragged breath, she followed him.

When they arrived, only Mortimer, Adrinée and Kaybin still fought. Renaud dragged his howling sister towards the shelter of the cart.

Fabien tossed a fragment of bone to Mortimer. He caught it neatly despite having taken an obvious and very bloody hit to the head. "Stab it with that! It works!" the young man shouted as he joined the fray.

Verenna paused and clutched her sides. Pain shocked through her torso with every deep breath. When she looked up Kaybin was at her side.

"That antler. I have an idea." He held out an eager hand.

With the boy's record of blunders thus far she wasn't keen to give it to him.

"What's the plan?"

As she asked, the beast lunged and caught Adrinée, her last shot flying uselessly skyward. It pulled her into its chest and crouched to the ground to protect its hard won prey.

"Give it!" Kaybin ordered, looking like he might fight her for it. She slapped it into his palm and he set off running for the beast. The Crier sensed his charge and readied itself to strike. He did not stop running. The boy barreled towards the beast as fast as his legs would take him. The Crier made a snatch for him but missed as Kaybin let himself fall back. He slipped below the blow, using the rain-slicked earth to slide underneath the creature. He vanished below its belly. The monster trembled and curled in on itself, crumbling to one side to reveal the antler shard sticking out of the place where a heart might be. And at the center of its heavy tracks, lay Adrinée and Kaybin, clinging to each other like frightened children.

Fabien was the first to let out a whoop of celebration. He was the only one with enough energy for it. He cackled and ran to Verenna, scooping her up and twirling her. "Now that! Was a fight! Woohoo!" He set her down and dashed after Mortimer to help the two young ones out of the muck beside the fallen beast.

Verenna smiled. A real smile. It seemed like weeks since the last time. She shut her eyes and turned her face up to the rain. They were alive, and so was Darius.

At the thought she bounded over to the cart. The twins sat together, Renaud finishing off tying a splint to his sisters leg. "What happened?" she rushed, her happiness buckling to concern.

"Broken leg," Thessa answered through gritted teeth. Renaud interjected, "Should be alright. We've got a splint and Godflower petals for pain. Once we get somewhere safer we can have a better look at it.

Verenna nodded and hopped onto the back of the wagon. "Darius?" she called, hoping he hadn't slipped back into unconsciousness. A weak cough answered her. He was trying to tell her something else.

"The head. Take the Crier's head. Before it. It's melted."

She looked up to shout the instruction, but caught the glint of Fabien's sword as he brought it down to decapitate the dead beast. The girl could just hear him saying something about a helluva trophy.

"That's been taken care of," she said with a grimace as Fabien marched towards them with the still bleeding head in one hand and a gleaming smile on his face.

"You're carrying it! I'm not sitting next to that bloody stump!" Thessa called to him. Fabien shrugged, taking the head by the antler and slinging it over his shoulder for travel. But when he saw Verenna crouched beside Darius he dropped the grisly prize to his side.

"Wait. Is he awake?"

Every ear perked. Verenna nodded a vigorous yes. The group gathered at the cart, all peering in to see the man they were sure was a corpse moving and speaking.

"We thought you might be good as gone," Mortimer said, climbing up onto the cart with them.

"You wish," the Doctor wheezed.

Fabien tried to hide the grin that threatened to creep across his face. "About damned time," he announced. "We could have used you. Look'it." He held up the disembodied head. "You ever seen the likes of this in one of your books? I think not."

"I think he has," Verenna interrupted. "He's the one who told me about using the antler to kill it."

Darius struggled out his own answer. "I study them. Very little known. That's mine when we're back."

Fabien slung the head across his shoulder with the most indignant expression. "We'll see about that. Where I come from, you kill it, you keep it."

"Look!" Adrinée let out a gasp and pointed one of the fallen creatures. Rain melted flesh away from bone, forming strange gray-blue puddles and streaking the ground around the beasts. Muscle and sinew disintegrated so quickly that the Crier Verenna had felled was already reduced to little more than bones. As the water struck the white protrusions they hissed and let off steam that mingled with the fog. Verenna grabbed Mortimer's arm as an eerie cry startled her. The strange, childlike cry of the beast rose from its remains. "It's not alive. It can't be." She whispered in hopes he'd assure her. The old man shook his head, took out his knife and crept closer to investigate.

At the base of the creatures neck lay a heart the size of a human head. And around it wrapped a squalling creature made of what she might compare to tar. It twitched and simpered. All of its appendages were irrevocably fused and twined with the muscle of the beast's heart.

Renaud shook his head against the sound, water flying from the tips of his hair. "I can't listen to it anymore. Drives me mad. You just want, you just, it needs help."

From her seat on the back of the cart Thessa snapped her fingers at her brother. "Listen you. Look at that. That isn't a baby. Doesn't matter how much it sounds like one. Look at it. Look."

He gazed with them at the pathetic entity, crying its last as it too weakened with the rain.

"But what is it?" Verenna said, her lip curling involuntarily in disgust.

"The demon that animates a Crier. That's the only thing it could be," Mortimer answered.

"It's so small though," Kaybin puzzled, still huddled with

Adrinée.

A shaky voice from behind her elaborated. "The souls of predators usually are." Darius had propped himself up against the side of the cart to look on with them as the monster evaporated. "Those. Come from Hell with a physical form. A portal must be opened for them. Probably Bronwell. They don't just seep up. Their souls are too heavy."

"Why?" Verenna ventured, her gaze never leaving the mewling thing.

"Because of who they were. Murderers. Those who prey on children. They become *that*. Or something like it. It won't last long now though. Not without its body."

She could feel the group around her cringe at the explanation.

Adrinée turned away in disgust. "Let's go. I don't want to watch."

The group heeded her request and got to work freeing the wagon. Once they'd finished packing the mud before the wheel with rocks, it took the combined effort of the whole party to shift the cart forward. Verenna had never been so glad to see anything roll. The cries of the fallen beasts fell away behind curtains of rain as the travelers forged on toward the abbey. Renaud said something about it being two days march before they sighted the town. She shivered at the thought of another night of fog, and shadows, and torches that wouldn't light, and swaying bows that took the shape of whatever her wildest imagination concocted in fear. As weary as they were, she knew they could not relent. With Darius, Thessa, and Renaud hurt, they'd need to reach Falseman Inn as fast as they could carry themselves.

As the day reached its zenith, the downpour relented, and the rain gentled to little more than quiet applause. But under the breezy hush of the woods, Verenna could swear she still heard the cry of the beasts. Or was it someone laughing?

Chapter 15

The trek dragged on for two days with frequent storms that turned the road to sucking mud that clung to everything it touched. The wheels of the cart sunk in so many times she lost count. Dislodging it became harder with the weight of both Darius and Thessa. The woman gritted her teeth as the road jostled her broken leg. She finally gave in to Kaybin's recommendation and accepted a few butter-yellow Godflower petals to chew for the pain. The delicate leaflets proved surprisingly effective and in an hour she'd dozed off.

As the third day dawned the weather changed from a nuisance to a danger. The wind picked up, especially at night, making a cooking fire impossible. The gale became so strong Verenna could feel welts where flailing locks of her own hair struck her face and neck. When darkness fell, they walked with one hand on the cart to be sure no one was lost.

The trees on either side of them heaved and sighed, as if the small light of the sap branch torches was the only thing holding apart two raging seas made of gnashing branches. Under the taut snapping of the wind-lashed leaves, when the storm breathed in to bluster again, Verenna could swear she heard someone laughing. She shook her head to clear any water that had gathered in her ears. The sound faded, but returned time and time again through the night. Unsure if the lack of sleep was finally getting to her, she reached a hand forward and found Fabien's shirt. She tugged it and he fell back to join her.

Between gusts she asked, "Do you hear anything?"

"Just the storm."

She waited for another lull. "No. Something like laughing."

"Not a thing."

A call from the head of the group stopped them all in their tracks. "What's that?" Adrinée pointed to a shape in the dark, blacker than the night woods around them. Renaud cried out, "Weapons!"

Verenna's hand shook on the hilt of her knife. They couldn't fight another Crier. Not at midnight with so little sleep, after being beaten by a storm, with every inch of them aching from travel. If another beast appeared, it might be the end of them.

Fabien drew his sword and pulled her in to his side. Up in front of the cart she heard Kaybin call out, "Wait here!" He dashed into the dark. Mortimer tried to snatch hold of the boy's vest as he vanished, but missed, catching only a handful of rain.

Lightning flared, casting the dark mass in a stark silhouette. They stood at the ready, gripping weapons so tightly their knuckles ached, braced to fight of flee.

Something darted out of the night. Verenna held up her knife, clasping the hilt in both hands. Relief nearly toppled it from her fingers when she recognized Kaybin.

"It's an outcrop!"

"We should stop," Mortimer shouted over the storm. "We could get on the lee side and wait out the worst of this. Exposure isn't something we can afford."

As they gathered together out of the wind, a memory surfaced in Verenna's tired mind. When she was young, and her mother and father would take her to the sea in the summer, they would stop in the shade of a gathering of boulders that jutted from the surrounding green countryside. As the troop pulled the cart alongside the rockface Verenna started to laugh.

"What could possibly be funny?" Thessa grumbled.

"This is Aster's Point. I played here as a child. We had picnics."

"Nice, but what's that got to do with anything?" Adrinée grouched.

"When it's light-" She paused as the storm buffeted the rock. "We will be able to see Canterford from here. We're so close."

Verenna almost forgot her exhaustion as she huddled between Fabien and Darius in the confines of the cart. Home was less than a day away. By noon they'd reach it. She tried to keep her hopes from rising too high. There could be no guessing what they'd discover. She could only pray there would be something left to find.

℘

At the first ashen moment of dawn Verenna scrambled to the top of the rock. The mist of last nights storm clotted into a near impenetrable curtain between her and the distant town. But as the somber sky grew white with veiled sun she could make out a faint smokestack, a single column that wove into the low hanging clouds. She nearly fell from her perch when she saw it. Sliding down the sloped back of the megalith she rushed to tell the others. They were just stirring, storm worn and weary.

"I can see smoke," she beamed, elated despite the lack of sleep.

Mortimer managed a weak smile but most simply carried on with readying themselves for the last leg of the journey. A faint but sarcastic comment told her Darius had regained consciousness. "Watching smoke. One of your favorite Canterford pastimes."

She shrugged off his jab and tried again to infuse anyone who would listen with her overflowing excitement. "Aren't you even the least bit happy? That means there's someone left in Canterford."

"Sure. Hopefully they're as excited for a visit as you are."
Thessa groaned.

"Of course! Canterford is so welcoming, and quaint, and...."

Renaud interrupted her. "We're strangers. We don't look like
them. Quaint isn't usually a good thing in this case. Even so, that
fire could belong to anyone. Looters, even."

This thought dampened Verenna's spirits but she refused to let
it kill her hope. Someone was there. Someone who would
recognize her and welcome all of them. She repeated this
uncertainty until it ballooned and felt like truth. There had to be
something good ahead. On sheer probability.

The woods broke into fields by mid morning. The outlying
reaches of Canterford smelled like wet earth and wheat. She
couldn't keep the smile from her lips. Even the rolling eyes of her
traveling companions couldn't quell it. The rain had stopped long
enough for their clothes to dry. Verenna could feel wild waves
forming as her rain washed hair curled up and bounced against
her back, free in the breeze.

Verenna fell back from the lead to walk beside the cart. She
peeked over at the doctor.

"What?" he moaned, his eyes still closed.

"You said I'd come back. You said one day, and that's today."

Darius opened his eyes and tried to clear the raspiness from his
voice. "I really wish your hopes weren't so high. We don't know
who or what is tending that fire yet. I'd keep cautious, if I were
you."

"There's got to be someone left. There's got to. Even if they've
all moved on, my parents will have left some kind of note about
where they've gone off to. Look!" Verenna pointed to a nearby
field, neatly fenced, with horses galloping together in play. "Those
are Mr. Winston's horses. He'd never leave without them. Never."

"I hate to eavesdrop," Thessa joined in. "But have you noticed that there is absolutely no-one out tending any of the fields we've passed so far? Some of the crops are ready. Bit strange, isn't it?"

Verenna struggled to answer this concern without deflating her mood. "Well, I'm sure some people left when they realized what was going on in Bronwell. But that doesn't mean all of them did."

"Hmm," Thessa's eyes shifted with suspicion to the herd of animals cantering around their enclosure.

Shaking off the well made point Verenna jogged to the fence and leaned against the wood, feeling the cool of the remaining rainwater soak into her shirt from the crags of the fencepost. She watched the horses frolic a while. Then she noticed something in the middle of the lot. Something smaller, weaker than the beasts circling it.

She stood straight and squinted. "What's that?"

"A foal?" Fabien suggested, joining her at the fence. The group slowed and collected to puzzle about the curious situation unfolding before them.

"Shouldn't be," Mortimer answered. "Wrong time of year. We're heading into Fall. Now's no time for foals."

"It's a deer." Adrinée spoke with no inflection, perfectly still and unblinking. Her cheeks had drained of color. "They're going to kill it."

"That's ridiculous. Why would they?" Renaud stepped closer to the scene, hand still clutching the reins of their own steed. It bucked its head and pulled, trying to turn away from the sight in the field. Kaybin patted the animals haunch. "Our horse doesn't like it, whatever it is that's going on."

"They're wearing it out," Adrinée said without taking her eyes off the circling herd. Verenna watched the girl for some sign of a joke and found none. Adrinée's voice was too hollow to hold humor. "How do you know?"

"They're not running together like horses do. As one. They're working like a pack. Like wolves."

"What on earth are you talking about?" Fabien made an unconvincing dismissal.

Verenna stepped up on the lowest board of the fence and strained for a better view. The chaotic cluster of animals whirled closer. She caught sight of a single doe ducking and dodging at the center, trying to find a break in the circle of horses. The frightened creature made a leap for freedom but ran into the well muscled chest of one of the mares. It toppled and the horses fell upon it. It was hard to see what ensued. The strong necks of the horses plunged again and again towards the unseen deer. It wasn't until a stallion raised his head with blood smeared on his muzzle that she understood what had happened.

She gasped and nearly toppled off her perch. Her back made contact with Mortimer, who kept her upright. Nothing seemed real. Not his hands on her shoulder. Not the far off heat of the sun struggling through the clouds. Not the mossy smell of the morning. Not the dirt beneath her. She shook her head with her hands over her mouth, sure the day must be a dream.

"Look there," Kaybin pointed to a few small doves pecking at the ground. But instead of insects, the group watched the tiny birds pluck pebbles from the earth, tilt their heads back, and let the fragments of rock fall down their gullet.

"I...I don't...what the Hell is going on here?" Fabien struggled.

"Something is playing with nature," Renaud muttered, checking the road ahead and behind as if he'd find the culprit.

"Malagrir?" Fabien suggested.

Mortimer stroked his chin. "Possible. But unlikely. According to Gawshire's notes on the map it looked like Malagrir was in Turim. Also, there's plenty of food here. The wheat is ripe."

Darius raised his voice as much as he could to add to the conversation. "Don't assume. Famine isn't always lack of food.

Sometimes it's the wrong food, or the inability to gather it."

Verenna shook her head in disbelief as the horses continued their perverse feast in the field. Silence swallowed them, save for the ticking sound of the birds pecking at pebbles and the grunting of horses scuffling for position over the empty remains of the deer. Verenna turned away in time to see something stir in the tall grass on the other side of the road. She grabbed Fabien's shoulder and pointed to the disturbance. The message passed wordlessly through the ranks until all eyes were on the subtly shifting grass.

Each took up their weapon with smooth, deliberate stealth. Adrinée strung her bow and nodded once to Renaud. The two stalked closer. The girl took careful aim, as the man weighed his axe in his hand. They steadied themselves. Then with a twitch so fast Verenna could hardly see it, Renaud let the axe fall.

A figure came tumbling from hiding with a frightened yelp.

Fabien swung for it but the mass rolled under the cart and missed the point of the blade. He ducked to grab the creature before it escaped but withdrew his hand and swore. A long gash gushed red along his forearm.

"Back! Back, all of you! Stay away!" a small voice screamed from hiding.

Verenna slid her knife away and called out. "Stop! I know him!"

The group stood back and allowed her to crouch next to the cart. "Willoughby?"

In the shade of the wagon, a familiar round face gaped, incredulous at their meeting. "V-v-vivie? Wha...h-how?" he stammered.

"Yes, it's me. You can come out. No one here will hurt you."

"I beg to differ," he pouted.

Fabien growled over his wound, "So do I."

"I said stop it. It's no good staying under there. Come out."

After considerable coaxing, Willoughby struggled to his feet and tried to dust the wet earth from his knees. It only smeared. His costly clothing had tears at all the joints. The decadent materials were swirled with several different shades of drying mud. A cracked monocle dangled uselessly from the pocket of his vest.

Verenna had never seen him with more than a strand of his scant hair out of place at a time. She looked him over, perplexed. "What happened to you?"

"I could ask the same. You look terrible!"

She rolled her eyes, to the tune of Adrinée's giggle. "Thanks."

"Did they hurt you? Don't worry, darling. You're safe now." He grabbed her hand and pulled her next to him.

Thessa let out a guffaw that drew a sour glare from Willoughby.

"Really, I'm fine. What are you doing here? I thought you would have left town by now."

"We did. Mother insisted. I had to come back for a few things before the looters got to them. Then the storm. My horse broke free and left me stranded. I had to strike out on foot. Now, my dear, we make our getaway!" He brandished an extravagant hat pin still tipped with Fabien's blood.

"Not if you announce it like that," Kaybin chuckled.

"Enough!" Willoughby barked. "You ruffians. You keep back, understand?" He took Verenna by the hand and began to back away.

"Little overconfident for a man with just a hat pin," Renaud noted.

Verenna allowed him to lead her a small distance and tried to reason with him. "Willoughby, you're the one who needs saving. You said yourself you're stranded."

"They've really gotten to you, haven't they? Poor dear. They've addled you. You don't know up from down right now. Come with me. It's for your own good. I'll take you to safety." He gave her another tug.

This time she resisted."I'm not going. Let go."

"Nonsense. You can't stay with these, these, vagabonds."

Red heat swelled in her ears. "No. Listen."

Willoughby ignored and continued his persistent tugging. "To think you've been being dragged all over God's green earth by this lot." One more sharp tug on her arm and Verenna snapped.

"I said I'm not going!" She ripped out of his grip and drew her knife.

The man looked winded, his mouth forming words without the air to sound them out. "I've been traveling with them. Willingly. You'd understand that if you'd shut up and listen." She pointed to her traveling companions with the tip of her blade. "They brought me back. They saved me. Countless times now."

He blustered but could not find language. Taking advantage of his silence, Verenna continued.

"It's all too much to explain now. But we're passing through Canterford. If you know what's good for you, you'll come with us. These woods, you don't understand what's in them. I'm honestly shocked nothing's eaten you."

Verenna noticed Fabien duck behind the cart out of the corner of her eye. Renaud followed him, dipping out of sight. Willoughby was too focused on her outburst to notice.

He took her gently by the shoulders. "Vivie. Dear. You can't be serious. These people, they…"

"They have kept me alive this long."

"They just want ransom!"

She tossed her head back and laughed at the notion that any amount of money would be enough to pay for their troubles thus far. "Oh, it goes way farther than that. I'll explain on the way into town." She tried to keep her gaze focused on his pudgy face as the two men appeared behind Willoughby and crept up on him. She kept talking to keep Willoughby's focus on her, rather than the two sneaking warriors.

"Just trust me. You do not want to be out on your own right now. Just walk with us a while. You'll start to understand. I'm fine."

Fabien stumbled on a dip in the road, alerting Willoughby. He turned and caught them crouched and ready to spring. "Wench!" he squealed. "You're working with them!"

"That's what she's been bloody well trying to tell you," Fabien blurted with an exasperated wave of his hand.

Willoughby went to reply but froze, mouth open. "What happened to the cut on your arm. I cut you. I saw it." He touched the end of the pin. The russet color of blood tinted his finger tips. "How is that possible? Where's the mark?" The words were more to himself than the others.

Fabien tried to roll down his sleeve but the damage was done. The hat pin hit the ground and Willoughby started a stumbling retreat, muttering. "That's not natural. Nothing heals that fast. Nothing. It's not human. It's the Devil's work."

"He's gonna run," Mortimer uttered close by. He was proven right almost instantaneously.

"It's the Devil's work!" Willoughby screamed and sprinted for town.

"Ah, let him go. He's useless," Adrinée said as she unstrung her bow. "If he wants to brave the woods alone, let him." But behind her, Kaybin took out his slingshot.

"We can't." Mortimer commanded. "If he gets to town first, he'll tell anyone and everyone what he's seen. He'll turn them against us."

"We'll catch him," Fabien slapped a hand on Renaud's back and the two took off after the departing Willoughby. But before they'd covered more than a few cart lengths of ground a swish, a delay, and a distant thud sounded and the sprinting frontrunner hit the dirt. He lay there mid-road, unmoving. The two men glanced at the others, confused.

"Got him," Kaybin shrugged and stowed his weapon.

"You're really starting to redeem yourself, boy," Thessa noted with a hint of surprise.

They marched to the place where Willoughby had fallen. Fabien hog tied him with the weak excuse of not taking any chances. It was overkill, but after the hassle no one objected. They loaded him on the cart and carried on. But a subtle tension had taken hold at the nape of Verenna's neck.

She spent a while walking next to Mortimer before saying anything. "We'll have to tell them, won't we? Whoever's there. If we don't, Willoughby certainly will."

The old man let out a deep sigh and ran his fingers through his graying locks. "I don't see a way around it. It'll be a gamble, but it's better people hear it from us than from an ignorant little pip who thinks we're devil spawn."

"Right," Verenna agreed, but the idea made her sick. If the smoke she'd seen came from a friendly source, if by some chance her parents were near it, how could she explain something so outlandish? The truth would be so much harder than a lie.

The teetering mix of nerves and hope rocked in her like troubled water as the wheels of the cart clattered onto the cobbles of main street. She felt she might shriek, boil over like a kettle as anxiety bubbled in her tightening throat. She wanted to run home, but exhaustion and suspicion kept her close to the group.

The window boxes were either dead or overgrown. Most doors had been boarded shut, shops closed and locked. Not so much as the pawprint of a stray cat rumpled the smooth mud of the sidestreets. The prognosis was grim. Especially as they turned into the wealthier part of town. Boards and shutters had been pried away, glass shattered; the looters Willoughby had feared had already taken their fill of goods from the empty houses. At least she hoped it had been looters, or at least someone human.

The entire town looked bruised like a fresh black eye, all red brick and purple shadows under the brooding sky. She checked every chimney, searching for the one still in use.

"Are you sure we should find that fire?" Adrinée whispered as if the houses might hear. "It's probably thieves. We're in no shape to fight."

Verenna was at the brink of agreeing with her when they came to the bend of her home street. The way to the Inn, to safety, lay straight ahead. But the street called to her in a way she could not resist. Down a ways she saw a little, white gate clinging weakly to the fence by a broken hinge. Unruly roses peered through the slats, the last of the summer blooms. And on top of the house, a thin line of smoke. She heard nothing but the slap of her own shoes as she broke into an all out run. The shouts behind her blurred into noise. The threat of collapse, the risk of stumbling upon enemies, all of it became meaningless as she raced for home just as fast as she'd left it. The windows had boards but the door remained unbarred. Gasping for breath she rounded the gate and stumbled up the few steps to fall against the front door, pounding on it for all she was worth.

She banged at it until tears welled in her eyes and her fists smarted like hornet stings. The others caught up in a panic. Mortimer rushed ahead and pulled her off the door. "You don't know who's in there!"

"It's them. It's got to be them," she wheezed and struggled to return to her furious knocking. "No one's answering. Why is no one answering?"

"Something's in the window!" Thessa cried, pointing high on

the house.

Mortimer scooped an arm around Verenna's waist and lifted her from the ground to take her back to the wagon. "Move," he ordered. But he could hardly be heard over Verenna's screams.

"Father! Mum! It's me! I'm back! Open the door! I know you're here! It's Vivie! Please! Open the door!"

She clawed at Mortimer's arm but the leather of his jacket protected him. Weariness weighted her limbs beyond fighting. Tears overflowed and she dropped in defeat. But when she looked up the door had been flung wide and a familiar voice called to her. Her father came rushing to the street, closely followed by a pack of neighbors armed with everything from cutlery to lamps.

"Verenna! Put her down!"

The old man let go instantly and Verenna flung herself against her father's chest. The smell of him, the creases of his eyes, the snow paths that age chased across his temples, the silk of his vest, all of it flooded her at once and she felt she might fall asleep there and then.

"I thought we'd never find you, Vivie. I thought we never would."

"I can't believe you're still here," her sigh of relief fogged one of his silver buttons. But before she could say more he'd pulled her to one side and taken a protective stance.

"Who are you?" She felt the words reverberate through him. "Explain yourselves!"

"They're friends," Verenna hurried to explain.

"Like Hell they are!" She looked up at him in shock. She'd never heard him swear. "That one was trying to drag you away."

"His name is Mortimer. He thought looters might be in the house. I ran up before I knew it was safe. It was stupid but I couldn't help it. He was trying to protect me."

Mortimer made a slight bow to her father and the mob behind

him. "I'm very sorry that was your first impression. I had hoped to return her under better circumstances, sir."

"Indeed. And, is that the flower boy?" Mr. Dellins pointed to Fabien, whose deep bow revealed the blade strapped to his back. "Why the devil has he got a sword?"

"That's him. The sword is a very long story. The Doctor's here too. In the cart."

Darius raised a trembling hand in greeting. "My, he's changed," Mr. Dellins whispered with a grimace at the healing burns on the man's face. "And these others?"

Verenna pointed in turn. "Adrinée, Kaybin, Thessa, and Renaud. They're all my friends."

"You sure?" A round woman wielding a frying ban narrowed her eyes to search them. Verenna recognized Mrs. Norworth.

Mr. Censington, shuffled forward under the strain of his pronounced slouch to comment. "The last time we welcomed travelers we almost lost our lives. One of them burst into sparks and near burned the house down."

She took a step back from her father and looked over the faces of the people she'd grown up knowing. They looked at her like a stranger.

"How do we know they're all...real?" A hidden sceptic argued. Grunts of agreement made the rounds through the gathered townspeople, lifted by a gentle swill of wind.

Mr. Dellins was quick to silence the criticism. "Because this is my daughter. Don't you think I'd know?"

Mrs. Babik, a doe-eyed friend of her mother's, took a few cautious steps forward and touched Verenna's arm. "She feels real. She's warm."

"I am real. So are they." Verenna took the woman's hands and placed them on her cheeks. "See? Test us all you like. We aren't Husks."

"Husks?" someone whispered.

"They look like people until they are about to die, then they collapse into ash and sparks. We've seen them too. I think we may have run into some of the same problems you've had here. We might be able to explain them."

A surge of breeze made the neighbors pull tighter together, their eyes darting like frightened mice anticipating an owl. Her father glanced back at the cluster of townsfolk. "I for one am willing to let them in and hear them out. "

"You're too trusting," Mr. Eeves broke in. His impeccable posture and drooping skin gave him the look of a long burning candle. He tilted his head in the way Verenna had grown to hate as a child; ever so slightly to the side with a raised chin, that managed at once to make him appear both stubborn and condescending. "Other than your daughter, we have very little knowledge of any of them. How could we know if what they tell us is the truth?"

A few calls of agreement answered the remark.

"We'll vote, then," her father shrugged. "But Verenna stays. That is non-negotiable."

Mr. Eeves fell silent and let Ms. Tiller, the string thin school teacher, call out the question. "We let the strangers stay long enough to explain. All those in favor?"

A forest of hands rose and were counted. Verenna tried to catch the number before they dropped.

"All those opposed?"

This time Verenna got a count. Seven against. There couldn't be many more than fifteen present. The margin would be slim.

"Well," Ms. Tiller sighed. "The yeas have it. They stay and tell us their story. Any weapons, leave them at the door."

Another gust of wind sent the people scurrying for the house. "If you're coming in, best hurry about it. Another storm's stirring up," Mrs. Norworth urged them.

Verenna beamed and turned to her companions. But none of them shared her enthusiasm.

"It's settled then," Mr. Dellins stated. "Inside. All of you. And tie the horse to the fence tight as you can. Something around here has them in a strange mood lately. Perhaps you can explain that as well."

Renaud helped Thessa from the cart and supported her to the house. Fabien took up Darius while Mortimer busied himself fixing the horse to a tree in the yard. Lastly, Adrinée and Kaybin quietly untied Willoughby and hefted his unconscious form towards the house.

Verenna watched her father's eyes grow round like twin moons.

"We found Mr. Porter, too," she mentioned, fearing he'd question how the man had come to be knocked out.

Mr. Dellins wrapped a guiding arm around his daughter's shoulders and moved her inside. He whispered to her as they walked. "They didn't hurt you did they? You can tell me now. They can't hear."

"No," Verenna rushed. She slowed her speech seeing her father squint with suspicion. "Not at all. I wouldn't be here without them. Except Willoughby. But they saved him too technically. He wouldn't have lasted without them either." But when she looked up, he'd been distracted by the weapon on her belt.

"Is that, do you...are you carrying a knife?"

"Oh. Yes."

"I hate to imagine why you needed it," her father groaned.

Verenna shuddered. "So do I."

"Heavens," he muttered, pushing up his spectacles to rub the bridge of his nose.

She almost laughed at the amount of consternation it caused him. But instead she grinned. "It's good to be back."

His concern broke into warmth. He squeezed her shoulder. "My dear, you don't know how good it is to see you. I may not know whose clothes you're wearing or who these friends of yours are, or why you're armed, but I would not trade any of it for the world."

Her good mood sank as they crossed the threshold. The house was darker than she'd ever seen it. All the curtains drawn, boards blocking out almost all signs of day, except for a few strands of silver light, like threads strung with dustmotes. The air inside did not move making for a stuffy, oppressive walk into the main parlor. Melancholy twisted awake inside her at the memory of her birthday party. In that very room only months ago she'd been filled with curiosity and questions she'd gone to great lengths to answer. Now, with the truth in hand, she wondered at the idea of a life without it.

"Where's mum?" she urged her father, as the group settled around the room, a somber version of June's celebration.

"Resting, dear," he told her and pushed an unruly lock of hair behind her ear. "Let's get this matter settled first." As soon as the words left his lips another voice took up and filled the room.

Mr. Eeves took the liberty to start the interrogation. "Well. I suppose I'll start. How is it you all came to know each other?"

The group glanced around for who among them would speak. Verenna answered first with a nod to indicate the cluster of Sarzen that had settled with their backs to the wall. "Well, I met the four of them when we crossed paths in the woods near their village."

"The Sarzen, I take it?" the man interrupted.

"Yes, sir," Adrinée's tone formed more of a question than a statement. "Not many know us by name. How do you?"

Eeves smiled down at his feet slightly, as if there were something quaint about her confusion. "Because my land produces much of the wheat in the area, among other valuable supplies. I used to send them to Bronwell to be sold. I have a memory of the occasional shipment going missing in the woods outside the city. It seems there are thieves."

Adrinée's jaw tightened. She locked eyes with Eeves. "I wouldn't know."

Verenna could see what Fabien meant when he mentioned their similarities. If she knew herself, she knew that the next words out of the girls mouth would be something irrevocable. "The Sarzen have been good to us. We wouldn't have made it back to Canterford without them. We didn't intend to stop actually. We thought everyone would be gone. We were heading for...well," Verenna seized up with the sudden memory of how those present felt about the abbey in the woods.

"Out with it," Mrs. Norworth insisted, hands planted squarely on her wide hips.

The girl swallowed. "Falseman Inn?"

A scandalized murmur cast around the room. Fabien, Darius and Mortimer all shifted with the discomfort of their secret coming ever closer to the surface.

"My, dear, you can't be serious," Ms. Tiller gasped, her long, kindly face going blank with terror.

"It's not what you think. When I went missing, I ended up at the abbey. I was badly hurt. The doctor there saved my life."

"I'll take that credit," Darius raised his voice just high enough to be heard over the disgruntled muttering. "You might as well know. I am in charge of the medical aspects of our home."

"Our?" Mrs. Babik inquired as she stepped out of the crowd to comfort the trembling school teacher.

The doctor fell silent under the weight of having revealed too much. Fabien begrudgingly elaborated. "Aye. We live there, too. Mortimer and I."

Mr. Censington broke in, pointing with a gnarled finger that shook with age. "We know you. You're the delivery boy. But him…" the ancient man eyed Mortimer. "You're that beggar."

Mortimer had no time to utter an explanation before Mrs. Norworth set upon him.

"That's right. He's that drunken beggar that's always about, isn't he? Sleeping in the street, dirty, staring off at nothing."

Mortimer's cheeks went flush as Verenna felt herself start to boil inside. She stepped to his side to defend him but Darius spoke first.

"That man is a king," the doctor stated.

The shock of Darius coming to his aid creased the old man's forehead into more wrinkles than Verenna had ever seen on his whole face.

"He is of royal blood. Not only that, he saved me from a Husk much like the ones you've seen. I owe him my life. And he was sleeping in the street to protect your daughter. Sir."

"I beg your pardon?" Mr. Dellins adjusted his glasses.

Fabien took up the explanation. "When Verenna vanished, did you notice anything strange around the house? Candles burning down faster than normal? Noises in the night? Dark figures where you didn't expect them?"

"Why, yes. How did you know all of that?"

"Because we've seen them too. A lot of them. Demons."

The room broke into an uproar echoed by the building storm they'd locked outside.

"This is too much!"

"Demons? You expect us to believe that?"

"If that beggar's a king I'll eat my hat."

"Everyone! Calm down!" Her father shouted to no avail. The clamor continued until Verenna noticed the vase on a discrete side table. Marching to it she knocked it to the ground. She felt a new type of freedom at the sound of it shattering. The noise shocked the crowd quiet.

"It's true. You know it is. You just don't want to believe it. Just like you didn't want to believe that the sickness in Bronwell would ever reach us. Well it did. It's called Cold Fever, and it's caused by demons when they enter a body and eat at your soul. I know. I had it. He saved me. You need to believe us. You can't afford not to. The demons were here looking for me. Mortimer was in the street to make sure I wasn't taken by them."

"And you lead them right back to us?" Mrs. Norworth squawked.

"No," Verenna faltered. "Things have, well, changed. They're looking for me but we lost them for now."

"For now," the woman scoffed.

"But darling, why you?" Her father's voice was smoothed by incredulity.

"Erm. Now. This part. This is going to be even harder to believe. There's a prophecy. And, well, I'm supposed to stop the Four Horsemen riding. Somehow. We stopped Souris, Disease, that is. He was causing the plague out of Bronwell. And we think that Malagrir, Famine, is in Turim. But we saw something strange on our way here. We saw the horses..."

Verenna stopped when low groans of despair grew from the crowd. "That was the first strangeness," Mrs. Babik bemoaned. "Mr. Winston's hired boy went out to tend the herd. All we found was a pile of bones. We thought it was wolves until it happened again to the next person who entered the field...Peter Censington. There were witnesses that time."

Mr. Censington rung his cap in his hands, clenching the fabric to hold back tears for his son. "Nothing's right anymore. It happened so suddenly. After all we've seen, is it really that much of a stretch to believe their telling the truth? I know we try not to talk about it, but we've all seen the shadows."

Mr. Dellins added to the tale with a distance that made it seem he might be lost in a dream. "It wasn't long after you vanished, perhaps a few days, and the town was flooded with dark creatures. People packed up and fled their homes in the middle of the night just to get away from them. Those that didn't...We came back a few weeks ago to see what became of them. To bury them. Now we're stuck. The horses we used to get here went rabid, or something close to it. And whatever's done it is laughing at us when the wind blows."

"What about the laughing?" Verenna pressed, with a sinking feeling she could not fight.

Mr. Eeves swallowed hard, making his prominent adam's apple bob in his roughly shaven throat. He gripped the arms of his chair to steady his voice. "When my wife and I made to leave town, as soon as we set foot outside, the wind attacked us. The dust rose up. At first we thought it was just a storm blowing in. But the gusts got stronger and picked up dirt until we could see a shape in it. A shape like a woman dancing. Her arms up, her hair flying. But no face to be seen." His words quavered and he took a sip of air. "It rushed all around us, blinding, scouring every inch of us with scraping sand. Then, it got hold of Angelica. I tried to hold onto her. I couldn't. It threw her high in the air. And when it put her down, she was dry and brittle like winter sticks. Old in my hands. She was gone. And so was the wind. All I heard was laughing."

Ms. Tiller placed a thin hand on his knee to comfort him.

"That's terrible," Adrinée whispered.

"So sorry," Renaud added under his breath.

The man brushed off the comforts and shook off the symptoms of his grief, his face returning to a composed picture of superiority. "Whatever it is, it has us trapped here. And we're getting low on supplies."

Mr. Dellins chimed in to agree. "Everyone brought what they had and holed up here for protection. We've tried to venture out for more. But the storms have become more frequent and less predictable. We hear the laughing almost every day now and especially at night."

The house creaked with the force of a massive gust of wind that set everyone clinging to the closest person to them. Some watched the boarded windows for signs of fracture, some whispered consoling kindnesses, others shut their eyes and mouthed silent prayers, their knuckles white in gripping each other's hands. Verenna stepped closer to her father, taking a fistful of his vest until the wind let up and the house began to settle.

She looked to him for some source of solace, but found an expression carved by fear.

"It's out there waiting. And we're running out of time."

Chapter 16

"You can't stay here," Mortimer insisted. "And neither can we. As Verenna said, we were heading to the abbey with our injured. They have plenty of supplies and wind will be much less of a threat inside stone walls. Please, you should consider coming with us."

Mrs. Norworth let out a splutter of laughter. "To a hospital for the incurable? We're supposed to be safe in a place like that?"

Her husband stood up from an armchair to join her in outrage. "We aren't stupid. We know what goes on out there. And we want no part of it."

Darius confronted them as best he could from his position draped in an armchair. "And how, pray tell, do you know so much? No one you know has ever been to our inn. Certainly not yourself."

"It's a preposterous idea," Eeves erupted. "That abbey is no place for god fearing people. How do we know that the evil we are faced with didn't originate there in the first place?"

The doctor rolled his eyes, "And now they think we make the weather."

Eeves rounded on him, "You're patronizing, mister..."

"DeFoe. And I'd prefer 'doctor'."

"Well, Mr. DeFoe, I do not appreciate your dismissal of our concerns. Our lives are at stake. We've already lost many. It isn't a joking matter to us."

"No it's not. Allowing your superstitions to prevent you from saving your own lives is the least funny thing I can think of and

I've recently been set on fire."

Mr. Dellins took over the conversation, taking his daughter by the shoulders, his thin spectacles sliding to the end of his nose. "Vivie, you've been with these people. You've come to know them. Do you think their home is truly safe for us?"

Verenna stared into her father's robin blue eyes, "Yes. It's the safest for miles. I keep telling you all, they saved me. Daddy, I was dying. I was stabbed. I have the scar to prove it. They kept me alive through all of this. Didn't you get the note I sent?"

Her father straightened his glasses and stammered, "Well, I, yes, but I thought they'd made you write it."

"I meant it. I was angry at the time, but they've treated me well. They're the reason I made it back to you. Falseman Inn is safer than staying here. They'll take care of us. They're..." Verenna was cut short by a waking snort from a fainting couch near the fire. Willoughby had awoken with a mind for vengeance.

"Monsters!" he cried. "They're monsters! I've seen it. If they're hurt they heal instantly. It's the devils work, I know it!" He rubbed the bump on the back of his skull where the slingshot knocked him out.

Eeves seized upon the little man's testimony. "See? How can we trust them? One of our own says they're demons."

"And I'm one of your own and I say otherwise," Verenna growled, eyeing Willoughby's smug, pouting cheeks and itching to punch one.

"You, dear girl, have spent entirely too much time with them for an objective opinion," Eeves snapped back. "There's something you're not telling us."

Every eye fell to her. Her former neighbors, the Sarzen, her father; each waited for an answer that would smooth the difference between her and Willoughby's conflicting tales.

She caught Fabien's eye and he gave her a knowing nod. Next

she looked to Mortimer, then Darius. Somehow it had become her task to tell the truth of what they were, without putting their lives in danger.

"Well, it's true that we heal quickly, but it's not for the reason Willoughby says. It's because, well, we can't really, um," She glanced at her father. His face held concern, confusion, but more importantly care. How much would her declaration change his kindly expression, and which parts might she never see again? But the first words were out. Every ear tuned to hear the finish of her message.

"We can't die," she let the words leave her like a sigh. They hung in the air, untouched by belief. No one made a sound. She scanned the faces of those who were once her neighbors as they looked to each other with speechless incredulity.

"We?" Her father murmured.

"Yes. Mortimer, Fabien and Darius. And me."

"Do you know what you're saying?" Mr. Dellins gasped with a hanging jaw.

"I do."

The motionless air in the room seemed to thicken even further without the stirring of words.

Finally someone coughed out, "Impossible. She's mad."

"Not really a way to prove it now is there?" someone else prodded.

"These people are insane."

Verenna held out her hands to stop the rising tide of protests. "Wait, I can show you. Just...watch."

With their weapons at the door she examined the room for another sharp object. A tinkling sound stirred at her feet. The shards of the broken vase would have to do. She chose a large one with a point and before she had the chance to think she drew the sharp edge across her palm. She clenched her jaw as a line of stinging fire ran across her hand. Ms. Tiller let out a squeal of dismay amongst the collection of gasps and surprised utterances. Before the cut could heal unseen Verenna splayed out her fingers and held it aloft for the room to view.

"Look! Look at what's happening! Tell me you've seen anything like this before. Tell me you won't believe me."

The less squeamish members of the group allowed themselves a tentative lean to get a closer look. Verenna hastily wiped the blood off on her skirt so that the thin, red line could be seen as it sewed itself shut from both ends. She'd never seen eyes so wide; her neighbors in disbelief, and her companions in the breathless terror of anticipation as they waited for the crowd to react. This would be either their salvation or undoing.

The wound crawled closed like a sand timer running out. Only an auburn smear indicated that anything had broken the skin.

"Incredible," Mr. Censington whispered. His hat dropped from his hands and he shuffled to examine her palm for a hoax.

"My word, what have we seen?" Mrs. Babik ran a hand through her hair to scratch her head in astonishment.

"How?"

"What the blazes?"

"I can't believe it. It's not possible."

The murmurs gathered to a peak but died as her father spoke. "Vivie, what are you?"

She hadn't thought that far ahead. "Well, I don't really have the right word for it." The crowd grew raucous, demanding an answer, demanding she define the condition she'd become. She knew the word she had to utter and what they'd think when they heard it. Every Canterford child knew the legends about the evil that lurked in the woods. And now it was her job to suggest it might all be real.

She stuttered and stumbled, watching anger swell in every face.

Her father stepped in front of her to shield her from the growing rage.

"Witch," someone hissed from among the mob.

"They're evil," another voice called.

"Throw them out!"

"Say it! Admit what you are."

Verenna couldn't stop trembling. She stammered for words but found nothing but thoughtless, cold panic inside. The gathered people began to rise from their seats and stalk towards them, jeering. The townspeople had advanced to only an arms length in front of them, when a breeze crossed the room and quieted the cacophony. It was nothing like the menacing wind outside. It held no fury, and carried with it the smell of wheat, and rain, and flowers, the scent of their town as it should be. It hushed them as a new voice summoned their attention.

"They are Nightbound." A gray clad man had inexplicably taken shape near the fireplace. Corvudeus had returned to them.

"And what would you know about it?" Someone piped with a dreamy slur.

What had been the beginnings of an angry mob had become docile and half-awake. Even her father had been overtaken by the irresistible peace. Death let out a sigh. They swayed like reeds as the smell of earth and home washed over them again. "I know plenty," he answered. "Nightbound are creatures that, unlike mortal beings, have a crystalline soul. Therefore they are unable to pass from this world, making them immortal. They can be injured. Grievously. But they cannot die. They survive forever, keeping to the night so that the sun doesn't beam through their crystal souls and burn them. As you can see from the charred one there," he motioned to Darius who scowled. "It's not a pleasant experience. The combination of their undying nature and their nocturnal habits makes Nightbound the most accurate name. You need not fear them. Their kind are more helpful to humans than you'll ever understand. These ones in particular, as much as I hate to admit it. I'd advise you to keep them until the storm dies down. Then, they will move on, with or without you. You have my word they mean you no harm. I'm sure everyone here would take the word of an old friend like me?" The breeze moved the crowd again. Their heads nodded like daffodils approving of Spring. "Good. Now that you're all relaxed, it's time for a vote. Ms. Tiller?"

The woman called to her companions in a tone that sounded fresh from sleep. "All those, erm, in favor of letting them stay through the storm?"

Not a single hand shot up. Not even her father's. Verenna's heart stopped. Until finally, like seedlings, one at a time, they rose. She could hear nothing but the pounding of her own blood echoing between her ears as hope ignited within her.

"Those opposed?"

A few half-raised votes, including Willoughby's, were all that accumulated. Mr. Eeves held his hand high. Even Death's spell could not sway his suspicion of them.

"The yeas have it. They stay."

The room loosened like a satin ribbon slipping free of a knot.

"Now, let's all be civil," Corvudeus reminded as the scent of home began to fade. "This was your vote. Your choice. I simply made you listen."

In the deep reaches of Verenna's mind she resented the gray gentleman before her and the patchwork of rules that determined when he was allowed to help. Nonetheless, as the moments passed and her neighbors drifted back to reality, they awakened considerably less hostile.

"Just until the storm breaks. No longer," Eeves grumbled.

Verenna glared as the man stalked off towards the study to

brood over the loss. Once he'd dismissed himself she turned her attention to the fireplace, expecting to see Corvudeus lingering there. He'd already vanished. Suspicion took hold in his absence. What had been important enough to bring him here?

From the way everyone went about their daily tasks she wasn't sure they remembered his brief presence at all. A Canterford man stoked the small fire, crouched exactly where Death had been standing. Others headed to the kitchen, some fell into discussion of the brewing gale outside or marched off to guard duty on the upper floor. Even her father seemed oblivious to the sudden appearance and vanishing of the stranger. He turned to her and pushed her hair out of her face. "I'll make you a cup of tea. I'm sure there's still some around. Just wait here, dear. I want to talk with you."

"But, I," she started, but he'd already hurried off.

Only when she saw the other members of her party did she realize how close they'd come to disaster. The sweat dappled brows, the leaning, the upcast eyes, all spelled out relief. Adrinée slumped against the wall and Renaud rested heavily on the back of Thessa's chair. She caught Darius in a glance that both congratulated her courage and insisted she never try it again. Fabien managed a smile. "I didn't think I'd ever say I was glad to see Death. Why'd he come?"

"Let's not question life's gifts shall we?" Mortimer pleaded.

Verenna agreed, but before she could celebrate the subtle victory with her companions, a whine sounded over her shoulder.

"So. You're like them now." Willoughby had arrived still rubbing the goose egg forming on the back of his skull. "What about us? What about all the time I've invested in you? How could you do this to me."

Checking that no one watched, she took hold of his collar and turned him so his mass hid the grip she had on him. "You nasty little toad. You called me a demon and practically incited a mob against us. What did you think we'd have between us after that? I'm so sorry about your investment. I was more focused on keeping us alive," she snarled.

"I didn't mean you were a demon. I meant them."

"Could have been more specific."

"What does it matter now? You are one of them. A freak. The girl I was set to marry…"

"You hadn't even asked!" She rasped, hardly above a whisper, tugging his collar tighter so it pinched and made him cough. She might have hit him but Mr. Dellins stepped between them.

"And if you had asked, I would have forbade it."

Verenna's eyes became perfect circles as she listened to what had to be the harshest words she'd ever heard her father utter. "With what I've just seen here, Mr. Porter, you'd be the last man on earth for my daughter. I've never known you to be much more than a simpering fool, but now I may add selfish, intolerant, ass to your description. My daughter has returned. Whatever state she has arrived in, you should be grateful. And if I ever hear you insult her under my roof again you'll find yourself without one."

Willoughby took in a deep breath that made his lower lip tremble.

"I-I never," he stammered.

"No. I suppose you haven't," her father finished. Unable to hold up under more criticism the little man waddled off to nurse his wounds in another room. As if nothing had happened, her father placed a warm cup of tea in her hands.

"You're alright with me not being normal?"

"Oh my dear, you never were. And I've been glad of it since the day you were born."

He tried to grin, but the corners of his mouth didn't rise the way they should. He gazed down at his clasped hands. It could have been a trick of the light, but Verenna thought she saw Corvudeus slip down the hall.

"Follow me, love." He guided her to his study, away from the commotion of the parlor. She caught a gray reflection in the grandfather clock. She checked over her shoulder but found no one there. Corvus must be watching.

Mr. Dellins took a seat in one of the armchairs and indicated she should take the other. She settled gingerly on its edge and set her tea aside.

"My dear, there's something I've got to tell you."

Her stomach did a flip. Some small voice inside her told her what he would say but she could not bear to believe it until the words had escaped his mouth.

"What?" It was less of a question than an attempt to dig her heels in and hold off reality as long as she could.

"Your mother."

"She what? What about her? What is it, why don't you just tell me, what it is?" Her voice cracked. She dug her nails into the upholstered arms of the chair hard enough to make the frame creak. Her father couldn't look at her, only down in a way that deepened the creases in his forehead.

"She's gone dear. About two months now."

Tears over flowed to wet her rage red cheeks. "No."

"She's buried with the family at Bellery Grove."

"Stop."

"She was very sick, Vivie. She's at peace."

"I said stop it!" the girl screamed and darted from the room without direction.

Instinct guided her up the stairs. A door hung open at the end of the hall. She raced for it without thought of her sore feet or tired limbs. She fell through the opening and steadied herself at the end of the empty bed. Undisturbed. The sheets tucked.

Freshly finished knitting coiled near the pillows. Everything lay in tidy readiness for a return that would never come. The whole room expected someone. Her body went heavy and she sank at the foot of the bed, unwilling to tarnish the crisp memories in the linen with hands so filthy from travel.

Verenna sobbed into her knees until the slightest knock made her lift her head. Corvus stood in the threshold between the hall and her mother's room. Her jaw clenched till her teeth ached. Her eyes stopped watering and refused to blink. All other surroundings were unimportant in the presence of the being that had taken her mother away.

"I'm very sorry."

"You're not," Verenna spat.

Death let out a sigh and took a step towards her. The scent of fields and flowers struck her but nothing shook her from her rage. Her hands trembled with the want to crush something more substantial than the fabric of her dress.

"Do you really think your magic tricks win me? I know what you did to her."

"You don't."

"You killed her."

"I did not."

"You killed her! I know you did!" The words scraped from Verenna's ragged throat as she sprang to her feet. "What else could have happened?"

Corvus folded his hands in front of him. "I do not kill. No one ever dies of death."

"What then? Cold Fever?

"Mercifully, no. One of her head colds turned into the flu. The demons never touched her."

"You could have left her! You didn't have to take her!"

"I think we both know better than that. The one time I

decided not to take someone, it created your kind and lead to the dire situation we're in now. Not my proudest moment."

Verenna's breath hissed through her teeth. Her hands balled at her sides as her eyes began to water anew with her lack of blinking. "You did this. All of it. You made all of this possible with one stupid mistake and now everyone else is paying for it." The girl balled her fists so tight she could feel her nails start to cut into the skin of her palm.

Death shook his head slow and gave a mournful sort of shrug. "You are absolutely right. All that matters now is what do we do about it?"

"No. The dead Sarzen matter. My mother matters," Verenna growled, taking slow deliberate steps towards the apparition.

"You confuse the things that are important to you for the things that are important in the grand scheme of the world. Sadly, they are not the same. Fight that fact if you wish, but it will not change. We have to focus on ending this before it gets worse."

"We? You abandoned us. Show up whenever you decide the rules allow it. You left us to face the other Horsemen alone. And we did it. We won without you. You are not part of 'we'."

"Oh, I am a part of everything. Like it or not. Personally, I don't. But here I am. Back with your little team. Can't resist really. You're interesting."

"We're your entertainment?" Verenna found she could not exhale. Her breaths came in tiny pants she could not calm. She seethed for revenge.

"Dear, when you exist as long as I have you take it where you can get it."

"So you think this is funny," Verenna's words were hardly audible. The air in her lungs refused to leave though her chest felt full enough to burst.

Corvus tucked his hands behind his back and began a leisurely pace around the room, examining with bright eyed curiosity the odds and ends her mother had so cherished. "Not funny, per se, but certainly fascinating."

He moved towards the dresser and leaned down for a look at her mother's silver brush, studying the mixture of gray and auburn hair tangled in its bristles. The girls whole body anticipated him touching it. She readied herself to spring and seize the object. But Corvus paced away to the boarded window sill that held her mother's neatly stacked books. Again her whole body tensed.

"Hardly in all of history, and I mean all of it, have mortal and immortal communities cooperated with full knowledge of each other's status as such." He stooped and read the titles with a half smile. Finally he stood to face her. By this time Verenna had flushed all the way down her arms. The room had narrowed to a tunnel with only Corvudeus at the end. She hardly heard him as he continued. "Watching you, your friends, all the little problems and struggles. Seeing all of you fight so hard for things that are so impermanent, it's inspiring. But I'd be lying if I said it wasn't also hilarious from time to time."

Verenna pounced. The knot in her chest unraveled into a gut curdling scream. She swung. Her fist landed on his jaw. Instead of the knuckle splitting impact of bone on bone, the blow sank into him, slowing like a pebble sinking in molasses. Then he evaporated entirely. The momentum of her punch sent her slamming into the wall behind him. He rematerialized a few feet to her right.

She lunged again, throwing her clenched hands wildly at his body. She could feel the thud of impact each time, the thick feeling of striking flesh, the slick fabric of his suit. But each punch ended the same way. The blow slowed down, digging into him before he vaporized to another point in the room. She charged anew every time he reappeared, clawing at him, trying to shred and bruise any part of him she could reach. Her breath went ragged but she fought on, screeching her fury for all of the things he'd let come to pass.

"Bring her back! You did it before! Bring her back!"

"You know I can't," the watery calm of his voice sent another wave of rage through her and redoubled her efforts to injure him.

"Coward! Stand and fight! I'll make you bring them back! All of them!"

The chase continued, the girl snatching at the shape of a man in empty air, until exhaustion forced her to the ground to gasp for air.

With Verenna subdued, Corvus took shape once more. He tidied his suit before kneeling next to her. "She was at peace you know. I told her where you were. What you were doing. Who you were becoming. She's proud. And I think she'd be honored that you literally took on Death himself with your bare hands to try and win her back. Not a bad swing you've got by the way. It may not hurt, but I can feel it. If it matters."

Verenna would have spat an insult at him but couldn't catch enough air to do so. She barely had the energy to keep herself up on her hands and knees. The girl kept her eyes on the tear dotted floorboards, one hand clutching the stitch in her side.

"I know it will take a while to believe me, but I am, as much as I can be, on your side. Because if you lose this fight, the world loses. It's a daunting idea, but with how hard you're willing to fight for just one person, I can see you fighting even harder for all of them. I'd bet on you. In a way, I already have."

Verenna rolled to one side and sat with her back against the bed, her eyes shut, feeling the hot, red, wave drain from her body replaced by the emptiness of true exhaustion.

"What's the wager?"

"I quite literally cannot say."

"Of course not," she mumbled on the edge of passing out. "What can you say?"

"That no one will have heard any of this. And that there's someone in the hall heading this way."

"What?" she grumbled, blinking awake to find herself alone, in a perfectly undisturbed room, as if she'd been fighting her own shadow. A muted knock came from the hall. The door hung open, but whoever had come to her stayed tucked around the corner.

"Who- what?" she muttered.

Darius emerged, leaning heavily on the wall for support.

She raised an eyebrow. "How did you get up here?"

"Adrinée was kind enough to help with the stairs. I insisted on tackling the hallway myself. I've got to start somewhere."

Verenna lay her head against the bedpost and studied him. He looked more himself now than he had since the incident in the tower. Most of his hair had grown back. Though his face was still badly marred he was for the most part recognizable. She found herself wishing everything came back as easily. "You're starting to look like you again."

Darius scoffed and staggered in, clinging to one piece of furniture, then another until he took hold of the bedpost and used it to lower himself beside her. It was the doctor's turn to study her. She could feel him looking her over but had no more energy to pay it any mind.

"He was here wasn't he? Corvudeus?"

She gave a single nod.

"I take it you fought him."

"He said no one heard."

"We didn't, but you're covered in sweat and look like you've been through a barroom brawl. Yet the room is utterly untouched. I'm familiar with the signs."

Verenna continued to stare blankly at the opposite wall.

"How's that?"

"I fought him too. Over my family, when they passed."

A softness she'd never heard from the man caught her attention and she turned to see if it could possibly be genuine. He stared at the tattered green hem of her dress as if watching the fluttering edge of some distant ocean, sitting back to ensure it did not consume him. "There aren't many things harder than watching the pieces of the life you'd planned fall away."

For once he held no venom, no sardonic advice, no orders. He'd gotten lost at a fraying edge of fabric. Perhaps noticing he'd strayed too far he shook his head and took a deep inhale before rattling off an awkward string of phrases. "That's over and done. Two hundred years ago, now. More. What I mean is, if you think about it, us, what we are...you just..."

He looked to her to see if she might be on the verge of understanding, but found her much closer to sleep. Darius fell silent. His expression, altered though it was by his injuries, told her there was some story he could not manage to tell. Then, without his former faltering, he said, "What I mean is, you are far from alone. And I'm sorry."

Verenna shut her eyes listening to the aches and pains of the old house, as the wind pummeled its sides, the creak of a board near the study, the dull hubbub downstairs, and when the voices died down the sound of the grandfather clock. Even the moan of the wind that crept under an ill-seated windowpane.

"Why'd you come up?" she blurted into the emptiness.

"You sat with me in the cart at night. Seemed fair."

It surprised her that he knew. But something bumping against her back from under the bed startled her more. She pulled away, expecting something monstrous, knowing she had no more power to run. But two soft white ears announced a different creature entirely. The kitten she'd been given emerged from its hiding place purring. It had grown considerably but seemed to recognize her, headbutting her arm in greeting. She held out her hand, letting the little cat stroll beneath so that the silk of its fur caressed her palm. She hadn't felt anything so soft since, well, the last time she was home. A fresh round of tears welled up and she turned away from Darius to hide them.

"It's alright, you know," he began and stopped himself. "Well, it isn't right now. But it will be."

"When?" Verenna's question was choked with her effort to hold back the flood.

"I'm waiting for that answer myself," he whispered.

Her shoulders started to shake and he placed a feeble hand on one of them. The cat continued its weaving path around her, nuzzling her hand to encourage her to scratch its head.

The sounds of the windstorm outside overtook the conversation. A low, smooth sound that at first she'd mistaken for someone downstairs struck up under it all. It grew, strengthening until she could distinguish a deep, satisfied, chuckle.

Darius's grip tightened on her shoulder and she reached back to grab his hand. The cat's fur rose in a ridge on its back. It stocked sideways, facing the eerie noise seeping in at the windowsill. The laughter swelled with ever strengthening gusts. Sudden strips of light beamed through the shutters. One of the boards nailed over the window tore off.

"What is that!?" Verenna screamed over the din. She could hardly hear herself much less Darius's answer. The whole house groaned under the force of the wind. Another board ripped away, letting in another shock of light.

The roar of the mocking wind built into such a din she couldn't even hear her own mind. Verenna crawled away in retreat until her back met Darius. She looked to him in a panic. He mouthed to her, "Cover your head."

She ducked, padding her ears with her hands and curled up as tight as she could next to him as the cat scuttled under the bed. The rush of the gale had grown so forcefully that the air rushing in through the crack near the sill sounded like the scream of a kettle boiling over. Darius placed one arm over her and hid his head with the other. Surely the window would burst. Or the roof would come off. The whole building shook with the effort of staying together.

When she was sure the structure could take no more, the storm slackened. Its fury exhaled a final dwindling laugh that died out as a breeze. Quiet reigned. Save for the ticks and cracks of a settling house, not a sound. In the sudden absence of noise a tin ringing sprang up in her ears. Verenna peeked her head up just a fraction to examine the room. It felt like something should be broken, but everything lay just as she'd last seen it. Then she saw an odd splash of color across the floor, a lighter brown against the dark boards.

Sticking a finger in her ear to rub out the ringing pitch, she rose hesitantly. Darius tried to keep her back from the stain that had appeared but his grip was not yet strong enough and she easily shed it. Stalking closer she felt grit below her shoes. Stopping at the edge of the color she knelt to investigate.

"Dirt," she whispered, tracing a line in it with her finger.

"Don't touch it! Why are you touching it?!" Darius's attempt at a shout set him coughing.

Verenna ignored him. "Sand and bits of bark and grass...it must have blown in under the window.

"Get a broom."

The girl shot him a scathing look. "I know how to clean."

"Maybe, but not what you're cleaning."

Verenna puzzled over his last remark, but he cut her thoughts short with another. "That might be more than dust. Get a jar. Get something. There," he gestured to her mother's dresser to an empty jar and broke into another coughing fit.

She hurried to do as he'd said. Without time to find a broom, she crouched above the dust and gathered it, scooping her hand along the ground until the majority of it lay at the bottom of the glass receptacle. "A book. Put a book on top as a lid."

Verenna snatched a heavy tome from the stack her mother kept. "This what you do when your study gets dusty?"

"No. Just when the wind starts laughing at us."

She clapped the book on top of the jar and set it on the dresser. She bent to watch for signs of life. "Nothing."

"Don't rule it out."

Distressed voices stirred awake downstairs. She could hear her father calling out to check on everyone. "I thought the house would come down," Verenna said, still in awe at the strength of the weather.

"To be honest, so did I. The sooner we can get out of here the better. This house can't hold up forever under these conditions...Verenna?"

She'd hardly heard him. Her gaze locked onto the jar. The dust lifted into the air, swirling into an enchanting spiral that gently caressed the sides of the container. The particles shrank together, gathering to dance in the center in a thin whipping shape of a woman. Her hair and arms flailed as if exploring for an opening in her glass prison.

Darius hauled himself from the floor to join her in amazement. "I have a feeling, that Famine isn't in Turim. It's here."

The thunder of running footsteps silenced them both as her father charged into the room, followed by a few worried neighbors. "Is everyone alright?"

"Yes, we're fine."

"We've never had a storm that strong. I can't believe it."

"Come downstairs," Mr. Tiller instructed. "If it's getting this bad around here we'll need to decide what to do about...What's...what's in the jar?"

"What's what?" Darius feigned ignorance and slid in front of the specimen.

Mr. Eeves pushed through the crowd and forced his way into the room. He marched with a ferocity that told the doctor to step aside or be thrown. Through gritted teeth he spat every consonant. "What. Is. That?"

Chapter 17

Darius settled against the dresser, determined to maintain his lie. "I don't know what you're-" a hard shove silenced the doctor and revealed what he'd been shielding.

"It's the creature," someone murmured. "The thing in the wind."

Eeves rounded on the Verenna. "You brought this with you. You were going to let it loose on us from the inside."

"No! It came through the crack in the window. We captured it. We didn't know what it was either, we just- ah!"

He seized Verenna's arm and yanked her face to face with him. "That thing killed my wife."

Verenna swallowed hard. A vein pulsed in the man's forehead. His teeth ground so hard she could hear it. Something told her nothing she could say would satisfy him. Her mouth formed shapes but the clutter of her mind kept them soundless.

Her father stepped in to separate the two of them. "Keep your hands off my daughter," he snarled.

"I warned you, Dellins. I warned you not to trust them. I warned you all. Now look. They've brought the enemy right to us!"

"It's not what it seems," he father defended.

"Don't you dare pretend to know. You've been lied to like the rest of us. Think about it, Dellins. Our horses turned cannibal. Birds are falling from the sky dead and full of stones. Our friends, our children, my wife, damn it half the bloody town has died or vanished and yet your little girl and her friends turn up here unscathed. How, if they are not working with the forces that threaten us?"

Mr. Dellins started to argue, but Eeves snapped to silence him. "Save it. Downstairs now. Bring the jar. Let's see how everyone votes when they see the truth."

ഔ

Verenna tried to swallow against the dryness of her nervous mouth. She and Darius had been thrust to the center of the parlor with her father and the rest of their companions. They were surrounded, encircled by distrustful faces, waiting to hear an explanation. The incriminating jar had been placed on a table so that all present could see for themselves the oddity that swayed inside.

"We think it's Malagrir, the Horseman that brings famine. Well, a piece anyway. We thought the next horseman would be farther away. It looks like we were wrong. That's why all the animals have been acting so strange. That's what's been trying to pull the house down."

"Tell it to stop!" someone cried from the back of the crowd.

"We can't. You don't understand. It isn't ours. We set out to kill it."

"Then get to it, why don't you? Destroy the damned thing before it destroys us," Mrs. Norworth demanded.

"It's not that simple," Darius interjected.

Eeves slammed a fist onto the table that made the jar wobble. "Why the hell isn't it?"

"We don't know how yet."

The man tilted his head back and laughed at the ceiling to keep the water in his eyes from tumbling down his face. "I see it now. How could we have been this blind." He whirled to address the room, mocking the doctor's voice. "'*They don't know how*'. Yet here they are. They arrive unscathed. We have the worst storm yet not an hour after they get here. They've got one of the monsters in a jar. And somehow, they still don't know anything about it. You're lying to us."

"There's no reason to lie," Mortimer added. He crept closer, his hands out in front of him to offer calm. Eeves made him step back with his snarling reply.

"You've got every reason. That creature in the wind, you brought it down upon us."

Verenna turned in a slow circle, looking for a sign of sympathy in any of her neighbors. She found only ire and confusion. Ms. Tiller let out a small sob.

Fabien took the lead to offer a solution. "We can, if you let us. We intend to destroy the beast and I believe we can if you give us a chance to try."

"And how do we know you'll be trying to save us? What if you're on the creature's side instead of ours?" Censington piped.

"It's too big a risk. We stand to lose too much," Mr. Norworth gruffed below his bristling mustache.

Mr Dellins straightened his glasses. "This is insane. What exactly do you intend to do with us? Throw us out into the next storm?"

"It's not out of the question," Eeves growled. "I think we've had enough of listening to you, Dellins. You're soft. You'll stand by your daughter's lies just because she's your child. The rest of us, we have our own lives to consider."

"It's not a lie!" Verenna cried. She felt like ripping out her hair. "We are your best shot at getting out of here. We need to get to the abbey. All of us. We can come up with some kind of plan when we're safe there. We can figure out how to stop the monster."

Eeves paused a moment, returning to his composed condescension. The spark of an idea had caught within him. "I think that's exactly what you'll do."

"That's what I said," Verenna commented, head tilting with caution. "What more do you want?"

He stepped in so that he towered over her and whispered, "I want my family back. But if I can't have that, I'll settle for the safety of those who are still here."

"And where does that leave us?" Adrinée inquired.

"The cellar."

"What?" Mr. Dellins spat.

Eeves sneered and circled them, "I say we lock you in with your little pet in a jar here, until you come up with a plan to do what you said you came to do. Kill the monster."

Verenna's father threw his hands up. "That's ridiculous! This is my house, you can't just-" his protest was cut short but hearty shouts of agreement form the crowd.

"Fine," Eeves agreed. "We'll vote."

"Fine," Mr. Dellins glared with all the venom he could muster. "Put it to a vote. If they're locked up, so am I."

"Perfect." Eeves turned with open arms to face the rest of the townsfolk.

"Who thinks we should let these strangers keep the run of the house? Who here honestly thinks we can trust them?" A few hands peeked above the crowd. Verenna counted three, including Mrs. Babik.

Eeves smirked and continued. "And who thinks that they should be locked up until they can give us something that helps us?" Up grew a forest of hands.

"There you have it, Dellins. Are you going willingly?"

Verenna watched her father's shoulders tense as he straightened his back. Chin high he responded, "If that's the vote, that's the vote."

Her eyes stung, welling with the frustration of helplessness. "You can't do this. We won't go."

ᥱᥗ

The door to the cellar closed with a gust of air that hit her like defeat. She sank onto the floor cross legged and slumped. Within a day of arriving back to the house she thought she might never see again, she'd become a prisoner in it.

The dim light from a thin window high on the wall lit the dust motes that tumbled about them.

"It ain't all that bad," Fabien shrugged with his hands in his pockets. "There's no way they're going to try and kill us."

"Is that the only thing that makes a situation bad to you? The threat of immediate violence?" Verenna groaned, allowing herself to flop back and splay out on the stone floor of the larder, absorbing its cool.

"It could be worse. They could have put us outside," Kaybin offered.

"They won't." Adrinée blew a piece of hair out of her eyes and took a seat next to Kaybim. "Not until we figure out some way to fix this, anyhow. I have a feeling they'll pick one of us to test the plan. Put one outside to see if it's safe."

Renaud helped Thessa ease down against a few sacks of flour piled against the wall. She hissed as she delicately slid her broken leg out in front of her. Her brother passed her another petal for the pain. "We haven't got too many more of these. Chew it slowly."

"Please tell me you were all serious about being able to defeat this thing?" Mr. Dellins pleaded, setting the whirling jar of dust on the floor in the center of the group.

Mortimer crouched beside him for another look at the tiny creature. "We're going to have to be."

"We'd better," Thessa warned. "May I remind you that not all of us here are immortal. If this house comes down we're just as dead as the rest of them."

Kaybin started the discussion with the most obvious problem. "Somehow I don't think we'll be able to outrun it on foot. If the horse survives, it can carry two of us at most."

"I'm sorry," Mr. Dellins stood to pace, furiously shining his glasses on his vest. "But how are you all so calm about this?"

"Been through worse," Verenna mumbled.

"I wish I hadn't heard that. Vivie, what on earth have you been up to?"

"Can we talk about it later?" she groaned and rolled onto her side to face away from him.

Mortimer made an attempt to soothe her father. "The best thing we could do right now is sit tight and think. Come on. All ideas welcome."

No one took up the mantle of making the first suggestion. In the quiet that followed Verenna traced a line between two stones with her finger. The texture of the mortar and the roughly hewn rock distracted her enough from the empty feeling in her chest that she felt something resting against her hip. A little, rectangular shape in her pocket. The book. She dove a hand in after it. She'd read it cover to cover by now, and nothing it held directly applied to the situation. But if the right eyes looked it over, perhaps it could offer them something.

"Here, flip through this. There isn't exactly a chapter on Horsemen, but we've got to start somewhere."

"I can't believe you still have that!" Darius exclaimed as he caught a glimpse of the cover. He took it up and began to search it.

By the time the light in the window turned the purple of evening the wind had raged against the house above them three more times.

Darius threw the book down.

Fabien growled. "Nothing? Not a single thing we've talked over sounds like an answer?"

"There are some good possibilities, but it warrants more discussion," Mortimer sighed.

"We have literally discussed all day. How much more can we talk?" Adrinée spoke her complaint into her hands as she clutched her face.

"I hear something," Thessa hushed and held up a hand for quiet. Footsteps approached the cellar. The trap door lifted. Backlit shadows crowded the top of the stairs. Ms. Tiller and Mrs. Norworth descended carrying trays with a few bowls of porridge.

Verenna sat up and hugged her knees, watching the two women with her sourest look. They refused to meet anyone's gaze as they set the things down and turned to leave.

"Feeling guilty?" Verenna griped. "At least you could bring us a candle or two. It'll be dark in minutes."

The two women paused and exchanged a nervous glance.

"Vivie," her father's tone reminded her of manners she no longer had any reason to abide by.

"What? Are we supposed to solve all your problems in the dark?" Verenna smarted again.

Mrs. Norworth shrugged at her younger companion who hurried up the steps, murmuring a request for light to the others. She returned and set a little lantern on the floor in the center of the room before scurrying back towards her peers. The cellar closed with a huff that almost put out the little flame. It sputtered and struggled, but came through.

"Here, my dear. You need to eat something." Her father

nudged her arm with one of the bowls of slop.

"That's actually part of the whole, not being able to die, thing. I don't particularly want to eat anymore."

"Surely you must eat something," he pressured.

The room went impossibly quiet. "I'll, em, have it in a bit," Verenna lied with a smile so weak she was glad the growing darkness hid it from him.

Verenna pulled her knees to her chest and watched the dust dancer in the jar as the group reviewed the collection of ideas they'd concocted. She noticed that Adrinée's voice was strikingly absent from the conversation. The girl sat a ways apart from everyone else, scraping the last bits of bland porridge from her bowl. Tired of rehashing the same ill fated plans Verenna scooted closer to the girl, just out of arm's reach, and slid her portion of dinner to her.

"Want it?"

Adrinée peered over the edge of her bowl with considerable scepticism that reminded her of Enra. After much silent deliberation she spoke. "Sure."

For a while they didn't talk. Adrinée kept a careful eye on Verenna as she ate. Tired of the standoff Verenna cut right to her best guess at the right thing to say. "I'm sorry."

The younger girl almost dropped the bowl. Her eyes narrowed. "For what?"

"Well, I sort of yelled at you I guess. On the night with the wolves."

"Don't mention it," she dismissed, pushing a dark curl behind her ear to continue eating.

A moment passed where Verenna considered taking her advice. But the weight of everything that had happened that day could not go unsaid. And the young one before her was most likely of all of them to know just how heavy things had become. "I also want you to know, that I'm very sorry about your brother. I didn't understand before and now I do."

The girl sensed something more genuine and set her dinner aside. "Why now?"

"My mum," Verenna rasped, tracing the lines on the floor.

Adrinée startled. "Today?"

"No. At least a month before we got here. Probably before we even met you. I just didn't know."

"Oh."

"Yeah."

"Sorry."

"Thanks."

They sat in another shared quiet, this time together.

"Thanks for the extra porridge," Adrinée said to move them before they could sink.

"Not a problem. It tastes like nothing to me now, being immortal and whatnot."

"It tastes like nothing either way, apparently," the younger girl remarked, picking her teeth with a nail. Verenna could remember getting in trouble at the table for such behavior. One good thing about such hard times was that no one had time to care for the little things. No one troubled anyone over manners when another storm was building outside.

Something thumped against the side of the house hard enough to shake it. Everyone capable of doing so shot to their feet in alarm.

"Was that the horseman?" Renaud hushed.

"Good god," Darius groaned. "A tree fell. Let's not get ourselves worked up before we have to."

The group returned to the spots they'd claimed as their own. Kaybin took slow backwards steps, never taking his eyes of the little window at the top of the cellar. But in doing so, he bumped into Fabien. The two stumbled but caught each other. A harmless incident, until they realized someone's ankle knocked into the jar trapping the swirling dust.

It wobbled, slid the book off its top, clattered to its side, and cracked. With a whoosh, whatever element it had contained was loose among them.

"Damned it! " Darius shouted.

Their clothes began to rustle around their bodies as a sourceless gust of wind bandied about the room. It changed directions, darting through their legs and weaving a tricky path in and out of the scant supplies. A jar shattered in the dark.

"Gather up!" Mortimer called to them. They clumped together around Thessa in the corner of the cellar with their backs to the wall. Verenna crouched with her father on one side, Fabien on the other, and Mortimer with his arms out in front of the lot of them.

The wind wrapped the old man's leg and took him to the ground, yanking him into the part of the cellar where the desperately struggling lantern light could not reach. Verenna lunged, taking hold of his hand and was hauled along with him. She heard another jar shatter and Adrinée scream.

Verenna hit the opposite wall hard, still clinging to Mortimer. She could see next to nothing. She lashed out at their attacker but there was nothing solid to strike. Even if there had been, she couldn't see it in the dim light. There would be no surviving this if they could not see the enemy.

Mortimer clasped her other hand and pulled her in to shield her. Another jar fell and split at their feet. Lard splattered her skirt. The old man shouted to her, "Hold on to me! It will be harder to drag us!"

But inspiration had struck the girl and she fought out of his grip, baffling the old man as she began to tear the outer layer of skirts from her body. She heard Fabien yell from somewhere in the mayhem but he was cut short as if choked. Ushered by that urgency she broke free from the fabric and pulled herself along the floor towards the lantern.

She curled around it to try and salvage its last spark. Utter blackness engulfed them and the fire winked once, twice, and out.

Despair turned to shock and pain as the oils in the material burst into light, singeing her fingers. Directly to her right, she caught sight of Fabien suspended in the air, held up by a larger version of the creature in the jar. The gray haze of an arm kept him aloft while the other seemed to be flowing down his throat.

Verenna took hold of the newly burning fabric and flung it at the startled demon. A whistling scream curdled the air. It dropped the young man into a limp heap on the floor as the fire raced up its spinning sides to devour it.

"Get down!" Darius commanded. "Don't breathe the smoke!"

The lot of them collapsed to the floor below the billowing gray fumes. But in seconds, the monster had been consumed, leaving only the flaming rag and a flurry of dust motes.

Hurried whispers ensued.

"Are you alright?"

"Who's hurt?"

"What happened to you?"

Most had minor cuts and scrapes from pieces of broken jar that had been set spinning around the room. Adrinée got the worst of it. One had shattered over her head. An ugly gash gushed blood down the side of her face. Darius rushed as best he could to tend to it. Kaybin passed him Mr. Dellins vest to use as a wrap.

"Verenna!" Her father seized her in a grateful embrace. "You're alright. Oh thank god. How did you know to do that?"

"I didn't. I made it up. Fabien...."

She skidded onto her knees next to him to try and shake him awake.

With a few slaps his eyes rolled open and she slumped beside him in relief.

"What the bloody…" he began before seeing Verenna's father hovering nearby. "Sorry. What was that?"

"That," Darius answered while tending Adrinée, "Was one, single piece of our next horseman. Consider that its little finger."

Verenna coughed, realizing that her smoldering skirt would soon fill the cellar with smoke. Holding her breath she rushed to the top of the steps to bang on the door, but before she could start knocking it flung wide, releasing the billowing fumes into the kitchen above.

"What on god's earth is the smoke about?" Someone cried from above her in the light.

Verenna wheezed a reply before anyone could stop her. "You wanted an answer? I think you've got it. We may be able to burn the creature. A piece of it got out and, well, we set it on fire and it's gone."

The combination of her onslaught of words and the puff of smoke had bewildered the crowd above.

"Right then…good," Mr. Eeves shoved his way to the front, trying to hide his confusion under a guise of stern leadership. "We will be packed by morning and be ready to leave. You'll get rid of the damn thing and we will be on our way. I suggest you rest. Your solution better work in the morning."

"Wait!" She shouted but the slam of the cellar door drown her cries.

Someone had put out the sizzling rag, and without so much as an ember left to relight the lantern, they plummeted into absolute pitch darkness. Verenna felt her way back down the steps and fumbled directly into Mortimer. He begged her pardon and helped her down the rest of the way. She could hear people moving but had no way of telling them apart until they spoke. She felt her way to a wall and moved along it until her foot bumped something warm. She jumped, but comfort came when Fabien spoke up. "It's just me. Sit."

Putting her back to the wall she slid down next to him. Somewhere across the room she heard Darius instructing Kaybin to keep Adrinée awake and talking in case of concussion.

"Everyone alright?" Mortimer asked the room, reciting one name after another. Once everyone had responded they settled in as best they could whispering to one another as not to scare away all potential of sleep.

Verenna felt herself nod when her chin hit her chest. "You can lean on me, you know," Fabien murmured with a smoke-hoarse voice. "Least I can do is be a pillow for the one who thought up a way to save me. You're smart you know that? Really smart."

Even in the cover of darkness Verenna was sure he could feel the heat radiating from her blushing cheeks. "Thanks. I just, I'm good at coming up with things when I have to. I guess."

"Well you're guessing has proved better than most peoples hard thinking," he added.

She would have been beaming if the last twenty four hours hadn't utterly depleted her. Her head was cluttered with everything from thoughts of her mother, to dizziness from the smoke, to the idea that tomorrow there was yet another horseman to face.

Fabien put an arm around her shoulders and she let herself lean against him. Soon she heard his subtle snores and knew he'd found peace. She'd almost fallen asleep herself when she heard Darius and Mortimer discussing the challenge of the coming day.

"But it worked," the old man insisted. "Fire has to be the answer."

"Sure. For a smaller version. The real thing is much much stronger. Nothing ever comes that easy. You know that."

The two men fell into their separate thoughts for a time before Darius's voice rose again.

"I think tomorrow will hold more trouble than we're ready for."

Chapter 18

Verenna spent most of the night with her eyes wide open. Not that it made much difference. The dark of the cellar was so complete that she couldn't tell if they were closed or not. She wanted to sleep like Fabien. But every fiber of her buzzed with anticipation. What if it didn't work next time? What if the fire couldn't consume a creature that size in time to protect them? Or what if it did work, what if the monster recovered in time to catch up to them on the road to the Inn? On top of that, how were they going to get close enough to light it?

Dawn crept in so infinitesimally she hardly noticed as the shapes of her sleeping companions emerged from the night, breathing softly. Save for three of them. Darius, Mortimer and Adrinée sat awake, whispering, and from the looks of it, assembling something.

She ground the sleep from her eyes. Taking delicate hold of Fabien's arm, she removed it from her shoulders and left it resting in his lap before crawling to the place where the trio worked. In between them glistened a multitude of jars filled with some small amount of a substance that clung to the sides of the glass. The two of them were cramming shreds of cloth into them and setting them aside.

"What's all this?" she murmured.

The three jumped at her stealthy arrival. "This is our way out," Adrinée informed her. "We light these, throw them, they catch the horseman on fire, then we run like we've never run before."

Mortimer took up the explanation from there. "We likely

won't have to run for long. The wind strong enough to do us harm doesn't last more than a half hour. The storms seem to die back around then. If we can keep it occupied for that long, we've got a good chance of getting out of this in one piece."

"There are two windows upstairs to throw them from," Darius informed her. "Of course, with the way the wind was blowing last night, there are probably a lot more without boards over them now."

Verenna scratched her fingers through her knotted hair, feeling the grime that had accumulated from the days of travel and rain. "Seems like the best shot we've got."

"That it does," Darius agreed.

Another prominent worry cropped up in Verenna's mind. "Will we have enough sun serum to get us to the Inn? I don't think we had the chance to bring it in from the cart."

"If it was out there it's gone now," Darius said with a note of disappointment. "We'll have less than a day to make it back to the abbey before we need it again. As if having Malagrir right behind us weren't enough reason to hurry."

None of what he said held anything she could use to comfort herself so she pressed him for more. "What about the horse?"

"I wouldn't count on that thing surviving the weather last night," Fabien added, joining them. "We'll have to make do without."

Verenna tried not to imagine the coarse, old mare becoming one of the flesh eating hunters they'd seen in the field on their way in. Even more disturbing was the thought of what would happen to anyone who chose not to run for safety with them. "Do you think anyone will actually agree to come to the abbey?"

Darius huffed in exasperation and set about prepping the last jar. "Good god, you're full of questions. How should we know? We've been locked down here all night too. I certainly hope for their sake they decide to trust us."

Verenna picked at a loose thread in her underskirts and watched the top of the stairs, straining her ears against the quiet of morning for the sound of someone coming to free them. Fabien nudged her with a shoulder. It was just light enough to see him smile. "I'm a good pillow, am I not?"

"Disgusting," Darius muttered. "We've got more important things to consider than your blatant flirting."

Before an argument could take shape, footsteps sounded above their heads followed by a waterfall of gray light as the cellar door swung wide. Mr. Censington called down to them. "Wake up down there! Up and out with you!"

Ascending the steps felt like a slow walk into cold water. The reception at the top was avoidant at best, and at worst icy. Verenna's former neighbors had all assembled, small sacks of items thrown across their backs or gathered in their arms. No words changed between the two groups save for the terse instructions of Mr. Eeves. "Grab your things. They're on the floor there. Quickly now."

Glowering they took up their items, checking that nothing had gone missing. Fabien strapped on his sword, Verenna found her belt and knife. The Sarzen took up their bags and varied weaponry. All under the watchful eye of the Canterford residents.

Eeves launched into a declaration of the events ahead. "The night has given us time to think it over. We will be heading south to Hartshire. After you kill or distract the creature you may go wherever you like."

Verenna couldn't withhold her concern. "Hartshire is too far away. You'll end up spending the night in the woods."

"So be it."

"So be it? Do you know what we've seen out there?"

"What I know, my dear, is that you are capable of constructing some lovely lie about it to steer us towards your den of freaks. All we need to know is that you and your friends do not share our interests. We will do as we see fit. Dellins, I suggest you come with us."

"I am staying with my daughter," he menaced, taking up Thessa's bag for her. The cat trotted to him, weaving its body around his legs. He scooped the little animal into the sack though it yowled in protest. "For your own good," she heard him murmur to it.

Eeves sighed. "A poor decision, but we can't make it for you. So. I take it you've put together some sort of plan to catch the damned thing on fire?"

Mortimer answered, "Down in the cellar. We emptied some jars. They've got lard in the bottom and a strip of fabric. Light it and throw it. It should work."

"That's the best you could come up with? You had all night," Mr. Censington grouched.

"And you can think of something better?" Adrinée sassed.

Three Canterford men trotted to the cellar to collect the jars. One of the windows in the front room had all the boards stripped off it overnight, either by the violent wind or by the efforts of the townspeople. They gathered the little fire bombs below it and set candles at the ready to light them. When another storm stirred outside, they were ordered to sit.

"Go on. Back to back. Middle of the floor. We don't want any trouble," Mr. Eeves instructed. His voice held authority but Verenna could see fear in his darting eyes every time the house creaked.

"I'm just as much trouble sitting," Adrinée snapped.

"Do as they say," Mr. Dellin's encouraged with an urgency that could not be argued. They sank to the floor in silence. Renaud offered his back as a support for Thessa, Kaybin and Adrinée huddled together and Verenna settled next to her father.

"Why exactly do we have to listen to them? They treated us like prisoners," Verenna huffed.

"Because we need them to listen to us. And if we want them to be reasonable, a good place to start is being reasonable ourselves."

"They've made up their minds that we're all freaks. They aren't coming with us."

"Verenna Dellins," he uttered. The stern sound of her full name caught her attention. "They may be less than hospitable but they aren't bad people."

"Then what are they?"

"Fearful. And they'll die if we don't convince them that we're right."

Verenna mulled over his wisdom to the sound of the swelling wind outside. She leaned so she could see a sliver of the front room down the hall. Three men crouched beside the window, each with a jar in one hand and a candle in the other.

The house took up its groaning again as the wind searched it for breaking points. The bones of the structure around them creaked like a ship on a rough tide. They waited in silence as the howl of wind transformed into laughter. A loud snap echoed through the house. Verenna clutched her father's arm. He placed a hand on hers. "More boards are coming off," she whispered.

He nodded. "I don't think the house will take much more if it gets stronger, the glass will break. Once it's in the house..." He halted, unable to stomach listing the possibilities. "Eeves," he called out. "The abbey is less than a days walk away. It's our best chance at reaching safety before that thing catches up to us."

The man shook his head, "I'm disappointed in you Dellins. Think about it. If we end up at that abbey we'll be trapped between the monster outside or the monsters inside. It's a deathwish."

Verenna took stock of the haggard faces surrounding them, clumped together for comfort, wide eyed with quiet panic. "I think they should be able to decide for themselves," Verenna stated over the chorus of groans from the straining house. "They can run with you, or they can run with us. Why not let them choose?"

"They can. But," Eeves turned to instruct his followers. "These people are injured, and they aren't from around here. They'll be slow. Going with them is just as risky if not more than following the group to Hartshire."

"Morice," her father pleaded. "I know you are just trying to do what's best. I know that because I am trying too. You won't make it to the next town. It's too far. Not everyone among you can make that trek under good conditions. And with the creatures we've seen, the animals...Falseman Inn is close enough for everyone to make it. We'd be there before nightfall. Let's not let anyone else die."

The gathering shifted uncomfortably, trying to read each other for like minds with subtle sideways glances. A shout from the front room sent a bolt of terror through everyone present.

"I see it!" one of the backlit figures pointed to the distance beyond the windowpane.

"Do you think you can make that throw?"

"We have to. Get it open."

The storm burst in as soon as they undid the latch. Cold wind engulfed the room raising shrieks from the startled, huddling figures. They threw their arms around each other to brace themselves against the onslaught. The laughter grew so loud they could hear nothing else.

The few jars they managed to light and launch yielded little result. Verenna could not see where they landed, but there were certainly no shouts of celebration. Only more scrambling to get the next flame lit. One after the other, the little bombs flew from the window and shattered. They lasted only long enough to bathe the faces of those who tossed them with orange light. Verenna covered her ears to keep out the violent buffeting. She counted the jars they threw, until they'd reached the last three.

A thunderous crack wracked the beam above their heads.

"The house may collapse! We need to get out of here now!" Mortimer shouted over the din.

"How? It's waiting outside?" Kaybin yelled.

"Could we survive a collapse here?" Fabien demanded of Mr. Dellins. He shook his head and pointed to the massive beam running overhead.

"We get out in the next few minutes or it ends here," Darius informed them. He grabbed Fabien's shoulder. "Can you carry Thessa?" He nodded once, his jaw set with a grim severity she'd never seen.

"Pair up! Everyone! You're responsible for making sure your group gets out of here intact! Hug the walls! It may collapse!" Mortimer screamed to the horrified clusters of townsfolk.

The group on the ground shifted next to the fireplace. Verenna felt the reassuring stone of the hearth. Then her back came into contact with something soft and warm. She looked over her shoulder to find Willoughby pressed between the wall and an armchair. She felt like elbowing him in the gut, but the abject terror on his tear streaked face was so pitiful she considered it revenge enough. The sound of shattering glass heralded a failed window upstairs. Then another. Another.

The men charged back from the front room to huddle with everyone else.

"It's not working," one of them despaired.

"It's not getting close enough!"

The chaos of the wind rattled room muffled all other talk.

Verenna's entire body hummed with the energy of alarm. Maigrir was trying to draw them out, staying back and shaking their only shelter. They'd either be frightened out or crushed inside.

The wind whipped through the house, pulling books from shelves, shattering dishes in the kitchen, making the curtains twist and snap like whips.

"Verenna. Vivie. I'm sorry," a small voice whimpered behind her. "I-I didn't mean it. I didn't want it to end like this. Th-th-there's so much more we could have become…"

She turned to him, vicious with contempt. "Shut up Porter, we're not dead yet."

There must be something to do. Something they'd overlooked. Verenna scanned the room for objects that might burn stronger than the substance in the jars had. She found the answer poking out of Kaybin's pack. One of the sap branches the Sarzen had cut. If it had held a flame through the rainstorm, it had the best chance of holding up now.

She took it without his notice and began scoring the end of it in some rough approximation of the elegant lines the Sarzen had cut in the others.

"I just need you to know, that, that I-" Willoughby continued close to her ear.

"Do me a favor. Explain once we're out of this."

"But we may not get out of this!" he wailed.

"Would you hold on!" she roared at him and finished the pattern of gashes in the bark of the branch. She reached it into the fireplace, hoping to catch the last of the flames before the wind blew them out. This caught the attention of those crouched around her.

"Good god! What do you think you're doing?!" Darius cawed.

"I know what to do."

"I seriously doubt that! Put that down!" The end of the stick sparked and caught as he said it. She kept it in the flames until the sap grew hot enough to color the flame blue and white. Her gut told her to say goodbye, but she wouldn't allow herself to admit that the odds of defeat were that high.

Her father had gone pale as her plan dawned on him. "Vivie, no."

She squeezed his hand. "When it's quiet again, run. I'll be back. I promise."

She stumbled and tripped her way out of the huddled mass, torch held high, its flame strong against the gale, and rushed towards the front door.

She'd hardly touched the handle when it sprung open. The force of the air rushing in nearly sent her tumbling back down the hall. Thoughts of family, the past, her town as it was, questions of who would make it out alive, who if anyone would she see again, all jostled for first place in her mind but she refused them all. Gathering her strength, she charged out into the storm.

⁊⁊

Every tiny rock and leaf in the tempest felt like the bite of a fly, stinging as they slapped onto the exposed skin of her arms and face. She planted her feet and leaned into the wind so it would not roll her away. Sheltering her eyes from the debris she looked towards the street. The vortex of the horseman's body spiralled up between the two crippled posts that used to hold the garden gate.

She tilted her head back until she squinted into the pale gray sky, aghast at the size of the elegant terror before her. The thin, winding body dipped into a delicate waist and drifted into broad shoulders. A featureless face, with arms dancing above seeming to draw down the clouds. It had constructed its entire form from a mixture of sky and the broken fragments of the world it had come to destroy. She now understood why the jars hadn't worked. Such miniscule flames would be squelched instantly by the force of the wind. The creature would have hardly noticed them. But it did notice her.

The wind calmed its raging ever so slightly and under the thunderous buffeting in her ears she heard a chorus of whispers so light she thought she might have imagined them. Word after word wove together, overlapping each other into a tapestry of messages.

"Stupid!"

"Tiny…"

"Brave."

"Alone…"

"Who will save you?"

"Willing."

"A sacrifice!"

"The end."

The voices died away as the woman made of wind bent to face her. Tendrils of cloud drifted after like strands of wildly whipping hair, keeping the creature attached to the heavens. Verenna froze to the spot, looking from the creature to the faltering torch in her hand and back again. The scores of voices picked up again.

"What does it want?"

"Why has it come?

"Make it die!"

"So small…"

"What is it carrying?"

Verenna had no breath left in her to answer. Cold terror had poisoned and paralyzed her. The creature stooped lower. The cloud of debris at its base fluttered like the edges of a dancers skirt as it slid towards her on its single, pirouetting toe. The girl considered throwing the torch and hoping for the best, but the only thing keeping it lit was the shelter of the leeside of her body.

She had to let it get closer. The murmurs welled up in her ears, this time with a frenzied enthusiasm.

"I know what it is!"

"The girl!"

"The Bright One."

"Sad fate…"

"Silly."

"Plaything!"

"Hell's toy."

"Speak."

The last word sent a painful rash of goosebumps up her arms. She tightened her grip on the struggling torch. It must come closer. She couldn't risk missing.

Malagrir drifted nearer, her head cocked as if listening, as if the faceless form expected to hear an answer above to roar of its own destruction.

"Speak!"

"Answer."

"Why is it here?"

"What does it hold?"

"Tell!"

"Now!"

The horseman lowered an arm and reached for her with the handless limb. It spiralled so close she could feel its pull, see down the funnel that lead to the core of its body. Verenna checked the flame at her side; only the smallest trace of fluttering blue left. One last bit of spark. There was no more time to wait. At this rate, it would be out before Malagrir closed in enough. Seeing her chance she lifted the branch. She didn't have to hurl it. It was sucked from her grip and into the main column of the entity before her. And it did nothing.

The monster didn't so much as flinch. Verenna went numb

with shock. Her hand went to her knife. But what good was that
to fight the wind?

The pull intensified. She leaned back and dug her heels in to
keep herself from falling into the creatures vortex. Despite her
efforts her knees buckled. She crumbled towards the ground in the
grip of the storm, tumbling like a leaf towards the funnel cloud.

Verenna tried to gain purchase, to keep herself from being
consumed. She grabbed onto grass, sunk her nails into the dirt,
even grabbed onto the base of one of the rose bushes, ignoring the
thorns plunging through her skin and ripping trails in her palms
as her grip began to fail her. She let go.

But instead of being thrown skywards, the torrent retreated. A
sudden and intense heat seared near her feet. The voices she'd
heard awakened shrieking. She turned over to see that the base of
Malagrir's body had gone up in flame. When the torch reached
the calm at the center of the wind it had been able to gain enough
strength to ignite the monster.

"Fire!"

"What is this?"

"Burning!"

"End it!"

"Kill!"

Malagrir reached for her once more but with a whoosh the
flames licked higher. The creature recoiled and writhed like an
injured snake. Verenna scrambled backwards and glanced towards
the house. Shocked faces lined the window. She could see her
father's in front. Several hands held him back. His breath fogged
the glass as his mouth made the shape of her name.

They'd need time to get out, time to put distance between
them and the angry horseman. She held up her bloody hand in
farewell and took off down the street just as she had the night it all
began.

At the end of the street she stopped and turned around to make sure Malagrir would follow. A tower of flame had formed at her center. The wind screamed with all of its formerly whispering voices. Verenna held still until Malagrir focused on her. As soon as the faceless head turned in her direction she took off around the corner and bolted towards mainstreet. This part she hadn't thought about. Where would she go? And how would she get there on foot?

Verenna tore down the town's main road, leaping over debris and the shatterings of shop windows, feeling the squelch of mud puddles and the pang of rocks under the thin soles of her boots. She did not dare stop. Not even to check over her shoulder. She could feel Malagrir's progress in the strength of the wind, hear the lapping flames, and see the orange glow of fire on the walls when the beast got too close.

She ducked down an alley. Searing heat pursued her. The two buildings on either side caught fire. The sweat on her shirt started to evaporate with the temperature.

Heat licked along the walls just slightly slower than she could run, always a fraction of a moment behind her. Smoke seared her lungs, making each breath raw and rattling. She fell out of the narrow path into a wider street. Crawling and coughing she checked each direction for the best escape. To her left, the road wound through town. To the right, she could see fields. No cover. She raced left until a section of the haberdashery crumbled into the street, blocking her way with fiery rubble.

The wind nearly swept her off her feet as she tried to turn around, but animal instinct kept her up and forced her forward. She made the mistake of looking back. The column of fire had reached Malagrir's middle. The monster plowed a burning trail of chaos in its wake as it rushed her.

She wouldn't be able to run much longer. But where to hide

that would not burn? A sound like rhythmic thunder occurred to her as she shifted course for the fields. At first she mistook it for the fluttering of her own heart, but as it grew closer she recognize the clatter of hooves. Running as she hadn't thought it could, the dusty mare they'd counted as lost arrived beside her.

Without time to think she threw her body gracelessly onto its back, barely managing to throw a leg over the animal's bony ribs before it bolted for the fields. It took all she had to hold on, having only ridden without a saddle on occasions where her cousins hid hers. She locked her knees to the horses sides and took two giant handfuls of its mane. The wind slackened. They were gaining distance, darting towards the shelter of the woods. She tugged the animals mane to slow it. They needed to keep ahead, but not so much that Malagrir might turn back and discover the others as they ran for Falseman Inn.

To her horror, what she discovered behind them was no longer wind, but pure fire. She watched as the flames she'd set to work reached into the featureless face, lighting the arms that spiraled towards the clouds as if begging mercy. The light gray that had been its hair had been turned belching black with smoke. Livid, Malagrir's speed redoubled.

"Go! Go! Go! Go!" she heard herself screaming to the horse. The pines at the treeline were already windbent at a wild angle as they entered the woods. A cacophony of snaps and cracks took up behind them as the sap in the trees erupted into flame.

The fire moved ever faster, turning the trail behind them into an inferno. All she could do was cling to the galloping animal. So far its frail appearance had been a disguise for otherworldly endurance. She prayed that it did not find its limit now.

Verenna had no idea how far they'd come. The path was such a blur that it was hard to tell the familiar from the strange. At a fork, the horse took a left. She knew where the road led but with the distraction of the gaining fire she could not remember.

Malagrir closed in. The flaming monster was only an arm's length behind them. She caught the acrid scent of burning hair. Embers had nested in the horses tail and the flapping edge of the girls skirt. She reached back to pat them out but almost lost her seat. She could feel the beasts sides heaving with the effort of carrying them ever faster. It leaped and cut off the path, bounding over a small creek and tearing up a hill.

As the mare burst through the woods it struck the girl where they were. There was the ruin of an old stone house nearby. She used to ride out to it with other children from Canterford. They'd dare each other to enter the roofless walls and peek down into the darkness of the abandoned cellar. No one had ever gone in. She'd have to be the first.

The horse came over the rise. The ruins lay dead ahead. Behind them the inferno had spread to the field, zipping across the distance in streaks of angry yellow. She spurred the horse faster as the distance between them and the horseman narrowed once more. As they drew near the old stones, the beast showed no sign of slowing. Verenna tugged the horse's mane to slow its gallop enough to dismount. It did not respond. They'd pass the house soon.

"Whoa!" the girl called. Still the horse sprinted on. In a few seconds she was looking at the ruin of the house over her shoulder with the fire in close pursuit. Seeing her last chance, Verenna let herself tumble off the animals back. She hit the ground and rolled. Something popped in her shoulder followed by blinding pain. She struggled up with a useless right arm. Clutching it to her chest, she ran for the only cover within a quarter mile. Towards the house. Towards the fire.

Each step sent a shock through her shoulder that made tears stream down her face. The blank, burning head of the monster rose out of the trees, spurring another gust that gathered the flames towards the building. Smoke choked her as she charged against the blast. Her eyes stung, her face went red from the heat. She saw the flames licking over one of the broken stone walls and pushed even harder.

Blind with smoke, she put her head down and ran for all she was worth. Just when she thought the heat might catch her clothes on fire, she tripped and plummeted down a rough slope into somewhere cool and dark. She'd made it to cover. Reaching out her hand she felt for the farthest corner of the little room and crouched there.

Tufts of burning weeds rained down the decaying steps. The storm outside roared so loud she could hear nothing else. Malagrir sat directly over the opening to her shelter. The air inside went hot; a heat so intense she thought it might boil the sweat right off of her body.

She took labored, gasping breaths as the fire consumed the air in the room. How long until it burned out? Would it at all? How close were the others to reaching the safety of the Inn?

Verenna pressed her body into the wall, trying to absorb its earthen cool against the kiln the room had become. With her last wisp of consciousness she smelled flowers, wheat, rain, and home. Someone spoke to her with a voice as familiar as her own, though she could not picture the one it belonged to. It seemed to speak from within her own mind; not over the wind, but from beyond its reach.

"Hold on."

Chapter 19

The next thing that reached her was the dull smell of smoke and the dusty scent of horses. Her body was draped over something rough and warm that rocked her gently side to side. The heat of the sun soaked through her clothes and onto her back. So much so that her skin was starting to tingle. A breeze moved her hair in a tickling wave against her neck. But above all else, she could hear the day. Birds, insects, the hush of grass dried by the dwindling summer. No storm. No wind. Not one of the hundred whispering voices.

She woke to an uncomfortably bright afternoon, devoid of the morning's clouds. Her smoke-sore eyes were near useless. She moved a hand against the warm object below her, ruffling short, bristly hairs. Somehow she'd gotten back on the horse.

Her lungs felt like bags of hot coals. She coughed, which put a strain in her neck that reminded her of the problem with her shoulder. Wincing, she tried to shift the arm it controlled. Nothing happened. She used the other to sit herself up and take stock of her new situation.

Only then did she realize that just ahead of the moving animal strolled a man in a gray suit. "Hello again," Corvudeus said over his shoulder, hardly looking at her. She wanted to have another go at him, but knew she was too weak to make it worthwhile. Instead she settled for rudeness.

"So now you're helping?"

"I don't know what you're talking about."

"Do you expect me to believe I got up here by myself?"

"It's not my job to tell people what to believe. I am a simple reality. A fact. They don't have to believe me. I am always true in the end."

"How sentimental," Verenna grumbled. It set her coughing again.

Corvus shrugged. "Call it what you like."

They traveled in silence for a while, Verenna scanning the trees for anything she recognized. They weren't on any particular path she could distinguish. Meadows stretched around them, interspersed with stands of trees. It all felt terribly familiar, yet there were no landmarks to tell her so.

"Am I dead? Is that where we are?" she grouched, cradling her limp arm.

"Not at all. You are, by an accident of your new, supernatural nature, very much alive. Very reasonable guess though. You should be dead."

"You'd like that wouldn't you."

"In theory, yes. Your kind should not exist. But that's my mistake to worry about. In reality, I enjoy you very much. Especially how much you bother that doctor. It's also nice to have someone around who can take the other Horsemen down a peg. They do get rather full of themselves."

Verenna's ears perked up. "So we won? It's gone? How are the others? Did they make it?"

"They are safe. Thanks to you. It was a brilliant plan, but executed with an idiocy I can hardly describe."

The girl tilted her grateful face skyward and let out a breath. If they made it to Falseman Inn it would all be worth it. But Death had more to say.

"As for victory, I wouldn't phrase it like that. You can't really 'win' over a Horseman. Not forever. Human behavior is what allows them to rise. In this case, your people were starved not because there was no food, but because they were afraid to collect it. Famine is clever, I'll give her that. My point is, until you erase all human vice, there is always the chance they'll ride again. But for now, you could say Malagrir has experienced a...severe inconvenience." He looked back with a glimmer in his eye.

"Well, where are we if I'm not dead?"

"On the way to the abbey of course. They'll be worried about you."

Verenna watched him walk, his hands clasped behind his back, taking in his surroundings with a leisure that would have suited window shopping.

"Couldn't have fixed my shoulder while I was knocked out?"

"That would be helping. I don't do that."

"You did, though."

"Not at all. I told you to get on the horse. You did it. And here we are. I did not aid you, I simply sped up an activity that you would have awoken and done anyway."

The girl let out a single humorless laugh. "How did you even catch the horse?"

"It came when I called. It's mine after all."

"What?" Her eyes would have gone wide, but the sun kept them in a tight squint.

"Do you really think any living animal could have survived so much?"

"So that's how it's kept going this long. That's why it healed so fast when the wolves attacked. "

It was Death's turn to laugh. "Actually, that is a very interesting story. You haven't heard it yet, have you? You should hear it from Darius, though. Ask him when you get back. He loves retelling it."

She didn't believe him, but curiosity etched the note in her mind.

"Look ahead," Corvus waved towards the distance.

A thin trail of smoke rose above the treetops. The same gray ribbon she'd watched from her bedroom what seemed like years ago. Tears welled up at the sight of it and a smile creased her face. "How far?"

"A few miles still. We'll be there by dark."

Verenna choked back a sob. "And they all made it? You mean everyone, right? Can you lie to me? Is that in the rules?"

Corvus chuckled. "I can lie. But I am choosing not to. There's no point. Especially because this is one of those rare occasions where the truth is what you want it to be."

A few hours later the sun curtsied onto the horizon in a stunning array of orange and fuchsia, leaving the purple ballroom of the heavens open for the waltzing stars. Crickets thrummed from secret places as a cool breeze heralded the first touch of the coming autumn.

Soon the formidable walls of the Inn loomed high before them like the curled body of some, ancient sleeping guardian. The only thing that kept Verenna from spurring the horse into a run was the knowledge that she could not hold on with her damaged arm. Her heart pounded so hard she thought Corvus might hear it. Behind the iron bars of the gate she could see lanterns bobbing towards her. She could hear her name.

Her father reached the gate first. She slid off the horse and ran to grip his hands through the bars until Lord Ren caught up with the key. Fabien came next, and Mortimer, followed by a host of other familiar faces. As soon as the gate opened they pulled her inside in a flurry of embraces and words of welcome.

"I thought you were done for, darling! They had to drag me away or I would have followed you," her father gushed with her face in his hands.

"We heard what you did, my girl. Very brave indeed," someone added.

"I can't believe you survived!" Adrinée exclaimed, bounding up with Kaybin in tow by a hand.

"You're not alone," Verenna retorted.

"Well done, well done," Mortimer repeated, his eyes sparkling.

Darius joined them too, wobbling up to the gathering with crutches and waving off Calla's offers of support. He stood at the back, a single stoic nod and a dim, distant smirk were all he would allow himself to show in the way of approval.

"You are brilliant! You have to know that!" Fabien managed to work his way through the hubbub and plant a kiss on her forehead.

"W-what's wrong?" Lady Ren stuttered, reaching a thin hand towards the girls cradled arm.

"I think my shoulder may be out of place. I fell off the horse at one point and hit the ground hard."

"Let me see that," Darius demanded, brushing people aside to get to her. He took her arm and weighed it in his hand, gently turning it over and rotating it. "Can you move it?

"Not really."

"Dislocated." He said it as if it were some minor scrape and continued to examine the arm. "We thought you were dead you know. At least until Corvus showed up and told us you'd made it. He wouldn't tell us how... How?"

"He wouldn't tell me either. But wait, how was he here? He walked me all the way back. He lead the horse." She checked over her shoulder. The horse had meandered inside and begun to graze, but there was no sign of Corvudeus.

"He's Death. He's in thousands of places at any given moment," the doctor dismissed.

She hadn't thought about that.

"There's a welcoming party inside as well," a voice injected from the back of the pack. "Your former neighbors would like to apologize."

"As they should. She saved their lives, too," her father scoffed.

"Well, except Mr. Eeves," Darius amended. "He says you're a reckless brat."

Verenna's ears went instantly red. "I am not a br-ahhhh!"

The doctor had used the opportunity to shift her shoulder back into socket. He let go to allow Verenna to wilt to her knees. "Nice to see you too," she snarled from the ground.

"And you as well. Oh, and he didn't say that. I did. You're a reckless brat."

The girl stood up with a fist cocked back, but her father caught her wrist. "Let's go inside. We thought you might like a bath."

Those were the only words in the world that could have calmed her.

ꝏ

Nothing in months had felt as good as the lukewarm water that waited for her. She stripped off the sweat stained, mud laced garments she'd been wearing for longer than she cared to recall, and plunged into the tub of fresh water, sinking below the surface in absolute bliss. Perhaps it was just her new-found healing abilities but everything from her sore feet to her smoke singed lungs felt better once she was clean.

Even when all the grime had come off she lingered with her eyes closed. She rested on the edge of sleep, her freshly brushed hair spilling over the side of the tub.

Her peace came to an abrupt end as she heard the door open without a knock. "I've brought you a few things."

Verenna splashed her way to sitting and found the intruder. Calla was draping some sort of dress across the back of a chair in the corner. "It's not as good as the last one. But I can't keep giving you my things every time you come around filthy."

Verenna didn't like the way her perfectly curved, cherry lips forced the word 'filthy'. "Um, thanks." She curled up and hugged her knees to hide herself.

"Calm down, dear, it's nothing I haven't seen before." The woman floated into the seat, crossing her legs so one foot twitched in the air like the tail of an annoyed cat, her stunning sapphire dress cascading from her exposed ankle like a waterfall.

She couldn't think of anything to say. Asking why she'd come seemed wrong, as she'd given a reason. But the way she'd settled into the chair told Verenna that she had intentions beyond a simple clothing delivery. She wanted to talk. Calla's black eyes and the stark contrast between her pale skin and immaculately groomed ebony hair lent a cutting sharpness to her appearance. She looked down at the girl in the bucket the way a cruel child might look at an old doll. Calculation painted with false kindness.

"Darius was worried about you. From the moment he got through the gate all he could talk about was what they were going to do to get you back. He and the beggar, and the blond boy almost set out after you. Not to mention your father. We could hardly keep him inside. If Corvudeus hadn't turned up at the last minute they'd have gone charging off like fools all over again."

"That's, I mean, nice of them," Verenna guessed. Calla's playful yet sinister poise revealed nothing about what she wanted to hear from the girl.

"Nice for you maybe. But Darius is very important here. Without a doctor to keep up the appearance of being a ward for the incurable, we are left incredibly vulnerable. Which I don't appreciate. None of us do, really. You have some sway over our doctor. A sway that inclines him towards rash decisions. Irresponsible. Stupid, some might say."

Verena swallowed hard. "I didn't mean to put all of you at risk. We just had to do something to get out of Canterford."

The woman placed an elegant hand over her heart. "Please don't think I'm criticizing your actions. You were very brave I'm told. But I think I can speak for all of us here at the abbey when I ask that this sort of risk not be taken again. We cannot afford to lose our doctor."

An accusation hung in the woman's words, but Verenna could not pin down exactly what it was. Emboldened by annoyance she remarked, "I'm really not sure what could have been done differently. I was miles away by the time everyone came back. I could hardly control anyone's reaction."

"Oh, come now. You don't give yourself enough credit. I've never seen him rushing for such drastic measures. You'd have thought he was on fire," she giggled.

Verenna cringed. It hadn't occurred to her that, because of how recently he'd bitten her, Darius would have felt everything she went through dealing with Malagrir. Perhaps that was why he seemed so angry with her when he'd set her arm back in place. He wasn't upset with her, he'd just had his arm twisted too.

"I know him," the woman continued. "He may have a temper, but he thinks things through. For you, however, he was ready to charge off into god only knows what. And in his condition? I mean, I suppose I can understand some hurry. You mortals do need all the help you can get."

"Well-" Verenna began to explain but stopped when she noticed the changes in the woman before her. Her hands, neatly clasped in her lap took hold of her skirts and twisted. Her eyes went ever so slightly wider, and the clever smile she'd worn broadened so that her perfectly white teeth peaked between her lips. Sitting straighter, she stared unblinkingly at Verenna.

"Oh. So you've been changed."

"Not quite."

"Dear, you either are or you aren't one of us. There is no in between. Which is it?"

"I was bitten twice. I'm like you. I just haven't gone through a dark moon yet."

Calla leaned back in her chair, swift intelligence replacing anger. "Interesting." Something about the fact seemed to satisfy her. It bothered Verenna that she couldn't know why. Fed up with the cryptic conversation the girl decided that the only way to end it was with blunt force.

"Listen, I don't know what you and the doctor are to each other but I want no part of it. Also, I don't know why we had to discuss this while I am naked. Whatever clothes those are, they're fine. I would like some privacy to get into them, however. Or were you sent to 'help' with that too?"

Calla tilted her head in cold amusement. "Well, I certainly didn't mean to disturb. You get dressed. We're all downstairs in the main hall." The woman rose, the picture of composure and drifted to the door. "They'll probably send someone to guide you, but I'd try to remember the way seeing as you'll be here for a while. Take your time. I'll see if we can arrange dinner for you. After all, you'll be one of our own soon."

The way she said it sent a chill down Verenna's spine that seemed to spread through the bath water, making her shiver. Before Calla departed she turned back, her perfect oval face hovering above her shoulders like a rising moon. Her fingers fluttered in the slightest wave and she vanished into the hall.

Verenna hurried dry and into the clothes. The woman was right. They weren't near as nice as the last ones. But the simple gray town dress would do just fine. She'd become so unaccustomed to checking her appearance, she almost forgot to glance in the mirror. The difference was striking. The last time she'd seen her own image her face had been full and young. Now, the hollows of her cheeks reminded her exactly how long it had been since she'd been hungry. It had been days since she'd eaten and still no appetite came. Her eyes were different too. Sunken and shadowed. The months away had sharpened every feature and drained the rose from her cheeks. For having been granted immortality, she'd never looked more dead.

She set about parting her hair when a knock sounded at the door. Mortimer waited outside, beaming to see her looking so well. As he lead her towards the meeting place he attempted to fill her in on what she'd missed while away.

"I'm afraid we're gathering for more than just social purposes," he informed her. "We need to discuss arrangements for your neighbors. We do have a mortal population here, but they'll have to be accepted. By everyone. It's going to be hard to make a case for themselves when they so obviously do not approve of us."

Verenna sighed. "They don't approve much of anything out of the ordinary in Canterford."

"Their idea of ordinary may be the problem then," he theorized.

"Definitely. They used to think I was strange. And now this place? I don't know if they'd stay if we begged."

"Oh," Mortimer grinned to himself. "I think they've had a bit of a change of heart. They decided not to run to Hartford. The sight of Malagrir changed their minds. After what they've seen today, you could say they're a little more open minded."

Verenna got the slightest twinge of satisfaction at the idea of Mr. Eeves wringing his hands waiting for them. She tried to keep a smirk off her face.

By the time they entered the main hall, Lord and Lady Ren had already begun their inquiries. They'd taken a few tables down from their places barring the entrances and set them up in a disorganized patch in the middle of the room. Those from Canterford clustered together facing the assembly from Falseman Inn, twitching at every sound like nervous hens.

Verenna took a seat in between her father and Thessa, who clapped her on the back in greeting and indicated her newly bandaged and splinted leg. "Can you believe Kaybin did this? He fixed up the bite on Renaud's arm, too. Boy might turn out a half decent doctor. Darius says I'll walk again just fine," she whispered. The girl smiled at her enthusiasm.

"You look splendid, Vivie," her father murmured.

"Thanks. How far have they gotten?"

"The story's been told. Now they're trying to explain themselves."

They settled in to listen as Ms. Tiller spoke, clutching Mrs. Norworth's hands for the courage to do so. "We didn't mean any harm. I regret participating now, but at the time, we were all so afraid. We thought that, maybe, they brought the storms or the thing that caused them. That they weren't telling us the whole truth."

"Please," Lady Ren protested. "Even if someone were p-powerful enough, who would have a reason? Canterford hasn't been the site of any major conflict for over two hundred years. What enemies do you think you have?"

Mrs. Babik answered, her eyes cast down to her lap. "It's the times. Everyone's been on edge. Not without reason, but that's not an excuse."

"If I may," Mr. Censington wobbled to his feet to address the room. "We had good information that our visitors might be a danger to us."

Verenna rolled her eyes, then scanned the huddled townspeople for Willoughby's face. He'd tucked himself into the crowd so that he could hardly be seen behind Mr. Norworth.

"And what information was that?" Lord Ren inquired, stroking the stubble on his chin.

"Rumors, most likely," Calla sighed. "That little town loves to speculate."

Verenna couldn't resist interrupting. "Oh, no. Willoughby lied to them." Seeing the little man duck in his chair she pointed directly at him. The whole assembly turned to view the culprit. "Mr. Porter there, told them that we were demons. That's what started most of the suspicion."

With nowhere to hide, Willoughby started hemorrhaging excuses. "Wh-wh-what was I supposed to think? I watched both of you heal instantly!" He waved a frantic hand between Verenna and Fabien. "The only way to get that sort of power is to sell your soul to the Devil. Everyone knows that. Besides, the storms got so much worse when they showed up. Anyone could have drawn that conclusion. Then they had one of those wind monsters in a jar. I mean, they could have been dangerous. How should I know what evil looks like?"

"Exactly." Mortimer stopped him. "How would you know?"

The entire room quieted. Then the scrape of a chair announced Mr. Eeves was ready to speak his piece. "It doesn't matter now. Maybe your kind aren't dangerous. Maybe you are. But whatever the case, you're not like us. What I'm concerned with, is whether or not you'll let us go with that knowledge? Are we your prisoners now?"

"Oh, n-no, please leave, if you like. We won't keep you. " Lady Ren told him and snapped open her lavender fan. Her voice remained calm but the flutter of her hand showed her frustration with him. "B-but for the life of me, I can't see what you're so eager to get back to. Your town is in sh-shambles from what I understand. Half of it just burned down. But please, take your leave if you must. No one here will stop you."

Darius interjected, "I'd also like to point out that you seem to be the only one concerned with leaving. I believe the rest of your number are looking to stay and shelter here until danger passes."

"We have room," Lord Ren considered. "We have the resources, if you're willing to share in the work. But this is a matter of safety for us as much as it is for you. You are strangers, that until just hours ago, were hostile to us. I think the decision on this should fall to ones who have known you longest and seen the most of your prejudice." The old man turned to Verenna and her father. "What say the two of you? Can they be trusted enough to stay in these walls?"

Every face looked to them for the decision. Her former neighbors clutching each other, tapping nervous feet, biting their lips and holding their breath to leave space in the air for the answer.

She looked to her father. "Go on," he encouraged.

Verenna considered her former neighbors. These people had been convinced of their wickedness so easily. They'd been so ready to blame anyone for their ills that they'd been willing to throw all of them into a dark hole and lock them there. Even those they'd known their whole lives. But before her now she saw none of that meanness. They looked like frightened children.

"I think," she paused to look directly into Willoughby's tearful face. "That they aren't dangerous. I don't think they're evil. I think they're scared. Just like I was when I came here the first time. And I think they should stay."

The crowd broke into whispered 'thank you's and 'you won't regret it's.

"It's settled then," Ren said with a clap of his hands. "As long as they agree to be peaceful and contribute, they can stay until conditions improve." The man gave a wave and three maids stepped forward from the back of the room. Verenna recognized them as the trio that had fixed her up and served her tea after her ill-fated escape attempt. The one she'd given the letter gave her a discrete wave.

Lord Ren instructed them. First he pointed to the Sarzen and her father. "Send five plates out here for our friends with life's appetite. Take these people to the kitchen, feed them, and show them where they sleep. The first floor, of course." He addressed the statement to Mr. Eeves. "So they can leave at any time."

The group ambled off with more shy gratitudes. Even Eeves went along, despite his bitterness.

"What now?" Verenna asked. It seemed like there should be some next step, another challenge right around the corner as there had been for weeks.

Darius shrugged. "You're home. You relax."

Something soft bumped Verenna's leg. The cat slipped by her and jumped onto Mr. Dellins lap.

"I can't believe how big he's gotten. Did you name him?" she asked.

"Not yet. I left that for you to decide when you came back. It helped keep alive the hope that you would." He ruffled the cat's ears and set it purring. Verenna let it sniff her hand with its petal of a pink nose. It headbutted her palm to encourage her to stroke it.

"Well isn't this a happy ending?" Calla stepped forward with a few wine glasses in hand. "I think there should be a toast."

"Excellent idea," Ren blustered.

Someone called out, "I'll get the wine," and scurried from the room.

Calla smiled, her lips a blood colored sickle. She set the glasses out one by one, leaving the last before Verenna. Their eyes met for the briefest second. The girls spine went rigid with the sense that there was a game being played and she hadn't been told the rules.

As the woman spun on her heel to go gather more cups, her hand tipped the glass before Verenna. It shattered on the floor. The sound cut through all conversation, rendering the hall absolutely quiet.

"Oh. How clumsy of me. Here," she stopped, then stood with a gasp, her hand sporting a long, crimson line. Slow drops of blood bulged and ran from the cut.

Verenna found herself staring at the injury as if nothing else in the world mattered. It was as if the rich red color had taken over her mind. A few months ago she would have fainted. But now, she wanted to watch the drops slide down the woman's arm. To see where the trails went. To touch it.

Verenna snapped back to reality at the sound of the cat growling. The little, white thing had puffed up on her father's lap, turning sideways and hissing at her. A strange change from its former friendliness. The girl reached out to pet it. "What's wrong? It's just me." But the cat swatted at her and bolted for cover.

"How odd," her father commented and adjusted his glasses.

A wave of nausea struck next. Not inspired by sickness, but as if something were trying to get out of her. Verenna covered her mouth.

"My dear, are you alright?" Calla worried in her silky tones, though her expression did not match the sweetness in her voice.

Verenna shook her head. Every fiber of her body wanted to turn back to the sight of Calla's bloodied hand. All of her insides were being pulled towards it. She wanted to taste it, to know what blood felt like in her teeth. The idea both revolted her and obsessed her in a way she had no words for. Her vision faltered, fading the world in and out of focus. But as one sense faded, the others came alive as if for the first time. She could feel the blood moving in the two people beside her, sense the distant rhythm of their hearts in the air around them.

"What's going on?" Adrinée hopped up from her seat to investigate.

Darius did his best to rush to Verenna through the tangle of chairs. "Look at me," he demanded, kneeling beside her. The doctor took one hand away from her mouth to check her pulse. His eyes grew wide. The others crowded around in concern.

"It's too fast." He put a hand to her forehead, then lifted her chin. "Good god, you've got pupils like saucers..." He pointed to Mortimer. "You. What phase of the moon is it?"

"I suppose it's almost dark. Might be dark tonight..." Then like a bolt, it struck the old man why he'd asked. "Oh no. Renaud, Kaybin, get Thessa out of here. Dellins go with them. Clear the room. If you have a mortal life to lose, clear the room."

"Why? What's going on? I need to stay with her," she heard her father demanding as he was hauled off by a few of the stronger residents.

"Blood lust," someone said. Voices she could not place swirled around her with an addling mixture of advice and questions.

"Is she one of us?"

"Who changed her?"

"Give them space."

"Who's going to watch her?"

"Get her to a safe room!"

Verenna could hear the scrambling, feel the warmth of the people next to her fade as they were whisked away by unseen forces. She could taste panic. But more than anything else she could smell the iron of Calla's blood.

"Leave. Now. Get out!" Darius roared at the woman.

"It's only a scratch. You act like I murdered someone on the dinner table."

"You know exactly what you did. Go or I will have you dragged."

Verenna's gaze cleared enough to see the woman fain indignation. She tossed her luxurious hair and swaggered from sight, murmuring, "Nice to see your true colors."

"OUT!" Darius thundered. Mortimer put an arm over Verenna's shoulders to calm her. Fabien took hold of her from the other side in a way that suggested he might try to restrain her. "It'll be alright. Everyone here knows about these things," the young man lilted.

She heard the words as if she were underwater. They were distant and muted, and though she could hear them she strained to understand. Darius knelt before her again and took her hands.

"We're going to take you somewhere safe. I want you to know that whatever happens, we expect it. There are no surprises in this for any of us. We know what to do. Come, follow me."

All she could do was stare at him. His features didn't make sense anymore. She couldn't make out any of the emotion in his words. Happy, upset, frightened, she could not tell the difference. Darius went to stand but when his hands encircled her wrists to guide her she ripped them from his grip and landed a kick to his stomach that flattened him. She hadn't meant to, it had happened like a reflex. He would take her somewhere away from this room. Away from the smell of the blood. She didn't want to go. More than that, she wanted to hurt anyone who tried to take her away. A few people sprung into action to help the doctor off the floor. "Hold on to her!" he croaked to the other two.

Mortimer tightened his grip and tried to reason with her. "Verenna, it's all right. We're going to take you somewhere where you can be comfortable."

But it was far too late for reason. Her whole world was made of echoing sounds, none of which made any sense as language though she know they must be. All she could understand was that the two men holding on to her wanted to take her away. She lashed at them, kicking, scratching, clawing, foam forming at the edge of her mouth. She flung Fabien off of her with a force she didn't know she had. He tumbled away from her. Chairs clattered to the ground around him. Mortimer still clung to her. But she knocked him senseless with a single strike.

She heard something growl. She felt the rumble in her chest but couldn't tell if it came from within or without. Noticing the shining shards of glass, still freckled with Calla's blood, she dove for them. Not just to touch them, to consume them.

Fabien blocked her. She took hold of his leg and pulled him to the ground, clambering on top of him and lunging for his throat. He managed to throw her off, only to set her springing towards Darius. Everything else was a blur. Reality became nothing more than shapes and noise. Instinct burned inside her, a drive to hunt.

She remembered next to nothing after that. Unsoothable rage, moving from light to dark, the cool of the night and the sound of crickets, the impossible swiftness of her own motions. If this was Bloodlust, she never wanted it to end. Freedom coursed through her like she'd never felt it before. All thoughts, worries, words melted away as she sprinted hard for the unknown. It felt like flying, like dancing, but above all, it felt powerful. Her mind fell apart. All she knew was the screaming, bone deep urge to seek, find, and kill.

Epilogue

Fumus lounged at Gawshire's feet, glutted and drowsy. The wraith stood at the edge of the moat where the drawbridge had collapsed to oversee his servants work. The gentle slosh of the water filled the overcast afternoon with a strangely restful song.

He'd had them working all night. Every servant he possessed had been summoned forth to construct the solution to the broken bridge. He congratulated himself on the genius of replacing human help. These creatures would work until they fell apart without complaint.

Gawshire watched as two of them lowered another piece of building material into the water, pushing it into place alongside the others without a splash. It had taken them a while to understand the consequences of disturbing the water. But by the third time the river banshees had come up to take one of them away, they understood the need for keeping the water peaceful. Of course once the banshees realized there was nothing truly alive to eat or shiny to collect, they left the project well alone.

He breathed deep and tried to drink in the tranquil day to soothe his impatience. He could feel each hour trapped in the confines of the moat draining away. Each minute spent in this insufferable stillness was a minute more his prey would be able to grow the distance between them. He must be calm. He must think.

Gawshire ran a finger down the center of Fumus' head, a single stroke, nose to the base of the animals skull. It shivered and licked its lipless chops. He spoke to it in Latin.

"No time for sleep now, my pet. We are almost ready."

Another piece of the new bridge slid into place soundlessly, but a ragged voice disrupted the moment.

"My lord, your things," a servant woman with hair that looked like a bird's nest stepped forward to present a pack to him.

"Carry it," he demanded, and she slung it over one shoulder. "You've remembered everything? My hunting kit? The map?"

"All save the map, my lord."

He rounded on the woman and stepped in close to snarl at her. "Did I not make it perfectly clear that I need the map?"

"Yes my lord," she answered with an utter lack of expression. "But the map is gone."

Gawshire blinked and leaned in to place his ear right next to the servant's mouth. "Come again?"

"It's gone, sir. It is not on the table in your study. I could not find it when I searched."

The wraith paced away from her, thoughts spinning. "Where else did you check?" The woman droned a list of rooms but Gawshire hardly heard. The map had been in his study, laid out on the table where he had left it. He'd had no reason to move it. "Who else has been in that room?"

"Those are your private quarters, sir. Only myself and the servants you permit. And of course yourself and the guest."

"What guest? I…" The truth of the situation rushed in on him. A deep growl rose in his chest and turned into a bellowing roar. He whirled and struck the servant in the side of the head. She crumbled to the ground. The commotion alerted Fumus, who raised its mammoth head to investigate. Gawshire waved the beast off. It yawned, letting its rows of talon like teeth glisten in the bright gray light before settling again.

Gawshire sank into the satisfying sting of a knuckle split by impact as the servant struggled to its feet. It made him feel a little better. Despite the lack of expression on the servant the blow must have hurt.

"The girl must have taken it. She must have." He put his hands on his hips and stared at the ground to calculate his prey's new advantage. "Unless they can find someone fluent in Latin they'll have a hard time deciphering it. We have no time to lose getting after them." He licked his teeth at the thought of the heinous things he'd plan for that little thief, for all of them.

He straightened up. "You have failed me. I need you to understand that the only reason I do not toss you into that moat for the banshees is because I am short on help. You will come with me, and you will do everything in your power to atone for the inconvenience you've cost me. Fail me again and you'll beg for the pit I pulled you from. Do we have an understanding?"

"Absolutely, my lord," the woman went to bow but he grabbed her chin, forcing her to look into his eyes. But the empty distance he found staring back at him did nothing to placate him. He wanted to see fear. He wanted to look into the face of a creature with a life to lose and revel in its terror. This husk was little more than a poor excuse for a pack animal. He released her with a shove.

Another servant ambled to his side, a hulking man with the same blank stare and a pronounced limp. "The bridge is ready, sir."

"Good. Has it been tested?"

"Yes, sir. Three times."

"Well done. Now gather the remaining servants and guard the place. No one comes or goes unless they are in my presence," Gawshire commanded the limping man.

"Yes, my lord," he grunted and called the last servants with a whistle. They left their tasks and followed the hobbling giant into the shadows of the building.

Gawshire strolled to the water's edge where he took in the masterpiece he'd had constructed. The corpses of a hundred servants, lashed together with rope, spanned the distance from one bank to the other. Their bodies forming a floating bridge over the springwater that fed the moat. A thin smile cracked Gawshires face at the sight. He called to Fumus who sprang to his side, sensing his masters glee. "Do you know what we're going to do?" Gawshire asked the beast.

In a long, guttural croak it issued the only word it knew. "Manducore!"

"Oh yes, my pet. Until there are none left."

About the Author

Alisar Eido's second novel, Night Bound, is book two of three in The Soulfire Series. Her work spans multiple genres including science fiction, psychological thrillers, dark fantasy, and realistic fiction. The author's inspiration stems from her many experiences with strange coincidences and unexplainable events, as well as battles with mental illness. She currently resides in Austin, Texas, with her pens and pencils.

Look for Wake of War, the third and final book of The Soulfire Series, in October 2019.